Iron and the Arrow

By

Wendy L. Anderson

ISBN-13: 978-1-64456-082-2
Library of Congress Control Number: 2019954561

Indies United Publishing House, LLC
P.O. Box 3071
Quincy, Illinois 62305-3071

"This book is dedicated to my mother, Linda,
who supports me and loves me always."

STORM RIDER

CHAPTER ONE

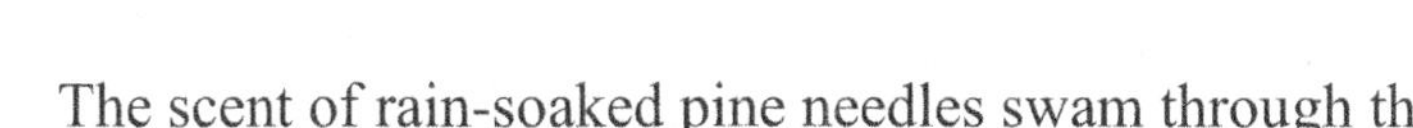

The scent of rain-soaked pine needles swam through the air. The sound of twigs snapping broke the twilight silence of the forest as Meurie pressed on through the black trees hoping to gain the village before nightfall.

Her clothes and boots were soaked through from the rain that had been falling most of that day, but she could not fret about that now, the important thing was to keep moving, and fast. Clinging to the densest part of the forest she avoided the well-worn trails. Still, she frequently cast watchful glances over her shoulder and kept her knife close at hand.

For days now, she felt as if she were being watched and followed. Telling herself that it was just the sentient nature of the Violent Mountains and that she was being silly, did not help her situation. An unfamiliar apprehension assailed her usually fearless mind.

The pack she wore was heavy and getting heavier with every mile as her weariness threatened to overtake her, but she pressed on. Consulting the mental map in her head, she knew that a small mountain village called Dade-Bend was just ahead. As she walked, the hill began to slope gently downward, and the faint smell of smoke reached her. She allowed a small sigh of relief to pass her lips. The village was close, which meant that the inn inside the village was close, which also meant that soon she could rest. The thought of food, a warm bath, a dry bed, and clean clothes appealed greatly to her, and she hurried her pace.

Darkness fell early in the Violent Mountains and though Meurie did not fear the dark, she was desperately tired.

These past many days, she had slept fitfully on the hard ground on only a thin bedroll, hunted for her food, and drank from ice-cold mountain streams she passed along the way. Her long, strong, legs carried her over many rough miles and would carry her the rest of the way home. As long as she avoided detection from *whatever* it was that followed her, she would be safe.

The thick forest opened up suddenly revealing a long, deep, green valley. Glowing, golden lamplights shone warmly from the many houses and buildings in the village that was her destination. Stopping at the edge of the forest to survey her final destination, she let her gaze wander fearfully to the wide open and the darkening skies above. It was some instinct that she could not explain that made her look up toward the sky.

Thick heavy clouds blanketed the evening as another spring storm threatened. Thunder rolled lazily across the distant skies over the mountains. Fatigue, cold, and hunger drove her on. Placing her steps toward the village, she darted out of the shelter of the thick forest.

The swift rushing sound of water met her as she lightly sprinted across the open space toward the village. The Dade River wound around the outskirts of the village buildings situated within the bend of the massive valley, giving the town its name, Dade-Bend. Flourishing gardens dotted the yards of the many houses. A dark blacksmith's shop sat empty and cold for the night and a large corral held many horses just to the side. A huge barn loomed in her path. Running swiftly between buildings, she hid in the shadows just in case the *thing* following her decided now, before she was relatively safe, was a good time to pounce. Casting quick glances around to make sure the way was clear, she hurried on.

Meurie startled suddenly as a brave fox burst from some thick bushes to her right. Black eyes stared at her for a brief moment before the animal disappeared back into the heavy growth. Its white-tipped tail flicked once, and it was gone. Dogs barked in the distance and the bleating of a goat gave the evening the impression that everyone and everything was bedding down for the night. It made her feel lonely.

Luck was with her as she safely made her way down the street unmolested. The creak of a wooden sign on rusting metal hinges drew her notice. Walking calmly, so she did not draw attention from the few people outside this evening, she walked toward the sound. The swaying sign advertised the 'Dragonfly Inn.'

Outside, the smell of pipe smoke, sweating bodies, and spilled ale assailed her delicate senses. Her mouth began to water as she also picked out the scent of baking bread and venison stew. Still skittish, she pulled her hood over her head and dared to place her hand on the rough wood of the door. Gripping her long dagger beneath her cloak, she pushed and went in.

The Dragonfly Inn was full of noisy patrons this evening. An old man with long, thin, graying hair played the lute while tapping a rhythm with his foot. Loud conversations did not miss a beat at her entrance and for that, she was deeply grateful. Smoke from numerous pipes wafted toward her and she resisted the urge to cough. Threading through the packed tables, she aimed for the long wooden bar at the back of the room. Her eyes darted everywhere taking in the layout of the place and the other patrons. Huge fireplaces crackled on both sides of the large room and a stairway opening made a tall dark rectangle in the rear.

Shifting her pack on her shoulder and holding the strap tightly, she was intent on getting to the wooden bar to ask about obtaining a meal and a room. She felt, rather than saw, the curious stares that focused on her. Someone half-heartedly snagged the edge of her cloak and made a rude invitation which she ignored. The roar of laughter followed her as she hurried on.

Finally, she achieved her goal. There was an empty stool and she eased up to it and waited to gain the attention of the man behind the bar. He was an older man with deep lines covering his worn face. He smelled like everything else in the noisy inn, of sweat, pipe smoke, and spilled ale. As he noticed her, he nodded his head once in acknowledgment. Then he went back to pouring two flagons before moving toward her.

Meurie scanned the room again, nerves on edge. Her wary eyes searched quickly from underneath her hood. There were three women busily working the full tables pouring ale and delivering steaming bowls of stew to the hungry men. The old musician in the back started to sing a tune. She turned toward him and noticed he had no teeth, but his voice was sweet, strong, and melodic. Meurie's eyes darted back as the barkeep finally walked up to her. She lowered her hood and greeted him with a nervous smile.

"What can I get for ya Meurie?" He nodded as he recognized her.

Meurie hesitated distracted not knowing why she was still so unnerved even now that she was out of the forest.

"Spit it out, I ain't got all night." The man asked slightly annoyed. Even though she was known to the barkeep, he was busy and did not hide his irritation at her delay.

"A room for the night, a hot meal, some warmed wine, and..."

"And?" He huffed impatiently.

"I don't suppose a hot bath is possible?" Wincing at the wistfulness in her voice.

"I can offer ya the room and the meal. No hot bath. Though I can send up a bucket of hot water and ya can make do, eh?"

"Yes, thank you." She smiled gratefully.

The barkeep started to leave but stopped next to a large, figure in a dark hooded cloak sitting on the stool one over from Meurie.

"An ale for you Sir?"

The big man nodded once.

"Ah," the barkeep scratched underneath his whiskered chin, "Around these parts, strangers pay upfront." The man slid a silver coin over the countertop. His hand was large and strong and drew Meurie's gaze. Meurie stared at it and did not know why the sight of this stranger's hand would attract her attention. She quickly looked away, embarrassed.

Meurie's supper and wine were brought in short order, and she slipped the barkeep a silver coin. He deftly pocketed the coin then dug in his other pocket and returned two bronzes and four coppers. Meurie slid the change through some spilled ale off the wooden bar and secreted them under her cloak.

After she ate her supper, the barkeep brought over a steaming bucket. If she was to have any semblance of a hot bath, she had to carry her own water.

"Yer room is up them stairs and down the end of the hall on the left." He said pointing and gave her an iron key.

Meurie made her way up the dark narrow stairs to the room she had been directed to. She held her pack on one shoulder and hefted the bucket of hot water with her other hand as she wearily climbed.

At the top of the stairs, she reached a long, poorly lit hall. Now that she had a meal and warm wine in her belly, she could barely move as the fatigue caught up with her and threatened to pull her down. Placing one foot in front of the other she told her exhaustion she was almost there. Passing the other closed doors quickly she made for her room. The hot water was cooling swiftly, and she did her best not to spill it as she hurried on.

Her hands shook as she pushed the iron key into the lock, turned it, and pushed the door open. Casting a glance over her shoulder, she looked back to make sure she was not followed. Earlier, as she sat at the bar devouring her dinner, the inhabitants grew rowdy with drink, and the stares and rude calls began to disturb her. She quickly ate the venison stew, stowed half the hunk of bread within a pocket in her cloak, and as soon as the barkeep brought her bucket of hot water and gave her the key to her room, she had gotten out of there. The sounds of singing and shouting drunkards assailed her ears, but she did her best to drown them out and concentrate on the soft singing of the old musician. She had above normal hearing abilities and even tired it was intensified. Being able to distinguish the sounds of his beautiful singing over the roaring laughter and boisterous conversations, was a blessing.

The room was as black as a moonless night, and she stumbled a little unbalanced by the bucket and her pack. Dropping both to the floor, she bolted the door and made her way to the small table and lit a candle. Breathing a sigh of relief, she realized she had finally made it. She had acted like a scared rabbit and shook like a frightened doe, but no one noticed her upset and now she was safe, locked in the room she purchased for the night. Embarrassment at her fear and weariness from her travel was so great that she could barely stand. An intense desire to sleep overtook her but she told herself, first and foremost, to get out of her wet clothes and into something dry. The water in the bucket, she so precariously carried all the way to her room, was getting colder by the minute.

There was a narrow wooden chair in the room. Moving it over to the locked door, she shoved it against the door giving herself an extra sense of security. She looked around. A narrow bed occupied the far wall and she decided to look that over later. The small stone fireplace had fresh wood in it. She lit the fire and watched as the dry wood swiftly caught and began to warm the frigid room.

By the soft glow of the candle and the warmth of the fire, she stripped off her wet clothes and hung them from pegs on the wall to dry. Her shoulders ached from carrying the pack for so long and her feet were tired from walking these many days. Her long legs had carried her swiftly, but her endurance had just about reached an end because of the fear. Completely undressed she shivered as she dipped a cloth in the bucket of tepid water and washed the day's tiredness away. The warmth of the fire helped her sore muscles and, for the first time in many days, she felt as if she had truly escaped whatever had been following her.

#

Storm Rider perched on top of a building across the street from a place called the Dragonfly Inn. He watched the dark windows of the upper floors and waited patiently. Soon enough the tiny glow of a candle grew and brightened a small room at the end of the second floor. Training his sharp gaze within that room he looked to see if *she* was there. She was.

Well disguised by his hood and cloak, he had listened carefully while he sat at the bar when the barkeep gave the woman directions to her room. After he found out where she was put for the night, he quickly downed the rest of his ale and left.

Now he continued to watch knowing full well that he had spooked her the last few days, but he did not care. A crooked smile of amusement curved across his lips as she placed the chair against the door. As if a thin wooden door and a puny chair could keep him out if he wanted to get in. He gave a low chuckle.

The object of his desire showed a strength of purpose and stamina that was impressive. She had hunted and taken care of herself as if she were born to a life in the woods. Storm Rider had seen her while flying overhead a few days past. Her long golden hair had attracted him, and curiosity won out, so he decided to follow the woman as she left Jior and went into the woods alone. His intent had only been to spy on her for an hour, but as the hours and then days passed, he continued to watch, fascinated. With her long legs, confident manner, and ability to fend for herself in the Violent Mountains, he became intrigued.

It was more than that he realized as he continued his vigil across the street from her window. *Something* drew him to her and he had no will to evade the temptation to follow her. Overhead, a spring storm brewed in the clouds and within his thoughts.

Storm Rider watched as the woman lit a fire in the small fireplace, stripped off her wet clothing, hung them to dry, and began to wash. The sight of her sleek, completely naked body almost caused him to swoop down, crash into the window and go to her right then, but he reminded himself he needed to be patient. Although, patience was not one of the qualities he possessed. He had a hard time not giving in to his baser instincts. The firelight made her fair skin glow as she stooped, wetted a cloth repeatedly, and then ran it over her arms, and legs, across perfect breasts, and over her flat stomach. Storm Rider had never seen her completely naked in all the days he had been following her and his blood fired. His breath grew heavy as he fought the arousal that threatened to overtake his better judgment.

As she turned away from the window Storm Rider's eyes suddenly trained on thin silver lines that glistened wetly across her back. The silver outline of *wings* graced her smooth skin from the top of her shoulders to the gentle curve of her lower back, as if the most talented artist had drawn them on using liquid silver.

"The ne'amh chomhara!" Storm Rider gasped in amazement and shock. He stared hard at the silver lines.

Storm Rider's interest hardened even more upon seeing those silver lines than he did from seeing her naked body. Everything made sense now he realized. She bore the ne'amh chomhara, *'Heaven's mark!'* She was Ny-Failen!

CHAPTER TWO

Meurie finished bathing and dressed in her other set of clean clothes then she moved toward the bed and listened. She strained her keen hearing to listen for bugs scratching through the well-worn mattress and coverlet, but she did not discern any. Even if she had, she was too tired to care about sharing her bed with flees or biting creatures. There were no mice in the room and she counted herself lucky for that. Climbing underneath the top blanket, she settled in, so grateful she was finally clean, warm, dry, and sleeping in a bed, she almost wept.

Outside, the call of a night owl reached through the darkness and penetrated her exhausted mind, she was too tired to be surprised. A night owl's cry had lulled her to sleep every night for the past week and it did not surprise her now. Rain began to pelt the window with muffled taps. Deciding she did not care, she rejoiced that she was warm and dry, and was too exhausted to think about it. She closed her eyes and fell into a blissful sleep.

As the rain began to fall harder Storm Rider continued to watch the window long after the girl had blown out the candle and gone to bed. He was in shock over what he had just learned about this girl. Rising to his full height, Storm Rider tilted his face to the rain and let it flow over him. He ran his fingers through his short, dark red hair and shook his wings, causing a cascade of water to sprinkle from his white feathers. Considering his next move carefully he lifted a hand to the side of his mouth and gave a cry. Mimicking the sound, he let fly the 'hoot hoo' of a night owl. It was reckless he knew and might alert her to his presence, even though she did not know it was he who followed. Part of him wanted her to know she was not alone. Spreading his wings, he lifted off of the roof and few across the street toward the barn next to the blacksmith's where he entered an upper window and bedded down in the hayloft. From this location, he knew he could watch her movements in the morning.

Sleep was slow in coming though as he thought long and hard about how he was going to meet this girl he had stumbled upon, and why he seemed obsessed with her so quickly. It was not just one thing he wanted from her, he realized. He wanted many things, but now the most important thing for him to consider was that she was Ny-Failen. Although she did not look like other Ny-Failen women, her skin was not pearl-white, she was fair-skinned but like a human. He was unsure of the color of her eyes, but she bore the ne'amh chomhara, Heaven's mark. He also learned the girl's name when the barkeep spoke to her. 'Meurie' he rolled the name around on his tongue. It did not suit her he thought, but her true name would be revealed to him in time.

His sister, Mercy Rose, always told him he pushed too hard when he wanted something. Storm Rider knew he was driven, intense, and only sometimes forceful. He wondered if this was one of those times if he relentlessly chased this girl on a whim, but he closed his eyes and pictured her bathing by the fire. The image of her naked body was burned into his memory, but it was the ne'amh chomhara that made his blood surge in his veins like a roiling storm gathering overhead. Her soft curves and lean body were as beautiful as he had imagined them. Growling with frustration, he crossed his arms behind his head and tried to get some sleep.

#

The far-off sound of a rooster crowing was like a stabbing screech in Meurie's ears. She cursed her overly sensitive hearing and covered her head with the musty pillow she lay on. Then she cursed her overly sensitive sense of smell as she breathed in the scent of the many people who had rested their heads on that same pillow. Her nose wrinkled in disgust. Her eyes felt dry and heavy. She just wanted to sleep, but anxiety woke in her mind and gave her a hearty shake to get going. She had slept in her clothing not only for warmth but as protection against any biting bugs that may move in, attracted by her warmth. The only thing that disturbed her, as she tried to fall asleep, was the sound of a night owl outside. That call had soothed her to sleep for the last few nights and somehow it made her feel *safe*.

Rising quickly, she looked out the window and saw the gray hand of dawn lifting the veil of night. Stilling, she listened and heard someone down in the main room scuttling about and the light thump of footsteps going down the stairs. She pulled her tunic over her shirt, cinched her wide belt around her waist, and pulled on her boots. They had dried by the fire overnight and were warm, but the leather had shrunk a little and now they were snug. Wrapping the laces around each leg tightly, she rose, grabbed her cloak, and searched the room with her gaze, making sure she had not left anything behind.

Leaving the room, she lightly stepped down the hall without making a creak or a scuff of sound. Descending the stairs her senses were assailed by the smell of baking biscuits and her stomach let out a growl of hunger. As she left the dark stairway, she decided traveling on an empty stomach would not be a good idea, and leaving the enticing smells without sampling, would be impossible.

The inn's main room which had been full of drunken revelers the previous night was virtually empty now except for a few other early risers. An old couple sat stooped over bowls of porridge at a far corner table. Two men she guessed were farmers, because they smelled like rich earth, sipped pints of ale, and munched on bread, jam, and sausages.

Meurie slid onto a bench behind a long table, her eyes trained hungrily on the kitchen door. Soon enough, a middle-aged woman who smelled of flour and bacon grease came out of the doors carrying a steaming mug. Without asking she sat the mug in front of Meurie and then walked away but came right back with a full tray.

Her attention, centered on the steaming mug of tea, was drawn away by the tray of warm biscuits, bacon, and boiled eggs now on the table. Disappearing into the kitchen for a moment, the woman came out again, walked over, and sat down with a bowl of berries, a small cup of cream, some butter, and jam.

Meurie felt like she had never eaten anything so tasty in her life. Lost in her thoughts, she fell upon the berries and cream with undisguised delight and reached for a second biscuit while spooning in another mouthful. Just as her hand grasped the warm bun it collided with something alive. As her fingers touched someone else's she startled, jerking her hand away, and looked up quickly.

"Helm!" She gasped in relief and surprise.

Helm laughed as he took the seat next to her. "What has you so distracted? You didn't even notice me coming up behind you." She realized he had come down the stairs, snuck up behind her, and reached over her shoulder to snatch away the same biscuit she had been reaching for.

Jumpy and nervous, Meurie stared at him for a long moment. He was young, clean-shaven, with long, straight brown hair that hung well past his shoulders, and he had deep blue eyes. He wore a long purple crystal on a thin leather cord around his neck. The inquisitive smile he gave her was sweet and loving.

"Come on, you can tell me why you are acting so distracted! I am your brother you know." He raised an eyebrow at her waiting for an answer.

"It is nothing. I just…" She took a deep breath and let it out before going on. "Well, on the way back from Jior, I thought I was being followed that's all and I'm a little spooked."

"Followed!" Helm looked alarmed. "By who?"

"I don't know. It's probably nothing, just the Violent Mountains. They are *haunted* you know."

"You've lived in the Violent Mountains all your life and never been spooked before. Tell me what happened." He continued to look at her with growing concern.

"I don't know really. I was on my way back from Jior, and the first afternoon after I'd left, a huge silence fell over the forest. Everything went quiet. At first, I thought nothing of it, but then I noticed the very air had stilled and there was *something* there. I felt a...a presence watching me. I tried to tell myself that it was my imagination, but it stayed with me the whole way. After traveling for three more days toward Dade-Bend, with the same feeling as if someone was watching and following me, well, I was very glad to reach Dade-Bend and the Dragonfly Inn. That's all."

"Maybe it was just a wild animal stalking you or who knows?" He shrugged, "It is a good thing I traveled out of my way to meet up with you. I'm sorry you were frightened, Sister." Helm smiled at her and then took the last biscuit with a playful grin.

"It's funny. I don't think whatever it was wanted to harm me, but I was on edge just the same. I kept hoping it would just step out of the woods and face me." She paused sipping her tea.

"You know," After thinking for a moment, she went on hesitantly, "it was like when you're on a mountain top and a storm is brewing around you but there are no dark clouds overhead. The air crackles with tension and your hair rises on the back of your neck, there is stillness in the air, and then suddenly lightning streaks across the sky and you feel the thunder shake your bones. That is what I've been feeling as if lightning is going to strike at any moment."

"Lightning can kill you if you don't take cover, you know," Helm warned. He was unhappy and his brow furrowed as he watched her.

Meurie just gave him a slight smile and nodded knowingly. While they finished breaking their fast Helm changed the subject and diverted her with stories about his travels to Gaunsig, a growing city on the coast of Vedt. It had been a profitable adventure, but they were both ready to return to their mountain home.

"I have the wagon provisioned and ready to go. I look forward to the pleasure of your company on the trip home, my Lady." Helm rose and playfully, gave her a sweeping bow.

She smiled and shook her head. Helm tossed two bronze coins on the table for their meal and then left.

As arranged, Helm met her outside the inn. He drove a small wagon full of tools and provisions. Meurie handed him her pack and he stowed it in the back. He offered her his hand to help her up onto the front seat of the wagon then made his way around the other side and nimbly jumped up beside her. Meurie stifled a small shiver as, once again, she felt eyes upon her.

Suddenly, the strange feeling of being hunted returned to her, and turning in her seat right and then left, she scanned the village. When she saw nothing untoward, she shook her head and told herself she was being silly but pulled her hood over her head as if to hide. The wagon jolted as the horses moved and pulled it down the street.

Storm Rider stood back in the shadows of the upper doors of the barn where he had spent the night. His wings lifted in agitation as he watched a young man, hand the girl up into a wagon. Where had he come from? His eyes narrowed in jealousy as the man touched her and he had to tamp down on the anger that overtook him as he realized that she might already be spoken for. Stepping back into the shadows so that he would not be seen as she looked around surveying the skies, he grinned wickedly knowing he was not daunted in the least bit. He would find out for sure what this man meant to her.

CHAPTER THREE

Helm was excellent company on the road home. As they traveled the muddy road, he kept up a steady stream of conversation. Meurie listened politely to his stories and covertly watched the treetops and surrounding woods, but there was no sign of the *thing* that had been following her. Even though she knew not what it was, she continued to look for anything out of the usual.

They stopped at midday for lunch and to rest the horses. Meurie was on edge and Helm sensed it.

"How was your trip to Jior?" He asked, handing her an apple. He watched his sister's every move. How her delicate hand cradled the red apple and how her slim body sat perched on the edge of a boulder. Looking away quickly he forced his attention to his luncheon.

"It went well. I sold all the crystals and raw gems I had with me, secured a guaranteed buyer for us in the future, and paid our tax to the King of Jior. It is a long way to go, though Jior is blessedly devoid of thieves and bandits. The terrain is difficult unless you keep to the roads."

"And did you see the object of your desire?" Helm teased with a winning smile.

High above, propped in the thick tree branches, Storm Rider tensed and listened intently to the conversation the two were having below. He perked up a little and waited for her answer to the last question.

"I did!" Meurie gasped wistfully.

Storm Rider's eyes narrowed in suspicion over what had her interest so acutely and he wanted to growl impatiently as he waited for her explanation. He listened.

"Oh, Helm!" She went on. "They are wonderful! Everything the tales say about them is true. They have huge white wings and *fly*! I saw the King of Jior himself, all dressed in black with his long white hair flying in the wind! There were two others all in brilliant white that were flying next to him. It was a wonderful sight to behold. One night, just before sunset, I saw another one flying alone. He was huge and had red hair, gigantic white wings and he flew straight into a rainstorm! Helm! Of all of them that I was able to glimpse that one thrilled me to the bones. He was the most beautiful thing I have ever seen!"

"I don't understand your fascination with those Jiorians," Helm grumbled then hesitated shaking his head with a furrowed brow. "But now that you've seen them and satisfied your curiosity that they are real, can you let it go? I mean, commoners like us never get near the royal family or any Ny-Failen for that matter. Living high in the Violent Mountains where we are, you'll never see one up close and you'll never…"

"Stop!" Meurie demanded, holding her hand up. She quickly rose to her feet and turned her back to Helm. "You've made your point!" She said, angrily crossing her arms over her chest and huddling into herself.

There was a long-reigning silence in the clearing. Helm finally sighed and quietly began to pack up their remaining lunch. It was many long minutes before Meurie finally turned and gave him a forgiving smile.

"And you?" Trying to gain back their light-hearted mood, she changed the subject. "Was your trip successful? Did you see your young maiden? Did you finally ask her?"

It was Helm's turn to frown now. "Yes, I saw her. No, I did *not* ask her."

"I don't understand what is holding you back?" Meurie grumbled as they stored their packs and once again climbed into the wagon. "You love Glenna, don't you? I know you want to marry and have children and you are of age. It is clear Glenna loves you too, the way she moons over you when we visit her father's farm. What is stopping you from asking her to marry you?"

Helm flicked the reins and guided the horses back onto the road before he ventured any explanation. Meurie was staring distractedly up at the trees once again and Helm looked intensely at her before he answered.

"Oh, I don't know." He continued to stare meaningfully at his sister, though she did not notice. He flicked the reins once again and the horses moved on.

#

Storm Rider did not follow the wagon as it moved down the road. He settled his back more comfortably against the tree trunk and considered what he had just learned. The girl, the object of his recent fascination, bore the ne'amh chomhara and was obviously Ny-Failen though she looked completely human. The young man with her was her brother, Helm. She had gone to Jior on business to sell crystals and gems and pay their taxes but seemed to have an ulterior motive and that was to spy out the Ny-Failen. Why she did not just fly to Castle Jior and make herself known, was a mystery. His family accepted all Ny-Failen, especially those with wings. Especially, *women* with wings as females with wings were rarer. Ny-Failen children had flocked to Jior in the first days when the Ny-Failen revealed themselves to mankind. Many of Storm Rider's family were winged, but he was also considered a rare anomaly among his kind because both his parents, Jagged Edge and Princess Lyra Song, were *not* winged. Among the Ny-Failen with two winged parents, giving birth to winged children was most prevalent. As the first grandchild to Forlorn Icefall the King of Jior, it had not been expected that Storm Rider would be born with wings.

So it was that the King himself taught Storm Rider to fly and his uncles, Vannier and Dark Star had helped. It was Storm Rider who discovered on his own, the joy of flying into storms, and thus he had been truly and deservedly named *Storm Rider*.

Now this new girl, looking more like a human, but bearing the ne'amh chomhara was not a new revelation as Storm Rider's father Jagged Edge, looked very human and was not winged but had Ny-Failen powers. The intense attraction Storm Rider felt toward her, had been a surprise.

Helm, the brother, was exasperated with his sister who seemed to have a fascination with the Ny-Failen. Storm Rider smiled at the information he had gained about Helm who had evidently been to see a young girl whom he had not the courage to ask to marry him. It pleased Storm Rider that he was Meurie's brother and not a husband and he questioned if Helm was also Ny-Failen. Although, Storm Rider did not sense that connection with the brother.

The thing that made Storm Rider's blood burn in his veins when he thought more deeply about it, was that Meurie, the girl he had followed now for over a week; *she* had seen *him* in Jior. In joyful abandon, Storm Rider shot into the air and spun like a tornado soaring into the highest clouds above.

#

Meurie and Helm reached their home high atop a steep mountain called 'Javelin Peak' in the Violent Mountains of Jior. They unpacked their gear from the long journey and stored away the supplies Helm purchased for them. During their supper together, Meurie regaled him with new stories about the Ny-Failen that she learned while in Jior. Helm tried to listen patiently.

Night fell and Helm had finally gone to bed but Meurie slipped from the confines of the cabin as was her nightly habit. Quietly closing the door behind her she slipped off into the night. A huge full moon glowed in the black, cloudless sky. She deftly made her way through the towering trees and down the side of the mountain. Meurie always had excellent night vision as well as an extraordinary sense of smell and hearing. Going down the mountain she easily traversed the well-worn trail. A light rain had fallen earlier and everything was washed clean and fresh.

The rich mineral smell of the hot springs greeted Meurie long before she reached them. She filled her lungs with the familiar scent and closed her eyes picturing herself taking a long soak in the hot waters. It would be the first real bath she had in days and the desire to wash her hair and thoroughly cleanse her body was overwhelming. A large owl passed through the trees far above her head, but she did not pay much attention as she was intent on her goal.

When she reached the natural hot springs nestled in the valley below her mountain home, she knelt on the ground and started a small fire in a ring of stones she always used. Then she stripped naked and paced confidently to the spring that was the perfect temperature for bathing.

The water was hot and eased the muscles that she had used so strenuously for the last many days. She dunked her head under the water and took a few long strokes across the deep, wide, pool. Her cares eased away with her soreness and she momentarily forgot everything.

#

The full moon lit up the clearing where hot mineral pools shimmered in its silvery light. Storm Rider crouched high up in the branches of a large oak and watched as Meurie undressed and slipped into the hot water. Once again, he had to reign in his physical desires and restrain himself from diving in to embrace her. His keen eyes detected the beautiful silver lines gracing her back as she lithely stroked across the pool.

Meurie swam and scrubbed her fingers through her long golden hair. As she enjoyed her bath, the watcher stared mesmerized by her. She seemed to dance in the moonlight as the water streamed over her sleek body and flowed down her long arms as they rose and gracefully dipped into the water. She languidly rolled onto her back and floated. Storm Rider could see from his vantage point how the moon caressed her white, wet breasts. Her arms reached through the water over her head and she slowly backstroked across the length of the pool. The sight was enthralling.

Later, Storm Rider watched as Meurie stepped out of the pool after her bath. The moonlight caressed her sleek wet body and he had a sudden revelation of her true name. She was *'Moon Dancer!'* The knowledge of her Ny-Failen name crashed through him as if it was shouted in the night. Why she went by the name 'Meurie' was a mystery to him as were so many other things about her. He could only think of her as Moon Dancer now that her true name was revealed to him. He watched as she strode over to the fire, drew out a large cloth she brought, and dried herself off.

After her bath, Meurie sat by the fire and dried her hair. She allowed her mind to wander and travel back to her adventure in Jior. Reliving the sight of the King of Jior and some of the other Ny-Failen flying above her head, she smiled and the firelight danced in her eyes. Then she allowed herself to think of the other one she had seen, the one with the red hair. She gave a heavy sigh as she thought of him and how the fading sun had touched him, turning his hair to flame red. Her heart beat more fiercely in her breast and she regretted that she had to leave Jior after such a short stay and regretted that she would never meet the wonderful being that made her heart leap.

Storm Rider continued to watch from the branches above. He wanted to howl with frustration. He longed to fly down to the clearing where his heart's obsession sat naked draped in a blanket, drying her bright golden hair by the fire. He wanted to look at her, all of her, and see the color of her eyes, and touch her soft skin. He wanted all of his questions about her answered but more than anything, he did not want to frighten her. So, he waited patiently, but vowed tomorrow he would meet her and hear her musical voice speak his name!

He called out to her disguising his voice like an owl and then he lifted off and flew into the night sky. Illuminated by the full moon, not caring if she saw or not, Storm Rider flew across the valley and landed high on the cliff of the mountainside just inside the highest tree line. There he gathered wood and lit a large fire. Situated on the opposite mountain face, Storm Rider knew that his fire would be visible for miles. More specifically, his blaze was bright enough to be seen from the barely distant mountain on the opposite side of the valley, *intentionally.*

As Meurie made her way back up the trail on Javelin Peak to the cabin she shared with her brother Helm, the sight of distant firelight drew her attention. The golden glow of flames illuminated the cliff face of a rock overhang. Meurie huffed in annoyance. This could only mean one thing. Another prospector had set up camp on the mountainside across from her and Helm's claim. Reaching the cabin doorway, she turned and stared in the direction of the fire anticipating a confrontation in the morning. As she stood there looking over the vast moonlit mountain range a tall shadow passed in front outlined by the fire's glow. Meurie could have sworn that, whoever had set up camp there, now stood on the edge of the cliff staring back at her.

CHAPTER FOUR

The following morning, over steaming cups of tea, Meurie told Helm about the fire she had spotted across the valley.

"I guess I'd better go and make sure this stranger is just passing through." Helm downed the rest of his tea and rose to grab his coat.

"I'll go with you." Meurie stood.

"No need. Perhaps he's already moved on and this will be a waste of time. You go back to the site and start digging; I'll check out our intruder and join you later. Best for you to start on the west face of the mountain, I think." He spoke as he wrestled a day's provisions into a pack.

"What if there is more than one? You could be in danger if they don't take too kindly to your shooing them off. I'm going with you." Speaking firmly in a tone that allowed no argument.

"Don't be stubborn. Both of us don't need to lose a whole day's digging."

"And don't *you* argue. I'm going! If you're so concerned with the digging, you stay and I'll go."

Helm hesitated irritated, looking back and forth from Meurie to his tools.

"Really, it makes more sense for me to go. You're the better digger. I'll go make sure our intruder has moved on, which I'm sure he has, and you stay and work." Meurie chided.

"I can't send you! What if they're hostile and overpower you? You could get hurt and I'd never forgive myself."

"Oh please! You know I can handle myself. Even against two men, I'm more than capable. Besides I'm fairly sure there is only one. I'll have my staff and you start on the west side. I'll be back before supper." Meurie turned without another word, grabbed her staff and pack she already prepared that morning, and walked toward the door. She turned back to Helm who stood still with a frown on his face looking at her.

"Don't look so angry. I'm not keen on digging today anyway and I promise I will be careful. I'll scout it out before I approach the camp, he'll never even see me. As you said, he's probably moved on and it will be a waste of time anyway." Meurie cajoled.

"Alright then, but I don't like it. You promise me you'll be careful and not take any risks."

She stalked back to Helm, stood on her toes, and kissed his cheek. "I promise." She bade farewell to Helm with a wave, reached for her long white, wooden staff, and left the cabin.

Meurie was ecstatic to be back on the mountain that was her home. She skipped along as she mentally greeted the landmarks she knew so well. There was a small meandering stream and a large rock wall with a well-worn deer path across it that she easily ran down. The birds in the surrounding trees chirped their greetings and her boots made a soft crunching noise on downed, dry, pine needles. Over the next hour, she made her way in the direction where she had spied the fire the previous night. She did not know why, but she was anxious to meet this stranger and had a feeling of great anticipation coursing through her veins. Not stopping to analyze her strange joyous mood she practically ran the entire way. Barely breathless, it took her most of the day, but she finally reached the bottom of the valley where a sheer towering cliff jutted out of the earth. She looked up toward her destination and resolved to be *very* careful.

The scent of a campfire and a thin wisp of smoke rose into the air above the high, sheer cliff. She momentarily wondered if, at the end of her search, she would find a man or a mountain goat. Looking to the right and left of the cliff face she searched for a way up. Not finding anything, she had to traverse the bottom of the rock wall until she found where it gently sloped upwards and she could safely climb up. Sticking her long white-wood staff in the loops on the small pack on her back, she nimbly climbed.

When she reached the bottom part of the cliff where she estimated the fire she saw the previous night was, she got the feeling of being watched. Many times, during her trek she wanted to whirl and catch the eyes she felt on her back. Convincing herself she was being ridiculous, she continued to climb up. She could smell the small fire burning above even stronger now. Her stomach gave a low growl and she realized she had not stopped for lunch. Deciding to press on toward her goal, she continued to climb.

As she reached the top, she knew her prey was just ahead. Pulling herself up over the lip of the rock face she silently leaped to her feet. If there were two or more ahead at the camp and if indeed, they had prospecting tools, she knew she would have to be cunning and stealthy. Drawing her staff free from her pack she crept silently toward the campfire just ahead. Stopping to listen she heard the sound of a man breathing. '*Good,*' she smiled to herself, there was only one.

Creeping forward she tightened the grip on her staff. She threaded through the thinning trees silently until she came to the rock overhang where she knew the intruder was. The rocks formed a natural shelf of sorts and she carefully placed one foot in front of the other intent upon sneaking up on the stranger. She peered around a rock overhang and saw a large man squatting next to a fire in a ring of stones. Beside him was a bed of pine boughs and he was feeding small sticks to the fire.

Meurie could not even breathe as she cautiously watched and it spooked her when he suddenly spoke.

"You can come forward. I heard you *stomping* up to my camp an hour ago." The man's deep voice rang out, though he had not even turned to look at her. She had to suppress a shiver the sound of his voice caused for some unknown reason.

"You must have excellent hearing because I was very careful," Meurie replied, irritated that he had insulted her tracking and stealth. Dropping any pretext of concealment now she stepped forward.

The camp was situated high atop a towering cliff and the vast mountain range stretched out in front presenting an impressive view. It almost looked as if only an eagle could reach it, but Meurie had easily climbed up. Though why he would pick such a spot so visible to the surrounding countryside, was beyond any reason she could think of.

"You've picked a poor place to camp. I spotted your fire from miles away last night and you easily could have stepped off the side of the cliff and plunged to your death in the darkness." Meurie kept her staff held at the ready wishing he would at least turn and face her. She got her wish. The man slowly stood unfolding his long frame, straightening and turned toward her.

Meurie saw many things in the seconds it took for him to fully turn and face her. First, he was one of the tallest men she had ever seen. He had broad shoulders, huge powerful arms, and large hands. Dressed all in black he looked menacing. The second thing Meurie noticed was that he wore a strange breastplate or light armor of segregated plates lined in silver and etched in strange patterns that looked like silver-tipped dragon scales. Each scale slid with his movements like a second skin. As he slowly turned and revealed his face to her, Meurie unwillingly gasped. He was a Jiorian! No! Not just a Jiorian, he was a *Ny-Failen*! He had dark red hair that spiked out from the back of his head as if combed by the wind and he looked like a majestic hawk. His pale, white skin, gently pointing ears, long nose, and sharp angular features further designated him as Ny-Failen. If his skin and features did not give his lineage away, the crest on his breastplate did. The silver Jiorian insignia of two wings caught the afternoon sunlight as his chest slowly expanded when he breathed deep. To say he was handsome, was a severe understatement, he was inconceivably beautiful and *divine*! What unnerved Meurie the most was his piercing dark green eyes. They stormed at her as if he were angry, dangerous, and threatening, but then softened and the anger was replaced by what she took as curiosity. She noticed the slightest twitch of his mouth as he tilted his head inquisitively and looked her over.

Storm Rider had waited impatiently all day while Meurie made her way toward his camp. Last night he had intentionally built his large fire here as a kind of signal. He knew that she would see it glowing against the night when she made her way back from the hot springs to her cabin. Now, here she stood, the girl whom he had followed for the past week. He had seen her naked body twice, had watched her bathe in the moonlight, had her true name revealed to him, but had never seen her face this flushed or looked this closely at the redness of her soft, full lips. Storm Rider's heart thundered in his chest when he saw she was even more beautiful than he had originally thought. Now he knew why he had gone to so much trouble to meet her and why he felt so drawn to her. With the exception of his Mother, Princess Lyra Song of Jior, this exquisite creature in front of him was the most beautiful woman he had ever seen. He could not help but let his eyes wander hungrily over her slim curves, long legs, and lithe muscular arms to land back on her full, red lips. The gentle breeze lifted wisps of golden hair from her brow and his eyes followed the strands down along the thick braid that fell over her shoulder and hung past her slim waist. She held a long white wooden staff in front of her as if it were a weapon.

They stood staring speechless at one another, for long, tense moments. Meurie almost jumped when he spoke again, breaking the silence.

"What brings you to my camp, my Lady?" His deep voice broke the trance she was under, just looking at him.

"I, ah," Meurie was suddenly angry that she was so distracted by this stranger and reminded herself why she was here. Despite his striking good looks, deep sultry voice, and tempestuous green eyes, she had business to attend to.

"You are trespassing upon claimed land. Didn't you see our markers? If you intend to mine here, I'm obliged to inform you that this claim belongs to my brother and me. I'll ask you to move on to another valley." To her ears, she spoke haltingly and sounded frightened and unsure.

"You claim this entire valley, my Lady?"

"I do!" She said defiantly. She did not like the way he called her *'my Lady'* as it caused her stomach to flip nervously. "We have the papers from Jior to prove the lease. We have sole permission to mine here from the King of Jior himself. You'd do well to move along now. You don't want to earn the ire of King Forlorn Icefall."

Storm Rider almost smiled as he found yet another thing to like about this girl. She was brave, defiant, and had no fear of him.

"You toss around the King's name easily enough, my Lady. I hope you can support your boasts."

"I can! And…and stop calling me, *my Lady*."

"Why?" He continued to stare openly at her as if devouring her.

"Because I'm not *your* lady. I'm not a lady at all and even if I was, I would not be *your* lady. So-so," She stammered even more now because of the way he was looking at her. "Just stop!"

"I don't know your name-*my Lady*." Storm Rider gave her a mischievous half-smile. "What else am I to call you?"

"My name is not important. What is important is that you move on and stake your claim elsewhere or I'll be forced to thrash you."

Storm Rider's eyes widened just perceptively, and he almost wanted to laugh, but she was too beautiful to laugh at and too attractively defiant. Her chin rose in a challenge and the wind-tossed wisps of her hair. Her cheeks blushed slightly pink as he silently continued to examine her.

Meurie was almost shaking with apprehension in front of this huge, foreign-looking Ny-Failen. Everything about him was different, from his skin to his hair, to his strange green eyes. He was fierce, menacing and so very attractive. All the years she had dreamed of meeting a Ny-Failen and memorized the tales about them, she never dreamed one would be this magnificent or standing in front of her.

"Alright." He said calmly. "Come and thrash me." Storm Rider invited, and when she failed to make a move, he leaned down and picked up a long thin piece of firewood. He gestured her forward and gave her that same half-grin that was not exactly a smile but was so alluring and *enticing* on his lips. Meurie's eyes darted to the silver short sword lying on the ground near where the Ny-Failen had been crouching by the fire.

She felt rooted to the spot, but then she realized he was mocking her and she became really angry.

"If I win, will you leave?" She snapped.

"I will not mine the land you claim if you can land one blow. If not, you will make me dinner, in your cabin, tonight."

Meurie's mouth fell open as she contemplated this bargain and then a smile took over her lips as she realized she could at least land one blow on this tall stranger. Hopefully, it would be on his arrogant head.

"Deal!" She shouted as she rushed toward him. Raising her staff, she sprinted straight at him and swung her whitewood staff at his head. The Ny-Failen did not even move but parried her strike easily making it look effortless.

Meurie's momentum carried her past him and she whirled making a backswing, but he was not there and she stumbled. Whirling in a circle she found him. It was then that she realized neither force nor surprise would earn her a strike. She tried speed, and began to whirl and dance, spinning her white staff in blurring windmills around her. Her lithe, muscular arms made the staff whistle as she battled with the air. The Ny-Failen just stood watching unimpressed and waited for her fancy antics to stop, but suddenly she sprang into the air and flipped to one side, as she landed, her staff swung in a wide arch about a foot off the ground. It whistled toward his ankles and any normal man would have had his feet cut right out from under him. Storm Rider was no mere man though and he nimbly leaped over the staff and, not to be fooled, he leaped again as the staff quickly swung in a backhanded blow missing him again.

Meurie was infuriated and began a frontal attack trying desperately to just touch him with her staff, but he repelled every trick she had and she could not so much as come near him. His eyes danced with humor and his lips held a tight, straight mouth as if he were holding back a grin. He parried her thrusts and stopped her swinging blows easily without giving ground.

As they fought, long staff to short stick, Meurie began to tire and it did not take long for her to realize she could not beat him. Not willing to give in just yet she redoubled her strikes. The sound of wood knocking wood reverberated over the cliff wall.

"Yield, my Lady." The Ny-Failen spoke calmly and was not even breathless.

Sweat began to run down Meurie's back and she gritted her teeth and attacked again. The tip of her weapon hit high and before she thought her opponent could block, she struck with the bottom of the staff and repeated those blows, rocking top to bottom, top to bottom. Still, he repelled every attack and halted any advance. Finally, Meurie admitted defeat and slowed her blows, and then stopped. Breathing heavily, she leaned on her stick, and without really admitting it, she yielded.

"A good attempt, my Lady. You are skilled, but you could use some discipline. Are you as good with the sword as you are with the staff?"

"I told you, stop calling me Lady!" She demanded between breaths.

"Come," The Ny-Failen held out his hand to her. "Let us go. You owe me dinner and I'm getting hungry."

Meurie cursed under her breath and looked at the long strong hand this strange Ny-Failen held out to her. She thought she had seen that hand before but could not place where. She stood staring for just a moment trying to remember and then shook her head back into the present. Suddenly remembering Helm, she looked a little perturbed at having to tell her brother that, instead of running off the intruder, they would host him for dinner.

"Alright then. Follow me." Meurie donned her small pack and started to walk past the Ny-Failen to return the way she had come, but he put out an arm to stop her.

"Why don't we just fly?" The words passed easily from his lips as he stepped in front of her and blocked her path with his huge body.

"*Ffly?*" Meurie gasped wide-eyed. "Perhaps you can fly, but I cannot!"

"You cannot?" Storm Rider looked down at the beautiful girl, the object of his obsession, and said quietly, "Or will not?"

"Cannot! Of course, I have no wings. The only way I'm going to fly is if you carry me!" Meurie jested with a nervous, tinkling laugh. Looking at him as if he were mad, she made to step around the Ny-Failen, but he once again stepped in front of her. This time she did collide with him. Like running into a rock wall, she stopped hard and then looked up into intense green eyes.

The Ny-Failen was looking down at her. She was tall for a woman but he was still a head and shoulders taller than her. She had not immediately noticed, but his arms went around her and he was holding her. Her body felt like she had been struck by lightning and she shivered in his embrace. He was warm and solid and she could feel him breathing and hear his heart beating hard and fast within his chest.

"Let me go." She whispered fearfully, but not very convincingly.

"Come, my Lady, tell me your name." He said very gently, his voice low and quiet, still holding her in his arms.

Meurie realized she was holding her breath and she said on an exhale. "Meurie."

The Ny-Failen reached down and gently pulled her wrists up and put her arms around his neck. He had been holding her storm blue eyes with his deep green gaze and just stood looking at her with her arms around his neck. The intimacy of the stance was not lost on her and Meurie felt as if her heart would burst because of the look he was giving her. Wanting to step back she found she was frozen to the spot by his presence.

She did not know where the outrageous thought came from, but it dawned on her that she had never been kissed before. As soon as she had that thought, she broke eye contact and looked at his lips. Blushing furiously again, she could not step back. Ordering her feet to move, just one step, she still stood rooted to the spot, then she ordered her arms to fall from around his neck and push away, but they refused to let go.

The Ny-Failen was still looking intently, hungrily at her and Meurie felt him shrug his shoulders and then shapeshifting from his back, huge white wings lifted and spread slowly.

"Meurie." He whispered as the wings gave a delicate pulse behind him. The white feathers glistened in the sun and almost seemed to glow. Bending down slightly he lifted her in his arms and she unconsciously pressed against him until they stood in a very tight, intimate embrace.

"We fly!"

"Wait!" She begged breathlessly, "What is *your* name?"

The Ny-Failen held her tightly and leaped into the sky as he proclaimed.

"Storm Rider!"

CHAPTER FIVE

Meurie's heart soared when the Ny-Failen told her his name. It was like a secret she always wanted to know had suddenly been revealed to her. She pressed her cheek against his shoulder and felt the movement of his body as they flew. She could feel the great wings pulse, lifting them higher and higher in the sky. He smelled like rain on the wind she realized, as she reminded herself to breathe.

"Look." He spoke into the wind, pointing with his chin and she turned her head and beheld the beginnings of a beautiful sunset. The blue sky gave way to brilliant golden clouds painted pink and orange. The sun was a blinding white crescent setting behind Javelin Peak and fingers of white gold reached toward them.

Storm Rider did not need to be told which direction to go because he already knew where her cabin home was perched on the side of the peak. He flew slowly for once, just so that he could hold Meurie in his arms for longer. The feel of her body pressed to him was intoxicating and he resisted the urge to lean down and rub his cheek against her golden hair.

The distance it had taken Meurie the better part of the day to traverse on foot was crossed in a few minutes with the Ny-Failen flying her. She closed her eyes for a moment and just enjoyed the feel of Storm Rider's arms around her and the wind in her hair.

Suddenly, he whirled and shot straight up into the clouds. They reached a dizzying height and Meurie fearfully looked around. They were high above the clouds hovering and she could feel the brilliant sun's warmth. Storm Rider turned onto his back until she lay atop him in the clouds. His gaze traveled over her hair as it glowed golden in the sunlight. His outstretched wings held them suspended in the sky for just a few heart-stopping moments.

"You fit well in my arms, my Lady." Storm Rider spoke close to her ear just loud enough to be heard over the rushing wind then he flipped over and plummeted back down through the clouds.

Meurie's skin tingled as the air rushed by her so fast that she clung more tightly to Storm Rider and hid her face against his warm neck. Every nerve in her body was aware of his body and she could feel the rhythm of his wings beating strongly and his arms flexing to keep her safe within his embrace. Too soon the flight was over and they skimmed along the treetops. Slowly, he descended to the clearing outside the cabin Meurie shared with Helm.

When her feet were solidly set upon the ground Storm Rider did not let go. Meurie was finally able to unclasp her arms but hesitated just a moment more before pulling away. The warmth of his body was gone and Meuric instantly missed his arms around her. Stepping away self-consciously, she smoothed wisps of hair away from her face where the wind had blown it loose. Disoriented from their flight and trying to catch her breath, she staggered a little as if being back on firm land was foreign to her legs then she turned and went toward the hut.

Behind her Storm Rider shrugged and shapeshifted his wings away. Now he stood there as just a very large and imposing figure of a man.

"Come this way." She bade him follow, and he did.

Inside the hut, Helm heard the door creak slightly when he heard Meurie enter.

"Well, did you get rid of our claim-jumper?" Helm was leaning over a pot of stew with his back to her.

Meurie leaned her staff against the wall and dropped her small pack onto the floor.

"Um, not exactly."

Helm straightened and turned toward the sound of Meurie's voice with a smile that froze on his face and then fell into a frown. He clenched the spoon in his hand until his knuckles turned white.

Storm Rider ducked his head to enter the small cabin then he was able to stand without hitting his head on the low roof, but just barely. He assessed Meurie's brother with calculating eyes and he noted there was no family resemblance. Meurie quickly stepped forward and stammered an introduction.

"Helm, this is Lord Storm Rider from Jior. It was his fire I saw last night on the cliff. He, um, he, well he's, I mean, I've asked him to come to dinner."

Helm just stood staring at the tall Jiorian taking up a large part of the kitchen.

"Lord Storm Rider," she turned and gestured, "This is my brother, Helm."

Helm nodded a short greeting but did not speak. Storm Rider placed his hand over his heart and tilted his head in the traditional way a Ny-Failen respectfully greets another. A long uncomfortable silence hovered in the small cabin.

"I'll set the table." Meurie stammered nervously, quickly breaking the awkward silence. "Are those biscuits I smell baking?" She went to a tall wooden cupboard and began to pull out wooden bowls and horn cups.

"Please sit down Lord Storm Rider." Helm gestured to the head of the table and Storm Rider folded himself into the chair.

"Your visit is well-timed as we've just come up from Dade-Bend and I have wine. Would you care for some? Or perhaps you'd prefer ale?" Helm's voice was strained.

"Just call me Storm Rider, Master Helm, and I'll drink whatever you are drinking. Lady Meurie was gracious enough to invite me and I do not want to be trouble."

Helm turned wordlessly and he and Meurie finished preparing dinner while Storm Rider watched them working side-by-side. As Meurie set the wooden bowls on the table, Helm reached into the cupboard and grabbed an *iron* spoon and knife. When they sat down, he dished the stew into bowls and placed a plate of biscuits on the table with honey and butter. Then, he placed the iron spoon and knife next to Storm Rider's place setting.

Storm Rider surveyed the iron eating utensils with interest and then looked up at Helm with narrowed eyes. Helm turned and hid his satisfied grin as he realized his suspicion was correct about the Ny-Failen at his table. He had an *aversion to iron*. Meurie did not notice the exchange between the two males, but as covertly as she could, scooped the iron utensils away and put them back into the cupboard drawer. She replaced them with wooden spoons not realizing Helm had intentionally tested their guest.

The uncomfortable atmosphere prevailed while Helm and Meurie waited for their guest to begin to eat first, as was only polite, but then he did the strangest thing. Storm Rider bowed his head over his bowl and said a word of thanks to the Creator for the meal. Then he reached for a biscuit and began to eat with impeccable manners. He avoided the stew which had been cooked in an iron pot.

"Lord Storm Rider is just passing through Helm," Meurie explained. "He's not mining and is not interested in our claim. I invited him to the cabin before he has to move on."

This news seemed to cheer Helm a bit and he picked up the conversation.

"What brings you to this part of the Violent Mountains, Lord Storm Rider? You're a long way from Jior."

"Please, just call me Storm Rider." Storm Rider's deep unemotional voice was polite but forceful. "I usually have no set destination. I often fly over the Violent Mountains in the spring." He looked meaningfully at Meurie then added, "I've been distracted from my usual path." His eyes sparked dark green desire as he looked at her.

Meurie held his gaze and blushed. Helm noticed the look between the two and it was his turn to sound polite, but forceful.

"When will you be leaving?"

Storm Rider looked away from Meurie and did not answer. He took a drink of the wine and a bead of the red liquid rested on his lips briefly before he licked it away. He was looking at Meurie again as if he would like to have her for supper. Helm could not fail to notice the way Storm Rider looked at Meurie and the way Meurie looked at him. He frowned into his cup of wine.

They ate in uncomfortable silence for a while, until Meurie spoke up as if trying to find something to talk about.

"Helm, did you have luck today? What did the earth reveal to you?"

"Yes, I dug up some grand crystals today. I've left them on the washing screen. Why don't you go and bring in a few of the larger ones to show our guest?"

"Oh? I, I suppose I can go get them." Meurie gave him a surprised and confused look. She had not touched much of her supper but rose to go anyway.

"I'll return in a few minutes, Lord Storm Rider."

Storm Rider had risen to his feet when Meurie got up from the table and when she left, he sat back down. Helm did not waste any time and, as soon as the door was closed, leaned forward.

"She doesn't know!" Helm whispered fiercely.

"Doesn't know what?" Storm Rider looked at Helm curiously.

"You must leave! Leave her be! You have no right to come here. I *know* you came for *her!*"

Storm Rider remained silent, knowing that in the man's anger he would answer many of the questions he had about Meurie, who was a mystery he was intent on solving. Keeping his voice very quiet, Helm went on.

"She doesn't know about the marks-the *wings* on her back. My parents always kept them secret she is not aware that she is part Ny-Failen! You must leave her be! Go now before it is too late! You will only hurt her."

"She is not your sister by blood. Is she?" Storm Rider tried not to growl. "Why have you kept this secret?" The hand he laid on the table clenched in anger. "She deserves to know who she is! Why have you not told her?"

"I've no time to explain and it really is none of your business just go and leave Meurie alone!" Helm spoke with finality.

"Give me the truth now or give it to me when she returns." Storm Rider demanded softly, a clear warning in his tone.

Helm closed his eyes and gave an exasperated exhale collecting his temper. When he opened them, he looked resigned as if he had known someday this moment would come. Taking a steadying gulp of his wine, he glared at Storm Rider.

"My parents found her when she was a baby. She is my sister in every way and I love her. I protect her from the world and men, who would use her and hurt her. They always told me that despite the markings, she would never fly and that is why she was abandoned as a baby. After our parents died, I just kept the secret because I saw no point in telling her. She can't see her own back so she will never know the marks are there." He paused and looked sad and angry.

"Despite my best efforts, she is obsessed with your kind, but she has no wings, and telling her about the marks on her back will only hurt her."

"The ne'amh chomhara is not something to be kept hidden. You have no right to hold her back from being who she is. She deserves to know she can fly! She should know her true name! Her Ny-Failen name!"

Helm sat back in his chair looking resigned then said in a sad quiet voice. "If you reveal who she is and find out for yourself she is wingless, you will tire of her and leave. You will break her heart and her spirit."

Storm Rider sat silently and glared at Helm who just glared back. When Meurie returned she found the two men sitting tense and angry like foes squaring off before a battle. Meurie lowered the roll of cloth she had in her hands and spread it out on the table.

"You see Lord Storm Rider; Helm has found riches beyond compare!" Meurie's eyes sparkled with glee as she lifted a long, milky-white crystal from the cloth. Moonstone spikes of many shapes and sizes glittered in the lamplight. Holding one up, Storm Rider looked at the opalescent object and gave Meurie a slight smile and nod.

"Most impressive Master Helm. The earth has revealed her secrets to you." Storm Rider held Meurie's attention and he went on. "Did you know when lightning strikes sand it melts into glass?"

"Yes, we know, Lord Storm Rider," Helm interjected angrily. "We are simple mountain folk, but the earth provides for us and shows us its many wonders."

"I must go." Storm Rider said as he slowly stood. He started to turn toward the door but stopped before opening it.

"I thank you for your hospitality, my Lady, Master Helm." He tilted his head again taking his leave of the angry young man. Stooping under the door lintel he stepped out into the cool night. Meurie followed him out into the blackness, puzzled to see him go so abruptly. She desperately tried to think of something to say.

Before Storm Rider left, he stepped close to her and gallantly lifted one of her small hands in his and kissed it gently, sending a small thrill up her arm. Then he shrugged and his wings expanded, pure, white, and glowing in the night. He flew away. Meurie watched his white wings beating strong in the moonlight, carrying him away from her. It was not until Helm gently put his arm around her shoulders and pulled her back toward their cabin that she finally looked away.

CHAPTER SIX

In the late night-time hours, Meurie rose from her bed. The events of the day had charged her blood and sleep would not come. She rose, grabbed a few things, and left the cabin. The moon was still large in the sky and lit the path to the hot springs. As she approached, she saw through the trees the faint glow of a campfire. She could not even allow a glimmer of hope or speculation as to who might be at the hot spring this late at night. It could only be one person. She crept forward stealthily. The mineral smells of the hot springs reached her and her other senses were attuned to *his* presence.

A nearby freshwater stream trickled close by and the night sounds of the mountain echoed through the forest. Meurie crept forward toward the glowing fire. She was as silent as her soft boots would allow.

"You can come forward." She heard the Storm Rider's deep voice speak gently from the darkness.

Meurie gave up all pretense of stealth and walked boldly forward. The fire's light revealed the dark pile of Storm Rider's clothing, boots, and armor. Her eyes moved from the glowing coals of the fire over to the hot pool where she saw Storm Rider. Standing up to his chest in the black water, his white skin glowed in the moonlight and his short hair was dark with wetness and slicked back. Meurie could barely move and was about to stammer an apology for intruding and leave, but Storm Rider's hand rose from the water and he silently beckoned to her. Like a frightened doe that has spotted a predator, she hesitated poised to run. That large hand beckoned again and before she knew it, she was bending over to remove her boots then the loose skirt she had donned to wear to the spring fell at her feet and she stepped out of it. Last, she cast aside her shawl and blouse until she stood in only a thin shift that covered her down to mid-thigh.

Storm Rider did not move when she walked slowly toward the water's edge unbraiding her long hair as she went. He just looked into her eyes as she moved forward. Meurie knew this pool blindfolded and placed her foot surely on the natural steps that had been eroded into the stone. The water embraced her as she entered deeper into the water and took Storm Rider's hand. He pulled her into his arms.

As when they had flown, Meurie's arms went around his neck and her body pressed against his. He was hugely muscled and his pale skin was smooth under her hands. She did not dare stare at his nakedness, but she could feel his body against hers and was glad for the thin shift that was all that separated them and for the darkness that hid her blushing face. He was intoxicating and she was supple and slim in his hands. For long silent moments, they just stayed motionless in the water staring into each other's eyes.

Storm Rider moved first. Lowering his head, he nuzzled her cheek until she lifted and met his lips. He kissed her softly and gently. She tasted sweet and as she parted her lips, his tongue touched hers and then delved deeper. His heart was thundering as his hands caressed her curves. Storm Rider wanted to haul her out of the water and bury his hardness deep inside her. He wanted to make them one, to make love to her like a raging storm and it was so hard to hold back, but somehow, he managed to. Swaying in the water he let his kisses travel down her neck. Pulling herself up against him Meurie wrapped her legs around his waist and Storm Rider growled as her intimate valley pressed against his bare erection. Then the kiss stopped as she leaned back supported by the water and swayed. Gently they spun a circular dance in the water. She smiled as she swayed in front of him and her breasts taunted him under the thin wet material of her shift. His hardness pressed against her and he was mad with desire, but he did not enter her. He leaned over and kissed her breasts, caressed her curving bottom, and just marveled at the feel of her in his arms, pressing against his body.

Meurie was dizzy from Storm Rider's kisses. Every place he touched her was shocked with lightning strikes and she was warm and her desire was potent, but he did not make love to her. As she leaned back and he kissed her breasts over her shift she regretted that she had not stripped completely wanting to feel his lips on her bare flesh. There was a small conflict in her mind some inkling of warning from a memory or a tale she had heard about Ny-Failen men making love to human women and then leaving them broken-hearted. It was a sad, harsh tale that taught girls like her that Ny-Failen men were something to be feared and kept away from. When Storm Rider did not take her innocence when they embraced, part of her was relieved and part of her was crushed with disappointment and overwhelmed with desire.

Meurie always had a strange fascination with the Ny-Failen and listened intently to tales or news of them. She hoarded information about them in her mind and her heart, she secretly wished to know them and live among them. Drawn to them like a moth to a flame she badly wanted to know what it was like to be Ny-Failen.

Storm Rider had slowed his kisses and now he caressed Meurie's breasts with his large hand as he looked at her with reverence. His desire burned in his eyes and pressed up hard between them. His control was astounding and he was surprised at his ability to hold back from taking her and finally making her his. Instead, he lifted her to her feet and tried not to notice the look of confusion and sadness that crossed momentarily over Meurie's beautiful features. When he released her, she stepped back, spun gracefully away so that he would not see the hurt in her eyes then she dove under the water. Swimming away from him, Storm Rider watched her long arms break from the water's surface and she came up across the pool far away from him. The warm water flowed over her as she emerged and her hands smoothed her hair back from her face. She could not look at him, because she knew how embarrassment from his rejection overtook her heart and mind, and she did not want him to see it on her face.

The moon cast the hot pool in bright, glowing light as Storm Rider climbed out naked as if nothing had happened between them. His wet, lean body was silvered by the moonlight and she could not help but gaze at him from head to foot. Her eyes traveled from the muscular thighs of his legs and up to the rippling muscles of his tight bottom and then up further to the broad planes of his back. She stared curiously at the intricate wings drawn in dark silver on his back and illuminated by the moonlight, she knew that never, in all of her days, had she seen anything so breathtakingly beautiful. To simply call him handsome was not enough. Her heart skipped a beat as the sudden realization hit her that Storm Rider had somehow changed his mind and he did not want her, did not want to make love to her. She turned her back to him because suddenly it was too painful to look at him. Clamping down hard on her hurt from his rejection, she closed her eyes and waited, hoping he would just fly away.

Moving to the other side of the pool and climbing out to sit on a rock, trying to get as far away from him as she could, Meurie waited until she thought enough time had passed and he might have gone. In her embarrassment, she could not face him and hoped that this first experience with a man would be her last because she never wanted to feel this devastated again. Then her logical mind awoke and slapped her thoughts away. Had he not called her forward? Had he not held out his hand to her? Had he not lowered his head to kiss her? He had, but this knowledge only made her feel worse as she realized something about her or something she had done, made him change his mind.

In the water, she had felt his desire for her pressing up against her belly and she wanted to moan with need, but he had stopped, exhibiting a control that she had not realized males possessed. Her first lesson in desire now ended in heartbreak.

The ghost of a breeze began to pick up and Meurie became chilled. There was nothing but silence on the other side of the long pool and she dared to look. He was gone. She stood feeling shocked, broken-hearted, and then furious at herself that she could think such a beautiful creature would want her. What had Helm said?

"Commoners like us never get near any Ny-Failen."

Suddenly glad she was not prone to weeping; Meurie just stared hard at the glowing fire. The wind blew gooseflesh on her arms and she embraced the cold mountain air and tried to let it seep into her heart.

Then the cool of the breeze was gone and she was embraced by warmth. Storm Rider was behind her wrapping her in the warm, dry blanket she had brought. His arms went around her and he held her against his body. She could feel his chest muscles against her back and she shivered, but not with the cold. He had let his wings out and now he wrapped them around her. He gently placed his cheek against hers and nuzzled her. She would not be fooled this time into turning to meet his lips. Storm Rider turned her in his arms and kissed her passionately. Meurie's arms were held tightly in the blanket he had wrapped around her and he pulled her closer, plundered her lips, and coaxed her tongue to dance with his.

After he kissed her breathless, he suddenly stooped swept her up into his arms and flew her to the other side of the hot pool. He set her down gently, shrugged his shoulders imperceptibly and his wings retracted into the silver lines on his back. He built up the fire and then pulled Meurie down by his side.

Storm Rider did not know what had made him refrain from making love to Meurie, but he knew he had to stop. He had to wait until some other matters were worked out between them. He would not just love her and fly off as he suspected she was thinking he would do, and he had felt her disappointment and hurt just now as she moved away from him. It further touched his heart that she was so strong and did not weep but had borne her pain courageously. Nonetheless, her pain was like a dagger cut to him. He wanted to do anything to take it away.

Storm Rider had donned his britches and boots and now propped one arm over his bent knee and tried to read Meurie's face, trying to catch her eyes. His brow furrowed because of what he saw. What Helm had revealed to him carlier was heavy on his heart and part of him wanted to throw caution to the wind and tell her who and what she was. He wanted to shout her name, '*Moon Dancer*' from the storm clouds and fly next to her while the lightning caressed her skin. He wanted to kiss her breathless and bury himself inside her, but he did not want to hurt her. Was it his right to give away a lifetime secret, no, a life-*changing* secret to this beautiful creature who had stolen his heart?

"My Lady." Storm Rider gently took one of Meurie's hands in his planning on telling her, what? "My Lady." He whispered gently, not knowing where to start or what to reveal to her. She took the choice away from him.

"You don't have to say it. I know what is stopping you from…I know how it is with the Ny-Failen. It is forbidden for you to mate with humans. I've heard the legends, the tales. I understand what is stopping you from making love with me. I am just a human, a commoner at that, and far, far beneath you in every way. I understand and I would not want you to break the laws of your people."

"I wish that it were that simple, my Lady." Storm Rider looked down at his hand holding hers.

"Storm Rider, I will have the memory of your kisses with me for the rest of my days. When you are gone back to Jior, this night will fill my dreams, and though I will be sad that you are gone and your kisses no more, I am forever grateful to have known you, even this little bit."

Meurie pulled her hand from his grasp and rose to her feet. She grabbed her skirt and boots and walked away whispering, "Goodbye, Lord Storm Rider."

Storm Rider rose to his feet as well and watched her disappear into the trees. Off in the distance, the soft sound of thunder warned of an impending storm. It called to him and he shrugged, his wings spreading out behind him. Bending at the knees he shot into the air, whirled through the black clouds of the gathering rain, and went to ride the storm.

#

It had been a week since Meurie had last seen Storm Rider and her heart ached with sorrow, but she hardened her feelings toward him. She told herself she had not known him at all and was glad that he had gone and her virtue was still intact. Each night as she left the cabin to return to the hot pool that was her refuge, she wished and hoped to see him again. Each night she looked toward the cliff where she had first seen his fire and hoped to see the glow of his flames, but each night she was disappointed.

Helm was furious that Storm Rider had brought this sorrow upon his sister, though he tried to be gentle with her. He knew deep in his heart why Storm Rider had left her and in truth, he was just as angry with himself. Still, he tried to cheer her. In the evenings, after the long days' work, he brought out a flute and would play her merry tunes. He had a beautiful voice and would sing songs to her and try and cheer her up. Finally, one day she did smile and Helm felt as if they had weathered the storm and now things would go back to normal. However, in the morning Meurie's quiet, sadness was back and Helm feared she would never be back to her old cheerful self. Somehow in the span of one afternoon and evening, Storm Rider had managed to steal her heart away and Helm worried about her. He wondered if he should tell her the truth but was afraid she would leave him.

Overhead the spring storms raged each afternoon and Meurie stood in the rain and watched as the lightning struck across the sky and the thunder shook the Violent Mountains. It seemed to her that there were more storms than usual this spring and the rain made digging on the steeply sloping Javelin Peak very dangerous. She worried about Helm getting caught in a rock slide and begged him to stop working until the heat of summer came and dried up the mountain.

At night Meurie would return from the hot spring pool with the memories of Storm Rider's arms around her. She told him that night before she walked away, that the memories of him would be enough to get her through her whole life, but she realized now that was a lie. Dreams of him, flying with him, kissing him, and seeing his body in its full glory, tortured her nights. In many of the dreams, she too had wings and flew beside him into the rays of the setting sun. She woke with tears drying on her cheeks and the flesh of her back burned as if she truly had flown all night.

CHAPTER SEVEN

Storm Rider returned to Jior feeling as frozen as a blizzard. He had watched Moon Dancer walk away from him and had respected what he felt was her wish not to see him again. His following her, finding her, their short time together, their short flight, the stolen kisses under the moonlight where she had danced in his arms to a mutual tune that was abruptly silenced, the dance unfinished, it all was for naught. Now her absence was like a dagger stuck in his chest.

He spent much time on one of the high towers of Jior's black castle and listened to the waterfall that cascaded from the rocks of the canyon where Jior was built. He spent a lot of time standing in the rain and more time riding the howling winds of the storms that raged over the Violent Mountains.

Storm Rider's family gave him wide berth knowing he was in a temper. No one could approach him, but his mother Princess Lyra Song and, though her presence calmed him, he would not reveal what bothered him, even to her. His father, Jagged Edge was just as frustrated because his oldest son's mind was one of the few that he could not read and he did not know how to help his son. He steered clear of his sister Mercy Rose who, in the past, had always been able to talk sense into Storm Rider. Lastly, Queen Lililaira with all her healing powers could not heal what ailed Storm Rider, though she knew somehow, he was heartsick.

When the rivers and streams in Jior and the surrounding mountains swelled over their banks and flooded the land because of all the rain, King Forlorn Icefall thought enough was enough. He decided it was time he approached his grandson.

Storm Rider stood on the high black crystal tower of Castle Jior and closed his eyes, seeing for the thousandth time, Moon Dancer's sleek, naked back and the ne'amh chomhara. He remembered how it glistened wetly in the lamplight that first night he saw her. He relived kissing her in the hot pool and his body stirred, unsatisfied and hungry. His lips curled in self-recrimination and he reminded himself again and again why he had left, and the secret Helm had revealed. It tossed his mind like a leaf in a tempest that she did not know who or what she was and that she was lost to him. She had turned and walked away from him. Anger, like a freshly opened wound, began to bleed in his heart and the clouds overhead turned black and roiled over the valley of Jior threatening another storm.

King Forlorn Icefall, also called King Lorn, approached the tower where his grandson stood shirtless not feeling the cold wind. He lifted his eyes to the sky and saw the building storm and decided enough was enough.

"Storm Rider!" King Lorn called over the winds. He approached his grandson and gripped his shoulder. "Cease this now or you will flood the entire kingdom!"

Storm Rider turned and looked up into his grandfather's eyes and his rage slowly dissipated. Closing his eyes, he concentrated. Ever since he was a young boy, he had been able to call the rain, the thunder, and lighting. He spent years under his mother's tutelage trying to learn to leash his abilities and calm his emotions so that storms did not constantly rage over the Kingdom of Jior. He had been highly successful in letting nature have her due and storm in season, but his desire and need to ride the winds of the storm and feel the lightning dancing over his skin grew so fierce he could not withhold it. So, he left Jior each spring and retreated deep into the Violent Mountains of Jior to let his power loose, to ride the storms. It was on the morning of his leaving this spring that Storm Rider had leaped from this same tower, had looked down, and had seen Meurie, *Moon Dancer*, looking up at him from the streets of Jior. As this thought once again took him over Storm Rider shook with the effort it took to settle himself and calm the skies. As the clouds blew away and the sun, in blue skies overhead, warmed the wet earth, Storm Rider turned to his grandfather.

King Lorn was fiercely proud and protective of his first grandchild and Storm Rider, more than any of the other grandchildren, took after Lorn. Like Lorn, he was prone to brooding and could fall into despair if not watched carefully. What struck fear into Lorn's heart was that Storm Rider was also like Lorn's father, Kullorn and he could be wild, violent, detached, and unemotional.

"Storm Rider, calm the storm and come with me! That is an order from your King!" Lorn leaped into the sky expecting his grandson to follow. Storm Rider also leaped into the sky and did follow, tamping down hard on the rampaging desire to call the lightning and strike. Grandfather led grandson and they disappeared into the dissipating clouds. They flew to the top of the raging waterfall at the end of the valley where the city of Jior sprawled and King Lorn landed near a small deserted stone building that had served as a watchtower in the early days of Jior's revival as a kingdom. Now it was empty, but for two wooden chairs and a small table. King Lorn shifted and put his wings away and ducked into the dark building. He lit a candle and stacked wood in the small fireplace to start a fire. This was more to set up a calming atmosphere than it was for warmth and Lorn used it as a distraction while he ordered his thoughts.

Storm Rider stood leaning against the doorway, looking back over the huge sprawling city and the vast stretching mountain range that was the Kingdom of Jior.

"Storm Rider, sit." King Lorn produced a bag of wine that he had brought and reached for two cups. He blew the dust from the cups and poured a measure into each. Then he sat down across from Storm Rider and pushed a cup toward him. Storm Rider reached for the cup but did not drink, he just continued to stare out the open door.

"Storm Rider," King Lorn began. "It hurts me to see you like this. Tell me what has you so upset that you unleash the storms and flood my kingdom as if you would make the very skies weep and cry out with your pain."

Storm Rider looked away defiantly and refused to answer. He had a stubborn look on his face, a hard set to his jaw that said he wished his grandfather would mind his own business.

King Lorn's fist slammed down on the table causing Storm Rider and both cups to jump.

"Must I thrash this out of you? You have your mother worried sick; your father is grumpier than a wild bear, and your grandmother has beseeched me endlessly to speak with you. In addition to that, I have farmers from all over Jior complaining that their crops are waterlogged. The summer season is short enough in these mountains without you drowning everyone in your misery. What is bothering you?"

Storm Rider's chin came up, he glared at his grandfather, and at that moment looked so arrogant and insubordinate that Lorn could almost swear that he saw Kullorn's face looking back at him.

King Lorn expanded his huge chest and faced Storm Rider. His violet eyes burned with a fierce glare that said he would not suffer further disobedience. Storm Rider looked away first and seemed to deflate. He gave an uncustomary slouch in his chair and his brow furrowed with sorrow.

"I apologize Grandfather. It is true, I have not been myself. I will calm the storms and let the clear skies reveal themselves."

Lorn understood this was Storm Rider's way of saying he was finally willing to share what was bothering him. Storm Rider took a deep breath and slowly began his confession.

"When I left for the distant mountains to ride the storms this spring, I saw a girl. She was down in the street below the castle, looking up at me as I flew by and I felt *drawn* to her. A short time later, as I flew over the forest, I saw her again. I could not let her alone and I followed her for days. I…" Storm Rider hesitated before revealing everything he had done, not knowing how his grandfather would react.

"I followed her to a small village and I watched from atop a building across the road as she bathed." Storm Rider swallowed and closed his eyes as his thoughts turned inward toward his memories. "Grandfather, I saw her naked body and I *wanted* her. She was so beautiful! Then she turned her back to me and I saw the ne'amh chomhara."

Lorn just grunted a little surprised but did not interrupt the story. Storm Rider went on. He described overhearing the conversation with her brother and learning her name.

"Her brother called her Meurie but that is not her name!" Storm Rider took a drink of his wine and then repeated stubbornly.

"That is *not* her name. Her name is Moon Dancer!"

"Go on Son." Lorn prompted when Storm Rider fell silent.

"I contrived to meet her and, Grandfather, my heart stopped when she looked at me and said my name in her sweet voice, it was like the soothing sound of distant thunder. I knew that I had to have her that she should be *mine*." Storm Rider's voice dropped to a deeper octave.

"Then I met her brother and he revealed the truth to me. He said Moon Dancer was wingless despite having the ne'amh chomhara. He said she was adopted by their parents and that they never told her she was Ny-Failen. They took her true identity with them to their graves. The brother asked me to leave and said if I pushed her, and revealed who she truly was that I would break her heart promising her something she could not have. He said she was wingless and did not know ne'amh chomhara was there."

Storm Rider's face was red with growing fury and, out of the clear blue sky, a bolt of lightning ripped through the air and struck the boulders outside with a crack. The air was charged with energy and the hair on Lorn's arms rose, but then everything stilled as Storm Rider took a deep breath and calmed.

He fell silent while Lorn thought over what he was saying. "Then what? You left her?"

"Not exactly," he hesitated, wondering if he should tell his grandfather everything.

"Storm Rider what did you do?" Lorn asked suspiciously.

"There is a pool there, a large, natural hot spring where Moon Dancer goes to bathe each night; it is where I first discovered her true name. It hit me like a lightning strike." He stopped remembering again and whispered her name softly, "*Moon Dancer*."

"That is when you left?"

"No," He looked a little sheepishly at his grandfather and then took a restoring drink of his wine. "I waited for her in the pool. I called her like I call the storms and she came to me. I kissed her-*a lot*. I touched her breasts, her body, ran my fingers through her long golden hair and I felt calm like a great storm had passed and I was satiated from riding it. At the same time, I felt like a different storm was building inside me and I wanted to…" Storm Rider stopped talking and stared out the door at the bright sunshine.

"Did you?" King Lorn prompted and tried not to sound angry.

"No," He said gently. "I couldn't. My body could, desperately wanted to, but my heart could not dishonor her. I could not reveal who she really was and risk hurting her if she truly is wingless as her brother said, but under the circumstances, I could not, *take* her."

"*That* is when you left her?"

"No, *she* left me. I could tell she was hurt that I didn't…well…and when I tried to explain, she said she already understood. She said she knew that we Ny-Failen were forbidden to mate with humans and that she was a commoner, beneath me in every way, and then she walked away and I didn't stop her."

Storm Rider hung his head in sorrow, his story finished. King Lorn rose and paced the floor thinking hard before he said anything. All his years dealing with problems as a king had not prepared him for this kind of situation.

"Storm Rider, you let this girl think that you did not love her because she was a commoner and not worthy of you?" King Lorn sounded very disappointed.

"It was the only way! If I told her the truth, what her brother revealed to me and it turned out she truly couldn't fly, couldn't ride the storms with me then…I don't know if I…and I had already…"

"You don't know if you could love her if she was *wingless* and it would be too late to turn back after you had taken her?"

"Yes!" Storm Rider shouted and jumped to his feet and paced angrily. He gripped his short red hair in anger and held his head as if to stop the truth from spinning around his thoughts. When he let go his hair spiked out in all directions and he looked wild and crazed, his green eyes flashing. He shouted again.

"I let her think she was unworthy of a Ny-Failen and that I didn't want her and I told myself it was for her own good! I flew away like a coward, afraid I could not control my body's desire to have her, afraid to commit to her. Now I cannot control my rage at *myself* and the storming blue skies remind me of the color of her eyes. The rain cannot wash the taste of her from my lips and my body aches for hers. The thunder's rumble cannot drown out the memory of her voice saying my name! I long for her like I long to ride the thundering storms!"

Another lightning bolt struck outside and the air was charged yet again. King Lorn paced over to his grandson and put his arms around him. He comforted him smoothing his hair and patting his back as he had when he was a small boy. Storm Rider dropped his head to his grandfather's shoulder and tried to calm his breathing before he caused a tempest outside that would destroy everything.

Finally, King Lorn released his grandson and led him to sit down, poured more wine, and leaned back in his chair. After a long time thinking the problem through, he began to speak.

"Storm Rider, I believe you are too hard on yourself." He began and raised a hand to stop Storm Rider's objections. "At the same time, you are correct, from what you've revealed to me, you may have let this girl think she was unworthy of you and that you didn't want her. That behavior is not worthy of a grandson of mine, but at least you held back from dishonoring her body. That is commendable." Storm Rider nodded his head and settled to listen to the king's judgment.

"Among the Ny-Failen, we have a belief that every Ny-Failen has a true soul mate. It is apparent to me, because you knew her true name and because of other *indications,* that this Moon Dancer is yours. Now, I think you have three options.

The first of your options is to stay away from this girl and remain miserable for the rest of your life. You will never mate and you will remain unhappy and possibly flood the entire continent with rainstorms. On the other hand, the brother will be happy, but Moon Dancer may never know she is Ny-Failen and I confess, I do not know the consequences of that for her though I suspect they are dire.

The second option is to take this girl to Everclearing to see Lost Morning or perhaps Mercy Rose will know. Lost Morning has special powers and can tell if she has wings or not and if she is truly Ny-Failen. But then you would have to reveal all to her and that everything she has ever known has been a lie perpetrated by the only family she's ever known. You could still break her heart. In either scenario, the girl stands to get hurt."

"And the third option?" Storm Rider rumbled unhappily.

"You can go back to this girl, bond with her, and live your life in happiness together whether she is wingless or not. I suggest you let your heart and your power guide you. When the time is right, you will know what to do. You will go against her brother's wishes and reveal the ne'amh chomhara to her, but in the end, she will know who she is and she will be *yours*. I suspect you would both be happy in that case."

Storm Rider rose again and paced the small chamber. His hands flexed into fists and loosened again as he weighed his options. He had to admit his preference was the option that made Moon Dancer his.

King Lorn watched his troubled grandson for a while and then refilled his cup with wine.

"It seems to me that the option you should take is clear. Come and sit down. Let me tell you the story about how I bonded with your grandmother." King Lorn's violet eyes sparkled with mischief as he waved over Storm Rider and began his tale.

"There is another hot spring that I know of, where I lay wounded after rescuing your grandmother from the castle of a Black Sorcerer. The cave walls were made of amethyst crystals…"

And so, King Lorn went on to tell the story of how he bonded with Queen Lililaira in an amethyst crystal cave, so many, many years ago.

CHAPTER EIGHT

Helm finally had enough of Meurie's sadness and decided that now was a good time for them both to get away. He still had hesitations about asking Glenna to marry him but knew in his heart he was wrong and did not care to analyze his reasons because they were wrong too. So, he suggested they both go see Glenna and for him to finally ask her to marry him. Though in his heart it was not what he truly wanted, what he wanted he could not have, and he would truly lose everything if he revealed that secret. One morning he and Meurie stayed in because of heavy rain and he broached the subject hoping the promise of female companionship and a trip, would break Meurie of her dark mood.

"Meurie, I think we should travel back down to Dade-Bend again. We can leave in the morning."

Meurie would not look up from the sewing she was doing and spoke in an uninterested monotone voice.

"Oh, are we in need of supplies?"

"No, I just thought that, well, I thought we could go and I would finally ask Glenna to marry me. We can be married within a week and then she can come here to live with us, and you will have another female for company. What do you say? It is about time and it would do you some good to get away from this place."

Meurie thought it over briefly and then announced her decision.

"You go, Helm. Take a moonstone and have a ring made for her. Marry Glenna. I hope you find happiness with her and that you have lots of children." Meurie tried a smile and failed.

Helm had been tying his long brown hair back in a queue but stopped and stared at her. "You won't come? You'd miss *my wedding* just so you can stay here and sulk about *him*!" His anger and jealousy got the best of him now.

Meurie looked away calmly and mumbled under her breath that Helm did not know what he was talking about. She had not told Helm what had transpired at the hot pool and so he was not aware of the extent of her heartbreak. She resumed her sewing.

Helm closed his eyes and under his breath, asked the Creator for patience. Then he grabbed a chair and sat down in front of her.

"It's my fault he left," Helm confessed. "My fault that Lord Storm Rider left so abruptly."

Meurie's head shot up and she glared at him confused.

"What are you talking about?" She whispered.

Helm gave another exasperated huff and cleared his throat.

"I told him to leave. More like, I *ordered* him to leave."

"Helm!" Meurie looked stunned. "Why?"

"When you left to go get the crystals I'd unearthed that day, I told him to leave. To go and not come back, I told him that you didn't know *what* you are and that by staying here he would only cause you pain."

"Helm! Why would you do such a thing?" Meurie's hand flew to her mouth and she closed her eyes in disbelief unable to look at him. Helm hung his head ashamed.

"I was afraid if he found out that you were, *wingless*, that he would leave you anyway and hurt you. I saw the way he looked at you and you at him. I hoped that, before you completely gave him your heart, he would go and you would not have the chance to fall in love with him. So, I stretched the truth just a little and told him you were unaware that you were partly Ny-Failen and said that our parents had kept it a secret from you."

Meurie rose to her feet and walked over to stare out the only window in the cabin. She wrapped her arms tightly around herself and thought about what Helm had done. This only made things worse. Since he had left that night Meurie had relived each moment with Storm Rider from the fight on the cliff where she tried to beat him with her staff, flying in his arms, to the night at the hot pool. She had stopped going there late at night because the memories became too painful and now, she had to sort through what Helm's confession meant.

Storm Rider had been told by Helm that she was not Ny-Failen. He had not wanted to make love to her knowing that and so she was right, he had stopped because she was a common human after all. The final blow to her heart was that Storm Rider knew she was wingless despite the strange wing marks on her back and it was that lack that made it impossible for him to love her.

Meurie finally took a deep breath and faced Helm. She spoke with a clear voice devoid of emotion and hurt.

"Thank you for telling me this Helm. Now, I think you should go. You should go and marry Glenna and be happy. Bring her here if wish, after you've married and we will forget any of this happened."

"You'll come with me? Please, Meurie! Come with me. Let's get away for a while." He pleaded, but in his heart, he was not sure he could go through with the marriage if Meurie was there.

Meurie went and hugged him then held him at arm's length, "No, I need some time alone and besides, you don't want your sister tagging along after you're newly wed. You and Glenna will need time *alone* together. When you get back, I will be over this and we'll put the whole business behind us. Now, go and pack and I'll choose the perfect stone for Glenna. You can stop in Dade-Bend and have the blacksmith set it into a gold ring." She kissed Helm on the cheek, hugged him again briefly, and then turned and left, but before she was completely out of the cabin she stopped and turned back toward him.

"Thank you for telling me this Helm," Meurie repeated, closed the cabin door behind her, and stepped out into the rain.

CHAPTER NINE

Blue skies and a shining warm sun were hanging over the city of Jior when King Lorn and Storm Rider returned to the castle. Storm Rider was charged with purpose and went immediately to prepare for his trip. He went to see his mother and father to tell them that he was leaving the next morning and would be away for a while, but that he would be back soon.

Just after sunrise the next day, rested and dressed in his light silver-tipped armor, Storm Rider launched into the summer sky. He flew straight up and called the high winds to aid him and they blew fiercely in the upper reaches of the atmosphere. He rode them toward Javelin Peak. Because of the speed lent him by the wind he thought he would make his destination well before the morning hours grew old.

#

The day after Helm made his confession to Meurie he reluctantly prepared to leave for Dade-Bend. Meurie followed him out of the cabin to say goodbye and handed him a pack full of bread and food she prepared. Helm took the bag, placed it in the wagon, and turned to take her in his arms. Helm held her then stepped back and looked her in the eyes for a long moment as if there was something more, he wanted to say. He searched her face for an instant longer, then gave her a sad smile and turned to jump up into the wagon. Without a backward glance, Helm clucked to the horses and they moved on.

Meurie was distraught over the strange goodbye with Helm but went on spending the rest of the day nursing her heartache. This morning when she had awoken the skies were blue and clear and the day promised to be warm. She was restless and decided to go for a walk. Something pulled her toward the hot springs and she gave in to the compulsion to go to what was once her favorite place.

She could not stop thinking about that one-night Storm Rider had kissed her in the hot pool and small shocks of lightning streaked through her body and left her breathless and aching for more. Now, as Helm had revealed to her, Storm Rider knew she was partly Ny-Failen, but still did not want her because she was *wingless*. That is what hurt the most because it was all true. Now as she made her way down the well-worn path, she scolded herself over how ridiculous she was being, pining for him. For in truth, she had only known him for one day, though she had seen him fly in Jior and had flown wrapped in his strong arms. Still, it was one wondrous day and one partially glorious night that ended in sadness, disappointment, and despair.

As she reached the hot spring pools, she smelled the heavy mineral scent permeating the air and heard the rustle of small animals in the leaves, the merry chirping of birds in the trees, the deep resonant sound of an owl calling out in the morning air. She stopped, struck with a new sadness, and was not sure why. Shaking herself loose of her self-pity, she walked on until she came out of the trees bordering the pools and walked straight into a solid black, silver-tipped, armored chest.

Storm Rider's arms reached around her and though startled, she was overwhelmingly relieved to be back in his arms, except she did not want to admit that even to herself. Pulling away slightly she looked up into his dark green eyes that stormed with passion as he looked back at her.

His deep voice whispered, "My Lady."

Then he dipped his head and kissed her passionately. All the weeks apart were washed away in that one kiss as he held her tightly. When Meurie was able to think again she shoved away and was instantly angry.

"Lord Storm Rider. You presume too much!"

"What do I presume? My Lady." He tried to stifle a slight smile.

"You presume that your presence and your kisses are wanted here."

"Before you send me away, will you at least do me the courtesy of hearing me out? The reasons why I went away."

"I know why you went away and it is hurtful. Helm told me what he said to you and I know you why you left."

Storm Rider looked at her for a long time as his mind reeled with what she was telling him. Helm had told her?

"Master Helm has told you that you are Ny-Failen? And that you have the ne'amh chomhara?" He looked confused and astonished. "*Now*, he reveals the secret they kept from you your entire life?"

She hung her head almost ashamed and could not look at him. "What Helm told you was not exactly true. I have known my whole life that I might have a *little* Ny-Failen blood in me. It is why I have been so enamored of your kind. I learned every story and every legend about the Ny-Failen from Jior and Everclearing. When I was in Jior, I waited a whole day on the street outside your castle just to catch a glimpse of one of you. Then I saw *you* and I could not forget." Her voice caught, but she went on. "When we met, here, the last time I saw you, and you rejected me, I realized that I would never be acceptable to you, your kind because I am wingless."

"There are many wingless among the Ny-Failen." Storm Rider rumbled.

"Storm Rider, you know I am more human than Ny-Failen. It is not just that I have no wings!" She punctuated those last words with painful resignation. "Look at my skin!

It does not glisten like pearls as I have heard is common among Ny-Failen women. My eyes are not violet like the king's. My hair is not silvery white like the queen's. I have no *aversion to iron!* I am human! I have no wings! If I jump off a cliff I *will* fall to my *death!*" Breathing heavily with emotion she stopped and her cry echoed through the clearing.

Storm Rider seemed struck by her last words and he stood there for a long-time contemplating. He took two strides toward her and realized what he had to do.

"My Lady, *do not doubt me* but believe me when I say your wings are there. I know it like I know a storm is brewing in the west! You may not look like other Ny-Failen women; you are more beautiful than they. Your hair is golden like the morning sun's rays and your skin is warm and fair. Your eyes are dark blue and gray like stormy clouds. Not all Ny-Failen have an aversion to iron. If you were to fall from a cliff, I would catch you."

He stepped closer to her and his hands slid up the sides of her arms. His pulse raced and his eyes darkened with passion. He wanted to sweep her into his arms and crush her in his embrace. To wipe away the memory of that other night, but he realized in her current frame of mind he needed to be gentle and calm the storm of his yearning. Like a frightened dove, she quivered under his hands, but then she jerked away and walked off a few paces.

"You rejected me. Now I must live with the memory of those stolen moments and the truth that you could not love a wingless human. These marks on my back, whatever they are, are just a cruel reminder of that!"

"Now *you* presume too much, my Lady." Storm Rider began to get a little angry, but she cut him off.

"Stop! I am not your '*Lady*!' And I presume nothing! I only know that I will never be good enough for you, never be able to fly through the skies with you, never!"

"My Lady!" Storm Rider went after her, giving her anger back. "*Both* of my parents are wingless! Are you saying that I do not love them?"

Meurie stopped and stared at him in shock with her mouth partially open. Her memory whirled through what she knew of the Jiorian lineage.

"Wh-who are your parents?" She stammered, her eyes going wide, afraid to know the answer.

"My father is Jagged Edge of the Ny-Failen from Celtica. My mother is Princess Lyra Song."

"Which means…your grandfather is…is…" She paled as the realization hit her.

"Forlorn Icefall, King of Jior." Storm Rider shrugged as if it meant nothing.

"OH!" She backed away from him yet again, terror, sadness, and awe painted her lovely features. "Then this is so much worse. You are royalty!"

"My father was not what you call royalty. That meant nothing to my mother, it means nothing to me or to any of us, you do not know us as well as you think. Do not let stories and embellished tales cloud your judgment of us." Storm Rider realized this conversation had gotten out of control and had not gone the way he planned. His power stirred within him and he felt ready to burst with frustration.

"Lord Storm Rider, you have had only one day with me. I do not judge you, only what I know about *myself*." Her tone was bitter.

"I know you, my Lady. I have been following you since the day you left Jior. It was my owl call that bid you goodnight during your travels. It was I who watched you from the skies and the treetops learning about you, about your strength and courage, seeing your beauty of spirit. I sat next to you at the Dragonfly Inn when you came in cold and hungry. I watched from outside your window as you bathed in front of the firelight. I never left you since I first saw you and I watched during those days and nights. I never understood why you just didn't fly after I saw your ne'amh chomhara, but now I know. I have known your true name since the first moment I saw you here bathing in the moonlight. You are *Moon Dancer* and I believe you can fly!"

These revelations left Meurie staggering as if he struck her. Suddenly, everything fell together in her mind and made a strange sort of sense.

"It was *you* following me all those days? You made the owl call?" Meurie stopped then took a deep breath. When he had said the name '*Moon Dancer*' something inside of her awoke and her heart soared. "Moon Dancer?" She questioned in awe feeling complete for the first time in her life.

"Yes," Storm Rider took her in his arms and lifted her chin. "Moon Dancer is your Ny-Failen name and Moon Dancer you shall always be to me. I want to reveal to you, who you truly are, and who you can become. If you will let me?"

Meurie knew what he was saying and tears filled her eyes. She shook her head knowing exactly what he was referring to.

"I tried once when I was a little girl. I tried to grow the wings, but they would not come. Storm Rider, I cannot ride the winds with you, could you still love *me, as I am?*"

Storm Rider closed his eyes, rested his forehead against hers, and sighed.

"My Lady, Moon Dancer, will you trust me?"

Meurie noticed that he had not answered the question. Realizing what she needed to do she turned away and hung her head. Nodding silently, she finally relented. The only way was to show him once and for all she had no wings. It was humiliating to her, but it would reveal the truth about how Storm Rider truly felt about her when he realized she was fully human and could not join him in the clouds as she knew he wished.

She heard Storm Rider exhale with relief, though she shuddered with fear knowing that he would now see her shame as if her very soul was bare to him. She turned resigned to her fate and faced him.

"What do you want me to do?" Her quiet voice was cold and resigned.

Storm Rider did not like the defeated look in her eyes, nor the sadness in her voice. She would not raise her face to look at him, so he stepped closer, and placed his hand under her chin. The pain in her eyes was almost unbearable as she looked at him. He spoke a little more forcefully than he would have liked to.

"Take off your shirt so that it does not tear."

Shocked, Meurie hesitated for a long time but finally did as she was told. Her mouth was a hard line and she looked like she was going to face death. She did not even blush knowing her naked breasts would be revealed to him in the bright daylight. She pulled off her top tunic and then the undershirt below and stood naked in front of him from the waist up. Thinking he wanted to see her back, she kept her eyes trained on the ground, so she could not look at him.

Storm Rider looked at her though. The perfect round globes of her breasts with full rosy nipples were bare to his green gaze. His eyes slid down her torso to rest on her flat stomach. It was late morning and the sun had risen higher in the sky and painted the clearing with golden warmth. He sensed that she did not realize how beautiful she was, standing full of sadness, in the clearing with the sun glittering on the water behind her and painting her with its glow. She was strong, golden, and beautiful, and he had to tamp down hard on his desire for her.

"Trust me." He said firmly, stepping forward he took her in his arms. Her bare breasts almost pressed against his chest. She bowed her head not knowing what he would have her do but knew that this was the final test she would fail and all would be revealed.

Storm Rider ran his hand up Moon Dancer's bare back. He could feel the silvery lines etched into her skin. His fingers played lightly over those lines, tracing them. She was tall, but he was taller and could see over her shoulder down to the gentle swell of her lower back. The trousers she wore were loose and she had become thinner over the last few weeks while he was away. Desperately he wanted to push them down and grab her round bottom and plunge into her. *'Time for that later,'* he promised himself, and he concentrated on his spell.

Storm Rider's power had been building within him and, just as his grandfather had predicted, he let his power take over and guide him. He suddenly *knew* what to do, instinctually.

Meurie felt Storm Rider's hands on her back and she tried to distance herself from the feeling. All of this was a mystery to her. A sound rumbled up from deep within his chest, her brow furrowed. She had never heard a sound like this before and it rumbled softly through his body making him vibrate like distant thunder. Suddenly, as his fingers traced the silver lines on her back, she felt an odd sensation across and through her shoulders. It coursed downward and the muscles in her back tensed, rippled, and began to pull. Gasping her eyes flew open and she tried to pull back, terrified, but Storm Rider held her tightly and continued to hum, it was becoming more like a deep purr, the sound of distant thunder. It called to her and connected them.

The sensation continued across the expanse of her back and then centered between her shoulder blades. Her skin began to itch maddeningly and his warm hands rubbed her and soothed her. She looked up into his handsome face and saw his eyes were closed, his brow furrowed in deep concentration as he continued to purr. The rippling feeling was soon replaced by small lightning shocks streaking up and down her back and it felt like hundreds of butterflies had landed on her skin and were beating her with their wings. Her mouth fell open in shock and awe at what she was feeling and Storm Rider suddenly awoke from his self-induced trance.

"It will hurt the first time!" His voice was husky as it rose more like a snarl from his throat. His body was rigid, his muscles tight and he shivered slightly.

Strange feelings were building inside her and her skin burned. Meurie concentrated on the sound he made and his hands on her back. Suddenly, it felt like the butterflies that had alighted on her skin were ripping and tearing her with a thousand sharp claws. She fisted her hands tightly at her sides, gasped, and arched back, jerking in his grasp. Storm Rider stepped away and his hands went to her upper arms and held her tightly as pain ripped through her. His intense green eyes burned her.

"Call the wings!" He commanded her in a loud voice.

Meurie gritted her teeth, the pain was almost unbearable. The thought came unbidden from her mind, "Wings!" Jerking and crying out, her head tossed as she arched back again her bare breasts pressing up, throat bared and muscles clenching, her breath heaving and rasping. Storm Rider held her up. His strength filled her. The final barrier tore out from between her shoulder blades and Meurie's head fell forward on his chest as excruciating pain ripped through her. She gripped his arms and clenched her teeth bearing the pain.

She could not see, but Storm Rider did as her wings pealed out of the silver lines and grew for the first time, stretching, fluttering. The wings were of white-gold feathers that spread and pulsed and flapped weakly. Freed finally, they stretched out wider and Storm Rider finally released Moon Dancer when she could stand on her own and stepped back.

Naked and beautiful, her wings reached out behind her. The sun painted the new wings with its warm glow. Panting she stood, arms stretched out in wonder and her face glowed with astonishment as she stood in front of Storm Rider in all her *winged* glory.

Moon Dancer cried out in excitement and experimented with flapping her wings and found the movement awkward and foreign. As her wings flapped, she became unbalanced and her feet wanted to leave the ground. Storm Rider quickly moved forward and caught her, stabilized her, and grinned with triumph. She was winged!

Storm Rider held on to her while she flapped around the clearing. Like a fledgling bird testing newly grown wings, Moon Dancer stumbled, rose off the ground a few feet then landed. Storm Rider's larger; more powerful and practiced wings spread out and steadied her, helping her learn the balance and the form of movement. Laughing giddily, Moon Dancer danced on tiptoes across the ground.

The pain was forgotten now and all that mattered was the sheer joy of the wings, the feel of them pulsing on her back. She learned to angle the wings and stretch her feathers and catch herself from falling face-first into the ground. All the while, Storm Rider held her and helped her, teaching, giving her direction as a good instructor would.

After a few hours, she began to ache. Her back and shoulder muscles were not used to this kind of exercise, though her strong legs could hold the weight on her back. Sweating, she gasped from the exertion, and finally, she stopped and folded her wings on her back. Breathing hard and smiling with glee, Moon Dancer rested.

"How do I change back? I don't want to, but I'd like to rest for a short time. The wings will *come* back, won't they? What do I do?"

"Saitya buri vaenga." His voice was gentle as he spoke to her, "In Ny-Failen it basically means *put your wings away.* Just think it and your body will react. The wings will go back into the ne'amh chomhara and from now on will be there when you call. It will be easier each time you do it. With practice, you will fly higher." Storm Rider was very pleased with her and very awed at her beauty. "At first, it is just like shrugging your shoulders and they come or go as you want. With time, you won't even think about it your wings will just appear knowing instinctually when you want them."

Moon Dancer stretched her wings straight back behind her and closed her lovely storm blue eyes. Concentrating, she shrugged her shoulders as she had seen Storm Rider do, and in a matter of a few seconds, the wings retreated into her back with a flutter brushing ripple across her skin. She suddenly felt much lighter. She felt sad to put them away then the breeze blew across her naked breasts and she remembered that she had been half-undressed in front of Storm Rider. Quickly bending, she retrieved her shirt and put it back on. She flushed red, thinking about fluttering around him bare like that. She was embarrassed that he had seen her half-naked then she remembered he had seen her naked before. She risked a glance at Storm Rider. He was staring hungrily at her and when he moved toward her, her heart thundered.

The afternoon sun shone brightly in the clearing and the birds were singing joyously as if one of their own successfully survived leaving the nest. So was Moon Dancer's heart. Storm Rider stood very close to her and stared. His expression was unreadable. Then he took her hand in his and kissed the palm. As he had their very first time they ever flew together, he pulled her arms around his neck and held her tightly. His wings carried them up into the air and he flew with her in his embrace. They raced around the sky free of all uncertainty and free of all pain. The question as to whether or not she had wings was answered and now he showed her the joy of the open skies. He also showed her that it did not matter if she had wings or not, he could still fly with her.

When they landed, Moon Dancer was glowing with joy. Storm Rider looked at her with such intensity she was almost afraid of him. Taking her hand in his he stood close and spoke to her, his deep, sensuous voice caressing her nerves like a soothing balm.

"My Lady, among the Ny-Failen we have a belief that every one of us has a soulmate and we mate only once, for life. There is a tradition of bonding within my family that Grandfather started and I would follow in his footsteps. It begins with these words." He stopped and took a deep breath.

"Moon Dancer, I want you to be mine forever. I bond to you, heart and soul. I make this vow to you that I will never willingly leave you, there shall be no other, and I am yours if you will have me."

Moon Dancer stared at him in shock, realizing what he was saying and she instinctually quoted back. "Storm Rider, I want to be yours forever. I am bonded to you, heart and soul and I make this vow to you that I will never willingly leave you, there shall be no other, and I am yours."

Storm Rider and Moon Dancer sealed their vows with a passionate kiss and now the storm was truly unleashed. He picked her up and swung her around. She laughed joyously and kissed him with abandon. When he set her on her feet, she was breathless.

Both of them sobered at the same time and Moon Dancer stepped back from Storm Rider and kicked off her boots and slowly peeled off her shirt and britches. Crooking a finger at Storm Rider she beckoned him to follow her into the hot pool where she stepped carefully into the steaming water.

Storm Rider had been watching her mesmerized and was not even aware that his fingers were busy with the buckles of his armor chest plate as it fell to the ground he finished undressing and then stood completely naked in the sun's light. Raising his face to the warmth he breathed deeply and then went to his lady. Diving in, he swam under the water until he came up in front of Moon Dancer. As he broke the surface, he gently took her in his arms.

"Now you are *my Lady!*"

They kissed as they had the other night replaying the scene under the blue skies instead of under the moonlit stars. Storm Rider tried to go slow but his control was beginning to slip. His hands caressed her heart-shaped bottom and his lips tasted her breasts. Moon Dancer's golden hair was a wet cascade down her back as he lifted her. Her legs went around his waist and he caressed her intimate folds with his length. He refrained from entering her just yet but spent time enjoying the feel of her sliding along him.

Storm Rider was overwhelmed by Moon Dancer's body and her aggressive response to his caresses. His own body was hard as rock and his need was screaming to be fulfilled, but he knew, just as with the first time her wings transformed that her body needed to be prepared. She was charged with her own passion as he touched her.

"It will hurt the first time!" His voice was husky as it rose from his throat.

Moon Dancer bit her lip seductively and arched under his caresses. She nodded assenting to what he was saying and closed her eyes desperate to have him fill the need aching inside her. Then his hand was guiding his hardness into her entry and he pushed, once just enough so he barely entered her.

"Call *me*!" He demanded softly as he held her.

"Storm Rider!" She gasped loudly as he pushed deeper and then, he plunged, broke through her last barrier to him, and thrust home.

Moon Dancer jerked and arched under him. The tearing pain shot up through her core and landed in her throat eliciting a small cry. Her eyes flew open and she looked at Storm Rider. His face was flushed with need and the set of his mouth said he was just barely holding on to control, his eyes turned dark and stormy with the desire to soar. She reached under the water and grasped his firm behind and pulled him deeper, spreading her legs wider, she bucked against him.

The storm that had been building within Storm Rider's body broke free as he plunged into Moon Dancer. They thrust together, the clear water of the pool flowing around them and the birds sang their wedding song. Storm Rider was insatiable and his hunger for her could not be quenched. Carrying her from the pool they lay in the cool sweet grass and he entered her once again. Now the water's cushion was gone and he plunged into her until she cried out in joy.

As he felt her inner sheath clenching his shaft, he recognized this was her pleasure. Moon Dancer felt Storm Rider's shoulders shrug slightly as he moved in and out of her then suddenly, he was lifting them both from the ground. With her legs clasped tightly around his hips connecting them, he kissed her with wild abandon and lifted them both up into the sky holding her with his strong arms and wings. She rocked against him as they flew higher and higher. Still joined, he flew them above the clouds and Storm Rider turned on his back, his mighty wings holding them in the air. Moon Dancer clung so tightly to him that her climax took her again and she cried out, laughing out loud in the vastness of the sky.

Storm Rider smiled and said, "You fit well in my arms, my Lady." Then he flapped his wings, bucked hard, and spun them down as his body exploded in ecstasy and he shouted out his joy through the skies.

After they landed, they returned to the hot pool and swam and played. They explored each other's bodies and laughed in the sunshine most of the afternoon. The second time Storm Rider made love with Moon Dancer he found his control was all but gone again and he had to fight his desire to storm, but it was impossible, like a maelstrom that had been brewing in the distance he broke. He rained down kisses on her lips, her neck, and more on her tantalizing breasts and smooth flat belly. He rubbed his thumbs along her nipples and smoothed his face across her soft skin. Moon Dancer was gasping and her skin warmed with his kisses and caresses. Then suddenly he was entering her again as they lay on the soft grasses in the clearing. He continued to kiss her breasts and his hands explored her body sending rippling lightning strikes through her. He was lost in the feel of her. His sculptured muscles twitched under her stroking fingers. He rolled over in the grasses and she fell across him. She kissed him passionately and rubbed her breasts against his bare chest. Her tongue danced with his while their mutual pleasure grew.

Moon Dancer straddled and rode him, arching over him. Her pleasure swept through her and she cried out again with completion. Storm Rider felt her climax and the walls of her tight valley clenched and pulsed around him. He moved, flipped her onto her back, and plunged in. Throwing his head back, he closed his eyes and centered his thoughts on the juncture of their bodies feeling the slide of his hardness in and then slowly out of her tight inviting sheath.

The rhythm they made was slow and hard, set at a pace so that every thrust was meant to increase their hunger, and accentuate their need and desire for each other. A storm began to build again, Storm Rider's breathing grew heavier, and his passion rumbled forward, his pleasure was like lightning striking. As building release thundered within him, he desperately tried to hold off. Moon Dancer cried out again as her tight walls pulsed and squeezed him stronger this time. He was deep inside her when his storm finally broke and his hot seed burst within her. He continued to thrust his hips making huge bucking motions between her legs and Moon Dancer held on to him and guided him through his raging storm.

When the tempest of their passion finally calmed and their breathing slowed, Storm Rider lowered beside her. He kissed her slowly, tasting her lips as if it were for the first time. It was as if the storm of his lust for her had calmed and now he wanted to savor her kisses as if they were something new.

Moon Dancer was overjoyed with those kisses and his sudden gentleness and took everything she had needed from him since she first saw him flying in the clouds above her. Lovingly, she smoothed her hands up and down his side and nuzzled close.

They were bonded! Her heart soared. She loved him and this felt *right*. She had no more doubts about being with him in body and heart and *she was winged!*

Storm Rider lowered his lips to hers almost touching and whispered forcefully.

"Never doubt me again, my Lady." Then more vehemently, "And *never* doubt that I love you!"

CHAPTER TEN

Moon Dancer and Storm Rider returned to the cabin high upon Javelin Peak and they spent the next few days together in joyful bliss. They rejoiced in their love for each other, made love frequently and Moon Dancer practiced strengthening her new wings. Storm Rider instructed her in the fine art of flying and spoke frequently about riding the storms. He described the different types of clouds and what their shape and size indicated as far as the winds were concerned. They discussed at length the capabilities of her wings and her body in the air. Moon Dancer carefully sewed slits in the backs of her shirts and a few dresses so that at any time, she could shape-shift without tearing all her clothes.

Storm Rider told her about his family describing his grandfather, the King of Jior. He spoke lovingly of his mother and father and about his two sisters, Mercy Rose and Rain Song who were both the image of their mother, though Rain Song was many years younger. He told her of his father Jagged Edge, his Uncles who were the Princes of Jior and their wives and children, and about so many others until Moon Dancer's head spun.

On the fourth day Storm Rider took Moon Dancer to the high cliffs where she had first seen his fire signaling her of his presence. It was time to practice her flying skills in earnest.

"Remember what I said to you. If you fall, I will catch you." Storm Rider spoke confidently to Moon Dancer as she fearfully looked over the edge of the cliff. "You will not fall though, you are strong. Let the wings carry you and do not overthink the flying. The wings will do as *they* know how."

Moon Dancer continued to look over the towering edge of the cliff then smiled at Storm Rider. "If you say I can then I will."

Storm Rider was looking out at the skies and saw the clouds gathering toward the west. The winds were higher than he would have liked for her first flight.

"I think we will have calm, blue skies for your first real flight." Then he closed his eyes and concentrated. Storm Rider unleashed his power and caused the winds to blow the clouds away. As the golden sun shone brightly across the mountain valley, he held his hand out to her. Imperceptibly, he shrugged and shapeshifted. His huge wings stretched out wide and brilliant white. He flapped them once then they settled on his back.

Moon Dancer shrugged and shifted till her smaller white-gold wings unfurled behind her and she gave a couple of practice flaps. Bending at the knees Storm Rider shot into the air and hovered above her. Turning, he beckoned. Like a bird taking its first leap from the nest, Moon Dancer flapped her wings, stepped toward the edge of the cliff, and leaped. This was the first time she had been so high up and she intended to go higher, but when the still air did not catch her, she flailed a bit in the air. Suddenly, Storm Rider was beside her. Though he did not touch her, he was there just to give her confidence and she dipped precariously low toward the ground and then her wings took over.

The white-gold feathered wings kept her slim body from hitting the ground and suddenly she was gaining altitude. Stronger and stronger with each flap of her wings she soared upward. Storm Rider led the way and she followed.

Moon Dancer had to resist the urge to flail her arms and move as if she were swimming through the air. She watched Storm Rider who flew effortlessly ahead of her, still and at ease in the sky, and mimicked his movements learning by watching. He gained altitude and she followed. They circled the highest reaches of the sky over Javelin Peak and Moon Dancer saw the land as she had never seen it before. Racing over the forests below and then back again, they flew through the skies. She never felt so free in her life and realized how long she had dreamed of flying and had denied that it was her deepest, dearest, desire-until now.

Storm Rider led the way through the misty clouds and they spiraled steadily upwards. The drafting air currents buffeted Moon Dancer, but she corrected naturally and her flying grew stronger and more confident. Her heart was soaring with her body as she followed Storm Rider. It became effortless to swerve and twist in the clear skies. Suddenly, he made a sweeping arch and came up over her. Moon Dancer craned her neck to watch him. Before she knew it, he streaked forward and off into the distance at a speed she could not yet match. She marveled at him, his beauty, his red hair smoothed back like feathers on the head of a red hawk.

Moon Dancer watched as Storm Rider became smaller in the distant skies. She followed more slowly in the direction he took until they were flying high above the jagged peaks of the Violent Mountains where no man had ever set foot. The air began to cool and she shivered, dropping lower searching for warmer temperatures. At this altitude, many of the peaks were still snow-covered. The sky seemed to carry her within a swiftly moving current like she was caught in a river made of air and she sped faster than she ever thought she could fly. Looking toward the direction where Storm Rider had sped off, she saw him flying straight at her. He was riding the upper wind shear, his wings held tightly against his back he plummeted toward her, lost in his joy of flying.

Panic struck Moon Dancer and she feared they would collide, but just before they met in the upper air currents, hers blowing toward him and his blowing toward her, Storm Rider tipped and sped past her, unrestraint evident on his face. Moon Dancer pulled up mid-air and was swept up into a swirling maelstrom of circling air. She let out a piercing scream as she was buffeted by the wind and sent spinning down. Her wings were pressed tightly against her back and body by the force of her fall. Tossed and turned in the sky she tried to pull out of her deadly spiral.

Storm Rider lived to ride the force of the winds and got carried away by the fast-upper currents. When he soared past Moon Dancer, he had not thought she would be caught in the circling maelstrom where the upper streams met the lower streams. His heart thundered in his chest as he saw her spiraling downward. Flying fast was almost the sole way Storm Rider ever flew and now it was no effort to catch her. Swooping under her, Storm Rider grabbed her and lifted her in his arms. Her wings regained their full spread and soon they were once again flying together, side by side at a more reasonable pace for Moon Dancer.

Moon Dancer headed back to the cabin and they lightly touched down. As they landed Storm Rider watched her face for fear or anger over what happened. He was surprised when all he saw was absolute joy! After shifting her wings away, Moon Dancer flung her arms wide and danced around in circles laughing giddily. Dancing across the mountain grass for a moment she did not stop until she was breathless.

Storm Rider had never seen such elation and watched her with undeniable happiness of his own. Next Moon Dancer flung her arms around Storm Rider's neck and kissed him with abandon.

"Are you alright?" Storm Rider asked checking her over for injuries now that she was standing still. Her breasts were heaving beneath her thin shirt and she could not stop her smile.

"Oh, Storm Rider! I've never been so exhilarated in my life. I loved it!"

"I was concerned you were afraid when the upper winds grabbed you. They can be unkind if you are caught unaware."

Moon Dancer sobered and stared at him. "Did you not say you would catch me if I fell?"

Then she went on her tiptoes and kissed him. Storm Rider's arms went around her and after a few more kisses, designed to light the fires of desire, they retreated into the cabin. They made love and fell asleep with Moon Dancer draped over Storm Rider's massive chest.

The next morning Moon Dancer woke early, started a fire, and began to make a morning meal. Storm Rider rose and slipped on his trousers and boots; they broke their fast and sat companionably discussing the day's flight plans.

A severe look suddenly crossed Storm Rider's face and he looked toward the door. Moon Dancer's keen hearing also picked up what had disturbed Storm Rider. Their peaceful morning was broken by the sounds of horse hooves and wagon wheels coming up the steep road to the cabin.

"Helm!" Moon Dancer rose slowly to her feet. "I forgot he was due back so soon." She gave Storm Rider a look that almost spoke of guilt and he narrowed his eyes at her.

"Master Helm's arrival should not hinder our plans." Storm Rider did not like the worried look on Moon Dancer's face. "You would have to leave him at some point to return to Jior with me. Am I not your husband?"

"Yes, but I had not thought about his reaction to my wings and I don't think I had considered leaving Helm. I mean, I know I shall eventually, but well, it doesn't matter. Let us go and greet him and Glenna his new bride."

Moon Dancer left the cabin. Storm Rider waited for the span of three deep breaths and then he rose to follow her. Before he left, he grabbed a blanket from Moon Dancer's bed and drew it around his bare shoulders. When he reached Moon Dancer outside, he walked up behind her and wrapped his arms around her so that the blanket enclosed them both against the cool, late morning breeze. Moon Dancer leaned back against him and waited as the wagon drew closer.

Storm Rider hugged Moon Dancer and watched Helm's face as he drew nearer and spotted them. Helm wiped away the scowl that began on his face and looked from Moon Dancer's face to Storm Rider standing so close behind her in the shared blanket. His mouth twitched in irritation.

The wagon pulled up and stopped. Helm set the brake and jumped down. Walking around the wagon he helped his new bride down and together, they walked up to Moon Dancer and Storm Rider.

"Lord Storm Rider." Helm greeted him warily and then looked at his sister wrapped so intimately in Storm Rider's arms in the blanket from her bed.

"Meurie, you're looking well." It was almost an accusation.

"Helm! I've so much to tell you!" Moon Dancer beamed and then left the shelter of Storm Rider's arms to go and embrace Helm's new wife. "Glenna! It is so good to see you! Now you are my sister! I'm so glad Helm finally got the courage to marry you!"

"Meurie! I'm glad to see you too. We missed you at the wedding." Glenna returned the embrace. "Helm said you were in a bad way, but you look happy to me."

Moon Dancer took her hand, turned, and led Glenna over to Storm Rider who now stood bare-chested and looking as ominous as an oncoming storm.

"Glenna, this is Lord Storm Rider from Jior. We've recently…well…that is…the happy news is that we have bonded and are soon to be officially married in Jior."

Storm Rider bowed his head and held his hand over his heart as he greeted Glenna in the Ny-Failen way. He saw a small girl dressed in homespun blue with long light brown hair. She had a ready smile and a pretty, heart-shaped face and though she appeared small and meek, she looked directly in his eyes and gave him a deep curtsey.

"You've what!" Helm gave a pained choke at their news and turned toward Moon Dancer.

"*Bonded*." Storm Rider cocked a half-smile and gave Helm a challenging look.

"Helm," Moon Dancer embraced her brother. "There is so much to tell, but please, you must have left before the sun was up having arrived so early this morning, come inside and have some tea."

More water was set to boil and mugs of tea were passed around. Meurie begged to hear all about the wedding and said she was sorry to have missed the festivities. Glenna related the story of the marriage proposal, the wedding dress, and details about the ceremony. When she looked at Helm her eyes were full of love and it was clear she worshipped her new husband. Helm only glared at Storm Rider and when Glenna was finished relating the wedding story, he chimed in revealing he understood the lie he told about Meurie was exposed.

"And Lord Storm Rider how is it you have asked my sister to be your wife? You left so quickly and suddenly we feared, because my sister is wingless, that you had lost your interest in her." Helm was blunt and leaned forward in his chair. "Not to mention you hardly knew her for more than a day." His eyes held accusations and contempt.

"Moon Dancer is not wingless." Storm Rider gave him a revealing grin.

"Moon Dancer? Who is that?" Glenna looked innocently around the table.

"I am Moon Dancer," Meurie stated proudly, and though she looked at Glenna when she began to explain, her words were meant for Helm. "You see Glenna. I was born with markings on my back called ne'amh chomhara which means, 'Heaven's mark' in the Ny-Failen language. Our parents always thought I was wingless because I could not…well, I had no wings. Lord Storm Rider and I met and he taught me how to *call* the wings and now I am named Moon Dancer. It is my Ny-Failen name given to me by Storm Rider."

"We are to return to Jior then Moon Dancer and I will marry more formally." Storm Rider informed them calmly.

The room fell silent after Storm Rider's last words until Helm slowly stood. Without looking at anyone he left the cabin. Moon Dancer rose and followed him out. Glenna was left alone in the cabin with Storm Rider who looked dark and brooding like gathering thunderheads.

#

"Helm?" Moon Dancer went after her brother and tried to gain his attention. Angrily, he stalked away and went to the horses and led the wagon away. His long brown hair fell loose over his shoulders and his head was bent down as if he was defeated.

"Helm, please wait!"

"What is it Meurie or must I call you *Moon Dancer*?" Helm whirled and spoke sarcastically.

"How dare you act so selfishly!" Moon Dancer raced after him. "My whole life I have felt like a part of me was missing and now I found it. I am complete and I have discovered love with Storm Rider and he has promised me the life I've always wanted."

"What was wrong with your life before all this nonsense? I thought you were happy?"

"I cannot believe that you would act this way! Have you not thought about what this means to you? If I am Ny-Failen, then you *must* be as well, for you are my brother!"

"NO!" Helm yelled and stood still; sadness replaced the anger on his face. He spoke more calmly. "No Meurie, I am not selfish! I am not Ny-Failen and you are not my sister."

Moon Dancer looked as if he had just struck her.

"What do you mean? Of course, I am your sister." She gave a nervous laugh. "We have the same parents. We were raised together. I've known you all my life! You are my brother!" Moon Dancer followed him into the barn where Helm began to prepare feed and water for the horses.

"Our parents," Helm took a deep breath then went on with sad resolve. "*My* parents found you when you were a baby. They never told me where. My father just showed up one day with you in his arms and told me you were my new baby sister and we had to take special care of you. I don't know where you came from or who your real parents are. When you displayed no ability to fly and we never saw any wings, our parents naturally assumed you were wingless. They said every Ny-Failen had the marks, but that not all could fly. When they died, they made me promise to take care of you and *I have*. I love you and I don't want to see you hurt. Storm Rider thinks you have wings, but I have never in all my life, seen them and I'm sorry Meurie, but I just don't believe that I ever will. I don't want you hurt and he should not push you."

Helm sat down heavily on a small stool and bowed his head in his hands. His long hair hung down and hid his face. Moon Dancer stood stunned listening to what he was saying and thinking about everything he was revealing to her. She took two steps back from him and stood in the doorway alight with the rays of the sun on her back. She gave a small shrug and shapeshifted. Slowly, she unfurled her wings until he sat in the shadow of their expanse.

"Helm, look at me." Moon Dancer said quietly.

As Helm slowly looked up, the shadow of Moon Dancer's wings shaded him, and his mouth fell open in disbelief. Moon Dancer's wings pulsed slowly like a butterfly and he stood staring at her in amazement as the sun painted her with its golden light. When she felt she made her point Moon Dancer shrugged and the wings stretched and gracefully went back into the ne'amh chomhara.

Helm walked slowly toward her and stood for a long time staring at her. His face showed the emotion and strain in his heart. Slowly, he reached forward and cupped her cheek, he lowered his head and kissed her, pressing his warm lips to hers for longer than a brother should. His arms went around her pulling her closer and holding her tightly as he moved his mouth across hers gently, lightly tasting her with his tongue. She stepped back suddenly, looking shocked and confused knowing this kiss meant something to him, but it frightened her to her core. His hands fell and he looked stricken.

"Then you really are lost to me," Helm spoke quietly, turned, and walked slowly up the mountain away from the cabin.

#

The sun was rising higher in the sky warming the hot spring clearing. Steam was rising off the surface of the still waters and in the distance the gurgling of a small brook made the morning seem calm and placid. After Storm Rider and Moon Dancer left the cabin, they spent the day at the hot spring pools and flew much of the day, strengthening her wings. It was the dark of the moon and Storm Rider pulled

Moon Dancer into the hot waters of the pool. He caressed her gently and stared into her sad eyes.

"What troubles you, my Lady?"

"Helm, he cannot accept that I really do have wings, he seems so sad and I don't know what to do. I think he is sad because I am leaving, but he hardly speaks to me and, well, I just did not mean to hurt him. I didn't think I would. I thought he would be happy for me."

"Master Helm has a conflicted heart. In time, he will come to understand and accept what you are and that you are mine. If it would please you, my Lady, we can come and visit him often."

"I am not sure we would be welcome." Moon Dancer rested her head on Storm Rider's strong chest. "He said I was abandoned by my real parents and that he is not truly my brother." Moon Dancer knew instinctively not to mention the kiss Helm had given her in the barn.

"I'm sorry he hurt you, but as I said he will come to accept the truth. He has a new wife to offer him companionship and time will heal his wounds. In Jior, you will become part of my family. I will teach you to ride the storms with me."

Moon Dancer looked up at Storm Rider and gave him a hesitant smile. "As long as I am by your side, I will be happy." Reaching up she ran her fingers through his red hair and kissed him. Storm Rider took her in his arms and loved her until her sadness was forgotten for a time.

CHAPTER ELEVEN

The beauty of spring hit the Violent Mountains with full force. Wildflowers sprinkled the landscape like the stars that shone in the night sky. Trees burst with leaves in every shade of green and the land was lush with thick grasses. Birds and animals of every kind populated the forest with their young and life bloomed everywhere.

Rain and spring storms lessened now that Storm Rider was bonded with Moon Dancer and his heart was at peace. They remained for a while at Javelin Peak because Moon Dancer was reluctant to leave until matters between her and Helm were settled. Storm Rider did not push for leaving because it was his time to ride the storms that naturally assailed the Violent Mountains. He had Moon Dancer as his bonded wife and he was content. They spent many of their days flying and Moon Dancer's wings strengthened. She learned to fly, honing her skills under Storm Rider's expert tutelage.

They spent their evenings with a reluctant Helm and a very welcoming Glenna who was just glad to have their company. They hunted and shared their meat and the two couples settled into a fairly harmonious truce. During the nights, Storm Rider and Moon Dancer returned to the hot springs where they slept together under the stars and left the newlywed couple to the privacy of the cabin.

Glenna covertly revealed to Moon Dancer, that Helm was an ardent lover, and Glenna's faint, *'Ah! Ah! Ahhhh!'* cries from their lovemaking were faintly heard issuing from up the mountain. Moon Dancer cursed her extraordinary hearing and Storm Rider distracted her by causing her own cries of pleasure to rival those of Glenna's.

Sadly, the time was swiftly approaching when they would need to go to Jior as Storm Rider was anxious to introduce Moon Dancer to his family. Before they could leave for Jior, there was one more lesson Storm Rider wanted to teach his bride and as the days passed, he became more and more impatient. It had been many days since he had ridden the storms and he desperately wanted to share that exhilarating experience with Moon Dancer.

He wanted to see her white-gold wings illuminated by the lightning, rain glistening on her skin, and watch as the wind folds her in its embrace. He wanted to guide her into the maelstrom of churning clouds and show her the deep colors of the storming skies high above the earth, and for her to feel the same passion and love he felt for the tempest. Storm Rider wanted her to dance to the rhythm of the thunder and race the fierce winds by his side.

As Moon Dancer listened to Storm Rider tell tales of how he rode the storms and flew as one with the wind, her skin prickled while her heart pounded fiercely with joyful anticipation. He spoke of the storms as if they were long-lost friends and it touched her heart to hear his longing. On the morrow, it would be the summer solstice and that was the day Storm Rider decided it was time. They spent a short evening with Helm and Glenna and returned to their camp to plan to ride the next day's storm. Storm Rider would call the tempest with his Ny-Failen power and Moon Dancer would follow Storm Rider into the gathering clouds. The wind would drive them high over the Violent Mountains far away from the peaceful calm of Javelin Peak. Into the dark skies, they would ascend and Moon Dancer would ride her first storm.

While he was explaining, Storm Rider showed Moon Dancer the special light armor he wore. It was made of the finest material from the Ny-Failen city of Everclearing. He called it *dragon scales* and mentioned that no human had ever seen the likes of that glorious animal, though myths and legends told of them. The dragon scales looked black, but in the light, glistened with fabulous emerald greens, cobalt blues, deep violets, and silvery hues. The material clung to him like a second skin. It was strong and rimmed in silver filigree that was deceptively decorative, but in reality, each silver-tipped scale acted as a lightning conductor. Storm Rider told how the shock of the lightning would be attracted to his armor and travel through his body making his blood sing like nothing he ever experienced on the earth. He shuddered with anticipation and went on to explain that, as Ny-Failen, neither of them would burn or be harmed, but would join with the lightning, like lovers join their bodies.

Lost and awestruck, Moon Dancer listened to Storm Rider and marveled at how passionately poetic he spoke of riding the storms. His face was transformed into a visage of pure love and joy. His eyes fired with anticipation and his voice rang with a fervor she had only heard once before when they first made love and he found his joy in her arms high above in the sky.

"Your wings will take you to leap from wind gust, to calm, and back again, and it will be like dancing! Keep your wings expanded, your arms by your sides, and let the storm take you. It will guide you where it wants you to go. You will experience the majesty, the beauty, and the thrill, the lightning in your veins, and the thunder echoing through your very bones. When the rain comes do not be afraid. It cleanses you like no earthly water can. The storm has a way of making you feel small and can overwhelm you, but you must not fight it, just find the wind current that is yours and follow. I will be right by your side. If you get lost or need rest, go into the eye of the storm and ride the calm winds within, until you once again can return to the arms of the storm."

Storm Rider stopped and closed his eyes. He gave another shudder of anticipation and seemed lost in his memories. Then he opened his eyes and Moon Dancer grew afraid of how they darkened to deepest green and looked like a tremendous storm was brewing inside him. He reached for her. His trembling hand closed around her wrist and then he was pulling her into his arms. His mouth descended to hers and his lips were cool, tasting of rain. The smell of crisp icy wind rose from his skin and Moon Dancer shivered at his touch as he smoothed his hand under her dress and onto the warm breast underneath. Pushing her clothing open with gentle patience, he revealed her to the night wind.

Moon Dancer arched under his hands while her lips and tongue danced with his. She ran her hands through his short red hair and pulled him closer, leaning back seductively, inviting him to come to her. While his mouth swept over hers in a passionate kiss, he lowered himself beside her and unlaced his britches. With one hand she pulled her dress up until her strong white thighs were bare to him. Storm Rider was ready and without undressing fully, released himself so that his bare erection could find her. As they slowly slid together, Moon Dancer sighed with relief as if she had waited overly long to be one with him again. He undulated slowly within her, loving her carefully, deliberately, with smooth calm thrusts as if he were taking his time to savor each moment. Feeling the slow strokes of Storm Rider's body within her, Moon Dancer slid her hands under the leather of his britches. Gripping, she pulled him in deep and felt the muscles of his backside tighten and release as he pushed. Just before her body clenched hard and pulsated, reaching the height of her pleasure, he gave one hard thrust that plunged her even further into a kind of delirium like she had never experienced before.

Storm Rider withdrew from his wife and finished undressing himself and then her. Before he joined with her once again, skin to skin, he drew a large blanket over them. The campfire crackled and spit sparks into the calm night sky. He spent quite a bit of time kissing her breasts and tasting the skin of her neck before covering her once again. Taking his time, he guided her to her completion before allowing himself to find satiation with one final, forceful thrust.

After their lovemaking, Moon Dancer stared into the night sky and watched as the stars wheeled above. Everything Storm Rider had taught her about flying, about the winds and the skies battled through her thoughts. She was not sure that she was ready to ride a storm. Fear clutched her insides and her blood ran cold as she remembered when she had been caught by Storm Rider's wind shear and had been at the mercy of the tumbling winds, plummeting toward the ground. At the time, it seemed almost like a game they were playing and she was thrilled. As she learned more and gained more knowledge of what she was and what Storm Rider wanted from her, the apprehension started to needle her.

Indecision and a lack of confidence were ruling her now and keeping her from finding restful sleep. Turning her head, she watched Storm Rider sleeping beside her, the rise and fall of his smooth, muscular chest. A faint smile played over his lips as if he was having a sweet dream. She wanted to kiss him, to taste those strong lips again and feel the strength of his arms protecting her, but she dared not. He would see her hesitation, her apprehension, and unease, and know she was afraid of riding the storms. In her heart, she wanted more than anything to please him and knew that she would do it, she would follow him into the black clouds as they churned across the skies calling her name.

\#

The summer solstice dawned in an expanse of pink and lavender clouds ascending from the deep violet of night. Storm Rider woke early and placed a few sticks on the smoldering fire. He turned back to the blankets and lovingly smoothed a hand over Moon Dancer's bare hip and up her side to wake her gently because he knew the day would bring enough violence. In truth, he was looking forward to taking his Love up into the heart of the sky where, finally, together, they would ride the storm he would call with his Ny-Failen powers.

Moon Dancer stirred and rolled over, opening her eyes to see Storm Rider leaning above her. He bent and kissed the warm soft skin of her neck and let his kisses travel downward. Before she was even entirely awake, he pressed his warmth into her and made love to her in the early morning light. Birds chided the lovers from the trees and the crackle of the awakening fire sent up a few lazy sparks, while thin blue smoke slowly swirled upward and mixed with the morning mist.

After their gentle lovemaking, they quickly bathed in the hot spring pool and ate a small meal of leftover bread, cheese and apples. When Moon Dancer could stall no further, she dressed and watched as Storm Rider did the same. He seemed distracted and impatient to be gone, explaining that they had a long flight ahead of them before they would find a place far enough away that he could conjure up a storm.

For this adventure, Moon Dancer had borrowed some old britches of Helms from years back when he was a boy. They fit snug and were of soft leather that clung to her slim curves. She tightly laced up a leather bodice and pulled on her boots.

After braiding her long golden hair, she looked around and realized there was nothing left to do but fly.

Storm Rider had donned his leather dragon scale armor and the tips shone silver in the morning light. He turned to her, held out his hand, and gave her the most beautiful smile, transforming his face into a vision of love, excitement, and assurance.

"Come, let us fly into the storm and see what secrets she will reveal to us."

Her lips trembled slightly as Moon Dancer smiled in what she hoped was an equally happy anticipatory smile and reached for his hand.

For a few hours, they flew, heading west over the Violent Mountains to a place where no man lived or had ever trod. This way, no one would be harmed by the violent tempest Storm Rider intended to call. He led the way toward the ever more darkening reaches of vast and expanding skies.

The air was exhilaratingly cool but not uncomfortably so and smelled crisp and clean with a heavy scent of rain. Moon Dancer followed close behind and peered down as she flew. Below them, the jagged peaks of snow-covered mountains sat unsuspectingly calm. When Storm Rider seemed to pause in the center of the sky, she knew it was time. Her heart skipped with anticipation as she watched him raise his arms and, floating on a soft breeze, wings spread wide, he closed his eyes and called to his power. Moon Dancer gasped as he began to glow golden and bright.

At first, it was hard to believe that the beautiful blue skies could so suddenly be covered in an ocean of clouds, but they quickly rolled in, racing toward them. They began to churn in a slow circle expanding outward, taking over miles and miles of sky. The afternoon sun painted the edges of the clouds gold but the building storm swallowed the brightness as the thunderheads gathered and towered above them. An eerie quiet was broken by distant rolling as if a huge great growling beast was swimming toward them through the ocean of clouds. Wave, after wave, the clouds came in like a violent tide.

Storm Rider's deep laugh echoed his joy and he beckoned to her as he flew higher into the building storm. Moon Dancer followed her Love, leaving behind her apprehension and embracing the excitement that was building inside her. The strength of her white-gold wings gave her courage as the winds whipped her hair back and the hint of rain began.

The thunder grew nearer and Moon Dancer noticed that the force of the wind worked with her wings and she startled herself by laughing as she seemed to leap from cloud to cloud. Her skin tingled and her ears buzzed as far off in the distance a bolt of lightning streaked across the sky like a bright silver streak. Banking hard to her right she followed at Storm Rider's side as he headed into the growing maelstrom.

Dark and ominous, the storm began to build on its own now and the golden glow that had enveloped Storm Rider subsided. She saw his intense passionate gaze and followed where he was staring. The skies were turning from deep violet to greyish blue to a stormy green. Moon Dancer marveled at the color of the greenish skies now and recognized it as the exact color of Storm Rider's eyes.

Moon Dancer was astonished by the abundance of color surrounding them. She had always thought storms were dark grey and colorless black, but this was an amazing swirl of violets and green, black and silvery-white on a background of deep cobalt lined with gold from the sun far above. Down below them, white billowy clouds clung to the tops of the mountains as if they feared the violence coming.

They flew apart and then together whirling around each other and playing in the winds, letting themselves be guided, gliding from gust to gust while the lighting and thunder drew closer. Side-by-side they soared and swooped laughing with abandon. When the winds reached a force that threatened to batter them mercilessly, Storm Rider banked hard and beckoned to Moon Dancer to follow. Every time he glowed with a golden light Moon Dancer knew he called to his power to strengthen the storm. She skipped along the currents with the strong beating of her wings and they flew higher than she had ever gone before.

The air grew thinner and cold, but Moon Dancer did not feel it, having never felt so exhilarated in her entire life. She watched as Storm Rider raced ahead of her and then had to stifle a scream when a bolt of lightning shot out and struck him. The thunder crashed with a deafening boom as the white light caressed him like a lover. The scales on his armor seemed to ripple and flash as the lightning danced, traveling from scale to scale, and now, he shone pure silver shooting across the sky, turning from silver to gold as he called the storm to swell and increase in power at his whim.

Elated, his laughter echoed through the skies and he glistened with rain and lightning and unfettered pleasure. Thunder rolled around them laughing back, in communion with Storm Rider's joy! It was the most beautiful thing she had ever seen! Moon Dancer had been so preoccupied watching Storm Rider she lost her concentration and the force of the wind suddenly caught her and flipped her over several times in the sky. Her wings wretched in every direction until she thought they would rip right from her back. Stifling a scream and fighting to control herself and find a calmer current, Moon Dancer flailed wildly.

She gasped as something hard hit her and she fought to understand what was happening. Storm Rider plucked her from her fall and held her tightly against his body soaring directly upward. His strength amazed her! Her wings gained control once again as he flipped onto his back and she rested in her husband's arms. Spinning impossibly slowly in the sky Storm Rider's mouth met hers and he kissed her passionately fueled by the joy of the storm. Holding her tightly the rain pelted them as he flew her to calmer winds within the eye of the storm.

Moon Dancer's breast was heaving as she tried to catch her breath. Storm Rider was flooding her senses with his desire and his kisses were like the tingling of the lightening on her lips. His strong wings kept them aloft while she rested in the deceivingly calmer wind.

"Are you alright?" He shouted above the screaming of the maelstrom circling them.

"I am! I just lost focus for a moment."

"Remember everything I taught you! Race with the winds at your back. Do not fight them. Let your wings guide you."

"I will! I am ready!" Moon Dancer shouted and smiled at him. He gave her one last devouring kiss and overwhelmed her already taxed senses.

"We must go! There is more to see, more to experience, more storm to ride! Follow me and be careful, my Love!"

With a final kiss, Storm Rider let her go and dove into the winds that began to wail as if calling him back to join them. He vanished below her into an ominous green and black bank of clouds.

Moon Dancer followed and as soon as she left the calm eye of the storm she was grabbed as if by two hands, but she was ready and tightened her wings against her back. As the force wrenched her, she quickly snapped them open and used the momentum to swoop back around as she had seen Storm Rider do before. Buffeted by another burst of air from a different direction, she flipped over and dove down yet again performing perfect pirouettes across the sky. She began to enjoy herself and danced through the clouds gliding from each gust to gust with unimaginable grace.

As she glided the air began to buzz again and Moon Dancer's skin tingled like before. She knew lightning was going to strike and she watched for Storm Rider to see if it would strike him again. He was far below her when the lightning struck. Crying out, she watched as he looked up and caught her terrified gaze as the shock flowed over her in a long thin bolt. It seemed to merge within her very veins replacing her blood, brightening her and shivering through her, making her skin tingle violently. Blinded by her own silvery-white glow, she twirled in the sky and gathered the light, like spinning a thread around her. She felt as if she was burning, but was not hot like fire. It jolted her with a force she had no name to give it. Devoured by the sizzling light, the thunder crashed around her and the force took her breath away. Looking around, Moon Dancer watched as the storm rushed by her. Like a flat stone on water, she was skipped across the sky at a violent speed. Flapping her wings as hard as she could she tried to catch herself and slow what she realized was a violent spiraling descent toward the mountains below.

Storm Rider had been lost in the rapture he always felt as he rode the storm. His power roared within him as he called the maelstrom to greater and greater violence. Thunder had been booming around them and the lightning flashed through the skies lighting up the dark green clouds with white streaks. He sensed that a bolt was coming close and looked toward it ready to receive the addictive caress that he always felt. When he looked for it though he saw Moon Dancer above him and marveled at the elation that had taken over her face. Her hair had come out of its braid and was waving around her. She was beauty incarnate! His joy quickly turned to fear as he saw the lightning had come for her and not him. Illuminated by the silver flare Moon Dancer jolted and then began to spin until she was wound completely in light. The bolt died and Storm Rider watched as she stiffened and was released like an arrow from a bow. At one with the lightning, she streaked away from him at an alarming speed he could not match. Horror took over as she began to flap her wings helplessly trying to compensate for the reckless speed. Her actions slowed her just enough so that she no longer streaked away, but seemed to skip across the sky. Then, she fell.

Chapter Twelve

There are some places on the Earth that man is not intended to see nor set foot upon. The towering peaks of the Violent Mountains are some of them. Jagged, rocky, and covered in snow year-round because of their height, they were massive, expansive, and awe-inspiring. It was said, among the Ny-Failen, that the Creator walked there and such was the beauty and majesty of those peaks that those of humankind were unworthy to see it or tread there.

It was to one of those high places that Moon Dancer, in and out of consciousness, hurtled headlong toward. Through the dangerous swirling greenish-black into the billowy white clouds. The ground seemed to rise as if it would embrace her. She crashed into the deep virgin snow on a high mountain top. Wings hitting first and absorbing some of the shock from her fall, the breath left her as she slammed into the deep hard snow. The impact drove the breath from her and the black of unconsciousness descended as the snow closed around her, burying her completely.

Storm Rider let go and anguished roar, *"NNNOOOOO!"* as he watched Moon Dancer crash into the snow and disappear into its depths. He had not been fast enough to catch her because the lightning bolt that hit her was faster. Keeping his eyes on the spot where she landed, he tightened his wings against his back and dove down. At the last second, he flared and came to an abrupt halt, landing in the snow. He shapeshifted putting his wings away and dropped to his knees shouting her name. Frantically, he shoveled at the snow throwing huge chunks aside, digging and clawing to get down to where she was buried. The mountain top was ominously quiet except for Storm Rider's heavy breathing and the wind blowing around him. It spoke to him and encouraged him to leave off his efforts, and come and play.

Ice-cold snow numbed his bare hands but he continued to dig, calling Moon Dancer's name. After too many silent minutes he finally clawed away enough snow to find a leg. She had been wet through from the rain and the cold of the snow had frozen her clothing. He continued to scramble through the snow opening a hole and working to make it bigger. As more and more of her was revealed Storm Rider quickened his pace needing to get the heavy snow off her chest and away from her face so that she could breathe. He did not allow the thought to cross his mind that the fall had killed her. It would not be!

When he finally got her unburied, he tried to assess the damage to her body. He put his head to her chest listening for a heartbeat. Nothing, not even the faintest flicker from her heart, and no breath issued from her lips. She was still.

Storm Rider reared up from where he knelt and cried out. Without realizing why, either in anguish or intentionally, he raised his hands to the sky and cried out to the Creator, and his answer was the lightning. It streaked down at his beckoning call. It was a small bolt, but directed to Moon Dancer's chest and it lightly touched her, scorching her leather bodice and shirt. When the flash subsided, he put his ear to her heart. The faintest flutter started within and after a moment, Moon Dancer gasped for air.

Moaning and crying out Moon Dancer tried to move. As she did, Storm Rider noticed a red stain spreading out from one of her wings. It was broken along the top edge and many of the quills were torn out and snapped. Blood splattered the beautiful white-gold feathers. The other wing fared better and lay curled around her protectively.

Storm Rider knelt beside her and ran his hands over her legs and arms, and felt behind her neck. Nothing else seemed broken. He took one of her hands in his and lifted it to his lips kissing her cold fingers reverently.

"Saitya buri vaenga." His voice was gentle as he spoke in Ny-Failen and told her, *'put your wings away.'*

Moon Dancer did not open her eyes, but her body began to rock slowly from side to side and as the wings shapeshifted into her back. Storm Rider carefully put his arms under her and lifted her. He held her tight against his chest whispering repeatedly. "Thior maithnanas dohlm!"

Even in her unconscious state, the words spoke to her heart and she heard his heartfelt desperate plea, *"forgive me!"*

Gently, Storm Rider lifted Moon Dancer in his arms, stood, and cradled her against his chest. Then he looked up, shapeshifted, and burst into the air. He hovered in the skies just for a moment looking in the direction of Jior and then Javelin Peak, trying to decide where he should take her. Then he streaked off.

The storm had continued to rage above and the rain pelted them as Storm Rider caught the swift-moving wind current. He sped back over the mountains so quickly that he flashed brilliant white and in minutes he was back at Javelin Peak. Landing he shrugged imperceptibly and shapeshifted. Then he went to the closed cabin door and banged against it with his boot.

Helm answered the door, alarm written all over his face. He exclaimed loudly when he saw his sister unconscious, frozen and bloody, cradled in Storm Rider's arms.

"Meurie! What happened!" Helm fell back and stepped aside as Storm Rider ducked past him and strode into the cabin. Stalking purposefully to Moon Dancer's bedroom he kicked open the door and laid her on the bed. He began to remove her boots and without turning ordered Helm to fetch hot water and blankets and to build up the fire.

Glenna came to the door and gasped. "Moon Dancer! What happened to her!"

Storm Rider refused to answer their inquiries, only continued to peel her frozen clothes off. Before too much of her was revealed he turned his head slightly and barked at Helm.

"Master Helm get hot water and blankets! Lady Glenna, please help me get her out of these wet clothes."

Helm turned and left the room while Glenna helped Storm Rider undress Moon Dancer. They got her sodden clothes off and Glenna gasped at the multiple bruises on her back, arms, and legs. As soon as Helm returned with hot water, they bathed her and covered her with numerous blankets.

Moon Dancer had not woken while they administered to her and Storm Rider's face looked as angry as a thunderstorm. Breathing shallowly, she appeared to be asleep. Glenna gathered the wet clothing and boots and silently left the room closing the door behind her. Storm Rider pulled up a stool from the corner of the room and sat down beside her, speaking softly in Ny-Failen, he closed his eyes and began to pray.

CHAPTER THIRTEEN

The next few days Storm Rider stayed by Moon Dancer's side. She had not awoken completely but cried out and moaned in pain at the slightest movement. Helm and Glenna hovered outside in the main room of the cabin bringing food she could not eat and hot drinks she could not swallow, helping where they could. Storm Rider would not reveal what had happened to his wife and the thunderous look on his face warned them not to ask.

Finally, Helm had enough, his patience was completely gone, he entered the room without knocking. Moon Dancer lay motionless in the bed and Storm Rider watched over her. He had not moved from her side once during her recovery. Helm narrowed his eyes as Storm Rider slowly turned his head and cast him a menacing look when Helm beckoned sharply for him to come outside. Storm Rider rose smoothly. He ducked out of the room and followed Helm out of the cabin. When they stepped into the morning daylight Helm whirled on Storm Rider.

"I demand to know what you have done to her?" Helm shouted a little louder than he had intended and Storm Rider just glared. "At least tell me if she will live? Glenna said she was badly bruised everywhere and there was blood on her. Tell me what happened to her?"

Storm Rider flushed with anger and a little embarrassment and when Helm opened his mouth to shout more he finally answered.

"I was teaching her to ride the storm. She was struck by lightning. Then the lightning drew her away from me and before I could reach her…" Storm Rider's voice caught and he swallowed before going on, "*she fell.*"

"Fell!" Yelling, Helm choked and his eyes went wide with shock, "She fell? How could you let that happen? Weren't supposed to protect her? How could you take her to fly into a *storm* when she is…?

Helm did not get to finish what he was yelling because Storm Rider was suddenly upon him. Grasping Helm by the throat, he lifted him off his feet with one hand and slammed him hard against the side of the cabin. The wood cracked and showered bark over them. Storm Rider's face was red with fury. Helm gasped for air as Storm Rider held him two feet off of the ground. Helm had taken to carrying an iron dagger and now pulled it in desperation and held it against Storm Rider's neck which began to smolder and burn where the iron touched his white skin. Storm Rider ignored the burning iron and brought his face close to Helm's and growled.

"You do not know of what you speak, *Human*!" Storm Rider let Helm go and stepped back looking at the iron dagger Helm threatened him with, but he showed no fear. Helm staggered on his feet and fell back against the cabin, his free hand grasping his throat. Red welts swelled up on Helm's neck as he tried to fill his lungs.

"I know you control the storms and you let it get out of hand. Didn't you?" Rasping and trying to gulp in air, he continued. "You endangered my sister's life for your selfish reasons and she is paying the price. Now you take your anger at yourself out on me! It was your own doing and now she lies in there fighting for her life!"

Storm Rider clenched his fists and looked as if he was going to pummel Helm, but Helm stood his ground. He straightened ready for a fight holding the iron dagger. The blows did not come and Storm Rider hesitated, eyes blazing with anger as he considered Helm's words, but then it seemed his anger abated. He took a deep breath and looked tired and worn. Running a hand through his wild red hair, he dropped his eyes and eased his tense stance. The welt from the iron dagger swelled, turning angry red and blistered. Helm sheathed his iron dagger.

"Master Helm, you speak the truth. I let the storm get out of control while lost in my enjoyment. Moon Dancer was doing well. She was a wonder to behold! But she was unprepared when the lightning hit her and…"

"You let *lightning* strike her!" Helm shouted accusingly and suddenly his fist shot up and bashed Storm Rider square in the mouth. Storm Rider's head snapped to the side a little, but other than that he did not react except to spit blood and dab at his split lip with the back of his hand. He made no move to engage in a fight, only continued with his explanation. His voice softened with dread; his eyes went glassy as he remembered.

"She was caught in the winds and fell. Before I could reach her…" he stopped as if he did not want to go on and recount the fall. Closing his eyes as if he were seeing it again, he rasped. "Before I could reach her, she struck the mountain. The deep snow cushioned her fall and because she is Ny-Failen and immortal, she did not die. One wing was broken and I suspect her head struck hard, but I dug her out of the snow and brought her here for help because it was closer than Jior."

"Snow cushioned her fall? You dug her out?" Helm continued to yell and shook his head barely understanding what he was hearing. Shaking with anger, he closed his eyes and took a deep breath gathering his courage to continue, facing the truth of what had happened to Moon Dancer. "Her wing was broken? Then…she'll never fly again?"

Storm Rider watched as the truths he revealed dawned in Helm's understanding and he narrowed his eyes knowingly. Helm's voice had sounded a little hopeful as he spoke his last words and Storm Rider smoldered inside. Stepping close to Helm he looked down at him and his split lip curled in arrogance.

"Human!" His eyes traveled over Helm in disgust. "The ne'amh chomhara is far beyond your ability to fully comprehend it. When she put her wings away, they will heal within the ne'amh chomhara and she *will* fly again. It will take time to heal but she will recover." He spat accusingly, "You would clip her wings and bind her to this earth and that will not be!"

Helm was speechless while they glared at each other and he swallowed words that might end his life. He could not deny Storm Rider's suspicions and, looking away, he did not want Storm Rider to see the truth in his eyes. The memory of the kiss he had given Meurie in the barn the day he and Glenna had returned home, flickered in Helm's mind. It had been a lover's kiss, a selfish indulgence on his part. He thought of his earlier accusation toward Storm Rider and his selfish reasons for taking Meurie into danger. He suddenly realized they had both used her for their egotistical reasons and desires.

Glenna opened the door to the cabin, breaking the tension, and spoke quietly to Storm Rider, telling him Moon Dancer had awoken and was asking for him.

Storm Rider turned and went into the cabin. Helm, turned and walked in the other direction without another word.

#

Over the next few days, Moon Dancer healed. She had awoken sore and bruised with a terrible headache, but she did not have any broken bones and appeared not to have any permanent injury. Storm Rider forced her to eat to regain her strength. They had long discussions about the ne'amh chomhara and Moon Dancer worried that her wings were lost and was anxious to shape-shift and see if she could fly again. Storm Rider urged patience and changed the subject. Instead, he told her he believed they should go home, to Jior. Javelin Peak no longer held any attraction for him and he wanted to escape the memories of most of what had happened there. He would not speak of that day and what transpired when they went to ride their first storm together but the look on his face filled in the holes in her memories of that day.

The first night she was well enough that he could sleep beside her in the bed, Moon Dancer was overwhelmed with emotion and desire for her husband. She coaxed him into making gentle love with her. Afterward, as he held her close, Moon Dancer felt his tears fall on her bare breasts and smelled the scent of rain.

#

They stayed at the cabin for another few days while Moon Dancer continued to heal from her ordeal, and they all tried not to talk about what happened to her. They spent time with Helm and Glenna and watched as the love grew deeper between the couple.

The day finally came when Storm Rider and Moon Dancer were meant to leave for Jior. He had been gone long enough and was anxious to return home. Moon Dancer healed completely and they walked down to the hot springs that held so many happy memories for them. She shrugged her shoulders and spread wide her white-gold wings in the warm, golden light of morning. Giving a few experimental flaps she tested them and gained her strength. The ne'amh chomhara had healed her completely. Bending slightly at the knees she shot up into the sky. When they flew together, Storm Rider used his power to whisk away the slightest breeze and the smallest cloud so that she would have peaceful azure skies to fly in. It was her smile and elation at being able to fly again that made him feel as if they had weathered the storm together.

The next morning, they flew up to the cabin and went to make their goodbyes. Glenna stepped out of the cabin and gasped in wonder as Storm Rider and Moon Dancer landed outside, illuminated by the morning sun. Her white-gold wings pulsed agitatedly as she looked around for Helm. They had argued over what had happened and, much to Storm Rider's surprise, Moon Dancer stubbornly refused to promise Helm never to ride the storms again. In the end, Helm and Moon Dancer agreed not to remain angry at each other and reached a tentative truce.

"Glenna…Helm?" Moon Dancer started to ask where he was but then turned as Helm came striding from the small barn. He slowed when he saw them standing there with their wings large and brilliant in the morning sunlight. As he approached, he scowled at Storm Rider, but his eyes softened as he looked sadly at Moon Dancer. No matter how hard he tried he could not remain angry with her.

"Meurie," he started to speak but was cut short by a low menacing growl from Storm Rider. "*Moon Dancer*, I will have to get used to calling you that. I see your wing is healed?"

She just nodded, too full of emotion to speak. Helm took her aside.

"I wish you well in your new life with your new husband." He brought out a small pouch made of doeskin and handed it to her.

"I made this for you. Perhaps it will remind you of me in the days ahead. Maybe you can wear it on your wedding day."

Moon Dancer took the pouch and poured out the contents. It was a silver beaded necklace strung with moonstone crystals set in a half-circle. She gasped as she looked at it and then tears filled her eyes. She threw her arms around Helm and kissed his cheek and whispered in his ear how much she loved him and would miss him. Helm looked a little embarrassed but hugged her back. Storm Rider growled again.

After a few moments, Moon Dancer went back into the cabin with Glenna to pack a small bag and Storm Rider took this chance to speak his mind to Helm.

"Helm, I know you love Moon Dancer, but she is not for you."

"Of course I love her, she is my sister. I only want what is best for her."

"You know of what I speak. I have seen how you look at her and that is not love for a *sister* that burns in your eyes. You have said more than once she is not your blood sister and I know your feelings of love are for the *woman* she is."

Helm stood still wondering if Storm Rider knew about the kiss in the barn and the tension built in the air until he finally relented and let out an explosive breath.

"Alright! Before you came along, I wanted to tell her she was not my sister by blood, but only the girl I was brought up with. I do love her, but I married Glenna and Meurie has you and we will carry on as before, as sister and brother!" He accused, "If you think *I* would have ever hurt her you are wrong."

Knowing that Helm was reminding him of Moon Dancer's fall, Storm Rider took a step toward Helm who stood his ground. The massive white wings sat calmly on his back, but his face was not calm. He clenched his fists.

"You humans bend the rules to suit your own needs and desires. You are like the storm winds buffeting and blowing in all directions. It is lucky you are that you never pursued her."

"And you Ny-Failen think you can do as you please and take what you want. Meurie is sweet and innocent and when you tire of her, I will be here to pick up the pieces of her broken heart…as a good *brother* should."

"Moon Dancer has given herself to me willingly and your bones will be dust in the dirt before *I* ever leave Moon Dancer." Storm Rider snarled.

Just then the two girls returned. Moon Dancer held a small pack with her few belongings and Glenna followed her outside smiling happily. The women looked back and forth between the two men squaring off and quickly interrupted.

"Helm, Storm Rider says the wedding can be held at the end of next month. You will come, won't you? Please say you will." Moon Dancer implored.

It was Storm Rider who spoke up not giving Helm the chance to answer. "Master Helm has already consented to attend with Lady Glenna." He held Helm's stare and dared him to reject Storm Rider's words.

Helm went red in the face with anger at Storm Rider answering for him. He opened his mouth to retort, but Storm Rider spoke quietly to him so that only he could hear.

"You will come to your sister's wedding because it will make her happy or I will truss you up and fly you there myself." Storm Rider was not smiling when he said this and so Helm could do nothing, but assent with a tight-lipped smile.

Moon Dancer said her goodbyes and hugged Helm for a long time. Then she let go, but before he released her, he pulled her aside and made some quiet proclamations of his own.

"Meurie, my sister, I will always be here for you if you need me. I hope with all my heart you will be *safe* and happy. I will miss you."

Moon Dancer's eyes filled with tears and she hugged him yet again and kissed his cheek.

"I'm glad you have Glenna to keep you company. I will think of you all the time and come to visit often." She smiled held her hand over the necklace Helm had given her and whispered a heartfelt, "Thank you, Helm, for everything!"

Moon Dancer and Storm Rider flew off into the late morning sun heading back to Jior to start their new life together. She was overjoyed to be heading to Jior with Storm Rider and start a new chapter in her life, but she was also sad to be leaving Helm. She knew that eventually; Helm would accept her marriage to Storm Rider.

They flew for most of the morning and when Moon Dancer began to tire and slow, Storm Rider swooped in, scooped her out of the sky, and held her safely in his arms.

CHAPTER FOURTEEN

Storm Rider and Moon Dancer flew north over the vast mountain range of the Violent Mountains. The thick evergreen foliage passed swiftly under them and they easily sailed over the jagged outcroppings of rock and towering granite cliffs. Soon the towers of Castle Jior appeared in the distance. Storm Rider had been through a lot after winning his bride and after what happened in the storm over the Violent Mountains, was surprised to find himself a little nervous to introduce Moon Dancer to his family. Though his grandfather, King Forlorn Icefall knew of Moon Dancer, he still felt anxious because he wanted his mother and father to love her as he did. His shame over what they had been through was like a hot brand in his gut, but he was determined that it should not ruin the love between him and Moon Dancer and their future together, whether or not they ever rode the storms together again.

They landed on a high tower that was connected to the black-walled castle by a high bridge. He took her hand and led her across and inside.

#

Jagged Edge always had a sense when his son was near and this time he sensed that he was not alone. He left the practice field where he had been at sword training with some Jiorian warriors of humankind and headed to the castle. He looked up in time to see Storm Rider flying overhead followed by a winged woman he had never seen before. The flood of her thoughts assailed him as he watched her and he had to shut them off before he learned too much. He went and found his wife, Princess Lyra Song, and informed her, *'the Storm approaches'* as he always did when he referred to his son's homecoming.

"Gather everyone; he's brought someone important with him." Surprised, Lyra Song looked up from her embroidery and smiled lovingly at her husband.

Storm Rider took Moon Dancer's hand and led her through the dark halls of Castle Jior. He had hoped to find his mother first and ease the way for his new mate. Introducing her to everyone at once could be overwhelming, but not surprisingly, his father knew and Storm Rider could hear that many people were gathered in the Great Hall awaiting them.

Moon Dancer's magnificent white-gold wings pulsed nervously on her back. Somehow having them there made her feel a little more confident and she consoled herself that Storm Rider had not put his wings away and guessed that she should not either. His large warm hand in hers made her feel safe and she nervously smoothed her hair and wished that she had braided it before they left. Picturing herself a wind-blown mess, she slowed her steps. After everything she and Storm Rider had been through, she feared her inadequacy was blatantly obvious.

As they came around the curve of the wide, winding stairwell, Storm Rider went boldly forward and opened the doors to the Great Hall. Moon Dancer fell in behind him suddenly terrified to meet Jior's royal family who all stood arrayed in front of her. Like stepping into a room full of giant men and delicate ethereal women of mythical legend, Moon Dancer felt as if she were caught in a dream. It had been one thing to spy on them from outside the castle walls and dream about the stories the Bards told of them, and quite another to be here facing them. Hiding behind Storm Rider she smoothed her hands over her faded blue dress and stood behind him using him almost like a shield. Her wings shivered behind her and she had the sudden urge to fly back to her mountain home where she came from. These next moments were what she had dreamed of her entire life. She was finally going to meet the Ny-Failen of legend!

As they entered, Moon Dancer's eyes flew to the massive King of Jior who noticeably stood towering above them all. Dressed in ominous black leather, his long white hair was held back in its customary long braid and his facial expression was impossible to read. Beside him was the most beautiful woman Moon Dancer had ever seen and she knew immediately it was Queen Lililaira Gem. The queen looked tiny next to her towering husband, dressed in a long flowing gown of dark amethyst. Her long silvery-white hair, described in legend as *spun silver*, hung in long intricate braids and flowing curls.

Storm Rider approached the king first, placed his hand over his heart, and bowing deeply to his grandfather, stepped forward and embraced him.

"Storm Rider you've finally returned! And you have brought someone with you." Knowingly, he crooked a half-grin.

Storm Rider turned and everyone in the room stilled and gathered closer to look at her.

"Grandfather, Grandmother, this is Moon Dancer. She is to be my wife."

Moon Dancer peaked from around Storm Rider's broad back and her wings twitched. She gave them a shy smile and dropped into a deep curtsey in front of the King and Queen as they stepped forward. Her white-gold wings tipped back and brushed the floor.

"Welcome, Moon Dancer." The Queen gave her a welcoming embrace. The King also greeted her with a masculine bow. Then suddenly she was being approached by a huge man with long red hair and a short red beard and

Storm Rider was saying something about his father, Jagged Edge and it was all she could do not to stare. Though Storm Rider's hair was short and multiple shades of red like the head of a red hawk, she thought the resemblance was uncanny. Moon Dancer's heart fluttered as did her wings.

"Do not be nervous Moon Dancer. We are happy and indeed grateful to you that you have calmed our Storm Rider." Jagged Edge gave his son a telling look and then turned and held out his arm to her as a courtly gentleman does to a Lady. Moon Dancer reluctantly took his arm and allowed herself to be pulled forward.

"Lady Moon Dancer, this is my wife, Princess Lyra Song." Jagged Edge introduced her to Storm Rider's mother who had the same silvery-white hair as Ny-Failen women and the luminescent pearly-hued skin like the queen.

"My Lady, I am very pleased to meet you." Moon Dancer curtseyed deep and felt her trepidation increase greatly when she looked into the violet eyes of Storm Rider's mother. She even blushed when the thought came to her out of nowhere that she had seen this gracious woman's son naked. Jagged Edge gave a small choke as the thought reached him and his eyes widened at his son. Clamping down hard on his ability to read the poor girl's mind, he turned and glared at his son. Storm Rider's chin came up slightly aware of the embarrassed blush Moon Dancer gave his mother and his father's sudden discomfort. Lyra Song embraced Moon Dancer and welcomed her with genuine affection.

Next, his two sisters stepped forward and Storm Rider's handsome face softened slightly as they approached his new wife. Moon Dancer beheld the two ethereal creatures with awe, but Storm Rider had spoken of them so fondly that she felt as if she knew them.

Mercy Rose let the much younger girl of approximately six years of age approach first. They called her Rain Song. Rain Song bubbled forward and praised Moon Dancer's beauty and poetically admired her white-gold wings. Then Mercy Rose stepped forward, everyone in the room stilled and turned toward them in silent anticipation. Moon Dancer resisted the urge to look around warily and wondered why the room had gone so silent. Even the King and Queen turned to hear Mercy Rose greet Moon Dancer. Storm Rider's face held a thunderous glare and he stood stiffly by her side as Mercy Rose took her hand.

The faintest blue glow passed over Mercy Rose's violet-colored eyes and Moon Dancer felt a tiny shock pass from the girl to her. Mercy Rose's silvery-white head tilted to the side as if she were listening then she took a deep breath like a seer about to give a prophecy and her eyes glowed brilliant blue.

"Moon Dancer, you are most welcome to the family." As if no longer speaking to her, Mercy Rose turned perceptively toward King Forlorn Icefall as if she were in a trance.

"Our Moon Dancer is a rare and precious find. She is second generation, either a grandmother or grandfather was Ny-Failen. To have wings…" She changed what she was going to say and went on, surprise suddenly coloring her eyes.

"I sense flight is new to you." Mercy Rose faltered a little before going on. "She has a kind spirit. Your love for my brother does you justice. Though your wings are newly found, you will do well among the Ny-Failen of Jior. I see many children and happy times ahead, though I warn you, my brother's love of storm riding may seem greater than his love for you at times. I urge patience with him. It appears you two have already survived a vicious storm together and come through stronger, as one. There is sorrow over a loved one I see, but he will find acceptance in his heart for your union with Storm Rider though they are both so alike I urge patience with him too for they are kindred spirits in their love for you."

Mercy Rose stopped and barely shook her head like she was just waking up. She released Moon Dancer's hand and as her eyes cleared, she looked at her with intense affection. "Storm Rider is lucky to have you, as are we. Welcome!" The two girls embraced.

The room seemed to breathe a sigh of relief. Storm Rider took her elbow and led her away, but before she could get many steps, Princess Lyra Song took her other arm and explained.

"Forgive our Mercy Rose she is somewhat like Lord Lost Morning, the Leader of the Ny-Failen, whom you've yet to meet. Her gift of reading Ny-Failen can be daunting sometimes and foretelling the future is somewhat of an after-effect of her powers. Once she has read one of us, it is done. Though Lost Morning has the final say." They paced forward and Princess Lyra Song gestured to a tall Ny-Failen standing in front of them. He turned and greeted her with a reserved smile and Moon Dancer was struck with the resemblance this Ny-Failen had to King Forlorn Icefall.

"Moon Dancer, this is my brother, Prince Vannier also called Little Wing, and his wife Lady Summer Rain." Prince Vannier was dressed completely in white, with a breastplate that shone with iridescent scales similar to Storm Rider's black armor. He bowed to her with his hand over his heart and Lady Summer Rain came forward. She wore a shimmering rose-gold gown and her white-blonde hair was so perfectly manicured that Moon Dancer gave another self-conscious pat to her own hair. Lady Summer Rain was a pearl set in gold to Prince Vannier's silver and she gave Moon Dancer a graceful welcome with a kiss on each cheek.

Prince Vannier gestured to the roof of the Great Hall and introduced his sons. Two identical twin Ny-Failen boys swooped down from the rafters grinning mischievously and jostling each other as they landed in front of her. Moon Dancer stifled a laugh and looked at the two youths who snapped to attention and, in unison bowed in respect, with hands over their hearts, as their father had.

"These are my nephews Winter Wolf and White Wing." The boys bowed in turn as their names were announced by Princess Lyra Song.

"And coming late to this joyous occasion is my niece, Autumn Day." Moon Dancer looked over and saw a little girl in a flurry of maroon silks rushing toward her.

"Autumn Day is one of Prince Dark Star's daughters. This is Moon Dancer; she has come from the Violent Mountains to be Storm Rider's wife." The girl crooked a finger at Moon Dancer who bent down to receive a kiss on the cheek. She murmured an apology for being late to Moon Dancer as Lyra Song directed a slightly chastising look at her, but she went on with the formal introductions.

Approaching them was a tall man with short white hair that spiked out in all directions. His cautious examination of Moon Dancer unnerved her and she barely heard Princess Lyra Song introduce, "Prince Dark Star, Storm Rider's uncle and his wife, Lady Dawn Rusher." Dawn Rusher was holding a small child of about three whose strawberry-colored hair made Moon Dancer smile, but Lyra Song was not finished.

"And this shy little one is Ariel Dawn." A little girl of about five years old peeked out from behind Dawn Rusher's golden-brown skirts. The violet eyes of the girl glittered shyly at Moon Dancer and she gave a squeak and hid again.

"Their eldest son, Blue Star, is somewhere around here. He's probably getting into mischief." Moon Dancer was not sure if she should laugh at that little joke, but she smiled, curtsied, and said how happy she was to meet Prince Dark Star and his wife and children.

While Storm Rider's mother took over the introductions his father took the opportunity to take him aside

"Storm Rider, she is what has been causing you to thunder around here like a winter squall?" Jagged Edge crossed his arms over his chest.

Storm Rider looked at his father with an unveiled challenge. Jagged Edge and Storm Rider had a close relationship, but Storm Rider seemed defiant now as he held the green gaze of his father with his own green gaze, so alike. It was not until Lyra Song had drawn Moon Dancer further away, making more introductions that he answered quietly.

"I only went after what was mine." Storm Rider grumbled, defying his father to argue or chastise him for going after Moon Dancer.

"Peace," Jagged Edge spoke calmly. "I only wish you would have come to me with your problems rather than keeping them pent-up inside and flooding half the kingdom before disappearing again. I warn you; a wife will not let you keep things from her or let you rage in silence. They have ways of drawing things out of you. Your experience with women is lacking and I recommend you be patient with her and open your heart to her. I only offer you this advice so that you can benefit from my experience. I hope it will help you weather any storm." Jagged Edge frowned and looked as if he would like to say more, but the look on Storm Rider's face stopped him.

A flash of memory struck Storm Rider as he recalled the still form of Moon Dancer buried in the snow after her fall and how close he had come to losing her. The habit of distant arrogance fell from him like a shed cloak and he spoke softly.

"I am sorry father. I should have come to you for advice. I just didn't know how to speak of such matters. I will come to you in the future. For now, my Lady looks overwhelmed and I must go to her." Storm Rider flushed with an overprotective instinct toward his wife and quickly embraced his father. He went to go and join his bride.

It was not meant to be though, as he turned to go, Mercy Rose stepped into his path and the look in her all-knowing eyes stopped him in his tracks. Jagged Edge gave both of his children a meaningful glare that said for the two of them not to start trouble and then he moved away to join Lyra Song.

Storm Rider faced the slightly angry look on Mercy Rose's face. Her normally soft and gentle features were hard and determined, and one eyebrow rose slowly as if that simple movement was all she needed to impart the depths of her ire. Storm Rider crossed his arms over his chest and met her glare challenging with one of his own, though his green eyes looked resolute as if he suspected he knew exactly what she was angry about. He momentarily feared she knew about the storm he had created and about Moon Dancers' fall. Everything he had been through just to be standing there in Jior with Moon Dancer by his side and to start their new life together, came crashing down upon him and he wanted to thunder in his defense. Storm Rider did not answer Mercy Rose's accusing glare immediately but continued the silent stand-off searching her face. Almost as if he was trying to judge how much she knew.

"I only went after what was mine." He said finally leaving out the rest she did not need to know.

"That's not what I'm thinking about and you know it." Mercy Rose stopped, took a calming breath, and reached out and touched Storm Rider's crossed arms. Her eyes implored and softened looking more concerned than angry now.

Suddenly, he knew fully what she was talking about and he almost breathed a relieved sigh because it was one of his actions he could easily defend.

"She had the ne'amh chomhara. I simply awoke what lay dormant. It can only be done once and I chose *her*."

Moon Dancer's tinkling laugh rang out from the group ahead of them and Storm Rider looked up to stare with intense green eyes at his new wife. He did not look down again when Mercy Rose dropped her hand from his arm and whispered with quiet intensity.

"Storm Rider, what have you done?"

The End

Aesir Blacknight

CHAPTER ONE

A tall dark figure slipped through the huge black gates set in the tall walls protecting the city of Jior. All that could be heard of his passing, was the rustle of the long, dark cloak that shrouded him. A swish of air ruffled the darkness behind him and a rasp and clank loudly echoed as massive pulleys slid huge bolts across the gates, sealing the city closed for the night.

A soft rain had been falling, and the streets were slick with water, washing them clean. The man moved on, taking long swift strides toward his goal. Rain did not deter dozens of other people from rushing here and there down the street seeking their destinations. Dogs barked in the distance, and a wet cat gave a woeful yowl from the steps of a tall building. Evening continued to descend.

Moving almost unseen, he continued, turning his steps toward the northernmost hill. Down the long streets, across vast courtyards and grassy lawns, he made his way toward the massive, looming, black fortress that was Castle Jior. Torches and hooded lanterns glowed and then burned brightly as the guards of the castle lit huge sconces in the battlements. Night fell swiftly in the deep Violent Mountains, but the ominous darkness and the gloom of rain existed peacefully with the inhabitants living among their peaks. The roar of the distant, goliath waterfall was a constant presence in Jior and, along with the rain, caused the river below it to swell and froth as the deep water rushed over menacing rapids. All around the city the sounds of descending nighttime echoed through streets and alleys, courtyards and gateways, to rise and vanish into the night.

Stopping in the shadows near the castle gates, the dark figure settled. His only movement was the slow turn of his hooded head as he surveyed the activity within. Soldiers leisurely paced the high walls and did not attempt to muffle pleasant greetings as they passed each other while making their rounds. In the distance, music echoed through the night. Strains of an elegant tune swayed back and forth through the evening air, strangely accompanied by the harmonious sound of the falling rain.

Iron spikes were erected to the height of a tall man's head, lining the top of the ramparts and encircling the walls surrounding the King of Jior's castle. These violent and twisted fortifications were remnants of the ancient past when King Kullorn reigned here with those of demon-kind. The watcher was not interested in architecture or fortifications, nor was he concerned with inattentive soldiers who should be wary of uninvited guests. His eyes burned from within his hood as he trained an intense glare on his goal.

The tall intricately carved gates in front of the castle were open, and small groups of people hurried through toward the brightly lit castle and the festivities within. Slipping silently from the shadows, the tall figure strode confidently toward the gates and entered unchallenged, trailing along in the back of one of the small groups as if he were part of their number. They hurried up the wide stone path lined with tall, twisted oaks that were only just starting to bud, signaling it was almost spring's time to reign. Huge iron cages held fires that brightly lit and warmed the pathway for attending guests. The rain began to falter, and the clouds overhead slowly glided away revealing the moon's bright glow. Now, the black stones of the castle glittered with rain-laced flakes of color under the bright moonlight.

Like stars on a midnight field, raindrops glittered on the watcher's heavy cloak and clung tightly as if holding on to keep from falling. Soundlessly, he shadowed the group ahead of him entering the Great Hall of Castle Jior. The sound of drums, pipes, harps, and flutes played unseen. In the center of the hall, men, and women dressed in colorful finery, paired up to dance. Swaying with the rhythm of the tune, they came together and then parted only to return to each other's arms in the intricate steps of the dance. The scent of freshly cut pine permeated the air along with rich smells of roasted beef, freshly baked bread, and other enticing delicacies. Vines of thick ivy climbed the tall pillars of the hall. Bundles of lavender roses decorated the brightly lit scene and also filled the air with their gentle fragrance. Laughter and the buzz of conversation swam through the air and gave credence to the joyful gathering.

The dark cloaked figure entered the Great Hall without stealth or hesitation and surveyed the scene. His head slowly turned, searching until he found the object of his desire standing next to the King of Jior.

King Forlorn Icefall was an impressive figure standing tall and regal among a group of richly dressed, heavily bejeweled men and women. He was calmly listening to one of the younger men standing beside him while he contemplatively stroked the short white beard on his chin. Nodding sagely, he turned toward a small, beautiful woman dressed in violet and diamonds. Long silvery-white hair fell in a curling cascade down her back, and the candlelight made her fair skin glow like lustrous pearls but it was her laughter ringing out that took her beauty to a new height. She turned her head slightly showing a peaked diamond crown that glittered on her head like a thousand stars, revealing her as Lililaira Gem, Queen of Jior.

Two guards suddenly stepped into the intruder's path as he advanced further into the room. Being the only one cloaked and hooded, they had been alerted by his dark sinister form entering the room. Now their long, sharp pikes crossed in front of the stranger and challenged his entry.

"Let me pass. I have business with the Queen of Jior." A deep male voice issued from the depths of the dark hood, impatiently addressing the guards before they could utter a word of challenge.

"You'll have to see the King about that and he's not available tonight. It's his granddaughter's nineteenth birthday celebration and I doubt you've been invited. You'll have to come back tomorrow if you want an audience." The guard took a menacing step forward, lowering the sharp pike he held, to point right at the stranger's heart.

"Nevertheless, I *will* see her, my need is urgent. Let me by or it will not go well for you." His deep voice sharply conveyed the warning.

Two more guards approached and the stranger was now surrounded by four Jiorian guards pointing deadly sharp pikes at him.

"Come back *tomorrow!*" The first guard spoke more forcefully.

Black gloved hands appeared out of the deep blue cloak. As the stranger raised his arms from the folds, low and menacing he spoke an ancient word, *"Blealdur!"* Blue fire flickered from the palms of his upturned hands. Suddenly, all the candles and torch flames lighting the large room flared flickered blue and cast the entire hall in a sapphire light.

This gained the attention of *everyone* within the hall. The music stopped abruptly and cries of shock and surprise rang out from the celebrants in the room. All eyes turned toward the commotion by the great doors and the *Blue Sorcerer* who had interrupted the birthday celebration. Dropping his arms and clenching his hands shut, the lights returned to their normal golden glow. Suddenly, like an approaching storm, the King of Jior was striding toward the interruption. At his side were two tall men who wore a resemblance so like the King's that it was obvious these were his two sons, Prince Vannier and Prince Dark Star.

The guards fell back to let the angry King approach but held their weapons pointed at the intruder. Not at all minding the sharp pikes pointing at him, the Blue Sorcerer pushed his way forward and met the King in the center of the hall. Everyone fell back to let them pass but then circled back in to watch the confrontation.

King Forlorn Icefall glared at the stranger with raging violet eyes. Fists clenching at his sides and his massive chest heaving, he stopped in front of the Blue Sorcerer. His deep voice thundered out and challenged him.

"Who comes wielding sorcery in my hall?" He demanded loudly.

The King of Jior was a giant among the males in the group. Dressed all in Jiorian black and silver with a twisted silver crown, he was a remarkable figure with his massive size, long white braid falling down his back, and tumultuous violet eyes. His two sons, Prince Vannier and Prince Dark Star were almost as tall as he and just as impressive, standing at their father's side.

Not intimidated at all, the Blue Sorcerer did not hesitate before answering the King's bellow.

"I come on urgent business and seek a private audience with the Queen of Jior."

As if summoned by his request, the Queen of Jior approached with two more strikingly beautiful women who came up beside her. She stood just behind the King and waited while her husband dealt with the intruder. Also, next to the Queen approached a beautiful young girl dressed in a flowing, iridescent, pale blue gown. Her head tilted slightly to the side as her amethyst eyes danced over the Blue Sorcerer confronting them all. Her gaze seemed to meet his burning eyes hidden beneath the hood. Suddenly, her pearl-white skin flushed with a pink blush and she quickly looked away, only to look back again. A shiver rippled through her body and her breath quickened.

"I think not!" The King of Jior growled loudly. "I do not let sorcerers anywhere near my family, and in fact, they are not welcome in my kingdom of Jior."

"I assure you; I mean no harm to the Queen or anyone else in Jior. If she will just hear my petition, my need is great."

Prince Vannier, standing next to the King, stepped forward and glared at the Blue Sorcerer.

"Show yourself, if you mean no harm." Vannier challenged.

The Blue Sorcerer seemed to hesitate, and the crowd held its collective breath. The lovely young girl in the pale blue dress nodded her head slightly as if she encouraging him and assuring him it would be alright to comply.

Slowly, the Blue Sorcerer raised his black-gloved hands, unclasped a heavy silver clasp at his collar then moved his hands up to the hood and grasped the edges. He slowly pulled the hood back and let it fall. As he did, the heavy garment seemed to come alive and slid from his body to pool at his feet. As if it possessed a life of its own, the cloak stirred and morphed into thousands of small, cobalt-blue birds. The brilliant birds rose in a tight flock, flew up into the high rafters of the Great Hall, and disappeared. The crowd had fallen back a little and gasped in awe, their eyes sparkling with wonder. Some even clapped in delight at the magical display.

Now, before the Royal Family of Jior, the Blue Sorcerer was entirely revealed. He was a young man, very handsome, and elicited a sigh of adoration from most of the females in the room. He had sharp striking features and the pale white skin of a Ny-Failen, but there the resemblance ended. With ice-blue eyes, he glared defiantly at the King and his sons, who tensed and stared back at the man's blue-black hair falling to his waist. His chin came up in challenge as whispers of, *'Ny-Komnir'* and *'demon-kind'* circulated throughout the crowd though in truth almost all of them had never seen one. Dressed impeccably in strange, dark blue and black clothing, he was clearly not a vagrant or a beggar and there were no signs that he had been out in the rain or had traveled from afar. The shoulders of his lightly armored vest were adorned with blue-black feathers, and the midnight blue shirt he wore underneath had a tall collar. Down to his boots, he was dressed all in shades of dark blue and black. Even the wicked blade sheathed at his hip had a large blue sapphire set in the hilt of bluish metal and was sheathed in black leather decorated in silver filigree. A soldier stepped forward and swiftly unarmed him. The Blue Sorcerer kept his gaze on the Queen as he held his hands up and allowed the soldier to take his sword and a matching dagger from his boot.

"Again, I ask who are you to come barging in unannounced to my granddaughter's birth celebration? And what is so urgent you must bring sorcery into our home?" The King spoke loudly. Beside him, Vannier narrowed his eyes at the intruder and grasped his knife hilt meaningfully. Dark Star took a step forward creating a protective barrier with his father and brother, in front of the Queen and the other women behind them.

"My name is Aesir Blacknight. I have traveled far through the Violent Mountains to speak to the Queen of

Jior." Taking a deep breath, he looked behind the King of Jior and addressed the Queen directly. "It is a matter of life or death!"

"It will be your death if you do not remove yourself from this hall. Sorcerers are not welcome here." Tightening his hands into fists, Prince Dark Star took another step toward the Blue Sorcerer.

Queen Lililaira Gem also stepped forward and gave the young man a beautiful, patient smile. Healing ailments was the sole reason people sought her out. Though she did not mind freely helping everyone who came to her, the many requests could become overwhelming. Indeed, with unfailing compassion, she was drawn to heal sick people with whom she came in contact. Now, the Queen examined Aesir Blacknight as if trying to sense an ailment. Before she finished her examination, however, he suddenly moved, startling everyone.

Aesir Blacknight stepped forward quickly and went down on one knee in front of the Queen. He bowed his dark head giving respect to her as was a queen's due. The bright candlelight glowed on his black hair causing a bluish sheen, and he was motionless before her.

"Please, Aesir Blacknight," the Queen moved away from her husband and sons' protective barrier. She beckoned with her hand. "Please, do rise." She smiled again.

King Lorn and Prince Vannier were just about to draw their swords and stand against any threat to her when they saw him on his knee bowing, vulnerable before her. All the Ny-Failen males in the hall stood tense and ready for a fight, should it come to that.

"My Queen," he spoke, still on his knee, his head bowed. "My need is urgent, there is a young innocent who desperately needs your healing power. I have come to plead for your assistance. Please, I ask you to come to my home in the mountains. Someone I love dearly is dying, and she needs you before it is too late.”

Prince Dark Star, still looming protectively at his mother’s side, spoke a little less menacingly. “Rise Aesir Blacknight and tell us where you have come from.”

The Blue Sorcerer rose to his feet, calmly folded his hands, and once again addressed the Queen.

“My Queen, I am from the far northern mountains of Jior, and one I love dearly is dying. If you will but...”

Prince Vannier stepped forward and interrupted. Though his face showed very little emotion, his eyes betrayed the anger and outrage he was feeling.

“Boy! You have interrupted a very special celebration. Can you not come tomorrow with the other supplicants and plead your case at a more appropriate time?”

Aesir Blacknight turned his eye to Vannier and narrowed his gaze considering but before he could answer, Queen Lililaira took the matter in hand. Stepping forward, she gestured toward the young girl in the shimmering pale blue dress.

“Aesir Blacknight, this is my granddaughter Mercy Rose and tonight is a celebration of her nineteenth birthday. You have traveled from very far. Perhaps your petition can wait just until morning? Please, won’t you take your ease, have some food and drink. You must be weary and hungry from your travels. I urge you to be at peace tonight. In the meantime, as I am sure your intentions are noble, you are welcome to join our celebration. Tomorrow, I will hear your petition.” The Queen turned toward her husband and entreated.

“My Love,” she spoke to the King. “Please convince our Guest he is welcome to join the celebration and that we will hear his appeal first thing tomorrow morning.” She smiled lovingly at King Lorn, and he frowned at her but then his features softened. After a brief hesitation, he wordlessly nodded his consent.

Aesir Blacknight hesitated. His gaze fell on Mercy Rose, and he surveyed her from head-to-toe before answering. His voice gave away his disappointment.

"My Queen, I will wait until morning, if I must. I accept your gracious invitation and offer my humblest apologies to Lady Mercy Rose for having so rudely interrupted her birthday celebration. I *have* traveled far and it has been many days since I've had decent food and rest." He held Mercy Rose's gaze in a long, captivating look before bowing deeply toward the King and Queen than to Mercy Rose.

Prince Vannier and Prince Dark Star closed in, shoulder to shoulder, in front of their mother and the other women forming an unwavering barrier. Recognizing that it was pointless to push his plight any further, for now, Aesir Blacknight turned and stalked away into the crowd. The music began to play again, and the celebration began anew.

Mercy Rose leaned slightly to the side. The rigid backs of her Uncle Vannier and Uncle Dark Star, blocked her view of the Blue Sorcerer disappearing into the crowd. All she could see was his long blue-black hair and broad shoulders disappearing into a crowd of girls who quickly surrounded the handsome young man and led him away presumably to find the refreshments.

Mercy Rose frowned a little and stood perplexed by her reaction to the Blue Sorcerer's appearance. Her frown deepened as she realized she had stood frozen through the whole altercation with Aesir Blacknight. Examining her feelings, she admitted to herself that the moment the deep blue cloak fell and revealed the handsome Blue Sorcerer, she had hardly breathed. Even now her chest rose and fell quickly as if catching her breath and her heartbeat was fast and uneven. Her bodice felt too tight across her breasts, and she was warm all over. A red flush of embarrassment crept up her neck and her cheeks burned as if from an internal flame.

She had, she realized, stared like an infatuated fool at the intruder and even felt a moment of jealous sadness when he mentioned why he sought an audience with her grandmother, Queen Lililaira Gem. Her memory echoed, and her warmed blood turned slightly colder as she once again heard in her mind what Aesir Blacknight said, *"one I love dearly, is dying."* She was even more ashamed because part of her heart fell when she realized he must have come here because of a woman, possibly his wife. Her reactions to him were not in the least bit like she normally reacted toward other people. Before she could contemplate the situation any further, she felt a looming presence beside her, and a strong hand took her firmly by the elbow and led her away.

Trail Blazer was a winged Ny-Failen from Everclearing. He had newly come to visit Jior with Mercy Rose's uncle, Blue Falcon. The two were long-time friends, but Mercy Rose suspected Trail Blazer's presence at her nineteenth birthday celebration was more preconceived than coincidence. It was his firm grasp that took her away now. Though he was a fine, attractive, sophisticated Ny-Failen, Trail Blazer tended to be intense to the point of discomfort toward Mercy Rose. She was only just now realizing this, as he possessively led her by the elbow out to the dance floor without asking if she even wanted to dance. She decided she did not admire that overly domineering characteristic in a male. Though, an inner voice whispered in her head that just that morning she felt an attraction toward that attentive aspect of Trail Blazer. Until that is, the moment when a certain Blue Sorcerer's eyes captured hers and made her heart leap.

CHAPTER TWO

Aesir Blacknight stood on the outskirts of the crowd at the nineteenth birthday celebration of the lovely Lady Mercy Rose, granddaughter of King Forlorn Icefall of Jior. Though he was furious at the delay in being able to meet privately with the Queen, *she* was an unexpected surprise to him. He sipped sparingly from a heavy silver chalice and watched as Lady Mercy Rose danced in the arms of a Ny-Failen male. The tell-tail slits in the back of the male's coat gave him away as one of the winged Ny-Failen. Aesir Blacknight wanted to snarl as he watched and for some inexplicable reason, he seemed to grow sulkier each time the dance steps sent Lady Mercy Rose into the Ny-Failen's arms. Before his incomprehensible ire caused him to do something rash, he tried to force his attention elsewhere.

The celebration was a crowded affair, filled with guests who were of Ny-Failen-kind and of humankind. It was not hard to distinguish who was of which race. The Ny-Failen had flawless attractive features. The stunningly beautiful women had fair, pale skin that shone with a soft pearly luster. The men were all tall, devastatingly attractive, and equally fair-skinned. Many of them, such as the Royal Family had long flowing white hair ranging in hue from white-gold to silvery-white locks. Those Ny-Failen without wings all had the same striking features with more human pigmentation but held a certain ageless *presence* about them that labeled them as Ny-Failen. Both types of Ny-Failen had ears that came to a gentle point.

Those of humankind appeared, well, like humans usually do with a variety of skin tones, hair colors, and more rounded features. Though, most of these humans could be considered the most attractive of that entire race. Being around the Queen, they were all the picture of health with not so much as a blemish or even a bad tooth.

Everywhere Aesir Blacknight looked, beautiful women were dancing with handsome men. An older woman, of humankind, with flawless nut-brown skin and rich brown, intricately braided hair, eyed him curiously as she walked by swaying her hips enticingly, in her elegant dark gold dress. This was the third time she had done so trying to catch his eye, and he knew what she wanted. She smiled invitingly at him with full ruby red lips. He almost entertained the idea of speaking to the woman, if only to bide his time until morning when he could petition the Queen of Jior to help him, but his better judgment told him he should remain inconspicuous. However, try as he may to distract himself elsewhere, he could not stop his eyes from wandering back to Lady Mercy Rose. Before he knew it, he was watching her again.

She danced as graceful and light as a cloud being swept along by the wind under a moonlit sky. Indeed, her pale, moon-blue dress flowed and shimmered with iridescence in the brightly lit room. Her hair was tightly braided and curled attractively under a silver threaded, intricately weaved, skull cap sprinkled with small moonstone pins. Opals and more moonstones graced her throat in a delicate necklace. She was the perfect picture of elegance and gentility overpowered by the huge hulking Ny-Failen who skillfully twirled her with a firm possessive hand. Aesir Blacknight finally gave in trying *not* to watch her and indulged himself, completely entranced by her beauty and the graceful way she danced. Her silvery-white hair was luminescent and sparkled with gems as she pirouetted across the floor. Each turn of her head, the violet glimmer in her eyes, and the blush of her cheek drew his eye and made something within his body smolder.

#

It was a magical night. Hundreds of silver filigree lamps hung suspended from the rafters in the Great Hall of Castle Jior. They twinkled like stars hovering brightly and lighting the celebration. Gifted by Prince Dark Star; thousands of lavender and white roses interspersed with giant, dark violet morning glories, and hung with thick trailing vines of ivy, were placed about the room in silver vases and tall stands. The music enchanted everyone at the celebration and swept the dancers into graceful sweeps and turns around the dance floor.

Mercy Rose had a hard time concentrating on her feet. Despite the magic of the enchanting melody, the complicated steps that were usually effortless to her, were now difficult to perform because she was distracted. The other couples danced around Mercy Rose completely unaware of her trepidation and swept along under the spell of the magical evening.

"My Lady, why do you frown?" Trail Blazer asked in a concerned tone as he tried to catch her eye and attempted to make conversation during the dance. Mercy Rose had to stop searching the room for a certain head of blue-black hair and replaced her frown with a slight smile.

"I am sorry," she thought quickly, "I, um…this is not of my favorite tunes. I did not mean to frown." The truth was, she frowned because she could not see where the mysterious Blue Sorcerer had disappeared to.

"Very well, my Lady. Perhaps we should stop for now and resume later when a tune more to your liking begins."

Mercy Rose just then spotted Aesir Blacknight leaning relaxed against the far wall. As the music continued, the dance swept her toward him. She almost missed a step when she realized his ice-blue stare was devouring *her*. Her heart fluttered and her breath stammered.

Mercifully, the music swelled and then came to a flourishing finish. The dancing couples bowed and curtsied to each other as the strains of the tune ended. Trail Blazer tried to take Mercy Rose by the arm again and lead her away, but she spied her mother, Princess Lyra Song in the crowd. Turning her steps in a different direction, she lithely slipped from his grasp. Absently thanking Trail Blazer for the dance, she excused herself and headed toward her mother across the room. Trail Blazer bowed slightly confused and watched fixedly, as she sped away.

"Lady Mercy Rose," her name was spoken behind her in a deep, unfamiliar voice and she turned to find Aesir Blacknight, the Blue Sorcerer. They stood staring at each other for the briefest moment and then suddenly he was taking her hand and pulling her into his arms. Her eyes went wide. His gloves were gone and she felt his warm, bare hand against hers. The Blue Sorcerer artfully swept her into the stream of dancing couples waiting for the music to begin the next tune. Effortlessly, he led her into place without asking her consent.

The music began. This particular dance was the Snowflake Waltz and required the male to hold onto the female partner throughout. His arm went around her slim waist as he swept her into the starting position. His hand was gently holding one of hers, and her other hand came to rest lightly on his shoulder as the first musical flourish brought her into the face-to-face position. As the tune swelled, he looked into Mercy Rose's violet eyes. This was one of her favorite dances, and she gave him a dazzling smile. Butterflies were already dancing in her stomach as she realized she was standing just an arms-length away from the mysterious Blue Sorcerer. His hand was warm on the swell of her lower back. The music began.

Aesir Blacknight swept her across the floor and, though it was the first time they ever danced, it appeared as if they were meant to be in each other's arms. So fluidly and skillfully did they dance together that she looked like a moonbeam pirouetting in the arms of the midnight sky.

When the song allowed, Mercy Rose swallowed her nervous tension over being in Aesir Blacknight's arms, and she blushed a little nervously. She surveyed his broad shoulders and noticed every detail of his strange light armor. The high collar of his cobalt shirt was delicately embroidered with black swans along the border. In vast contradiction to the swans, two wolves' heads faced each other across the expanse of his chest decorating his fine leather breastplate. Mercy Rose took a deep breath and found the courage to speak to him.

"Who is this loved one you seek healing for?" In a gentle compassionate voice, she boldly asked with an inexplicable curiosity.

He did not answer her right away but searched her wide innocent eyes with his. So light was the color of his eyes that they looked almost white with barely a touch of crystal blue.

"Who is the hulking Ny-Failen who leads you so possessively by the arm?"

Mercy Rose was flustered but flowed through the dance moves without the slightest effort and Aesir Blacknight flawlessly guided her among the other dancers.

"You did not answer my question?" She finally responded.

"Answer mine and I will answer yours." His deep voice was warm, caressing, and slightly insistent.

Mercy Rose was more aware of his hand on her waist than she was of her feet executing the dance steps. She felt as if she were floating on air, held up by the music of his voice and the power of his very presence. Without understanding why, she braced herself before answering.

"He is Trail Blazer, from Everclearing. A friend to my Uncle Blue Falcon."

"Who is he to *you*?" Aesir Blacknight leaned a little forward and glared at her almost as if he were angry.

Taken back by his intensity, she fumbled for an answer, "I, he is just someone I've only recently become acquainted with, and you didn't answer my question before asking another. Who is the loved one you seek healing for?"

Aesir Blacknight took a moment to contemplate his answer and then he leaned forward, almost touching his lips to her ear as he whispered, "She is my beloved." Then he pulled her closer, and they waltzed across the room as if they were the only dancers on the floor.

Flustered even more by his contradictory behavior, Mercy Rose did not know why his answer bothered her so much, but she was determined not to let her ire show. She had only just met this man and had no right or reason to be interested in him or his, "*beloved.*"

After a few moments of waltzing across the floor in his arms. Mercy Rose felt the stares of the other party guests on them and the glares of the males in her family, but they danced on. She smiled radiantly. He pulled her closer until her breasts were almost pressed up against him.

"You hold me too tightly, Sir." Mercy Rose whispered and delicately looked away from her dance partner, trying to hide her embarrassment at speaking to him in such a forward manner. Without any preconceived artifice, she tilted her head slightly to the side and blushed softly.

"Is that a protest?" He purred and grinned like a wolf. The music swelled and her every graceful movement enchanted him.

Mercy Rose's eyes snapped back at him, and she saw the laughing challenge in his ice-blue, cunning, wolfish eyes. She was going to answer him, but she was distracted by the curve of his lips, the perfectly trimmed black beard that hugged his luscious mouth and chin, and the smooth white skin of his neck. As her eyes traveled on, she rested her gaze back on his lips which were curved into a slightly crooked smile waiting for her answer. She continued looking upwards and traced the arch of his high cheekbones, over to his ears which she noticed were gently pointed. Finally, she boldly looked him straight in the eyes because it was what she wanted to do. The seconds passed in silence with his question still hanging in the air between them.

Locking her gaze with his, she ever-so-slightly squeezed his hand tighter, flattened her palm against his, and interlocked their fingers. Then she leaned in, so close to him that her breasts did press against his chest. His arm went tighter around her waist as he pulled her against him, even closer. Challenge accepted, they danced as if they were of one body and all the while he never took his eyes from hers. Breathing deeply, she caught his scent which reminded her of snow dancing on winter's breeze. Her heart pirouetted within her breast.

When the song changed Aesir Blacknight did not relinquish his hold on Mercy Rose, he just effortlessly led her more toward the center of the dance floor without missing a beat. They danced for two more songs, close and then apart as the music dictated but never releasing their touch, her hand in his or his arm around her slim waist. As the last strains of the tune rose, it whirled the dancers into a turning figure-eight, placing one of the male's arms around his female partner's shoulders arranging him behind, her arm across her body while still linking their hands. The tune ended, and Mercy Rose tilted her head up and back, staring at Aesir Blacknight who was looking down at her with a slight devouring smile and an intense gaze. The crowd began to disburse, but they held their position as if they were two statues made of one stone.

Aesir Blacknight parted his lips as if he were going to speak, but then they heard someone impatiently clearing his throat. Mercy Rose was caught under Aesir Blacknight's gaze and startled from the trance she was under. Looking over, she saw the frowning face of her *father*.

Jagged Edge stood red-faced and angry with his hands on his hips and glared at the stranger holding his daughter in his arms in the middle of the dance floor. With growing agitation, he had been watching the strange man and his daughter, as they whirled across the dance floor. Internally, he marveled at the arrogant confidence of the Ny-Failen King who allowed this intruder to enter their home. Even surrounded by armed guards and highly competent Ny-Failen warriors it was inconceivable to Jagged Edge that a Blue Sorcerer had been allowed to stay and join in the celebration. He took a menacing step closer to the couple.

"*Daughter*, if this young pup is finished pawing you across the dance floor, I'd like a word with him."

Aesir Blacknight gently, covertly, squeezed Mercy Rose's hand as if imparting a secret message through his touch. Then he slowly released her altogether and reluctantly took a step away with a slight bow. Mercy Rose drew breath to say something, but Jagged Edge interrupted her with an impatient glare and growled in his deep accent.

"Go to your mother."

Mercy Rose dared not glance back at Aesir Blacknight but did as she was told and walked slowly away. Aesir Blacknight watched her slender form as she reluctantly disappeared into the crowd. Drawing himself to his full height and unflinchingly, he looked back and met Jagged

Edge's unspoken challenge. Jagged Edge moved slowly and stood almost toe-to-toe with the Blue Sorcerer.

Jagged Edge's Ny-Failen power was that he could read minds and sense danger. He had been watching the dance and heard the boy's thoughts, his captivation with Mercy Rose was like blue fire in the boy's head. The Blue Sorcerer had been deeply engaged in the feel of Mercy Rose in his arms and was fascinated with the way the light caressed her pearl-hued skin, the way her body moved with his and with the swell of her breasts. It was at that point Jagged Edge had enough and decided to put an end to the dancing.

"I step away for five minutes, and I come back to learn a Blue Sorcerer has barged his way into my daughter's birth celebration and is helping himself to my daughter no less." Jagged Edge's fists were on his hips, and he glared. Aesir Blacknight glared back and opened his mouth to answer, but Jagged Edge interrupted him.

"Don't bother lying boy; I can read your mind like an open book. I know your thoughts were far from *only* enjoying a dance with my daughter. Now, what do you think you're doing with my daughter?"

It had been *exactly* what Aesir Blacknight was going to claim, that he was only enjoying a dance with this man's daughter. Years of study had heightened Aesir Blacknight's senses, and he had felt an intrusion into his mind during the last song he danced with Lady Mercy Rose. As Jagged Edge approached, he sensed where the intrusion had come from, and inside his mind, he spoke a few words and threw solid blue walls around his next thoughts. He knew immediately what this angry Ny-Failen was capable of.

"If you can read my mind then I need hardly waste my breath telling you what I was doing. At the very least you could see with your own two eyes, I was dancing with the lovely Guest of Honor." Aesir Blacknight crossed his arms over his chest and smirked.

Jagged Edge drew closer and whispered menacingly, "I know what you were doing and what you were thinking. I also know you are barely here at the indulgence of Queen Lililaira, not that you gave her any choice. It was either that or spoil the celebration with *your bloodshed.*" His green eyes glittered with malevolent mirth at that suggestion.

"The Queen did invite me. I have traveled for many days and many miles and I am not leaving. In the morning the Queen has agreed to hear my petition. Until then, I have no choice but to bide my time at the celebration." Aesir Blacknight closed his eyes, gathered his patience, and dropped all animosity from his voice. He placed his hand on his chest and bowed slightly to Jagged Edge.

"My name is Aesir Blacknight. I am here on a matter of supreme urgency. I've no desire to cause trouble; my mission is too important. As I have said, I am only biding my time until morning when I can formally address the Queen and ask for her help. If I have overstepped my bounds with Lady Mercy Rose or offended you in any way, I do pray for your forgiveness. It was not my intention."

Jagged Edge narrowed his eyes at Aesir Blacknight and saw only swirling blue when he tried to read the boy's mind now and assess if he was telling him the truth or if he was just saying what he thought might deflate the situation and get himself out of trouble. Hardly mollified, he could only give in and admonish the boy to steer clear of his young daughter.

The Queen had asked Jagged Edge earlier to make lodging arrangements for Aesir Blacknight. Now he took this opportunity to instruct him where he could stay for the night but made sure to note that his daughter's chamber was on the *other* side of the castle right down the hall from Jagged Edges' room.

CHAPTER THREE

Mercy Rose stood by her mother's side and watched the confrontation between her father and Aesir Blacknight, the Blue Sorcerer. She bit her bottom lip in apprehension and wished she had been allowed to stay and listen or at least had been able to assure her father that Aesir Blacknight had treated her honorably. Though her body still reverberated from his closeness, the warmth from his touch and her heart still trembled from his nearness. Mercy Rose was unaccustomed to being so flustered by anyone's presence and she marveled at her reaction to this stranger. Her attentions were suddenly alerted to her Uncle Blue Falcon and Trail Blazer making their way toward where she stood with her mother and her aunts. Acting quickly, she grabbed her brother Storm Rider by the arm and made him dance with her to avoid Trail Blazer.

Later, after an elaborate dinner and some performing acrobats, the crowd gathered to watch Mercy Rose receive gifts from friends and family. Much attention and approving exclamations were made over a white bow and arrows with pearl inlay sent from her great-grandfather Dark Moon. She received a beautiful silk shawl from her Aunt Summer Rain, and her Uncle Vannier gave her an elaborately decorated leather-bound book of Ny-Failen poetry. Next, nineteen of Mercy Rose's family and friends filtered by her one at a time and placed in her arms a single white rose until she had nineteen, a gift marking the right-of-passage from a young girl to womanhood. Her grandparents, the King and Queen of Jior, stepped forward last. They each kissed her cheek, and the King placed over her head a strand of long, pale blue pearls with a single large pearl droplet suspended from it.

Mercy Rose gasped at the beautiful gift and thanked them both with kisses and exuberant embraces.

The celebration continued until the hour grew late. The last song was played, and Mercy Rose joyfully spent the final dance in the company of her father, Jagged Edge. The King and Queen bid their many guests a good night, and everyone began to slowly disburse heading to their homes or their rooms if they were guests at Castle Jior. The final swells of music died to be replaced with the sound of a gentle rain beginning outside.

Mercy Rose glowed with happiness. She took her father's arm as her mother joined them and they headed out of the Great Hall. Covertly, she spared one last glance back looking for Aesir Blacknight who was not to be found.

At the door to Mercy Rose's bedchamber, she kissed her mother and father goodnight and thanked them for the one-hundredth time for the wonderful birthday celebration. Brimming with happiness, she twirled and waltzed around the room lighting the lamps with a long taper. Last, she lit the candle on a small mirrored vanity by her bedside. One by one she placed the nineteen white roses in a tall vase and stopped to admire their fragrance and beauty. She worked at the multiple opal pins in her hair and unclasped her moonstone and opal necklace. The jewelry was a gift from her brother Storm Rider and his wife Moon Dancer which they gave her to wear for the party. Memories of the happy night assailed her, and she sighed contentedly and bent to blow the candle out so that she could undress and go to bed. Slowly breathing in, she pursed her lips to extinguish the candle when the flame suddenly flared *blue*. Her breath caught. She straightened and whirled around to see Aesir Blacknight, the Blue Sorcerer, standing not two long steps away.

Aesir Blacknight closed the distance until he was standing *very* close to her. Astonished, Mercy Rose looked up into his ice-blue eyes, and he looked down at her. He saw troubled surprise, curiosity, and the first blush of desire in her lovely, violet eyes. Boldly he reached up and cupped her cheek then ran his thumb over her full bottom lip. His other hand rose to her other cheek, and slowly and hesitantly he lowered his face to hers. His lips nudged hers in a gentle and slow, sensuous kiss. One arm dropped and went around her waist, the other hand went to her nape, and he pulled her closer still and deepened the ravishment of her mouth. Mercy Rose ran her hands up his back and embraced him while he tantalized her lips with his and touched his tongue to hers. Tasting, they explored each other in a sweet, gentle kiss.

The kiss ended too soon for him as Mercy Rose pulled away from Aesir Blacknight and stepped back. Her hand went to cover her tingling lips as she struggled to catch her breath. The candles in the room burned natural golden now, and for the first time, she felt fear in his presence because of the intense devouring look he was giving her. She knew all she had to do was scream and her father would come to her rescue in mere moments, but she did not want to scream.

"Why?" was the first word she could manage to utter and then the questions came pouring out. "Why the dancing? Why are you here?" She swallowed and whispered, "Why the kiss?"

"Why indeed?" Aesir Blacknight's half-smile faded and he took her hand and laced his fingers with hers. He never looked away from her eyes. His face turned serious as he asked in his low husky voice, "Do you know what a man and woman do, alone, *together?*"

Mercy Rose blushed at the audacity of the question and could not answer. Her breath caught, and all she could do was tremble. She could not answer him then her temper flared a little because she realized he must be teasing her.

"Am I to understand that you do not?" Aesir Blacknight's voice was sultry, mischievous, making Mercy Rose want to…she was not sure what she wanted to do, but then another realization hit her.

"Would you betray your Beloved?" she whispered. Gaining courage, she went on.

"Why would you come here to ask for Grandmother's help only to then dishonor her granddaughter?"

Aesir Blacknight narrowed his ice-blue eyes that sparked and suddenly turned dark, looking a little annoyed. After a tense moment of silence, he relaxed and smirked again, and asked, "Why are you such a surprise?" Then confessed quietly, "An unexpected flower I've found on my journey." He stood for a long time his hand laced with hers as he had not let go. With his other hand, he lifted a curl of her hair and brought it to his lips while she remained silent, still, and resolute.

"I simply did not get the opportunity to give you your birthday present." Aesir Blacknight broke the tension between them and gave her that crooked smile that so easily graced his lips. Reaching behind her, he plucked a rose from the vase on the table. He cupped the perfect bud in his hands until it was completely hidden. Softly he spoke an ancient word, and when he opened his hand, the delicate white rosebud had been transformed into one that looked as if it had been carved from a single, deep blue sapphire and grew from a live green stem.

Mercy Rose gasped as he handed it to her. She stood staring fascinated at the lovely gift. In front of her eyes, he touched one long finger to the stem, and it crystallized into a green-leafed emerald stem. Reaching around her and with a wave of his hand, he changed the other eighteen buds into sapphire roses on emerald stems, shifting the white to blue, the living to precious gems.

"I don't understand," she began again, but stopped, unsure that she wanted to know the answer as to why he had come to her like this and why he had kissed her. Why he would not answer any of the questions weighing so heavily on her intrigued heart.

"Goodnight, my Lady." Speaking a little sadly, Aesir Blacknight started to turn as if he would go, but then stopped, turned back, and gently drew her back into his arms. Once again, he kissed her softly and slowly. Then he released her, lifted her hand to his lips, and placed one last kiss on the fluttering pulse inside her wrist as if he knew her desire for him pulsed hotly through her veins. A very confused Mercy Rose watched him leave.

In the peaceful loneliness of her bed that night she contemplated her first kiss from a man and her heartbeat so fiercely it took her a long time to fall asleep.

CHAPTER FOUR

King Forlorn Icefall was in a foul mood. Today was the one day of the week that he dreaded most and was one reason he never wanted to be named *'King'* in the first place. It was the day when people from all around his kingdom came to the castle and asked him to give advice on their problems, rule on their disputes, and judge their legal cases. This morning was especially vexing because he knew he would have to deal with that Blue Sorcerer and he *loathed* sorcerers. Lily fell into step beside him and took his offered arm as they made their way down from their tower chamber.

The ghosts of the past still lingered in the halls of Lorn's mind, and he badly wanted to fly away with Lily, to escape and forget his responsibilities. His ne'amh chomhara itched on his back, and he had to hold back the desire to shapeshift. As she walked beside him, Lily began to hum a tune. He watched her from the corner of his eye. Never had she stopped amazing him, and this morning, she was so lovely he wanted to carry her back up the staircase to their bedchamber, lock the door behind them, and love her until she cried out in her passion.

Sensing his dark mood, Lily gave him her most radiant smile and squeezed his arm playfully. She always seemed to read his thoughts or maybe it was the look of unquenched desire burning in his eyes. She smiled and purred, *"later!"*

#

Word had spread about the Blue Sorcerer in Jior who would be petitioning the King and Queen, and the hall was filled with people who wanted to see what was going to happen. Many of the Ny-Failen had delayed their departures after the party to remain until they knew Queen Lililaira was safe. They too were suspicious of a Blue Sorcerer within the castle walls.

Castle Jior's Great Hall, gaily decorated for the birth celebration held the night before, was cleared of all but the tall flower-filled vases and vine-covered pillars, and once again served as the meeting hall. A large throne was placed at the head of the room, and though King Forlorn Icefall disdained such formalities, his loyal subjects expected it. The Queen's chair sat next to his because today the Queen would be in attendance. Upon his head sat the King's intricately twisted silver crown. Claimants with petitions to bring before the King lined up and waited their turn to speak.

Mercy Rose dressed carefully in her favorite rose-colored dress, decorated with copper and bronze embroidered roses and leaves, and long flowing wine-colored ribbons. Her white hair hung in loose waving curls, and she wore the strand of pearls her grandparents had given her for her birthday present. She skipped her morning meal, raced through the halls, and down the stairs to the Great Hall, forgetting completely that she was a woman now and not a young girl. Trying to be as inconspicuous as possible she slowed and made her way through the people gathered in the hall. She spotted her Uncle Blue Falcon and Trail Blazer standing amongst the crowd, and she ducked behind a group of people, avoiding them. Finding the best spot to watch the proceedings she stood near her Grandmother's chair and waited. Prince Vannier, Prince Dark Star, and Jagged Edge attended today, as well. They were more heavily armed than usual, and their hands rested on the hilts of their swords as if anticipating danger.

The crowd stilled as King Forlorn Icefall arrived without undue fan-fair. After guiding Queen Lililaira to her chair, he sat down in the chair beside her. The supplicants began to come forward one by one, to make their petitions to the

King. A human chamberlain guided the proceedings announcing the business at hand and recording the judgments as they were made by the King.

Mercy Rose anxiously searched the faces in the crowd but did not see the handsome Blue Sorcerer, Aesir Blacknight. After a tedious hour of listening to miners and farmers with boundary disputes and patrons who claimed they had been swindled by dishonest merchants, an older nobleman came forward. Along with him was a young girl around Mercy Rose's age. He roughly jerked the girl by the arm like a wayward child. The man was the girl's father. Today he sought the King's judgment on the girl who refused to marry the man the father had chosen for her. A young soldier quickly stepped forward, bowed formally to the King and Queen, and declared that he and the girl were in love and that she had promised to marry *him*. The furious father wanted the girl to marry an older man who was wealthy and of his choosing. He insisted, as her father, he had the right to command his daughter to marry the man *he* had chosen, and it would not be a young, penniless soldier. As he angrily told his tale, he shook the girl by the arm. She winced in pain and hung her head. Now, they all stood before the court and sought the King's judgment.

After listening to both sides, the King spoke directly to the girl, "Did you promise to marry this soldier?"

"Yes," cried the girl, tears streaming down her face. "I love him, not the man who is old enough to be my grandfather. My father only wants me to marry him so he can get his money!"

"My King," the father interrupted the girl. "It is my right as her father to decide who my daughter marries. The girl is disobedient, unrepentant, and defiant, too young to know her own mind. I know what is best for her and I demand she marry as I have arranged! You must make her obey, bow to my wisdom and obey me as I am her father." The father looked mightily pleased with himself thinking he had made the best argument and that the King would surely rule in his favor.

In the end, the King found for love and decreed the girl had to marry the soldier and keep her promise to him. The father, knowing he was now bound by the King's ruling, was furious and turned red in the face loudly declaring his daughter was dead to him if she did marry the penniless soldier, and shouting that she would have no dowry from him. King Forlorn Icefall accepted the father's decree and agreed to pay *twice* the dowry himself with the stipulation that the father did not get one coin. The happy couple left the hall to get married immediately. The father left a very disgruntled man.

Next, two Jiorian soldiers came forward. They were dirty and rough-looking from swift travel on the road. Bowing to the King and Queen, they reported demon sightings near the soldier's barracks situated in the hills of eastern Jior.

"It was demon-kind alright," one said firmly in a rough accent. "Seen-em with me own two eyes. Black as night they all are. One grabbed a man and *melted* right into the ground! Oy can still 'ear the screamin in me dreams. The worst part is the women go willingly like they was under some kind of spell or in a trance. They just follow them demons away and are never seen again."

"My Lord," the other soldier stood at attention with his helmet under his arm and spoke eloquently. "No one but you can deal with these fiends. Will you come? Our need is urgent. There are children, and families in that barracks, and no one knows why the demon-kind have suddenly started appearing. We're all in fear for our very souls."

The Soldier went on to describe in detail the brutal deaths and terror brought by the Ny-Komnir at the Eastern Barracks.

King Forlorn Icefall sat forward and listened intently. The demon-kind were called Ny-Komnir, *the descended*, and were subordinate to Ny-Failen. The King of Jior was the most capable of dealing with the threat of Ny-Komnir. When the soldiers finished their account of the trouble, he promised he would look into the matter personally as he did have the most experience with those of demon-kind. Plans were made to leave the next day and address the problem immediately.

It looked as though the soldiers were the last in line to address the King. Before he could draw breath, sigh with relief, and close the day's proceedings, the great doors at the end of the hall opened. The tall, handsome Aesir Blacknight strode forward. He had been given back his sapphire-hilted sword and approached confidently. The crowd stirred noisily and perked up as the man they had all come to see, arrived. Mercy Rose took a few steps forward to the edge of the crowd and also watched as he approached. He noticed her watching him, and she saw one side of his mouth twitched just slightly as if he was pleased to see her there.

The King rose to his feet as Aesir Blacknight approached and he towered above everyone in the room. "So, you've come." Looking down from his raised dais, he crossed his arms over his chest and waited expectantly. His face was not too angry looking, but he was not happy either.

"I have, my King." Aesir Blacknight spoke loud and confident. "Will the Queen hear my petition now?"

Before King Forlorn Icefall could answer the Queen spoke for herself.

"I will." She beckoned him to step closer to her throne.

The King just frowned deeper as Aesir Blacknight approached and stood alone before him and the Queen.

Again, Aesir Blacknight glanced at Mercy Rose, and only the Queen caught the encouraging smile she gave back to him. Lily tilted her head as a sudden realization dawned on her. Intrigued, she tried not to smile at the two who apparently seemed to be starting an attraction toward each other. Mercy Rose moved forward to stand closer to the Queen, her eyes glittered with anticipation.

"King Forlorn Icefall, my Queen," Aesir Blacknight began formally, bowing in acknowledgment with his hand over his heart, "as I informed you last night, I seek your help for someone I love who is gravely ill. I've no power over sickness and…"

"Just what *do* you have power over, Blue Sorcerer?" Prince Vannier spoke menacingly and stepped forward interrupting Aesir Blacknight.

All eyes turned to Prince Vannier who glared at Aesir Blacknight. His violet-blue eyes flared with cold, protective animosity. Aesir Blacknight realized quickly he had chosen his words poorly. He closed his eyes and calmed the frustration rising inside his mind, over yet another delay. At first, it seemed as if he would not answer the Prince and then he nodded once as if deciding.

"I am no longer a Blue Sorcerer. I discontinued my education when my loved one fell ill."

"You did not answer the question." Not to be put off, Vannier insisted, "what *kind* of power do you have?"

Taking a deep breath Aesir Blacknight fought for control over his impatience.

"I have some skill with manipulating elements." Aesir Blacknight growled back impatiently after another short hesitation. He lifted a hand, and the torches in the chamber flared with blue flames again. The crowd gasped in admiration. "Childs play that is all. I assure you I am no threat to you and yours."

King Forlorn Icefall who had watched the altercation between his eldest son Vannier and Aesir Blacknight, finally spoke.

"Just what are you if you are not a Blue Sorcerer? Of humankind or something else?" Everyone in the room knew the King was asking if Aesir Blacknight was Ny-Komnir, of demon-kind.

Aesir Blacknight became very agitated but dared to get irritated with the King. "That hardly matters, what matters is…"

Now the King interrupted forcefully. "I've no patience for those who will not tell me what I wish to know and I must know for the safety of my Queen. Lord Lost Morning, the leader of the Ny-Failen has a way of answering these questions, but he is not here. I want to know who and *what* I am dealing with, especially when my Queen and sorcery are involved." He gestured behind him. "There is another I can call on. She is like Lost Morning, and she will find out your secrets if you will not willingly divulge what I want to know."

"No!" Jagged Edge shouted and stepped forward, daring to go against the King's command. "We don't know what this Blue Sorcerer could do to her!"

Aesir Blacknight seemed rattled. "This is hardly relevant." He spoke through gritted teeth and then tried to appeal directly to the Queen. "My Queen, if you will *just* hear me out."

"Mercy Rose!" The King bellowed before Queen Lililaira could respond. Mercy Rose jumped a little when her name was shouted but stepped forward and walked toward Aesir Blacknight. She held his ice-blue gaze and tried to assure him with a look that all would be well as she approached him.

Jagged Edge started to protest again, but King Lorn silenced him with a look and a chopping gesture. They all turned and watched.

"Give me your hand." Lady Mercy Rose held out her hand to him and assured him quietly in her sweet voice, "it will not hurt."

Aesir Blacknight searched her face for a moment and glared at the King and then at Jagged Edge. Finally, he reached out his hand. Lady Mercy Rose slowly placed her hand in his. Sliding her palm against his, she wrapped her slim fingers around his hand. He was warm and strong, and she was cool and delicate. The intimate moment was rife with suggestive pleasure as they stood, looking into each other's eyes as if they were the only two people in the room.

The crowd hushed and watched as Lady Mercy Rose called upon her power. Her violet eyes began to glow blue as she delved deeply. Aesir Blacknight tried momentarily to resist her, but then released and like a floodgate opening, let her control him.

Aesir Blacknight felt a small shock when Mercy Rose's power overtook him. Like a slow-moving wave of energy that flowed over, it wrapped around him gently. Had he not been so attuned to such energy he would not have noticed it but her energy flowed into his like two rushing streams converging into his very veins. He shivered slightly, seduced by her nearness, captivated by her beauty, and intrigued by her control. She melded her power with his blood and sought to answer the question, what was Aesir Blacknight?

Those watching who were of humankind, only saw Lady Mercy Rose clasping the hand of the Blue Sorcerer and her glowing blue eyes. Those of the Ny-Failen saw not only her eyes but a golden glow that seemed to envelop Aesir's arm and then crept up slowly, covering his whole arm and shoulder beginning to encase him completely.

For Mercy Roses' part, she delved deeply and saw everything, saw what Aesir Blacknight did not want the King to know. On the surface, Aesir Blacknight was distantly Ny-Failen and human as were most of their kind. She could not recall the last time she felt this particular combination. Her power revealed he had a grandparent who was partially Ny-Failen. However, as she prodded deeper, she found it was his father who was mostly Ny-Failen. Deeper still in Aesir Blacknight's bloodline, something with the mother?

This was how Mercy Rose's power worked. It started with the distant heritage and moved forward in the family lineage. She was more startled the closer she got. There she felt a thin strand of…Mercy Rose froze as a sudden vision enveloped her mind and she saw a wounded swan. She felt as if she was kneeling beside it as it bled, so close to death. Then her vision changed and a snarling black wolf leaped at her.

Mercy Rose gasped and pulled her hand away quickly stopping the vision. She shared a quick look with Aesir Blacknight that indicated she had learned his secrets. He dared her to reveal them with a slight narrowing of his eyes. Slowly, Mercy Rose turned toward the King. Her eyes had returned to their normal violet, just like her mother's and her grandfather's. She stepped in front of Aesir Blacknight almost as if she would protect him and then she gave her pronouncement.

"Grandfather," she smiled sweetly. "Aesir Blacknight is, well, he has ancestors who are Ny-Failen, but I sensed, a little something *extra*." She only hesitated a moment when she felt Aesir Blacknight move slightly closer, almost looming menacingly behind her. "There is the possibility that he has many distant Ny-Failen ancestors in both his mother and father's lineage and somewhat beyond that, but he is predominantly of *Ny-Failen-kind*. And, as he said he has the power to manipulate the elements, earth, water, stone, metal, and fire. That is all." She practically felt Aesir Blacknight's tension flow out of his body and the gentle brush of his breath in her hair when he exhaled as if he had been holding his breath.

"That is all?" The King exclaimed surprised.

"Mercy Rose, nothing of his future?" The Queen sat forward and inquired, voicing her surprise.

In addition to having the power to discern if a person was Ny-Failen, Ny-Komnir, or human, Mercy Rose could foresee parts of a person's future when she unleashed her power on them.

"No, I only saw a white swan. I think it was injured." Now it was Aesir Blacknight's turn to gently gasp in shock behind her.

Trail Blazer stepped forward and imposed on the proceedings. "He is wingless?" He stood tall and sure of himself, an arrogant sneer on his lips. His question sounded more like a statement and a question at the same time as if he already knew the answer.

The room's atmosphere flexed taut with tension, and people leaned forward to hear the answer.

Mercy Rose parted her lips to answer, but Aesir Blacknight answered first.

"I am wingless." Aesir Blacknight looked as if Trail Blazer had just revealed his greatest shame as he made the admission.

Jagged Edge had reached the end of his patience and, holding out his hand; he motioned to Mercy Rose, "That's enough! Come, Mercy Rose." She dutifully moved to her father's side, and he placed a protective arm around her shoulders. Aesir Blacknight did not look at them but moved forward a step and once again went down on one knee in front of the Queen.

"My Queen, while I respect the King's need to know everything about me for your protection, I assure you, I present you no harm. Please, I will beg if I must. There is an innocent girl deep in the Violent Mountains that is dying. I've come to ask you to go to her and heal her. She is in grave danger and her time runs short. Will you come to my home in Hoarfrost Range? Come and heal her?" His voice sounded desperate as he pleaded.

The Queen leaned forward. Concern showed on her lovely face. "How many days' ride is it to your home?" She asked.

Aesir Blacknight rose, and his face took on a hopeful look but then fell a little as he realized his answer might not be well received. "It is five days' ride on horseback if we go swiftly. I would have liked to wait for fairer weather to seek you out but time is precious. Many of the peaks are still covered in snow. Hoarfrost Range is high in the Violent Mountains and is always covered in snow and ice. If we leave in the morning, we can be there roughly in five short days, but in all honesty my Queen, I feel I must warn you. The way is fraught with obstacles and some can be dangerous, but I will protect you with my life." Aesir Blacknight spoke passionately hopeful.

"Why did you not bring this person *here* for healing?" Vannier asked before the Queen could ask anything further.

"She is too ill to travel. It would have assured her death to bring her all this way." Aesir Blacknight snapped back at him as if the answer was obvious. The two looked as if they would soon come to blows but Mercy Rose spoke first. Stepping out of her father's protective embrace, she moved forward and spoke loudly.

"Who is this loved one? Who is she to *you*?"

Aesir Blacknight turned, looked at her, and held her gaze as he spoke. His eyes sparked with mischief and icy fire, "She is my beloved."

Mercy Rose's face fell a little as if he hurt her with his answer but then he turned to the Queen and spoke directly to her, "she is my beloved younger sister. Only an innocent in every way and sick unto the very gates of death." His voice grew angrier and louder. He turned to glare at Prince Vannier and Trail Blazer and raised his voice, "Too sick to travel, and I cannot fly her here on wings I do not have. No physician has been able to help her, no medicine, no magic has helped. We have no parents, no family, no one to help us and so I have risked *all* to come here to beg *you* to come with me and heal her. My Queen, her time runs short and you are my last hope." The final words were stained with despair.

The room was still and silent as everyone tried to understand what Aesir Blacknight had just said. The Queen gracefully rose to her feet.

"I will go." She spoke with kind finality.

The hall erupted. Some in the room cheered for the Queen, happy with her decision to help the sick girl. Startled, Vannier and Dark Star both exclaimed, "Mother, No!" in unison. The King turned and gave his wife a stern, shocked look. He of all people knew that Lily could not say no to a sick person, let alone a young innocent but his fear for her safety was plain. Everyone shouted at the same time.

In a small circle of calm, Mercy Rose went back to Aesir Blacknight's side and smiled at him. She placed a consoling hand on his arm as he exhaled and closed his eyes, overcome with relief. The noise in the room grew loud, and the King of Jior roared for quiet. His wings abruptly appeared in an instant of rage, spanning out behind him, and he commanded order. Everyone stilled as he loudly addressed his wife.

"Lily, you cannot go with a Blue Sorcerer to a strange place we know nothing about! This could be a trap!"

"My Love! I will be fine," she paused and turned and said with knowing finality, "and I will take Mercy Rose with me!"

Pandemonium erupted in the room again. A smiling Queen Lililaira held her hand out to Mercy Rose who quickly went to her side and they turned and left the hall together. Aesir Blacknight followed.

CHAPTER FIVE

The rest of the day was a whirlwind of arguing, planning, and preparing. The King and his sons, and even Princess Lyra Song, Mercy Rose's mother, argued with the Queen over the wisdom of leaving the security of Jior and heading off into the Violent Mountains with a stranger. Jagged Edge was livid and barely trusted himself to speak at all but when he did it was only to shout. He glared daggers at Aesir Blacknight and tried to break through the blue walls surrounding his thoughts. Jagged Edge's sensitivity to danger was flaring every time he was around the man, but he could not pinpoint if it was actual danger or a father's protective instincts toward his eldest daughter. He had not missed certain *looks* passing between Aesir Blacknight and Mercy Rosc. While everyone else was protesting over the Queen agreeing to go into the Violent Mountains on this quest, Jagged Edge was dreading his daughter going along. Watching, inwardly he sensed the growing attraction between the two. In addition, to fearing for his daughter's safety, he feared for her virtue. To nay-say the Queen, however, was to admit that she did not know what she was doing or that she would needlessly endanger his daughter.

King Lorn protested the loudest because, just before Lily had agreed to go with Aesir Blacknight, he had committed himself to go with the two Jiorian soldiers and investigate the Ny-Komnir sightings in the east. Lorn pulled Lily aside to have a private word.

"Lily, you cannot go traipsing off into the most dangerous part of the Violent Mountains with a stranger at a time I when cannot be there to protect you!"

"You do not need to come! We will be fine! Mercy Rose will be with me for company, and I'm sure Aesir Blacknight is a noble young man. I sense no danger from him, and his efforts for his young sister do him great credit. Besides, we can take Vannier, Dark Star, or Jagged Edge with us for additional protection if you insist."

"I must have one of them here in Jior while I'm gone. With Sorell Brand and Lady Umber in Krickgold with their sons, there is no one else I trust to rule while I'm gone. On top of everything else, Skogur is disputing boundaries to the southeast, and I've got to send men to Dade-Bend to handle trouble they have been having there."

"My Love," Lily approached closer to Lorn and reached up to place her hand over his heart. "Go and deal with the Ny-Komnir problem in the east. Send Dark Star and Storm Rider to Dade-Bend to handle the trouble there. Vannier can stay here and mind things while you are gone, and Jagged Edge can accompany us. Will that relieve your worries?"

"No," he growled, "I would not be happy unless the entire Jiorian army went to protect you both. As much as I admire and have confidence in Jagged Edge." Lorn lowered his voice, "He has no wings, and I would want someone with wings who could fly you and Mercy Rose to safety if needed."

"Alright," Lily consented. "We will take Vannier, and Jagged Edge will stay here and rule Jior in your absence."

After long, tense moments of consideration, the King gave an exasperated exhale.

"Agreed," he agreed reluctantly, "Vannier will go and twenty Jiorian soldiers as well!"

"Then it is settled. Now, I must go and pack. We leave in the morning." Her face fell and reflected her worry. "I'm so very worried that we will not make it to the child in time."

Lily turned and left the room where they had all gathered to argue over the trip. Lorn stared after his beautiful wife and tried to find consolation in the knowledge that Vannier was going along to protect her. He called his sons and son-in-law together to tell them of his decision and they spent the evening planning for the different troubles they were all faced with.

#

Mercy Rose was smiling so much her face hurt. At times she had to bite her lower lip to keep from giggling. She raced around her room throwing practically every item of travel clothing she owned on her bed so that she could decide what she would need for the trip to Aesir Blacknight's home. She stopped and contemplated the new knowledge that his *sister* was the "beloved" he had spoken of. He was unencumbered, and this seemed to answer her earlier question as to why he kissed her.

Standing in the middle of the floor, she touched her fingers to her lips and remembered the kiss she shared with Aesir Blacknight the evening before, in this very room. Her heart fluttered as she daydreamed of possible opportunities to share more kisses.

Suddenly, feeling a presence behind her, she froze in place. Strong, warm hands smoothed over her waist from behind and then someone was pulling her close and wrapping her in an embrace. Mercy Rose took in a startled breath and smelled the scent of a crisp winter morning and knew instantly who was bold enough to take her in his arms. She relaxed back against him and barely resisted a girlish sigh.

Aesir Blacknight held her in his arms for a moment before he bent his head to kiss her cheek. Mercy Rose tilted her head to the side, and he kissed lower across her jawline to her neck, hovering there over her fluttering pulse. She was breathing heavily under his kisses, and her skin warmed. Turning her head toward him, he coaxed her mouth into a kiss. Warm fluttering tingles raced through her veins and Mercy Rose was swept away. Aesir Blacknight turned her into his arms and crushed her mouth in another devouring kiss. Her arms went around his neck, and she clutched him, utterly consumed by a need for more.

Aesir Blacknight had one thing driving him, and that was to return to his home in the Hoarfrost mountain range with the Queen of Jior to heal his sister. However, unexpectedly, he had stumbled upon the Queen of Jior's beautiful granddaughter who was just reaching the blush of womanhood. He gave in to his desire to taste the lovely Mercy Rose. His heart was singing because the hope of healing his sister was finally going to become a reality. His body was singing because this unexpected beauty was in his arms. She tasted like sweet nectar, and her body under his wandering hands was responsive and warm. His heart thundered in his chest, and other parts of his body grew hard with wanting.

Mercy Rose let go. Aesir Blacknight was kissing her, and she did not want him to stop. While her lips concentrated on his, her body thrilled to his touches as he smoothed his hands across her lower back and then over her hips. He pulled her into him, and she could feel his lean body against hers. He went slow and did not press her but for the unfamiliar pressure building inside every inch of her body because of his mere presence. These feelings were new to her and intoxicating. She wanted more! He was her first romantic encounter, and she was afraid all of her control would snap, and she would melt to the floor with him and be lost.

Aesir Blacknight traced Mercy Rose's lips with his tongue and lightly plucked her lower lip, pulling sensually. A demon inside his head began whispering heated demands for him to seduce her. The thought had been slowly forming in his mind since the night he first saw her, but he had to stop and think this through without her slim hips pressed against his. He stopped kissing her and leaned back a little searching her eyes with his. He gave her that crooked smile again.

"You never answered my question." His voice was rough with desire while his ice-blue eyes burned into hers.

"I," Mercy Rose searched her mind. Had there been a question?

"Do-you-know," he said between more carefully placed kisses, "what a man and a woman, do alone, together?"

"I," she tried to speak again but only shivered, and her eyes closed dreamily as his kisses swept away her resolve. She could not think and did not know how to answer his question. She knew basically what a man and woman did alone together, but she had never actually…

A knock echoed in the room, and Mercy Rose stepped back and turned toward the door, glad it was tightly closed. Frozen, she could only stare as she realized whoever it was would find her there, *alone* with Aesir Blacknight. She turned back to him to tell him to hide, but he was gone. Whirling around she looked for him, but it was as if he had never been there. The knock came again, more insistent the second time.

"I'm coming!" she cried. Mercy Rose ran toward the door smoothing her hair and skirts and pulled it open only to find *Trail Blazer* standing on the other side. He gave her a curious look that crept up and down the length of her.

Mercy Rose's eyes flew open wide in shock as she halted by the door. She did not open it wide enough for him to enter in hopes that he would leave. Aesir Blacknight was hiding somewhere in her room; she did not want him to be found out.

"My Lady," Trail Blazer bowed deeply at the waist with his hand over his heart. "May I be so bold as to ask if I might have a moment to speak with you in private."

Mercy Rose blushed, nodded once, and stammered before she realized she had no choice but to let him in.

"Ah, for just a moment, as you will see I am packing for the trip with Grandmother." Mercy Rose allowed Trail Blazer to enter and, with narrowed eyes, he looked around the room a little suspiciously. Mercy Rose quickly scanned the room as well and was relieved that it appeared, she was completely alone.

"Who were you speaking to? I thought I heard another voice in here with you." Trail Blazer did not look happy as if he knew someone had been there with her moments before he knocked. He walked around a bit, searching.

"I was packing. Talking to myself as I went over the list of things I need. I have much to do." She said firmly hinting.

Trail Blazer seemed satisfied with this explanation and stopped his scrutiny of the room. Nodding, he focused his intent gaze on her and approached. Mercy Rose took a few steps away, keeping distance between them.

"My Lady, Mercy Rose, I know I have no right, *now*, at this present time, to ask you this," Trail Blazer hesitated. Mercy Rose gave him a look of horror as she feared what he would say next. She took a stuttering breath to speak and stop him from going any further, but he pressed on. "My Lady, I have come here to ask you…"

"Trail Blazer, please, I do not think…" Shocked, she interrupted but he would not be daunted.

"Lady Mercy Rose, I do not think you should go on this trip with your grandmother!" He finished quickly and firmly.

Mercy Rose stood perplexed and was quite relieved. She had feared he was going to ask her something else entirely, something much worse. Narrowing her eyes at him, she tried not to show her irritation when she asked, "Why?"

"I do not trust this *Aesir Blacknight*. I think he has desires that encompass more than just having the Queen heal his sister. I think he desires *you*."

"I am accompanying Grandmother." Mercy Rose began to get very affronted at his presumption.

"This trip will put you in harm's way. In *his* way, and I do not think you should put yourself in danger by going."

Mercy Rose stretched to her full height and narrowed her eyes at Trail Blazer. She no longer wished to hide her irritation, and in fact, she was quite angry at his assumptions.

"Trail Blazer, your coming here assumes a familiarity, a connection between you and I that is not present. It is certainly not proper that you have come to my bedchamber and your concerns are not warranted regarding Aesir Blacknight."

"Never-the-less, I do not trust him, and I do not want you to go with him." Trail Blazer was frowning at her, and he took two steps toward her, crowding her possessively. He examined her carefully, and Mercy Rose was afraid that somehow, he could see Aesir's kisses lingering on her lips or that he could tell she was flushed from his caresses. She looked away and could not meet his eyes, but she did meet the eyes of someone else.

Aesir Blacknight stood in the doorway as if he had just arrived. His hand was on his sword hilt, and he looked as if he were about ready to draw it and face Trail Blazer.

"My Lady, are you in need of assistance?" His menacing tone was like steel rasping on stone.

Trail Blazer whirled around and shielded Mercy Rose as if she needed his protection. Aesir Blacknight loosened his sword in its sheath as he and Trail Blazer angrily stalked toward each other. Mercy Rose raced forward as nonchalantly as she could and placed herself between the two men who looked as if they were about to come to blows.

"Aesir Blacknight!" She looked guilty. "Thank you, no. Everything is fine. Trail Blazer was just…inquiring about our trip." Aesir Blacknight's eyes flew to her face, and he looked shocked that she seemed to be protecting Trail Blazer with a lie because he had obviously been upsetting her and had been standing far too close. Now, he looked angrier than before. Trail Blazer for his part, looked a little surprised and pleased that she would take his side. He smirked at Aesir Blacknight and placed a proprietary hand on Mercy Rose's arm.

"The Queen wishes to see you *immediately*. If you have no objections, I came to escort you."

Aesir Blacknight's voice was flat as he held his arm out to Mercy Rose. She quickly strode forward to accept it, her other arm slipping from Trail Blazer's grasp. Aesir Blacknight looked furious and tilted his head toward the door.

"After you." He spoke to Trail Blazer who had no choice but to proceed them out of the door. Aesir Blacknight gave Mercy Rose a stern, meaningful look and they left the room. She could feel him trembling with anger as if he were about to explode.

#

Later that evening they all gathered for dinner in a small intimate dining chamber. The arrangements to leave first thing in the morning were complete and the family convened before they all parted to go on their separate journeys. In attendance, with the heads of the family, King Forlorn Icefall and Queen Lililaira Gem were their two sons Prince Vannier and Prince Dark Star with their wives, Lady Summer Rain, and Lady Dawn Rusher. Jagged Edge with his wife Princess Lyra Song, Mercy Rose, and Aesir Blacknight attended.

Also, joining them were the two soldiers from the eastern barracks, Blue Falcon and Trail Blazer.

Serious conversation passed the evening as the groups discussed their respective trips. Aesir Blacknight was seated next to Mercy Rose whose father was on her other side. He was moody and distracted. He ate very little and stared daggers at Trail Blazer who sat across the table from him. The tension was distracting to Jagged Edge, and he stared moodily at both Aesir Blacknight and Trail Blazer. Normally he could block the thoughts of others, but when he was agitated, and the thoughts were about his eldest daughter, he had difficulty shutting them out. Tonight, his head was throbbing from his attempts to break through the walls blocking Aesir Blacknight's thoughts. Trail Blazer's angry accusations flying around in his head did not help. Lyra Song smiled lovingly and placed a cool hand on his and eased her husband's pain as only she could.

Queen Lily sensed the tension in the air, and when Lorn was in deep conversation with Vannier, she leaned forward and grabbed the attention of everyone at the table when she spoke.

"Trail Blazer," she smiled coolly down the table.

Trail Blazer snapped to attention and looked pleased to be addressed by the Queen.

"Yes, My Lady?" He tilted his head in acknowledgment and smiled.

"I was wondering if you would have the time to do me a great favor?"

"Anything my Lady wishes, I will do." Trail Blazer preened thinking that the Queen was going to ask him to accompany her on their journey. Aesir Blacknight held his breath, wary of the same thing and not very pleased at all.

"Blue Falcon this concerns you as well." Once she had their attention, she went on. "As you know, we are all going on separate journeys in the morning, and there could be unavoidable dangers. I was wondering if I might ask you both," she stopped and looked at Blue Falcon as well and after a brief pause continued, "I was wondering if you *both* would accompany *my husband* to the Eastern Barracks to address the problems there. I believe two extra sets of wings would be an additional deterrent to any Ny-Komnir in the area. It would ease my mind greatly to know you two were there to lend your assistance." She gave them both a sweet, expectant smile.

Ny-Komnir are subordinate to Ny-Failen, and it was a valid and prudent request to have additional winged Ny-Failen along to help deal with them. Though, Lily knew Lorn was more than capable of dealing with the threat alone.

His eyes darting across to Mercy Rose, the arrogant assurance left Trail Blazer and he looked less than pleased because he had assumed the Queen was going to ask him and Blue Falcon to accompany *them* on the journey to Hoarfrost Range. Because he had just claimed that anything the Queen wished he would do, he was now obligated to do as she wished.

"Of course, My Lady." He tried to mask the disappointment in his voice. "It would be a great honor to assist the King."

The Queen gave a satisfied smile and thanked him graciously. King Lorn was about to protest, but she gently laid her hand on his thigh under the table, and he silenced.

Aesir Blacknight was tense, staring at the meal in front of him, and had not bothered to raise his eyes when the Queen addressed Trail Blazer. He had pretended he was not listening, but Mercy Rose sensed the tension in him ease subtly. He had not spoken to her since the confrontation with Trail Blazer in her bedchamber, and he still seemed angry. Mercy Rose was too edgy herself to eat but cast her grandmother a look of such gratitude that the Queen could not help but smile knowingly.

"Mercy Rose," the Queen addressed her calmly, "eat your supper. We have a long road ahead of us tomorrow, and you'll need your strength."

#

The dinner party finished quickly, and all but the men disbursed for the night. The Queen and the other women went to bed, and Mercy Rose accompanied her mother, Lyra Song, to her bedchamber.

"Mother, I was wondering if I might speak to you about something of a *personal* nature."

"Of course, Mercy Rose." Lyra Song directed her to sit down in a comfortable chair across from where she sat on a small couch, and she smiled affectionately at her daughter.

"I, ah, we've never discussed certain *matters*," Mercy Rose began but did not quite know how to go on.

"Matters? About?" Lyra Song prompted curiously.

"Well, will you tell me about the first time you and Father, well," she got the words out quickly, "made love?"

Lyra Song paled, and her eyes went wide, and her mouth fell open a little. A rush of memories of her first time with Jagged Edge came flooding over her, and she blushed furiously. Taking a deep breath, she thought quickly about how to answer Mercy Rose's request. Lyra Song could not exactly tell her daughter that she gave herself to Jagged Edge when he was her jailer to bribe him to help her escape an undeserved death sentence. So, she delayed that story with a distraction.

"Mercy Rose, is this about Trail Blazer? I knew he was courting you, but I had not thought that matters had progressed to this stage of, of, *affection*?"

It was Mercy Rose's turn to blush, and she shook her head silently before avoiding telling her mother exactly *who* matters had progressed with. After a moment of collecting her nerves, she went on carefully.

"No, it is just that I am nineteen and a woman now, and I wondered how it is supposed to be between a man and a woman when they are *alone together*." She stressed some of her words, trying to impart what she was trying to say without really saying what she meant. Mercy Rose stared at her mother expectantly.

Lyra Song smiled patiently at her daughter and began. "When a man and woman have certain feelings, feelings of love and their hearts become one, the hope is that they love each other enough to want to get married. *After* marriage, *matters* progress to physical love-making love-and eventually children come along. Does that answer your question?" She knew it did not, but she hoped she had avoided telling her own story to her daughter.

"Yes, somewhat. I knew marriage preceded children. I just didn't know, when two people are physically attracted to each other when they come *together*, does that mean that they have to get married? I mean, I had heard Uncle Dark Star and Aunt Dawn Rusher made love before they were married and they weren't even in love at the time. I've heard the whole story about how…"

"Mercy Rose," Lyra Song laughed nervously, "what is this *really* about? Are you thinking of getting intimate with Trail Blazer or?" Lyra Song interrupted her daughter before she could go on. "Has he pressured you to…?"

"*NO!* I just want to know how it all works, how is it supposed to be? Between a man and a woman. Should you be sure you love the person first? I've read Ny-Failen law that one of Ny-Failen descent does not mate with humankind, that it is forbidden, and I had heard tales of Grandmother and Grandfather that they bonded rather than formally marry, as did Uncle Vannier and Aunt Summer

Rain before their actual marriage ceremony. I know my brother Storm Rider well, he and Aunt Moon Dancer bonded, then um…but I had not heard *your* story. I truly want to be prepared *should* the time come. I want to know, what is the right thing to do? If I have strong feelings for a man, should I give myself to him without words of love or the promise of marriage first?"

Lyra Song looked stunned gazing at her daughter for a long moment. She saw how mature and beautiful Mercy Rose had become and knew that men would be attracted to her outer and inner beauty. Mercy Rose had always been an intelligent, calm girl, cool, patient, and seemingly wise beyond her years which is why this subject was so surprising coming from her. Also, because Mercy Rose had glimpsed many people's futures with her power, Mercy Rose frequently came across as not needing any kind of instructions on many of life's trials and tribulations.

Lyra Song reached forward and drew Mercy Rose onto the couch beside her. She took her hands in hers, looked her straight in the eye, and began to tell her the story of how she met and fell in love with Jagged Edge.

"It all started a long time ago at the former King of Krickgold's funeral." Lyra Song wove a story of danger, fear, desperation, and love. When she finished telling her story, Mercy Rose wiped tears from her eyes. She said quietly to her mother, "So your first time, you didn't really love Father?"

"No, it was a desperate situation. One I would not wish on anyone. It is true, love came a little later in our story. As I remember back to that time, I do believe your father's protection and care for me drew me to him. This does not mean that it will be the same for you. You need to follow your heart. If you are asking me what I think you should do, I would tell you to do what is right, and that is, to *wait* until you find the man who will be your husband. Giving your body to a man for the first time is temporarily painful and can be enjoyable, but if you give it only to him, along with your heart *and your love*, at the same time…well, then it is special beyond description."

They spoke for a while longer changing the subject to the trip Mercy Rose was taking with her grandmother, and Lyra Song admonished her daughter to be very careful. She gave her a final embrace and wished her goodnight. Then Mercy Rose went to her room feeling more educated and slightly more confused at the same time.

Closing the door to her bedchamber, she trembled with nervousness wondering if Aesir Blacknight would come to her, hoping he would, fearing he would, anxious that maybe he would not. Hoping possibly, he was already in the room waiting for her but it was empty, but for a crackling fire in the fireplace.

Mercy Rose paced the floor wringing her hands. She desperately wanted to explain what had transpired with Trail Blazer. She knew Aesir Blacknight was angry with her; he had not spoken a word to her since earlier that day when she had almost lied to protect Trail Blazer. She had not, she only spoke the truth and said what she had to avoid a possible physical confrontation between the men, but she could see how Aesir Blacknight could misconstrue her actions.

As the hour grew late, she despaired of him coming to her, and so she prepared for bed resigned to the truth of it, that he truly must be angry with her. Letting her hair down, she blew out the candle, and the room went dark but for the firelight that cast strange shadows. She turned. Just as she was about to untie her robe, take it off, and climb into bed, two warm hands slid over hers and stopped her. As before, Aesir Blacknight had come up behind her and embraced her. The difference now, was that he was ridged behind her and taut with anger. His hand over hers was firm and not caressing. He stood there for a long time and remained silent, his anger permeating the room and gripping her.

Mercy Rose slowly turned in his arms and looked up into his handsome face half-hidden in shadow, half illuminated by warm firelight. She did not smile or apologize but met his anger with courage. Truly angry, Aesir Blacknight looked down at the beautiful Mercy Rose and parted his lips to speak. Before he could say anything, Mercy Rose touched his lips with her fingers silencing him, and stood on her tiptoes initiating the kiss this time. He gave in, and his arms went around her, and he kissed her hungrily. Pouring his anger into the kiss, he branded her with complete possession of her mouth. His desire for her spilled out, and Mercy Rose thought she would be carried away by the force of him. She met him kiss for kiss and clung to him pressing her body against his. When his fury was spent, his kisses slowed and stopped. He touched his forehead against hers and waited while his breathing slowed, his heart settled.

With a small wave of his hand, the candle by the bedside ignited and cast the room in a sapphire glow then it flickered and changed to warm gold, bathing Mercy Rose in its light. Aesir Blacknight took a step back and then reached up and pushed the robe off her shoulders. It fell to the floor in a whisper of silk and velvet. Mercy Rose's breath caught as his hand parted her nightgown. He pulled it apart just enough to glimpse her bare breasts painted in the golden candlelight. Now it was time for his breath to catch and, reaching forward, he caressed one of her breasts staring transfixed at her beauty.

The pearl-white skin of her breasts warmed with his touch and Mercy Rose closed her eyes, overwhelmed by the sensual feelings he was causing in her. His other hand reached out, and Mercy Rose again gasped quietly as he skimmed his fingers over her other breast.

He bent to kiss her, gently now. His long hair fell over his shoulders in a black curtain as he tasted her, running his lips over hers and sucking gently on her bottom lip. Mercy Rose thought she would shatter with the rising tension he was causing in her body. Then his hands stopped caressing and embraced her completely, holding her against his chest. His strong arms made her feel safe and secure. He leaned back and with one finger tilted her chin up. He kissed her sweetly and then rested his forehead against hers closing his eyes. Once again slowing his breathing further, he tried to find some control and calm the jealous beast within. For a few moments, they stood in the embrace then he stepped back and looked at her. His ice-blue eyes were dark with desire but then sparked brilliant blue. He finally spoke.

"Mercy Rose," he whispered her name without smiling. "I think you will be mine."

Releasing her, he took two steps back, and a strange blue light grew up around his feet and encased him completely. Like slowly immersing in dark water, he vanished into the floor and was gone.

CHAPTER SIX

Nineteen Jiorian soldiers waited at disciplined attention beside their mounts as the Queen of Jior approached. Jagged Edge was speaking with Joziah Caulder, the Captain of the Queen's Guard, as the company prepared to leave. Queen Lililaira wore a long, dark violet riding dress and a heavy gray riding cloak lined with white fur. Her long silver hair had been braided tightly and hung long down her back. She pulled on a pair of gray riding gloves as she walked. The King of Jior followed right behind her. His face was a thundercloud of annoyance. She turned to him, and his face softened as he spoke quietly to her, telling her things only she had a right to hear. Then he lifted her onto a white horse after he hugged her tightly and kissed her goodbye one last time. He admonished her to be careful and then went to speak with Jagged Edge and the Captain of the Queen's guard.

Captain Joziah Caulder was one of Jior's best warriors of humankind. He had won his position through gallant deeds and unfailing service to the Queen. He was tall for a human, with striking good looks, a full head of wavy dark blonde hair, and sensual blue eyes. He struck a handsome figure in his black and silver Jiorian uniform and light silver armor. Mercy Rose's father, Jagged Edge, was requesting Captain Joziah watch over his daughter as well as the Queen and especially keep an eye on Aesir Blacknight. Secretly, Jagged Edge was glad such a handsome young man was going on this trip and hoped Mercy Rose would find him a distraction away from Aesir Blacknight, despite the fact that he was human. He would deal with that problem later *if* it arose.

Mercy Rose had spent a restless night contemplating everything her mother had told her and everything that Aesir Blacknight had said and done last night. This morning, she awoke with some resolutions firmly placed in her mind. She had dressed for cold weather in a black and copper-colored riding dress, with a black cloak lined in rust-red fur. She also wore tall fur-lined boots to keep her feet warm in the snowy mountains. She went over the promises she had made to her mother and father, and herself. Despite her frustration over what had happened late last night with Aesir Blacknight, she was determined not to let him see her as a petulant, inexperienced little girl. Also, upon waking this morning, she realized she had not been herself since meeting Aesir Blacknight and she had not come to any intimate decisions about him. Though, now she knew how he got in and out of her room so clandestinely. The only course forward was to find the self-confidence and cool detachment she used to have and not moon over such a confusing man.

As if summoned by her thoughts, Aesir Blacknight stepped up to her. His long hair was braided into a single long black rope down his back, and his gently pointing ears were revealed making him look even more like a Ny-Komnir. Wordlessly he helped her mount her horse. He held her hand overly long, and before he let go, he gave it a soft squeeze and stared meaningfully into her eyes. Turning away, he went to hold a brief conversation with the King, in which the King threatened Aesir Blacknight with a fate worse than death if anything should happen to his wife or granddaughter. Not daunted in the least, Aesir Blacknight mounted a new horse, a blue-black stallion who tossed his head and danced spiritedly over the stones in the road. Then they were off. With ten Jiorian soldiers in front of them and ten behind, Mercy Rose rode beside her grandmother and smiled wide, actually starting to look forward to a long journey.

Aesir Blacknight rode, straight-backed and tense, impatient to be off. He was in the front column of travelers with Captain Joziah Caulder, and they rode out of the city and toward the huge raging waterfall to the west of the city of Jior. Overhead King Forlorn Icefall flew with them for a few miles and was a comforting presence until they left the valley.

Vannier also rode at the head of the procession with Aesir Blacknight and Captain Joziah Caulder. Mercy Rose watched Aesir Blacknight's straight back and broad shoulders and marveled over how the sun shone on his black hair highlighting it glossy midnight blue. She remembered what she had learned when she read him in the Great Hall, and she shuddered a little. Last night, Aesir Blacknight had revealed what she already knew, he was part Ny-Komnir, and today, but for the white skin, he looked likc it. Most Ny-Komnir had blue-black skin she knew, though she had never seen one herself. The legends of them were frightening and she stifled a shudder.

They traveled all day and stopped briefly for a cold lunch, then moved on. Vannier and Aesir Blacknight consulted a map that Vannier had brought. The two men appeared to have reached a temporary truce in their volatile relationship. The animosity that always tainted Vannier's voice when he spoke to Aesir Blacknight back in Jior, was now gone and they got along amicably. For part of the journey each day, the plan was that Vannier would fly overhead to spy any danger ahead. He made frequent reports to Queen Lily but privately with her, remained slightly suspicious of their quest. The Queen had to remind Vannier often that this trip was at her consent and for the good of a sick child. Vannier relented because in his heart he truly wanted to help.

Night fell swiftly in the Violent Mountains as the sun gave way and painted the clouds blood red. An ominous cool breeze blew. After a long day on horseback, the party stopped in a pleasant clearing with fresh water nearby, and Captain Joziah directed the soldiers to set up camp. He also assisted Mercy Rose in the construction of the Queen's tent and then helped erect the smaller tent for Mercy Rose. Aesir Blacknight watched the young Captain's attentiveness to Mercy Rose. A covetous wolf inside him began to growl menacingly, and Aesir Blacknight had to remind himself of the importance of his mission so that his jealousy would not cause trouble and endanger everything he worked so hard for.

Vannier spent time with the women during their supper and then went to scout the mountains from the sky afterward. Shrugging his shoulders, he shapeshifted, spread his huge white wings, and leaped into the air. He shot up into the clouds and was gone from sight.

As the evening ended, Lily instructed Mercy Rose to get some sleep, and she did as she was told, after making sure her grandmother had everything she needed. Mercy Rose departed and went to her tent, prepared for bed, and threw more sticks on her brazier. Though it was springtime, the air was still cold in the mountains, and the small fire barely warmed her tent. She crawled under her blankets and furs and tried to go to sleep, but sleep would not come. Aesir Blacknight had been absent from dinner and Mercy Rose was afraid he was still angry with her. Recalling her resolution not to act like an infatuated fool, she admonished herself yet again to stop thinking about him.

The night was peaceful and a cold breeze gently swayed the sides of the tent back and forth. The fire flickered warmly in the brazier. It was quiet and dark. Outside, two men on guard walked by making their rounds. Their boots made soft crunching noises on the frosty ground. Mercy Rose's bedroll was comfortable, and she burrowed under her furs and blankets trying to fall asleep, but it was useless. Just as she rolled over yet another time to try and get comfortable, she felt a slight coolness as someone lifted and slipped under her blankets.

Mercy Rose inhaled sharply and the scent of falling snow assailed her. She rolled over into the arms of Aesir Blacknight. He leaned over her and kissed her gently and then more urgently, his hand slid under her shirt and across her ribs. He stopped after a few caresses, and closed his eyes, trying to find his control. When he finally did, he laid back and pulled her across his chest, into his arms. Although, he had to use great restraint because he wanted to do more than kiss her. She rested her head on his chest and quickly fell asleep.

Aesir Blacknight felt Mercy Rose's warm womanly figure next to his and marveled at how perfectly she fit alongside his body then he too fell into a peaceful sleep.

Early the next morning Mercy Rose awoke alone. The gray of early dawn was starting to push back the night, and she rose and quickly packed her few things and went to help her grandmother. The rest of the camp was waking, and after a quick morning meal, they all started back onto the trail heading for Hoarfrost Range.

After they stopped for an afternoon meal, Vannier took to the skies to scout ahead, and Aesir Blacknight rode alone in front of the party. Mercy Rose had come to a decision that morning upon waking alone and decided to act upon it. Nudging her horse forward, she rode alongside him. They were far enough in the lead from the others that she did not fear their conversation would be overheard.

"Why did you not tell me that it was your *sister* whom you called, '*beloved*'?"

"Why did you let Trail Blazer into your bedchamber and then defend him when he was trying to intimidate you against me?" His reply was tinged with irritation.

"Why do you always answer my questions with another question or vague responses?"

Aesir Blacknight gave her a strange, devouring look but did not answer.

"Do you realize," she began again when he did not answer, "that we have never had a full conversation since the night we met."

"True enough," it took a moment, but he finally answered, "but I do believe we have communicated in *other* ways." He gave her that crooked smile and looked as mischievous as a cat who was playing with a mouse.

"I know so very little about you." She mused.

"Is that true?" He had been looking forward, but turned and looked at her with narrowed eyes. She knew he referred to the day in the Great Hall where she read him with her Ny-Failen power and discovered almost all his secrets. When she failed to respond, he went on.

"What would you like to know, my Lady?"

"Who are you? Where do you come from?"

"I am the wolf-born and the swan's wing. I come from the wind frost." He looked completely serious when he answered her, and his wolfish eyes dared her to challenge him.

Mercy Rose was silent for longer this time wondering what that could mean, what he revealed?

"You speak in riddles and avoid answering me. You seem to want to play this game of evade and deflect." She bravely went on because she had forgotten all her questions while looking into his eyes and handsome face, so she fell back on the benign. "How old are you? How long have you lived in Hoarfrost Range?"

"I will reach my twenty-sixth year when the leaves begin to turn gold this fall. I have lived mostly in Skoria then I moved to Hoarfrost Range seven years ago. Now you must answer *my* question."

"What question is that?" Her words stumbled as she asked, baffled yet again.

"The question I asked you the very first night we met?"

Now Mercy Rose knew which question he was referring to because he had asked her more than once. She blushed furiously remembering the things her mother had told her.

"I believe you already know the answer to that question."

"Now who is evading?" He chided even though she was right and he did know. Something within him wanted to hear her confession from her lips.

"Alright, I will answer your question and the one that naturally follows. Yes, I have some idea of what a man and woman do when they are alone together, and no, I have never...I have never *been* with a man in the sense that you are asking about."

"That is what I thought." Aesir Blacknight grinned wolfishly. Mercy Rose fully expected him to lick his lips and reveal sharp teeth like a hungry wolf.

"Why does it matter?" They came to a large boulder in the middle of the road, and Mercy Rose had to lead her horse around it. When they came back together, she blurted out, "Why did you kiss me?"

"Because it just does and because I wanted to," he quipped, answering both of her questions.

"Why did you, the night before we left Jior, why did you...ah...stop?" A thrill ran through her breasts as she remembered his touch.

"Because of your other question." Aesir Blacknight seemed to grow a little angry again.

Searching her memory, Mercy Rose finally had to admit defeat and asked irritated, "What other question?"

"To be quite straightforward, my Lady, you said lying with me would be dishonorable and implied I was ill-using your grandmother."

"Oh," Mercy Rose blushed, truly embarrassed now for many reasons.

"*Oh,* indeed." Aesir Blacknight said flatly.

"Aesir Blacknight," she began defiantly. "I had only just met you, and I was protecting Grandmother. Not only that but, in my family when a man *lays* with a woman who is not his wife or intended, he dishonors her. Though I have heard of instances where the man and the woman were betrothed or bonded and they…well, it is a lifetime commitment." Hesitating only a moment, she then rushed on. "It is not a new concept; surely you know this."

Mercy Rose looked away with contrived dignity and tried to look mature beyond her age. Thinking she had outdone his argument this time, she momentarily felt proud of herself.

"Then you should be glad I stopped when I did, my Lady. Your honor is intact and as I am not ready to make such a commitment," he shrugged insolently and let the statement hang in the air. They rode in silence for a long while.

"I dreamt of you last night." Mercy Rose quietly ventured, though, she felt strangely wounded by his last words.

This seemed to please him and his lips slowly curved, "tell me of this dream."

"I dreamt that you came into my tent last night and into my bed. You kissed me sweetly and then I fell asleep in your arms."

He looked at her seriously this time as if here were done playing.

"What a wonderful dream. Perhaps you will have that dream again tonight."

CHAPTER SEVEN

Sharp peaks towered above and surrounded the group as they rode deeper into the Violent Mountains. The tops of those mountains were covered in snow and frost, though the deep valley they rode through below was blooming green, drenched in new springtime growth. The rocky trail wound up through the valley meandering through budding grasses and short shrubs sprinkled lightly with snow. Below them, a river at the bottom of the valley gave its rushing call as it wound its way alongside them. The miles passed quickly and where the land allowed, they galloped their horses to make better time. Aesir Blacknight was anxious to cover as many miles as possible and drove them as hard as he dared. Just as the sun was going down, they camped for the night.

Vannier and Mercy Rose once again attended supper in the Queen's tent, and Aesir Blacknight was invited to join them. They discussed what Vannier had seen on the road ahead, and Aesir Blacknight told them of dangers they might encounter. The next day, the path would take them out of the long valley they had been traversing through, and they would begin the ascent up the winding mountainside. As they gained altitude the weather was growing colder as winter had not yielded completely to spring just yet. The potential for avalanches and rock slides was great and cautionary measures were foremost on everyone's minds. Aesir Blacknight mentioned that there might be outlaws in the area, but twenty heavily armed and armored soldiers should be enough of a deterrent and perhaps they would not be bothered.

Queen Lily paused in the conversation and directed her attention to Aesir Blacknight.

"Aesir Blacknight, tell me the nature of your little sister's illness." She asked him pointedly. Both Vannier and Mercy Rose gave him their attention also.

"She was wounded and fell ill with a terrible fever." Aesir Blacknight spoke haltingly but seemed to sense that he needed to tell the Queen more. "The wound would not heal, and the fever would not break. She grew very frail, and so I moved her to Hoarfrost Range in the Violent mountains hoping the cold would help bring her fever down."

"Wounded?" Vannier asked concerned.

"By an arrow-an *iron* arrow." Was the only clarification Aesir Blacknight would offer as if it revealed everything. After a few moments, he went on to explain, "She has an aversion to iron and fell gravely ill because of it. I believe it has poisoned her blood."

"My mother cannot tolerate iron either." Mercy Rose offered and blushed a little recalling Lyra Song's story, but went on. "I can't imagine what would happen if an iron weapon wounded her."

"It is true." Queen Lily offered. "Lyra Song has been unable to go near iron for as long as I can remember. Once when she was much younger, she was *unjustly* caged in an iron cell, and she grew very weak, and it was a horrible, terrifying experience for her."

"She told me about it. Mother said it was like her very blood was poisoned." Mercy Rose added gravely.

"Then you can sympathize with our plight and why I have come to you for help. I have no way to heal my sister though I have tried endlessly. The iron has poisoned her, and the wound will not heal." Aesir's voice was very sad and his eyes took on a far-away look as he went on. "My sister and I have a *special* bond. We share the aversion to iron, and I know how badly my sister has suffered."

"I am sure Mother will do what she can for the poor child," Vannier spoke up and even his normally hidden demeanor was stricken with compassion.

"I am in your debt." Aesir Blacknight spoke with deep emotion. Placing his hand over his heart he reverently bowed his head to the Queen. When the sad moment passed, he offered a slight smile and turned to Mercy Rose gladly changing the subject.

"Lady Mercy Rose, it is a very fine evening, I was wondering if you would like to accompany me on a walk before you seek your rest?"

Mercy Rose looked a little surprised by the offer but turned to look inquiringly at her grandmother who answered for her.

"Yes, Mercy Rose, you've been in the saddle all day, and I believe a walk will do you good. For a short time, it cannot hurt, and I am sure Aesir Blacknight will make sure you are safe."

"I'll take a flight before bed. I would like to assess the weather and make sure all is well. Goodnight Mother, Mercy Rose, Aesir Blacknight, I will see you all in the morning." Vannier kissed his mother's cheek and then disappeared out the tent flap and into the cloudless night. Mercy Rose likewise kissed her grandmother goodnight and followed the men out.

Aesir Blacknight offered Mercy Rose his arm when they were out of the tent and into the cool night air. They walked through the camp where the soldiers had set up surrounding the women's tents, and Aesir Blacknight led her out into the woods. He walked slowly until they were out of sight of the soldiers and then he took her hand in his and pulled her deeper into the woods. They walked through the trees until they reached a steep gully in the mountainside and the trees opened up to reveal a tumbling brook that made a series of low waterfalls down the mountainside. The moon was almost full, and the clearing was a glittering wonder where the spraying water fell in sparkling droplets on the icy moss, bushes, and rocks.

Aesir Blacknight paused, and Mercy Rose turned her face toward the sky and let the white light of the moonshine on her as if she were enjoying the warmth of the sun. Aesir Blacknight spoke a few ancient words, and with a gesture of his hand the clearing lit up with tiny sparkling lights that seemed to flit and flutter around the clearing turning it into a magical place. He was staring at her bathed in blue light as she beheld the wonder of his magical illusion. Then he moved forward and took her in his arms. Opening her eyes wide, she looked at him while her heart fluttered in her breast like a frightened bird.

Aesir Blacknight kissed her gently and then more urgently. He pressed her back against a tree trunk and plundered her mouth and traveled down her neck. Mercy Rose felt swept away by his passion. Their lips danced, and his hands roamed over her curves. Finally, Mercy Rose had to stop kissing him and pull away, or she knew they would never be *able* to stop.

"Mercy! My Rose!" He almost begged, "You torture me with the sweet taste of your lips and the feel of your soft curves. My heart beats so fiercely in my chest it hurts. My blood sings around you, and my body cries out for yours."

"Aesir, I don't know what to do." Mercy Rose was afraid of the sensual tension between them, and at the same time, she knew exactly how he felt because her body cried out for his too. "I also long for your touch, but I cannot give myself to you."

He backed a few steps away from her. "I am sorry. I swear I am not pressuring you to do something your conscience will not allow." His voice filled with frustration and anguish. "My sole concentration should be on getting your grandmother to my sister before she…"

Mercy Rose went to him and placed a consoling hand on his arm. She stood very close, looking up into his haunted eyes. He looked away as if he could not meet her gaze.

"I am impatient to get to my sister and anxious to see her well again. I'm afraid I am not in complete control of my emotions. Again, I apologize, my Lady."

Seeing him so vulnerable and revealed, caused Mercy Rose to speak carefully and hesitantly.

"After, when Grandmother heals your sister, what will you do then? Will you stay in your home in Hoarfrost Range?"

"My sweet Mercy Rose. I do not exactly know. I had not thought past the healing and having my sister well again. The truth is, it is very dangerous for my sister to be around humans and so I keep her hidden at Hoarfrost Castle. Before this journey began, I had not counted on meeting *you*."

"What does your heart tell you?"

Aesir Blacknight knew at some point that he would have to tell the truth. "My heart is stone Mercy Rose, and my body is ruled by Ny-Komnir blood. Every moment since I first saw you, I wanted to touch you, to seduce you. My desires have become intent on the ultimate victory over your body, but I am not free. I am poisoned. When my sister is healed, I will be healed." He turned toward her and fisted his hands by his side. His ice-blue eyes burned in the moonlight and he wanted to howl like a lonely wolf.

"Then, when this is all over, I will not be denied unless you are saving yourself for someone else but until then I will be satisfied with your kisses only."

He cupped her face with his hands and rubbed her bottom lip with his thumb then kissed her gently. "My heart tells me I must *have* you or I must leave you. However, there are things you do not know, things I've done that I hope you will eventually understand and forgive. I am a Blue Sorcerer, and there is demon blood in me and my sister. My mother was a wolf-born Ny-Komnir and there is no place for us anywhere, and I don't suppose your father or your grandfather would approve of that!"

"You told Grandfather that you were not a Blue Sorcerer and that you never finished your training." She spoke so innocently that it made her sound like a child.

"I lied," he growled almost viciously, his lips curled like a snarling wolf, "I would have said anything to get the Queen to come with me to heal my sister, and you were there, delving into my secrets, seeing straight through me, into my very blood."

"It was not exactly a lie and told for a good reason." Mercy Rose felt partly responsible for that lie. "I would not have told them *all*. I didn't tell them all, but I am asking *you now* to tell me all. Why did you come to my room that first night? Why did you kiss me? Why were you so upset over Trail Blazer? Why did you touch my breasts and say what you did? Why did you sleep with me last night and not try to…what does 'wolf-born mean?' Ahh! I want to know what it *all* means?"

Aesir Blacknight looked at her intently for a long moment. He took her hand and raised it to his lips, kissed the racing pulse in her wrist then held her hand against his cheek.

"All will be revealed, my Rose. For now, just know that from the first moment my eyes met yours back in Jior, I wanted you. You take away my pain, you make my blood sing, and my body hardens with yearning. I desire to be close to you every minute of every day and at night, I want to touch you and join with your body. I want every restraint of honor, morality, duty, and obligation to fall away, and I just want to make love to you and forget everything. When I saw Trail

Blazer standing so close to you in your bedchamber, I wanted to kill him for his audacity. You protected him with your words, and I was jealous of your relationship with him. If you are betrothed to him, I don't know what I would do." He hesitated, stepped closer to her and his voice was low and soft. "I came to you last night because I can't bear to be parted from you and it helps me sleep just being with you. I can calm the howling wolf within and lay next to you without taking you because you ease me and give me *mercy*." His last words were a whisper that thrummed across her heartstrings.

"Aesir, I care for you, but I cannot give myself to you no matter how badly I would like to. I want a love like Mother and Grandmother have. Love, passion, companionship, forever, I want it all." Her voice fell away.

"You *care* for me?" Aesir Blacknight looked a little shocked and upset, "just *care*?" He scowled as if the word were a bad taste in his mouth.

"You say wonderful things that make me want to dance with joy, but it is what you are not saying that is the most important. I don't want you to say it if you do not mean it or just so that you can lay with me for a short time. *Care* is as far as I am willing to let my heart go and I'm afraid kisses are as far as I am willing to let my body go."

"My Lady, I…" he started and then stopped, changing what he was going to say. The soft look on his face hardened, "come it is getting late. I will take you back to your tent and your sweet dreams." He smiled sadly and took her hand.

Mercy Rose followed him back, but once she was within the safe boundaries of the campsite, and in the watchful eyes of Captain Joziah, he bowed deeply and said goodnight. He turned and disappeared back into the forest. Mercy Rose went to her tent, removed her boots, threw more wood on the fire against the cold, and went to bed. She fell asleep alone and dreamed of wounded swans and snarling black wolves.

CHAPTER EIGHT

Once they passed out of the deep valley, their path led them through a dark forest that was struggling to come awake after the winter sleep. Patches of snow still covered the ground and the air was chilled but tranquil. The pine trees grew so thick they obscured the view ahead, and that is where they were ambushed. Vannier had taken to the skies and flew ahead. Aesir Blacknight had Vannier's horse's lead tied to his saddle. The closed canopy of trees above and the thickness of the foliage sheltered the party and caused them to travel two by two on the narrow shadowy trail. When the outlaws jumped out with swords, knives, and arrows drawn, the party was spread out in a vulnerable line.

Mercy Rose rode next to her grandmother and concentrated on the path in front of her. When the sound of yelling men came from behind them, they stopped their horses and turned in their saddles to see what was happening. Dirty men dressed in rags and camouflaged with leaves and branches, wielding long knives, wooden staves, and slightly curved swords, jumped out at them and tried to grab the women's horses' reins. Jior's soldiers were trained better than the outlaws, and they soon had the women protected against the attack. They held them off and the sound of swords clashing rang out. When it was clear to the outlaws that they attacked trained soldiers, they turned and fled.

Captain Joziah and ten of his men surrounded the Queen and Mercy Rose, while the rest of the men rode to the rear to protect the wagons with the gear and supplies. In front, Aesir Blacknight viciously engaged one of the outlaws with his blue metal sword and succeeded in wounding the man who turned and vanished into the woods. The outlaws seemed more interested in the women and the supplies and concentrated their attack against them.

They thought they were free of the outlaws until arrows started flying at them. Two soldiers fell, wounded by arrows before the Queen and Mercy Rose could quickly dismount and find cover among the bushes. Surrounded by men with shields on horseback and Jior's best soldiers, they were safe enough from flying arrows.

Once again, the desperate outlaws charged out of the forest and made another attempt at the women, shouting and brandishing weapons as they came in a concentrated wave. Aesir Blacknight gave no mercy as he fought his way back to the Queen and Mercy Rose. He lurched forward as an arrow struck him in the back. It passed straight into his shoulder and lodged there, the arrowhead protruding out the front, but he kept fighting. Mercy Rose grabbed the bow and arrows off her saddle, and now she stood shielding her grandmother and shot arrows into the trees where she spied the enemy's arrows were coming from.

Vannier descended from the skies and the attack did not last much longer. The outlaws quickly disappeared when they saw a winged Ny-Failen. Aesir Blacknight called to Captain Joziah, and they took five of the men and searched the area around them to make sure all of the attackers were truly gone. The rest of the soldiers surrounded and protected the women with drawn swords and long pikes.

When they returned, Aesir Blacknight went back to make sure the Queen and Mercy Rose were unharmed. He leaped from his horse and ran to where the Queen was tending one of the wounded soldiers. Another soldier had died instantly with an arrow through the throat, and she was devastated that she could do nothing for him. A few other of Jior's soldiers had minor wounds but most had come through the fight unscathed.

"Are you all right." Aesir Blacknight addressed them both. The arrow protruded from his bleeding shoulder, but he hardly seemed to notice it. Mercy Rose ran to him.

"You've been shot." Her face went ashen when she saw that the arrow tip was made from iron.

"I'm alright. Are you hurt?" He asked Mercy Rose after looking over to make sure Vannier was with the Queen.

"*I* am fine, but we must get that arrow out of your shoulder." Mercy Rose pulled him by the good arm toward Queen. "Grandmother, Aesir Blacknight is wounded."

"No! I will be fine." Blood oozed from the wound. He sheathed his sword. Just enough of the arrow stuck out in front where he could reach it and he took the iron tip in his left hand. His hand sizzled and burned as he broke off the iron arrow tip and tossed it into the bushes. He walked over to Vannier.

"Prince Vannier, will you assist me?" He calmly turned his back toward him, and Vannier placed his hand on Aesir's back, took the arrow by the shaft, and with a quick jerk, he pulled it from his shoulder. Aesir Blacknight let out a pained, "huh!" and staggered a bit. Blood poured freshly from the wound.

The Queen was using her power to heal the other wounded soldier. The bleeding stopped, but she did not get to finish. Vannier pulled her to her feet and shielded her with his wings from any further attack.

"Mother, we've got to get you to safety. We will help the wounded, mount up, and let's get out of here." Vannier snapped at her almost ready to fly her home, but he knew she would protest and would want to continue the journey. Queen Lily swung up into her saddle and gathered her reins, but made sure Mercy Rose was safely mounted before they once again took to the path.

The entire party rode hard through the trees hoping no more arrows would be shot at them while they made their escape. They rode deeper into the forest until they came to the bottom of a steep cliffside where soft snow was beginning to fall from white skies.

Aesir Blacknight swayed in his saddle bleeding from his wound. The iron arrow passed through his right shoulder and had burned his hand when he hastily broke off the arrowhead. When they felt they had made it far enough away from the outlaws, they stopped near a place where a rock wall towered steeply above them. The soldiers swiftly set up camp while the Queen finished tending to the wounded. Some of the soldiers had cuts or minor wounds. Aesir Blacknight dismounted and went to order the watches with Captain Joziah while the others made camp. Night was swiftly falling, and they needed to be secure from the outlaws before the darkness fell. A couple of the soldiers gathered wood for fires while the rest stood guard. Vannier once again took to the skies and surveyed the land from above looking to see if any of the outlaws followed. His great white wings beat the falling snow as he trained his hawk-like eyesight on the area surrounding the camp. He searched carefully for miles to make sure that his mother and their party were truly safe.

Below, swiftly pacing the perimeter of the camp, Aesir Blacknight began. Throwing his black and cobalt cape back with his good left arm and with sharp gestures and ancient words he worked his sorcery. Around them, he used his blue magic to form a perimeter of tall stones that suddenly thrust up from the ground. Thick thorny trees magically grew up closely spaced until the camp area was fortified. The thickness of the trees and the stones would keep them safe from arrows and further attacks. When he was sure that they were secure, he sought out the Queen and Mercy Rose.

They had started a fire, and the Queen was finishing healing the worst of the wounded men. Mercy Rose was assisting her by making hot tea and cleaning and bandaging small cuts on a couple of the other soldiers.

"How many men did we lose?" Aesir's shoulder was oozing fresh blood, and he looked even paler than he already was. A sheen of sweat was on his forehead, and he swayed slightly.

Mercy Rose looked up from tending a small wound on another soldier and saw the state he was in. Leaping to her feet, she went to steady him.

"Grandmother!" She cried, "come quickly. Aesir needs you!" Mercy Rose helped Aesir Blacknight as he slid to the ground and sat with his back to a rock.

"Ironic, isn't it?" He winced in pain and then almost laughed. "It is almost the same wound as made my sister ill."

"Grandmother, he is burning with fever. Can you help him?" Mercy Rose's eyes filled with tears as she dabbed his sweating forehead with a cool damp cloth.

The Queen went to him, and she and Mercy Rose helped Aesir Blacknight peal his coat off. Underneath he wore a thick leather vest that had been little deterrent to a sharp iron arrow. His hand was badly burned where he had broken off the arrowhead, and it was hard for him to use it. His deep blue shirt was soaked with sweat and had a blood-stained hole in it, his skin was badly scorched, and he was bleeding a great deal.

Queen Lily placed her hands on Aesir Blacknight's bleeding shoulder and started to call her power, but then she slowly pulled her hands away. A shocked quizzical look took over her beautiful face. She hesitated as if she did not want to touch him.

Aesir's eyes were closed against the pain and did not see her shock, but Mercy Rose saw the look on her grandmother's face as soon as she touched Aesir Blacknight. She gave her granddaughter a look that said, *'why didn't you tell me'* then she steeled herself to touch him again. Pouring her healing energy into Aesir Blacknight, she worked to heal the iron arrow wound. The wound was easy to heal, having been so recently received. The blood soon stopped flowing, and the wound closed from the inside and then slowly healed toward the outside and leaving a red welt and a small star-shaped scar. Keeping her hands on his shoulder, she swept the poison from the iron and the arrow out of his blood. She took his hand and placed hers over the burned one and healed it. The fever slowly fled and his burning skin cooled. Aesir Blacknight relaxed with the healing as the pain and heat left him.

Though the Queen had used her healing powers on Aesir Blacknight, he was exhausted from the fight, the iron arrowhead, and from using sorcery to create the protective boundaries around the camp. His exhaustion was evident, and he was pale from the loss of blood.

Mercy Rose tried hard not to cry but seeing Aesir Blacknight in so much pain she could not help it, and two sympathetic tears fell down her cheeks. Holding his good hand, she knelt beside him, and he opened his eyes to look at her. Leaning forward carefully, she kissed him gently, and this is how her Uncle Vannier found them.

CHAPTER NINE

Vannier was furious with himself for not spotting the outlaws before they ambushed their party. The place where they attacked had thick tree coverage and a heavily leaved canopy that saturated the trail in darkness. He finished surveying the area around the place where their party had set up camp and determined that the outlaws were truly gone. Swooping down to make a landing near his mother, he saw the wounded Aesir Blacknight resting against a rock and his niece leaning over, kissing him right on the lips. When the kiss ended, she did not look up because all of her attention was on Aesir Blacknight. He was gazing back at Mercy Rose as if he were a starving man and she was the meal.

Vannier exchanged a quizzical look with his mother, and she just shook her head and smiled weakly. They finished tending the few other wounded and once the camp was secure and tents were set up, they went about making dinner. Mercy Rose helped Aesir Blacknight to her tent.

In her tent, Mercy Rose helped Aesir Blacknight take his blood-stained shirt off. This was the first opportunity she ever had to see him this much undressed. His skin was pale like most of the men in her family, except for her father who had skin like a human. If Mercy Rose were to compare now, she would say Aesir Blacknight was more Ny-Failen than human in appearance. He was unbelievably beautiful like a creature from the Heavens would be. Muscular and smooth, his long black hair was stark against the white of his skin. Dipping a cloth in warmed water, she carefully wiped the blood from around the area where the wound had been. It was still sensitive to the touch, and he was stiff, but he was healed.

Aesir Blacknight was weak from the iron arrow wound, and he remained quiet, watching her while she tended to him. He had lost a lot of blood, and the iron had done its work poisoning him, so he had to allow her to take care of him, and was soothed by her presence.

When she finished, he laid down on her bedroll. After giving him a relieved, meaningful kiss, he fell fast asleep. Mercy Rose washed the blood out and stitched the hole in his shirt as best she could. She watched Aesir Blacknight as he slept. His black eyelashes were thick and long. His cheekbones were high and his nose slim. He was beautiful and had definite Ny-Failen features all the way to his gently pointed ears. His throat was smooth and masculine as was the rest of his body down to his perfectly sculpted chest and long firm legs.

Mercy Rose sighed and was startled as someone came to her tent. Vannier lifted the tent flap and quickly looked over the scene to make sure she was alright. He quietly motioned for her to follow him out and she did. They went a short way down the path and entered her grandmother's tent. Judging by the look on her Uncle Vannier's face she knew he was displeased with her. She had let her feelings for Aesir Blacknight show in front of her grandmother, her uncle, and half the soldiers in camp. Not ashamed in the least, she stood tall and ready for them to voice their disapproval.

"Mercy Rose, please do come in and sit down." Her grandmother smiled at her, relieving some of the discomfort she felt. "Little Wing! Sit down; this is not an inquest!" Turning to Mercy Rose, she smiled, "my dearest Granddaughter, how is our patient?"

"He is sleeping quietly. I think he is mostly exhausted. If it wasn't for your healing, I shudder to think what would have happened to him."

Her grandmother smiled at her and relieved some of the tension Mercy Rose was experiencing.

"Mercy Rose, we couldn't help but notice that you seemed to have grown rather, *fond* of Aesir Blacknight." Her grandmother inquired choosing her words carefully.

"I do care for him," she answered slowly. "We have become quite good friends."

"*Care*?" echoed her Uncle Vannier loudly. "That is all? The kiss I witnessed looked a little more than friendly!"

"Mercy Rose," her grandmother took over the conversation, "what your Uncle Vannier is wondering, is just how far your friendship with Aesir Blacknight has progressed? Has he asked you to marry him?"

"No Grandmother," Mercy Rose said quietly, "I do not think he is in love with me. His only thought has been for his little sister. They are very close, and he is desperate to help her. I know that falling in love is the last thing on his mind right now."

"Then what was all that kissing! And he is in your tent! Sleeping! Your father will have my head when he finds out!" Vannier was on his feet pacing angrily. "And what about Trail Blazer? I thought you two had formed an attachment?"

"Little Wing please, why don't you leave us alone for a while." Lily used the most gentle, motherly but queenly tone on her son. It was as if she were trying to impart a message to him that he needed to calm down. Vannier stood defiantly for a moment but then reluctantly placed his hand over his heart and bowed his head to his mother then left the tent. Outside his shadow darkened the tent entrance as he spread his great white wings and shot into the air.

Lily turned toward Mercy Rose. Her brow was drawn and she looked very disapproving of the situation with Mercy Rose and Aesir Blacknight. As soon as she was sure Vannier was far enough away and could not overhear, she took Mercy Rose's hand and looked her straight in the eye with deep concern.

"Now," she began, "why didn't you tell your grandfather and me that Aesir Blacknight was Ny-Komnir or at least partially of demon-kind? I felt it in his blood when I healed him."

Mercy Rose blushed but held her chin up and looked bravely into her grandmother's eyes. She briefly wished her mother was there because Lyra Song always had a way of smoothing things out.

"Grandmother, Aesir Blacknight has some Ny-Komnir blood, and I did tell the truth that he has relatives on both sides of his family that were Ny-Failen. Ny-Komnir used to be Ny-Failen after all. He is just different than anyone I've ever tested before. Besides, I did not think it was important at the time, and I…he is very dear to me. I wanted you to help him."

"Mercy Rose, do you love him?"

Taking a deep breath, Mercy Rose teared up a little and choked, "Oh! Grandmother, I do not know! Part of me is afraid of him because of the way he makes me feel and the other part of me can't stay *away* from him because of the way he makes me feel. He says such wonderful things and my heart sings when I am with him, but he has told me he is not ready to commit to me. Everything balances on his sister getting well. There is a special bond between them that I do not quite understand and he is desperate to get you to her. He said I am helping him get through this, in a way. I do not know if he loves me and I am not quite willing to admit if I love him or not. I just don't know." Mercy Rose laid her head in her grandmother's lap, and the tears started, but she went on. "When Aesir was wounded, I thought if he died, I might die too. If his sister does not get well, I do not know what will happen to him."

"Mercy Rose, I believe you are too young to be in this situation, and while Aesir Blacknight seems honorable enough…"

Mercy Rose sat up quickly and interrupted. "Too young? Grandmother, I am practically the same age as you were when Grandfather rescued you from the Black Sorcerer's tower. At that time, didn't you think Grandfather was of demon-kind? But yet you loved him just the same! I am old enough! Is it too much to ask to want to know his heart before I reveal mine?"

Lily was speechless because, after all, Mercy Rose was right.

"My darling girl," Lily did not quite know how to answer and hesitated for a few moments. "It is getting late, and we both need our rest. You can stay in here tonight, and we will sort all this out later." She gave a short laugh and hugged Mercy Rose. "Actually, these affairs of the heart have a way of working themselves out in the end."

Mercy Rose remained in her grandmother's embrace while her tears dried. Finally, she pulled away and pleaded.

"Grandmother, I want to go to Aesir. I am worried about him. He is sound asleep, but I want to be there if he awakens and needs something. Nothing will happen between us, I promise."

"Alright my dear, but if you change your mind, you can come and sleep in here with me. Goodnight, my Little One."

Mercy Rose kissed her grandmother's cheek and hugged her tightly then left the tent. She was very glad when she did not see her Uncle Vannier waiting outside. Hurrying back to her tent, she slipped in as quietly as she could and tied the tent flap shut from the inside. Aesir Blacknight was breathing deeply in a sound sleep. Mercy Rose quietly built up the fire against the cold and then sat next to the bedroll where he slept. Cautiously, she reached forward and touched

Aesir's forehead checking for signs of fever, but his skin was cool. He was in such a deep sleep he didn't notice her attention. Mercy Rose took her boots and her heavy cloak off and sat cross-legged by the fire so that she could watch Aesir Blacknight and be near in case he needed anything. The fire was burning well and warming the tent. After a while, she grew sleepy and laid down on her side facing the fire but close enough that she could help Aesir if he stirred. She had not meant to, but she fell asleep. An hour later she woke snug and warm next to Aesir. He had pulled her against him and was sound asleep with her in his arms.

#

By the next morning, Aesir Blacknight was almost completely well though he was weakened. The Queen's healing had worked wonders and saved his life. He arose from Mercy Rose's bed and all that he could see of her was her white hair fanned out over the pillow, the rest of her was hidden beneath the warm blankets and furs. Standing for a moment, he surveyed her sleeping form. It was almost domestic the way he felt, natural, at ease, and right, waking next to her. It truly gave him pause, and he realized he had a lot to think about where Mercy Rose was concerned. For now, he had to concentrate on getting to his sister and getting her healed, everything centered on that.

The light in the tent was beginning to brighten with the morning sun, and there was something so comforting about waking up next to Mercy Rose, rising from her bed, and seeing her sleeping form. Taking a deep breath, he could smell her scent, and her warmth beckoned him back to her side. He knew the taste of her lips, the curves of her body, the soft feel of her breasts, and the gentle swell of her hip. Though he had not joined with her yet the promise of her sleeping figure was an assurance that he could and would have her. That knowledge had to be enough.

Gingerly pulling on his shirt, his leather armored vest, and grabbing his cloak, he slipped out of Mercy Rose's tent. Aesir Blacknight went to check on his horse. He had completely forgotten about his black horse after he sat down next to the rock and the Queen healed him the evening before. The rest of the camp was still sleeping, though five sentries paced the perimeter on duty. Aesir Blacknight found his horse with the others, and he also found Prince Vannier.

Vannier was calmly leaning against a rock face where the soldiers had created a temporary corral for the horses. Vannier straightened up, his arms crossed over his chest, and waited until Aesir Blacknight was in speaking range. As Aesir Blacknight approached and saw Prince Vannier waiting for him, he steeled himself for the discussion he knew was inevitable.

"Aesir Blacknight, how is your shoulder?" Vannier's voice was low and calm, but his eyes were smoldering.

"Prince Vannier," Aesir Blacknight placed his hand over his heart and tipped his head in polite greeting, even though he would rather avoid speaking to Vannier at all. "I am well thanks to the Queen's healing. I am deeply indebted to her. If anything were to happen to me, my sister would be doomed."

"Aesir Blacknight, I will come straight to the point. What are your intentions toward my niece, Mercy Rose?"

Aesir Blacknight hesitated for a moment wondering just how much Prince Vannier knew, but before he could speak to defend himself or disassemble, Vannier went on.

"I saw her kissing you yesterday, and I saw the way you were looking at her. Just how far has this *relationship* gone between you two?"

"Prince Vannier," Aesir Blacknight began, but Vannier held his hand up and interrupted him again.

"Just call me Vannier."

"Vannier, my sister and I share a special bond. My sole purpose in life right now is to get the Queen to her so that she can be healed of this deadly illness. Mercy Rose is innocent of any wrongdoing if that is what you are assuming."

"I assume nothing. I only know I saw her kissing you and you looking at her as if she were water to a man dying of thirst. Forget not that I was once young like you but rather than dishonor my wife Summer Rain, I reined in my desire for her until we were bonded."

"But you did *desire* your wife. Perhaps, I am not as strong as you in this, and Mercy Rose is stronger than you think." Aesir Blacknight faltered and could not go on because he did not quite know exactly what she was to him. "Vannier, I can promise you this, I have not dishonored her in the way you are implying."

"Aesir Blacknight, I know that love unrequited is worse than death. Mercy Rose is too sweet and innocent in the ways of the world. Do not hurt her or you will have me to answer to and be assured, you'll get off easier with me than you would be dealing with her father, Jagged Edge."

Narrowing his eyes at Vannier, Aesir Blacknight cooled his rising temper before he could respond. Still, his voice remained strained and anger tinged the edges of his patience. Narrowing his eyes, he took a step forward and spoke as quietly and as controlled as he could muster.

"Prince Vannier, I would rather take a thousand iron arrows in the back, than hurt Mercy Rose. And, while I am not quite ready to explore the depths of my feelings for her, you have my word, I will not hurt her."

"I think you are too late. I saw the look on her face when you were shot. Despite what she claims, I am convinced she loves you, and there can be only two choices, you marry her or you leave her."

CHAPTER TEN

The valley they traveled through the next day, became rockier, steeper, and more covered with snow. Soon they would leave the tree line altogether. They frequently had to dismount and walk the horses up steep inclines. A cold wind began to blow, and the air grew thinner. They went a full day without any mishaps and Aesir Blacknight quickly regained his strength. He pushed them hard and was impatient, scowling at the slightest delay. That night it snowed and dusted the trail ahead in white. They pressed ever onward toward Aesir Blacknight's home.

Eventually, the trail they traveled on became completely covered in heavy spring snow. They could see farther ahead that they were approaching a steep mountainside deeply blanketed with snow. It was agreed upon that they would keep moving and not stop for a noon meal, but press on traveling as far as they could as the conditions harshened. Vannier, who could sense the weather, told them a storm was brewing. Not wanting to be caught on the mountainside in a blizzard, they pressed on. The sky overhead was white, and the clouds moved slowly, heavy with snow that was ready to fall.

By mid-afternoon, they came to the steeply sloping mountainside that they spied and the party halted. Aesir Blacknight and Vannier advanced cautiously. Aesir Blacknight strongly advocated for the group to go across and Vannier pushed back, that they needed to check the safety of the slope before risking a crossing.

Forward, across the snow-covered expanse, was going to be dangerous and the only way to reach Hoarfrost Castle. Going down and around could be just as dangerous and very time-consuming. A mile up toward the top of the mountain, a precarious crest of snow and ice hung above them. Vannier took to wing to survey how stable it was from above and if it was safe to cross. Aesir Blacknight waited ahead watching while the rest of the group retreated far back onto safer ground. They watched from the safety of a few widely spaced trees.

Suddenly, without any warning, the snow seemed to burst, and, as if sentient, a crack streaked toward Aesir Blacknight with the speed of a lightning bolt. Underneath, the snow of the mountainside loosened, and the massive mountainside began to slide. The snow broke into huge slabs and boulders. White waves of snow roiled down the mountainside snapping off thick trees as if they were twigs. Everything became buried in the white frothing mass as it moved while huge clouds of white snow crystals billowed in the air.

Aesir's horse reared and screamed in terror as the snow gave way beneath his hooves. The Queen, Mercy Rose, and the soldiers could only watch as the avalanche of snow-swept Aesir Blacknight and his horse away.

Mercy Rose screamed, jumped off her horse, and raced forward before the snow even stopped tumbling, she scrambled to where she had seen Aesir Blacknight go down buried under a mass of snow. He had been thrown off when the horse reared and tried to gallop through the snow as if he were in water. After they rolled down the mountainside, the horse managed to escape through the snow and reached the other side of the mountain. He stopped running and stood quivering and exhausted, favoring his foreleg. Aesir Blacknight was gone, buried under the wall of snow.

Mercy Rose was screaming his name trying to find where Aesir Blacknight was buried, the soldiers behind them dismounted and ran forward to begin searching. Vannier had witnessed the avalanche from above and flew over the mountainside trying to spot any sign that would reveal Aesir's position. They all knew that if he still lived, in a matter of minutes; Aesir Blacknight would be crushed under the weight of the snowpack and suffocate.

As they all frantically searched, a huge patch of snow farther down the mountain, began to glow blue. The soldiers stopped and stared in disbelief. Mercy Rose leaped over the snow and slid her way toward the place she had seen the glowing. Aesir Blacknight slowly rose surrounded in blue light, lifted from the snow as if by an unseen hand. She thought he was unharmed, but as she got closer, she saw he was bleeding from a head wound. As soon as he had completely risen from the snow, he collapsed on top gasping for air.

Vannier had watched everything that happened from the air, and when Mercy Rose reached Aesir Blacknight, he immediately flew across to check on his mother. The Queen had been back far enough from the slope that she was completely out of harm's way.

"Mother, are you alright?" Vannier landed and embraced her in relief. She nodded her head but could not take her eyes from where Mercy Rose knelt in the snow cradling Aesir's head in her lap. Captain Joziah and some of the other soldiers finally reached them but stood uncertain as to what to do.

"I'm fine. Is he alive?" Queen Lily was afraid Aesir Blacknight lay dead or dying. "What about Mercy Rose? Is she alright?"

"Mother, did you see that? Did you see how he escaped the snow?"

"Later Little Wing, we'll discuss it later. For now, my son, please take me to him."

Vannier lifted his mother in his arms and flew her across the expanse of snow and over to where Aesir Blacknight lay unconscious. Mercy Rose was weeping silently next to Aesir Blacknight and could not even speak to ask for help.

Lily knelt in the snow and placed her hands on the unconscious Aesir Blacknight. The golden glow of healing passed through him, and she gave an account of his injuries.

"He has got a nasty cut on his head but no broken bones, thank the Creator. A couple of bruised ribs. He has just fallen unconscious from the tumble he has taken." Everyone stood by while the Queen worked.

Moments later Aesir Blacknight awoke with a sudden gasp and looked into the teary eyes of Mercy Rose. They helped him to his feet, and he shakily brushed the snow from his clothing as he looked around for his mount. The poor horse had been able to get away from the crushing snow but stood a few feet away favoring his leg.

Half of their party was stuck on one side of the mountain and the other half that had gone to search for Aesir Blacknight when he was buried, was almost to the other side. One of the soldiers went to catch the wounded horse. Aesir Blacknight was a little unsteady on his feet, but the Queen had healed his cut head, and he was able to stand and make it the rest of the way to the other side. Vannier helped his mother and Mercy Rose helped Aesir Blacknight. When they got to the other side of the mountain, Aesir Blacknight wordlessly went forward one hand pressed to his ribs. Closing his eyes, he began to conjure a spell. The snow parted and melted as a hot fissure of steam erupted from the ground. There was less snow uphill after the avalanche and now it turned to a solid wall of ice rooted deep within the ground where suddenly a wide path appeared on the mountainside. The rest of the party with the horses and wagons was able to pass safely across.

The Queen went to the wounded horse and spoke quietly to him petting his nose and soothing his fears. He stood still while she moved her hands over him and then her hands moved down his leg. The golden glow of healing enclosed the horse's fractured leg, and he was soon healed as well. Aesir Blacknight had grown very fond of the horse and was very grateful he survived. He cast a relieved look at the Queen for saving his life and his horse, though his brow furrowed in consternation.

"My Queen, forgive me. In my impatience to get to my sister, I endangered us all. I should have…well, I hope no one else was hurt because of my carelessness."

Mercy Rose knew he was concerned about his sister and what would happen to her if something happened to him. There was nothing they could do about what had transpired except turn toward their destination and press on.

The rest of the way, Aesir Blacknight rode behind Mercy Rose on her horse, letting his horse rest after its trying ordeal. The day had been eaten up by the avalanche and the search afterward, so they found a safe place at the foot of Hoarfrost Peak and they camped for the night.

Jior's soldiers who had accompanied them on this quest, gave wide berth to Aesir Blacknight though they looked at him with a combination of fear and respect. After the camp had been established, the guards posted and dinner was underway, everyone calmed down after the day's revelations. Aesir Blacknight had used blue sorcery to make the trail across the mountainside and by revealing his Ny-Komnir powers to escape suffocation under the crushing avalanche, everyone was wary and on edge. He sensed their fear of him and left them alone. He stood at the base of the mountain staring up toward the high peaks of Hoarfrost Range where the last part of their journey would finally take them to his sister and, with the Queen's healing, the end of her sickness.

#

After the day's harrowing events, Vannier once again sought out his mother. Wrapped in warm furs and staring into the fire of her brazier, she rested inside her tent. She missed Lorn greatly and was swamped with worry for her granddaughter. The look on her face spoke loudly of her concerns. Before Vannier could say anything, she spoke first.

"Little Wing, I fear I was wrong bringing Mercy Rose on this trip. I knew she was forming an attraction for the boy, but, until I healed him, I had no idea he was…" she hesitated as if she could not speak the word.

"Ny-Komnir," Vannier said as if it were a curse.

"Possibly Ny-Komnir." Lily sighed. "When I met your father, I thought he was half-demon. At the time, we didn't know that the Ny-Failen existed and so I willingly gave my love to someone I thought was half-human and half of demon-kind." She hesitated and shook her head, "I keep asking myself, why should Mercy Rose be denied that love if she wants him? Aesir Blacknight deserves love too, despite the fact that he has Ny-Komnir blood. What I fear more is the *sorcerer* in him."

Vannier nodded and sat down. His protective instincts were screaming. Reaching for some warmed wine, he collected his thoughts before he revealed his fears to his mother.

"I spoke to him about Mercy Rose. I am not convinced that he loves her, but I *am* convinced that she loves him." Vannier also looked tired and worried. "The fact that he spent all night alone in a tent with her, though he was exhausted from fighting outlaws and being wounded, despite the fact that we all understand and are familiar with someone having an aversion to iron, despite the fact that he has some Ny-Failen in him, despite it all; Jagged Edge would have my head if he knew that they spent the night alone together. I promised him I would protect her. She is so innocent and compassionate, merciful beyond reason. He will break her heart!"

"You can't know that for sure. Something tells me there is a lot more to Aesir Blacknight than meets the eye."

\#

The following morning bloomed brightly under a clear azure sky. The horses were saddled, the tents and provisions stowed and everyone was about ready to move on. Mercy Rose patted her horse's neck and was about to mount. She felt a familiar presence as Aesir Blacknight slipped in behind her. He put his arms around her and placed his cheek next to hers. They stood together in the crisp morning air slightly swaying, and he closed his eyes and nuzzled her affectionately. Now that the word had spread that there was something between them, Aesir Blacknight did not bother hiding his affection for her. Though they had not openly slept in the same tent since Aesir Blacknight was wounded by the iron arrow, everyone knew that he had claimed Mercy Rose for his own.

Behind them a deep, disapproving throat cleared, warning the couple that they were no longer alone. Their actions indicated that the two were closer than they had been before the avalanche and even before the arrow wound. Somehow something seemed changed between them, and indeed it seemed as if they truly had become lovers.

"Aesir Blacknight," Vannier spoke, very uncomfortable with the way the two stepped apart as if they had been caught doing something they shouldn't. "The weather will hold fair today do you think we will make it to your home before nightfall?"

Aesir Blacknight helped Mercy Rose mount her horse and then turned to confront Prince Vannier. His eyes held a challenge that dared Vannier to say anything about him and Mercy Rose.

"Yes, part of the way up, the wagons might not be able to make it because of the hoarfrost and snow, and we will have to see about the horses. We may have to walk up, and the way can be treacherous, but we should reach my castle before the sun sets."

The party headed out. Queen Lily and Mercy Rose were wrapped in their warmest cloaks and gloves. Overnight the winter weather had strengthened. Everything was covered in snow, but now the sky was a clear blue, and the sun shone brightly, though it seemed to become colder as they ascended. Aesir Blacknight moved as if the cold did not affect him. Vannier did not fly in the freezing air but stayed close to his mother, an ever-protective presence. They traveled all day across tough terrain. Trees became sparser and giant slabs of rock and ice thrust up from the ground like huge sentinels guarding the way. In the distance, they could see Hoarfrost Peak where Aesir Blacknight pointed and told them his castle was at the top. The sun was shining, and the bright white reflection on the untouched snow made it sparkle like trillions of diamonds. Everywhere they looked, they were surrounded by boundless, treacherous beauty.

By mid-afternoon, they reached their destination. The wind had blown sharp, frost spikes pointing in every direction and it looked like they were traveling through a forest of ice daggers and swords. In many places, the hoarfrost covered the rocks and the minimal foliage as if they were shrouded in blankets of white crystalline fur. They approached a towering mountain, and as they emerged from its shadow, they saw Hoarfrost Castle pristine and shining in the golden sunlight.

Cut out of the side of the mountain, huge sharp spires flanked the main castle, and the surrounding walls looked as if they were entirely made of giant blocks of snow. The battlements dripped with ice cycles, and the mortar holding the bricks together looked like black ice. Huge crystals and gigantic sparkling snowflakes adorned the sides of the spires. Goliath frost-laden gates revealed the only entrance. Indeed, to Mercy Rose, it looked like only birds could reach the castle. The team of horses had a difficult time pulling the wagons up the snow-covered trail and they made slow progress and fell behind.

As they finally rode closer, they saw a huge glittering bridge arching across a large chasm. The bridge was a thing of great beauty in itself, glimmering in the afternoon sun with a myriad of colored prisms cast through clear ice. Hoarfrost also covered the bridge that spanned a vast chasm filled with white fog, and it was impossible to tell how deep it went.

Finally, they arrived at Hoarfrost Castle. Aesir Blacknight, the Queen, Vannier, Mercy Rose, and ten of the soldiers went ahead. They approached the huge bridge and could see that it was, in reality, gray granite covered in layers of snow and hoarfrost. Thick ice blanketed the way too, and it was clear that the horses would not be able to make it across easily. Though the bridge was wide enough for the wagons when they arrived, it looked treacherous to traverse because of the thick, slippery ice. The going would be very slow.

Aesir Blacknight dismounted and went over to help Mercy Rose off her horse. Vannier helped Queen Lily. Walking forward she peered out at Hoarfrost Castle from the hood of her fur-lined cloak.

"It looks deserted." She quietly spoke to Vannier who had also noticed that not a single soul stirred on top of the battlements.

"It looks like a trap." He said testily.

Aesir Blacknight was helping Mercy Rose as they all approached the entrance to the bridge. Then he left her side and walked ahead of them, throwing his arms out in joyous abandon. His head was thrown back looking across the chasm up to the huge castle.

"Finally!" Aesir Blacknight whispered with passion, "I am home!" The others watched as the relief of reaching his destination transformed Aesir Blacknight's face into a mask of elation. His joy at having the journey over was obvious to everyone and relieved the trepidation that had assailed them all during the journey and upon first seeing a deserted castle. Aesir Blacknight whirled and smiled at them all, but he went to the Queen. Suddenly, his brow creased with concern, and hand over his heart he bowed to the Queen.

"My Queen, I beg your indulgence a little longer, and I ask that you trust me."

This request seemed inappropriate and also a little strange at the same time to Queen Lily, Vannier, and Mercy Rose, considering how far they had come. Then Aesir Blacknight was whirling and, stalking forward, he went to the threshold of the bridge. Midnight blue cloak waving in the wind, he raised his arms again and called out in a loud voice.

"Watcher! I have returned!" He drew his long sword and stood in a fighting stance.

In a matter of seconds, the ground in front of Aesir Blacknight began to glow a sickly green, and out of the hoarfrost-covered ground arose a blue-skinned demon. The Ny-Komnir looked at Aesir Blacknight and bared stark white fangs from the blackness of his beautiful face giving a menacing hiss. He stood almost completely naked in the frigid air except for a black cloth tied around his lean hips, but he did not seem to feel the cold. Holding a long black spear at his side and tilting his head inquisitively, he looked over the group behind Aesir Blacknight. He averted his eyes away from Prince Vannier who suddenly shapeshifted and spread his white wings behind him, protecting his mother and Mercy Rose with wing and drawn sword. The rasping sound of more drawn swords rang out as the soldiers all raised their weapons and stood ready.

The enticingly beautiful Ny-Komnir bared fangs from his luscious mouth and hissed again in anger and warning. His ice-blue gaze returned to Aesir Blacknight.

"Aesir Blacknight, you have returned. It has been many a long days." The Ny-Komnir spoke around his wolf-like fangs, in a tone that sounded as if the demon was not happy to see him.

"Imda! Ig-losa-fieng!" Aesir Blacknight shouted out in a strong voice as if he were speaking the words to a magic spell. The Ny-Failen in the group understood the ancient language. Aesir Blacknight had said, *'I release you!'*

"Imda no wish to leave, Ny-Failen."

"You cannot deny me entry to my own castle Imda, by foot or by sword you will leave. I will fight you if I must. You are released from your post."

After a long pause where the Ny-Komnir's stare rested on Vannier in all his winged glory, he finally addressed Aesir Blacknight.

"No wish to return to Underworld," Imda growled and took his spear in both his hands as he crouched into a fighting stance.

It is the nature of all Ny-Komnir to be perverse, unreliable, and typically act in their own interest. So, it came as no surprise to anyone that the watcher Aesir Blacknight had used to protect his castle was now betraying him by not wanting to leave and denying them all entrance.

Raising his sword Aesir Blacknight snarled like a wolf, "Have it your way!" and he attacked. His long strides took him into single combat with the Ny-Komnir. Imda raised his black spear and grinned in anticipation showing his sharp fangs. The weapons struck with a resounding ring and the fight was on. Aesir Blacknight deftly leaped out of the way as Imda made a slashing blow with his spear. Quick to respond, the blue metal sword flashed around and struck hard against the demon's weapon. The slash and parry of sword and spear rang through the air and echoed down the chasm making it sound as if an entire army were at war.

Behind them, everyone watched while Aesir Blacknight fought for entry to his castle. He struck with vicious intensity as Imda kept him from his goal. Mercy Rose stood pale and frozen, struck with fear for Aesir Blacknight. His long blue-black hair had come loose from its braid and blew out around him as he fought. It looked as if he fought his dark twin as Imda's long black braid swung with his movements. The blows continued and the two were equally matched until Aesir finally struck through Imda's defenses and landed a long wounding slash across Imda's ebony chest. Deep red blood splattered across the brilliant white snow. Imda staggered back and looked down at the wound in his lean sculpted chest. He wiped at the blood oozing from the wound, and then looked at his blood-covered hand.

"Yield and I will show mercy." Aesir Blacknight stepped back from the wounded demon. Imda was breathing hard but did not appear to be in any pain and his wound bled down and dripped into the snow. Finally, he lowered his spear and bent his head in submission.

"Imda go, but you is warned Ny-Failen sorcerer, not to call on Imda again."

The Ny-Komnir's beautiful face turned, looking over the group one last time before he gave a final defiant hiss, then melted into the ground through a sickly green mist and was gone.

Aesir Blacknight sheathed his bloodied sword. He did not hesitate any further but beckoned to the others before striding forward onto the great bridge. The wind came up and his cloak billowed out behind him like dark wings.

Vannier took Captain Joziah aside and quietly warned him to be vigilant. Mercy Rose and the Queen followed behind. The Captain directed five men to go and the rest to stay and wait for the wagons to make it up the mountainside. They waited with the horses on that side of the bridge until the others secured the castle.

As they walked across the long bridge, they heard a kind of music in the air where the wind strummed the hoarfrost spikes, and the sun warmed the glittering ice, together making a hauntingly beautiful, tinkling symphony. Beneath their feet, the breaking delicate hoarfrost fur shattered the stillness and tranquility as they strode upon it.

As Aesir Blacknight and the others approached the far side of the bridge, they could see that hoarfrost had completely sealed the gates closed. Aesir Blacknight raised his arms and blue fire danced from his hands. Placing his blue flaming palms against the huge gates, he gave a mighty shove and spoke a magical command. The ice sealing the gates cracked, splintering down the long seam. Released air gusted out and, with a shower of misty ice crystals, they slowly opened.

"Welcome to my home! Come!" Dusted with tiny glittering ice crystals, he beckoned to the others, and they cautiously followed Aesir Blacknight into his castle. He stormed forward as if he were a Winter King entering his icy domain.

The sight that met their eyes took them all by surprise as they entered a huge corridor with a high vaulted ceiling. The outside of the castle was smaller than it appeared it could be on the inside. It was dark in the hall, but a dim glow seemed to emanate from the pale stone floor. Suddenly, one by one huge towering torches flickered and flared with blue and white fire following as Aesir Blacknight strode swiftly down the huge hall. Every surface was piled with ice and snow. Every pillar and ornament was decorated in ice and frost. Snow mounded in the corners and ice cycles grew from the high ceiling. Outside their breath misted and was so cold it felt as if their lungs would freeze, but the huge hall was only pleasantly cool. It became more comfortable the further they went in, and they realized it was getting warmer. The smooth walls were made with white marbled granite streaked in silver and quartz. Aesir Blacknight had explained to them earlier that his castle was built upon a sleeping volcano although it still offered warmth from deep down in the earth. It fueled his sorcerous power which was something he did not mention. At the same time, the high altitude kept parts of the castle cold and covered in ice. The pure elemental power was intoxicating to a sorcerer such as Aesir Blacknight.

Striding purposefully down the dark hall and sharply waving his hands through the air, sconces lit with blue fire as Aesir Blacknight passed them. Vannier held the Queen and Mercy Rose back until they were flanked by the ten Jiorian soldiers. They followed cautiously. Vannier went in front leading them with his silver sword drawn and his great white wings pulsing slightly with agitation.

After they walked down the long hallway, they came to a circular chamber brightly lit with blue flames. The ceiling of the room glittered with many facets, and it appeared as if the entire dome was made of millions of large diamonds and dark blue sapphires. The walls were constructed of the same polished white quartz run-through with thick veins of silver as the long hallway. In some places, they could almost see through the walls to the outside. The wind sang around them unseen and played its tinkling symphony, but the beauty of the chamber was dimmed by what stood in the center of the room. It was a huge platform and, on the platform, was a large statue.

The statue itself looked as if it were made out of a single diamond carved in the shape of a huge swan. Each feather glittered with realistic facets. The swan was frozen in place, wings spread out as if it were about to take flight. Its beautiful neck stretched long, and the beak was slightly open as if it were about to trumpet. The black around the eyes of the swan was made from onyx and gave the hollow, haunted impression that it watched them with ruby eyes. The detail of the statue was so intricate that each crystal feather was proportioned and exact as if the crystal swan could take flight. The only flaw was below the swan's neck where it met the wing. The sculptor had carved into it and placed a large ruby. The red was a grotesque addition to the utter perfection of the piece, and the ruby looked almost as if it were spreading into the diamond. Some trick of the light made it look as if it was a wound in the facets and it bled. Aesir Blacknight fell and knelt on one knee, his head bowed as if worshiping the statue.

Without needing an order, the five Jiorian soldiers circled the room. Spanning out, they stood at attention watching as the Queen, with Mercy Rose and Vannier, approached Aesir Blacknight. Captain Joziah stood close on the other side of the Queen. Though Aesir Blacknight felt their presence behind him, he ignored them and started speaking to the statue.

"Swan, I have returned." His voice caught a little and he was swept up with the emotion of his homecoming. He was breathing hard, but the look on his face was of triumph!

Watching in amazement, Lily darted a look at Vannier as he spoke in an irritated tone.

"Aesir Blacknight, if you will take us to your sister now."

The Ny-Failen have no patience with those who worship false gods, and his voice was intolerant as it broke the silence of the room.

Aesir Blacknight rose to his feet and turned. His ice-blue eyes almost looked feverish in the blue glow of the room. "My Queen, I asked you to trust me. Please do so now!" Then his arm swung toward the huge statue, and his voice rang out, "*My sister*, Swan Glory!"

The Queen gasped in shock as did Mercy Rose. Vannier snarled and raised his sword. He was at the end of his tolerance, and he lowered the sharp tip toward Aesir Blacknight's throat.

"Aesir Blacknight, what have you brought my mother here for?"

Aesir Blacknight ignored Vannier and the sword pointing at his throat. Looking a little crazed, he pleaded with the Queen.

"My Queen, this *is* my sister, Swan Glory. I had to place her under this spell because it was the only way to keep her alive and stop the iron poison spreading from the wound and killing her. Once I release the spell, and she transforms into a human again, you must not hesitate to heal her but do it quickly. You see, in my desperation, why I *had* to do this. She was dying! I could not let death take her!" Aesir Blacknight spoke with pleading desperation. Mercy Rose stood by, motionless and frightened for him. The terrified look on her face suggested she thought Aesir Blacknight had gone mad.

"I understood that your sister was a child. A young innocent you said." The Queen was calm but perplexed.

"You assumed she was a child and I would have let you believe anything to get you here to heal her. My sister and I share a special bond, and I feel her pain as acutely as if it were my own. We are both imprisoned! She needs you

Queen Lililaira, and *I* need you. Will you do what you came here to do?"

Mercy Rose gave a terrified look at her grandmother with pleading eyes as if she were willing her to do as Aesir Blacknight asked. The Queen removed her gloves and spoke quietly as she folded her hands in front of her.

"I am ready to do what I can." She spoke surely but looked doubtful.

"As soon as the spell is broken, you must start her heart." Aesir Blacknight spoke urgently.

"Aesir Blacknight," the Queen gasped, "I cannot bring back the dead!"

"She is not dead!" Aesir's voice rang out. "She is frozen!"

Mercy Rose had a sudden recollection of Aesir Blacknight telling her *he* was frozen, and she watched with intense fear for him.

Aesir's eyes closed momentarily as he was overwhelmed with relief that his ordeal was almost over then he whirled away. He stripped off his cloak and flung it aside then raised his hands in victory and began to chant. His voice rang clear accompanied by the symphony of the wind, the blue torches in the room flared, and the light brightened. Aesir Blacknight transformed into the Blue Sorcerer in front of their eyes. His long black hair blew in a strange wind and his voice rose from a whisper to a shout as he wove his spell. Finally, he cried out, "Beyaka vila minum!" which meant in ancient Jiorian, '*bend to my will!*' As soon as the echo from his last words faded, there was a shifting in the atmosphere of the room.

Slowly, the statue in the center of the platform began to crack and melted like ice shattering under intense heat. The crystal shattered and turned pure white as it transformed and revealed beneath pure white feathers. After minutes of shimmering and crackling the diamond fell completely away. Then suddenly before them, the wounded swan cried out with a terrifyingly human-sounding scream.

Astounded, everyone in the room watched as the wounded swan's wings flapped weakly and she shapeshifted. It shimmered and rippled with magic and in moments, standing in front of them, was a beautiful girl with a horrible bleeding gash on her shoulder that trickled new blood. Staring upwards her long neck was exposed, one arm reaching high where a wing had been. She looked drenched in icy water and stood completely naked with long blue-black hair cascading down her back to brush the backs of her knees. Her beauty radiated from her as she stood statuesquely, arms raised then outstretched, but only for a moment before her large black eyes faded to blue, fluttered closed and her legs gave way. She gracefully folded and fell.

Aesir Blacknight was there in a flash and caught her. Carrying her from the platform, he laid her at the Queen's feet.

"My Queen, please hurry!" His voice croaked with strain as he pleaded with her. The veins of poison that spread from the bleeding wound had been held off by Aesir's spell until now. It seeped over the girl's white shoulder and began to creep up her neck in sickly blue tendrils as she shivered in Aesir's arms.

The Queen knelt and was slightly taken aback by the identical resemblance between the girl and Aesir Blacknight. His *twin* had the same features with high cheekbones flushed red with heat, but her eyes were closed and her wet skin burned with fever. Lily did not hesitate. Laying her hands on the girl, the golden glow of healing spread over her and flowed into the wound. Lily could feel the feverish heat of the girl's sickness. Indeed, the iron had taken hold in Swan's blood and had poisoned her. As if sentient, it did not want to let go. The wound itself was deep and infected, and the girl had been sick for a *very* long time. She was thin and weak shivering almost violently. As the Queen's power spread through the girl, she glowed goldenly, and her heart began to beat faintly.

The only other time in Lily's life where she needed to expel this much of her power was when she was forced to heal the King of Skogur during the Great Jiorian War. Lyra Song had been three years of age, and her life was at stake when Bower of Skogur forced Lily to heal him. He was deathly ill by Lily's hand, and she had to undo what she had done to save Lyra Song's life. Now, the Queen's energy drained into the girl, and she began to falter. Closing her eyes, Lily poured everything she had into the dying Swan.

As if Lily's mind was whisked back through time she was swept up by another memory, a different time. She was suddenly back in Jior lying in her bed. She was struggling to give birth to her first child, Vannier, and her energy was completely drained. The despair and fear that they would both die was about to overtake her. When her Love, was inexplicably next to her and pouring his energy into her. Her hand was on Lorn, and she *pulled* using his energy, she restored her own and made it through the birth of their first child.

Seeing her grandmother weaken, Mercy Rose quickly knelt beside her and placed one hand over the Queen's hand and one over Swan's heart. Her eyes glowed blue as she called her power. Mercy Rose did not have the power to heal, but she had energy, and as she poured that energy into the Queen and into Swan, they created a triangle of vitality and healing.

Lily did not know where she was, but she felt her husband's presence as if his spirit were there in the room lending her strength. *"Lorn!"* she whispered as the memory took her but even with Mercy Rose's added strength helping, it was not enough. Swan Glory was so close to death; after so much sickness there was much healing to be done and the iron had a tight grip on the girl who was unlike anything any Ny-Failen had ever seen. Trapped in the memory of Lorn, as if drawn to him, she reached forward with her other hand and gently cupped Aesir's face. Now she *pulled* and felt the same Ny-Komnir energy as she had from her husband all those years ago. All together they upheld her and Queen Lililaira morphed their combined energy and poured her renewed healing power into Swan Glory.

The poison slowly fled from the girl's blood, and the wound finally closed until all that was left was a thin star-shaped scar. The fever abated, and the Queen searched through the girl's body, healing all and making her well again. Being frozen was not the same as being ill, but it had caused its damage, and that needed to be healed as well.

Aesir Blacknight felt his energy being pulled from him and he did not fight it. All he knew in those moments was that Swan was healing, becoming whole again, returning to him!

Swan Glory gasped in Aesir's arms, and now her shivering was from the cold. Mercy Rose took her cloak and covered the naked girl while Aesir Blacknight cradled her in his arms and kissed her forehead. He cried tears of joy and rocked her, "Swan! My Swan! You've come back to me!" The girl raised a thin, weak hand to his cheek and in a barely discernable voice whispered, *"Brother!"*

Queen Lily released her healing from Swan Glory and slowly stood, smiling down at the happy scene. Her work was done. Then, in a slow falling motion, her eyes closed and she gently crumbled. Vannier had been watching her like a hawk and was there in less than an instant and caught his mother as she fell, completely drained of energy.

Aesir Blacknight lifted his sister in his arms and cradled her against his chest. He was very weak from the Queen having drained his already taxed energy, and he swayed weakly. Captain Joziah was suddenly there beside him and took the girl from his arms as Aesir Blacknight staggered. Mercy Rose was beside him and pulled Aesir's arm around her shoulders, as he pointed the way and led them from the room. As weak as he was, he bade Vannier follow and showed them to chambers off the main hall where the Queen could rest. Vannier took his mother into a room and stayed to keep watch over her.

Captain Joziah was directed to a room across the hall, and he placed Swan Glory in the bed and covered her with soft blankets. Aesir Blacknight was trying desperately to shake off the lethargy and the weakness that wanted to take him down into blackness. He shook his head trying to find the strength to go to his sister's side, but the Queen had taken much from him to finish the healing.

Captain Joziah addressed Mercy Rose, "My Lady, I can stay and tend his sister. She's only sleeping now. You go and take Aesir Blacknight to rest."

Mercy Rose was having trouble holding Aesir up as he was much taller and bigger than she and he swayed on his feet. "Thank you, Captain Joziah. I will find a room just down the hall. I will come back to look in on Grandmother and Swan Glory as soon as I can."

She turned to lead him away but Aesir Blacknight suddenly stopped. He cast his burning gaze on Joziah. "Captain Joziah, I will *kill* you if you hurt her, and trust me…I will know."

The Captain nodded once in acknowledgment of the threat.

Mercy Rose led him away to the last room at the end of the hall. Sapphire light shone through blue crystal windows and painted everything with its radiance. A large bed in the center of the room looked as if it was ornately carved from huge blocks of clear ice. It was heaped with cobalt pillows and sheets, and black furs. Mercy Rose helped Aesir Blacknight stumble to the bed, exhausted. She pulled off his boots and then leaned over him and pulled a blanket up to cover him. She turned to leave him to rest, but his hand shot out and grabbed her wrist. He pulled her down into his arms, and she laid her head on his chest, listening to his strong heartbeat.

"*Finally*, my Swan and my Rose." His body relaxed, and he was asleep.

CHAPTER ELEVEN

The following day found Mercy Rose waking alone in Aesir's bed. She looked around the blue room and realized he was gone. Not sure of the time of day, she quietly slipped out, intent on finding her grandmother. Unfortunately, she found her Uncle Vannier first. He was standing out in the hallway leaning against the wall with arms crossed over his chest as if he knew she had been in there and had waited for her to come out. He looked her up and down staring at her wrinkled clothing.

"Good Morning Uncle," she tried to force her voice to sound tranquil and not betray the nervousness she felt upon seeing him waiting for her. Smoothing her hand over her hair nervously she tried to act calm.

"Mercy Rose," Uncle Vannier pushed away from the wall and walked up to her. He sounded disappointed in her and she winced. "We need to talk." He pointed back the way she had come, and Mercy Rose turned around and went back into the room. The morning was swiftly growing lighter as the sun rose outside and the room glowed blue from its rays shining through the sapphire crystal windows.

"What is it, Uncle? Is Grandmother alright? Has anything happened?"

"That is what I was going to ask you." Vannier paced into the room and lowered himself into a chair by the cold fireplace. "Come and sit down."

"Uncle Vannier," Mercy Rose began and looked toward the door as if she would like to escape but did not quite know what to do or say. Lowering herself to the edge of the opposite chair, she crossed her hands in her lap.

"Mercy Rose, I question your loyalty. Ever since Aesir Blacknight has come into your life, you have changed. You used to be a level-headed girl who never let wild emotions rule her or allowed herself to make improper judgments."

"Question my loyalty? To Whom?" Mercy Rose jumped up alarmed, her hands gripped in front of her, and struggled to understand what her Uncle Vannier was telling her.

"Your grandmother!" Uncle Vannier sounded exasperated. When Mercy Rose continued to look lost, he filled in the pieces. "Yesterday your grandmother fainted from using *all* of her energy to heal that girl, and your first thought was to go to *him*! Then you disappear into his bedchamber and spend the night!"

"Nothing happened between Aesir and I. He was completely spent, exhausted beyond any capability for anything but sleep and I stayed with him. He needed me!" Mercy Rose's face fell, "I am sorry about Grandmother, but I knew you were taking care of her, and Captain Joziah was taking care of Swan Glory. Aesir Blacknight had no one and I didn't know what else to do. I was swept away by everything and…"

"We were all swept away by his lies! Aesir Blacknight has lied to us from the beginning. He let us believe we were coming here to heal a sick child and she is a grown woman! His twin no less. We risked Mother's life under false pretenses. Lost a soldier to outlaws along the way and an avalanche almost killed all of you. I'd fly Mother and you out of here right now if it weren't so infernally cold and far away, and I don't want to risk the other men's lives."

"Aesir Blacknight never lied. It is his way not to offer information and be a little vague that is true, but he did not lie, exactly. Surely, you can understand his desperation! To what lengths would you go to save my mother, your own sister's life? You would stop at nothing. You have twin sons yourself and understand the strength of the bond between them! Aesir did what any good brother would have done. I am sorry about Grandmother last night. You are right, but I...” Mercy Rose felt horribly guilty, and she realized her Uncle Vannier was right about everything. “Where is Grandmother? Is she alright?”

“She is with Swan Glory. After everything that happened during her ordeal, the girl remains very weak. Mother is caring for her now.”

“Where is...” before she could continue her question Uncle Vannier spoke.

“He is with his sister. He returned to her bedside at some point during the night, and he has not left her since.”

Mercy Rose turned and looked toward the door as if she wanted more than anything to go to him.

“Mercy Rose, you know that my concerns for you are solely based on the fact that you are my niece and I love you. I also told your father I would watch after you and not let Aesir Blacknight do anything to dishonor you, but despite my best efforts, it seems I am too late. At this point, I have no idea what to do next except demand Aesir Blacknight marry you.”

“Uncle Vannier, I swear to you I have not allowed Aesir to-to,” she just could not say the words, to deny what her Uncle was accusing her of. “I have not-we have not-I mean he has kissed me of course, but we have not, I told him I *would* not.” Mercy Rose stuttered and stammered her explanation.

Uncle Vannier turned a little red with embarrassment. “Niece, I know that you will find this hard to hear, but I spoke to Aesir Blacknight the morning after the iron arrow wounded him and I discovered that you two had deeper feelings than I’d previously believed. It makes me very sorrowful to tell you that I do not think he loves you. His only thoughts were for his sister, and he did not strike me as having very deep feelings for you." He did not want to say those words but had to tell his niece the truth.

"Believe me when I tell you that I know how it feels to be mistaken about things you see and sometimes are led to believe. I don't want you to be hurt when we return home, and Aesir Blacknight stays here in his beautiful castle with his twin sister, and lets you walk out of his life."

Mercy Rose was stunned by her Uncle's words and that he had spoken to Aesir Blacknight about her. Her heart was wounded because of what he was saying, but she had to accept the possibility he spoke the truth.

"Uncle Vannier, I…what would you have me do?" She sounded resigned.

"Go and stay by your grandmother's side for the rest of our time here. We will leave as soon as possible, and you can put all of this behind you. Your virtue is still intact, and I know that Trail Blazer is very fond of you, perhaps it will be easier when you are home for you to let go of a situation that is not all what you had hoped." Vannier could not go on because of the look on her face, and he felt sorry down to his bones. He stood and took Mercy Rose into his arms and gave her a fatherly embrace.

The rest of the day Mercy Rose spent by her grandmother's side. After the first initial shock of seeing a very gaunt-looking Aesir Blacknight with his twin sister and the worried look on his face, she decided her Uncle Vannier was right. He had not even noticed when she had entered the room. She began to suspect she had only been a diversion for him during their trip. Convinced his feelings for her had changed or never were what she thought, she avoided meeting his eye which was easy because he hardly seemed to notice she was there.

Swan Glory was an exact twin to Aesir Blacknight. Her features were soft and feminine where he was masculine, but the almond shape of the eyes, the pointed ears, long blue-black hair, and pale skin were almost identical even to the curve of their eyebrows. Aesir Blacknight sat next to Swan Glory holding her hand. Mercy Rose watched him from across the chamber. The anxious look on his face was as close to fear as she had ever seen on him during their short acquaintance. It was clear that the bond he spoke of between his sister and himself was deep and unbreakable. Mercy Rose felt like a gullible fool but resolved not to let it destroy her.

Queen Lily tended to the sick girl. She could not determine exactly what was wrong with her but concluded it was only weakness or possible after-effects from having been a statue. At times, Aesir Blacknight paced the room while the Queen tended his sister and continued to pour healing energy into her. He even offered more of his own energy. Mercy Rose left the room and went to find food for them all. After discovering a fully stocked kitchen she and one of the soldiers, who had cooked for them all on the trip, prepared a large meal. Arranging a tray with some broth and bread, she took it up to Swan's room.

Aesir Blacknight took the bowl of broth and tried to get Swan Glory to drink it. She was too weak and lethargic, so he had to sit with her propped up against him and coax small drops onto her lips. Thus far, Swan Glory had not spoken and had barely moved or opened her eyes.

Eventually, Queen Lily, Mercy Rose, and Vannier left the room and went to the kitchens to sup. It was a cheerless meal, and Mercy Rose could barely eat. Her heart was heavy, and though there was nothing she could do about Aesir Blacknight, she could do something about her grandmother.

"Grandmother, I am sorry for my disloyalty. I didn't help Uncle Vannier with you after the healing when you needed me. I was…I was swept away by all of this, but I promise you I will stay by your side and help you from now on. When we leave and put all of this behind us…well…we will leave and put *all* of this behind us."

"My dear child!" she reached across the table and took Mercy Rose's hand, "Disloyalty? No! Never! I didn't think it at all. In fact, without your extra strength to help me, I would not have been able to finish the healing. I shudder to think what would have happened! You helped me immensely by supplying energy when I most needed it."

Vannier cleared his throat and looked a little embarrassed, "Mother, when can we leave? I am anxious to return home to Summer Rain and my children. I know if Father has returned, he'll be looking for you. I think for everyone's sake," He paused and looked meaningfully at Mercy Rose, "we should be on our way as soon as possible."

"You're leaving!" Aesir Blacknight stood in the kitchen doorway and looked from face to face with his saddened eyes resting on Mercy Rose. "So soon?

Mercy Rose stood from the table; she had not touched her supper. She could not look at Aesir Blacknight but made to move past him in the doorway.

"I'll just check on Swan Glory." She mumbled as she tried to leave but was blocked by the broad chest and imposing presence of Aesir Blacknight.

"Captain Joziah has volunteered to stay with her." He grumbled not looking happy about that at all, "He was most adamant that he could be of help. Why are you leaving?" Acsir Blacknight looked sad and angry, and he was speaking directly to Mercy Rose.

It was the Queen who spoke up first though. "Mercy Rose, please come sit down and finish your supper. Aesir Blacknight, do come and get some food yourself."

Vannier got up and ladled some stew into a bowl and set it in front of Aesir Blacknight. He had not taken his eyes from Mercy Rose's face, and she had not looked up.

"My Queen, Prince Vannier, I cannot express enough my deepest gratitude for everything you've done. You have crossed the Violent Mountains and entered the dangerous Hoarfrost Range to help Swan Glory and I can never repay you for all you have done. I know I wasn't quite straightforward about her being my twin, but I did what I had to do to save her. I hope you understand that? I was desperate!"

"We do understand Aesir Blacknight and any one of us would have gone to such great lengths to help one of our loved ones as well. We hold no ill will toward you."

Vannier had spoken up and then went on with a little more warmth in his voice. "However, we think we should be on our way as soon as possible. I am anxious to get home to my family. Mother, I'm sure, will need a long rest after this journey, and Mercy Rose," he paused choosing his words carefully, "has *obligations* of her own waiting for her in Jior."

"Does she?" Aesir Blacknight's eyes turned glacial as sudden understanding hit him. He looked enraged, but then he cooled his temper slightly after another moment and turned toward the Queen, anxiousness replacing his rage.

"How long can you stay? I was hoping my sister would be a little more lucid before you left us. She is still not well and *must* be able to shapeshift into her swan form *before* you go. It is the only way we will be assured that she is completely healed and no longer needs you. There is no sense in coming this far only to leave prematurely."

"I will stay as long as it takes. Though we do miss our family back in Jior, I am confident Swan Glory will be well very soon, and I hope to be gone in a few days." The Queen spoke quietly.

"Thank you, my Queen." Aesir Blacknight rose from the table not having touched his dinner, and he quietly left the room without another word.

CHAPTER TWELVE

Mercy Rose was dreaming. She was trapped in a sapphire box without seams or a door and no way out. She was screaming for help. Aesir Blacknight was standing watching her with an angry look on his face as she beat her fists on the box but he would do nothing to help her. Suddenly, he grew and grew enormous, while she shrank to a size smaller than a mouse. Her cage, which turned into a sapphire rosebud, he then placed into a giant vase and then he turned and walked away. Watching as he left, she saw Aesir Blacknight transform into a huge black wolf that loped away into the forest leaving her imprisoned and alone.

Mercy Rose woke up startled, looked around Swan's room, and met the beautiful almond-shaped, ice-blue gaze of Swan Glory herself. It was very late at night, and it was Mercy Rose's turn to stay and watch Swan Glory, but she had fallen asleep. Now, the girl was watching her which meant she was finally awake after her long ordeal. She sat up and gave Swan Glory a shy smile.

"How are you feeling Swan Glory?" Mercy Rose spoke quietly to her.

"So, you are the one he loves?" Swan's voice was whispery from not having been used for a long time during her sickness, but Mercy Rose heard her.

"I, who?" Mercy Rose was afraid to ask what the girl was talking about, was she dreaming this too?

"Aesir, my brother. You are the one he loves."

"I am Mercy Rose." The two girls stared at each other for a moment then Swan Glory gave Mercy Rose a beautiful smile.

"He's not a black wolf. His heart is not black." Swan Glory smiled reassuringly.

"How did you know what I was dreaming?" What the girl was saying did not make any sense to Mercy Rose.

"Maybe you said things in your sleep?" Shrugging, she gave an evasive answer and looked away.

"How do you know he loves me?" Mercy Rose could not help but ask.

"Mercy Rose is a beautiful name you must tell me sometime how you got it." Swan Glory winced a little and moved her shoulder. "There was a beautiful woman with silvery hair here. I think she healed me. Where is she? I would like to thank her."

"It is very late at night and everyone else is asleep right now. It is my turn to watch and care for you. Shall I wake Aesir Blacknight and tell him you are awake?"

"He is in pain. You should go to him."

Mercy Rose did not know what to make of what Swan Glory was saying and then remembered their twin bond. She wanted to ask her so many questions but did not want to tire her.

"Can I get you anything?" She prompted. "Some water, tea, or food? You should eat."

"Who is the young soldier who helps care for me?" Swan Glory looked around the room.

"I think you mean Captain Joziah Caulder. He is asleep down the hall. As I said, it is my turn to stay with you, and everyone else is asleep."

"Oh," she sighed and paused for a moment, thinking. "I am not very good at subtlety Mercy Rose. I would like to see Captain Joziah even though I know he sleeps. He dreams of me." Swan Glory smiled again and blushed prettily. "I do wish you would wake him. I feel so *real* when he holds my hand. I wish you would send him to me. Then you must go to my brother Aesir and ease his heart."

Mercy Rose stood slowly, and her heart flipped at the thought of going to Aesir Blacknight and being alone with him in his bedchamber during the deep of the night. She brought Swan Glory a glass of cool water and then went to wake Captain Joziah who arose at once and rushed into Swan's room closing the door gently behind him.

Now Mercy Rose was alone in the hallway and her heart wanted to give in and go in the direction of Aesir's room. She had promised her Uncle there would be no more spending the night with Aesir Blacknight. Her lips momentarily quivered remembering his kisses, and her memory took her back to that night in her room in Jior when he touched her naked breasts. She desperately wanted to go to him, but then the reality that she would soon be leaving him slapped her across the face, and instead she turned and went to her room.

The room had a warm crackling fire burning. Mercy Rose had been in the same clothes for two days, and she stripped them off and washed in a large sapphire bowl of clear water. The room was surprisingly warm, and she was overwhelmingly tired and crawled between the soft blue sheets and black furs of her bed and closed her eyes. Immediately, she was sound asleep, and she was dreaming of *him* again.

In her dream, Mercy Rose walked naked down to the end of the long hall. Her bare footfalls on the cold stone were silent, and the brush of her long white hair whispered on her flesh. Pushing open the door to Aesir's room, she slowly walked toward his bed. Golden warmth from the fireplace bathed the sleeping man in its light as he lay still. Lying face down, his head resting on his folded arms, she looked at his body in repose. Long, blue-black hair lay fanned over his back, and the expanse of his smooth white skin was revealed to her wondering eyes. The deep blue sheet was folded down to his hips and Aesir's long, white back, and lean body were relaxed in slumber.

Her eyes followed the line of his broad shoulders down to the curve of his smooth hip. There was something sweet about watching his face in peaceful slumber. Her hands ached to touch him, to pull the sheet all the way down and look at the full length of his beautiful masculine body. She longed to brush his hair back, to kiss his shoulder, to slide in next to him and lay her naked body alongside his. While she stood watching him sleep, Aesir's brow creased, and he whispered in his sleep. Mercy Rose could not make out the words but it sounded as if he were casting a spell.

Suddenly, she was whisked away by a misty tide and was standing outside in the cold hoarfrost, next to a large lake with huge gusts of mist. A large white swan was leisurely gliding through the center of the lake, and the rising sun was making the mist glow gold and pink, as it rose in thick swirling wisps off the water. Behind her, she heard Aesir call out to them both, Mercy Rose and the swan, then in a smooth, graceful motion the white swan spread her wings, lifted into the air, and flew. As she landed atop the high balcony, she shimmered and transformed into Aesir's twin, Swan Glory. They turned and walked away together leaving Mercy Rose alone, frozen, a crystalline statue by the lake.

#

Aesir Blacknight woke from a dream of Swan gliding gracefully across a lake brightened by the morning sun. He suddenly felt as if he were not alone and rolled over onto his back, hoping to see Mercy Rose standing at his bedside. He could have sworn he felt her presence there. Aesir's hands clenched, and a thrill shot through his body as he thought of holding her, but he was alone with only the crackling fire.

The long flickering flames cast the room in a golden glow, and where the light did not touch, it was deep black. His disappointment was great, and his heart yearned for her but for the thousandth time he remembered Mercy Rose had *"other obligations"* back in Jior. Aesir knew it would be wrong of him to force their relationship any further because of his obligations and because of *secrets* he had yet to reveal. Though his heart yearned toward her and his body longed for hers. In his dream of Mercy Rose, she had been draped only in her long white hair, standing at his bedside watching him. Instead of trying to go back to sleep, he rose, pulled a deep blue sheet from the bed, and wrapped it around his naked hips. He walked over to the fireplace and threw another log on. Before he could consciously arrange his thoughts or decide what to do, he was melting into the floor, passing through stone and ice then rising from the floor beside Mercy Rose's bed.

She was asleep laying on her stomach, her arms wrapped around a pillow and her brow was wrinkled in distress. She mumbled and began to breathe hard, caught in a nightmare. How badly he wanted to go to her, wake her from the bad dream and ease her distress, caress the fear from her brow but she was naked, as was he, and he knew he would not be able to stop himself if they were to lie skin-to-skin. When she whispered his name with a gasp, he could no longer hold back from going to her. He lowered down beside her and gathered her into his arms and held her close. Her naked breasts pressed against his bare chest, and it was almost his undoing as she held him tightly, her arms going around him.

Mercy Rose was so beautiful. His fingers wandered of their own accord as she fell into a more peaceful sleep. Gently, careful not to wake her, he smoothed his hand over her shoulder, down her arm, and down over the slope of her bare hip. It was hard not to awaken her, roll on top of her and impale her. To feel her pearl-white skin against his, to pull her long, firm leg up over his hip and thrust, and thrust. He thought he would lose his mind if he did not have her. His heart and his body raged, and the wolf inside howled with unsatisfied lust.

His touch lingered on her hip and slowly caressed the smooth skin there. Her leg moved up over his, and they lay entwined like lovers. Mercy Rose slowly opened her eyes, tilted her head back, and looked up at him. Her hand, which had been lying across his chest, moved slowly, her palm flattened against him and inched downwards exploring his warm skin. When she touched the sheet wrapped around his waist, she frowned a little, confused.

Moistening her lips, she whispered, "Are you here, or are you a dream?"

"Which would you prefer, my Rose?" Aesir's voice was a husky whisper, but his heartbeat was like a loud drum in his chest. As her fingers traveled over his lean stomach, he quivered with desire, with need.

"A dream. Because then I could make love with you with no fear of reprisal or obligation, no permanent consequence, no heartbreak."

"You fear I will break your heart?"

"You already have." Mercy Rose reached up and touched his cheek and stared into his ice-blue eyes.

"And you are faultless?" He growled just a little angry. "You and your, '*obligations back in Jior*'?"

Not responding to his anger or insinuations, she deflected the subject.

"Swan Glory told me, I was your love, that you loved me?"

He evaded her question. Took a deep breath to calm his rage and his desire.

"Mercy Rose, this is not a dream. I am here."

Bathed in the firelight, Aesir looked at her for a very long time not daring to move, and she was tense beside him, her face tilted up toward his. It would be so easy to kiss her and stop all the deflecting and evading. It would be so easy just to say the words so that they could move on to what he really wanted to be doing, but her violet eyes would not be denied. His chest was tight with need. His whole body was hard and desperate for her. Knowing that as soon as he said the words, he could have her, he still hesitated.

For him, he knew he was not free to lay with her just so that he could quench the raging hunger to join with her body. Something deep inside him knew that just once would never be enough. The lustful wolf inside him gnashed its teeth and howled! He wanted to kiss her, to stop her questions but to take Mercy Rose, the Granddaughter of the King of Jior, a leader of the Ny-Failen, to join his body with one of them would be to bind himself to her *forever*. That is what his Rose seemed to want, but his uncertainty made him hesitate.

At his silence, she slowly released from his embrace and sat up turning her back to him, her white hair cascaded over one shoulder. The tantalizing slope of her smooth back and the pearly glow of her skin called him.

"Dreaming or awake, I must go on without you. My home is in Jior with my mother and father, my family and…"

"And Trail Blazer?" Aesir sat up next to her; jealousy turned into a raging demon within him slashing with claw and talon, tearing at his restraint. He closed his eyes and took a deep breath, calming both the howling wolf of his lust and the raging demon of jealousy inside him, and took control. Going on with a more patient but strained voice, "If I say the words you long to hear if I make love to you, my Rose then there will be no going back to Jior as you are, no keeping obligations. Is that what you want? The gift of your body once given cannot be taken back."

Mercy Rose did not rise to his jealousy, and she did not deny his insinuations. Aesir knew she wanted him to admit that he loved her. She wanted the words to weave a spell, to make the bond that would seal the future with him. There were too many questions that needed to be answered and, more importantly, she had not said the words to him.

She turned toward him. Her nakedness was revealed to him. "It will be like living in the Hells if I am not with you. One night will not be enough." Her eyes glistened with tears, "I have lost my heart to you Aesir Blacknight, and I am afraid to risk everything for one night. I want it all! I love you!"

A log in the fireplace crackled loudly, snapped and a shower of sparks flew up the chimney, breaking the silence where her last words echoed. Her glittering eyes were like dark amethysts, and she was trembling. Aesir slid his arm around her waist and pulled her closer. Her soft breasts pressed against his chest and fired his blood anew.

"Love *is* risk. It is risking everything body, mind, heart, and soul. Saying the words weaves an enchantment between two hearts and the joining of their bodies completes the spell. Once cast, you cannot undo what has been said and done. You have ensorcelled me, and I cannot deny that I do love you, my Mercy, my Rose, my Love."

He slowly pressed her back and kissed her deeply then he looked at her again and whispered, "I love you." He kissed her again, stopped, looked into her eyes, and whispered, "I love you," over and over with each carefully placed kiss.

Mercy Rose's heart was taxed to the breaking point with the joy she was feeling. Aesir loved her and was telling her over and over again as he placed kisses on her lips, her eyes, her cheeks. His kisses traveled down as his hand went from cupping her face, lingered on her breast, and then slid downward. As Mercy Rose's feelings soared, she let go of all her fears and doubts and concentrated on Aesir's fingers tracing a path down her flat stomach. She gasped as he finally cupped her most intimate place and rubbed the moisture there. His lips breathed flames in her heart, and his hand fanned the blaze, catching her body on fire.

Another gasp escaped her lips as his kisses traveled down her neck and then he was kissing her breasts causing shocks of pleasure to shoot through her body. Her own hands were moving down his sides and pulling the sheet from around his waist. Suddenly, she stopped him and pushed him back just enough so that she could look at him in his full glory. The lean muscles of him and his firm skin beckoned. She pushed him back further until he lay completely flat on his back and then she looked her fill.

Perfection! He was long, lean, and muscular. His fair skin was almost hairless but for silky dark curls between his legs. Aesir's body was so beautiful she wanted to weep, but instead, she reached out and touched his hardness. She caressed him while he let out a long, relieved breath, dropped his head back, and closed his eyes, relaxing with her presence but tense with her touch.

Smoothing her hand over his length, she felt astonished at her first touch of his maleness, and he let her explore. His control began to slip and rising, it was his turn to push her back. He paid homage to her breasts with his lips and then the moment had come. Moving over her, he settled between her slim legs. His warm length rubbed her moist valley as he kissed her.

Mercy Rose's heart beat so fast she thought she would faint. Aesir's beautiful body was atop hers, and his weight on her was so delicious that she wanted to laugh with surprise at this new feeling. Her hands smoothed over his back and grasped his firm buttocks as she spread her legs and positioned him between.

Aesir was kissing her, pulling gently on her lips, and tasting her. Suddenly, he was guiding himself into her, pushed just so far as to wet the tip with her moisture. He pushed a little further and then he warned.

"I can be denied no longer, my Rose!" and he plunged!

Pressing her head back into the mattress, Mercy Rose stifled a cry, biting her lip while the tearing pain shot through her womb. Aesir threw his head back and bit his lip as he pulled out and then thrust more deeply inside her. Then he was moving and what glorious movement it was. He started slow, kissing her and undulating inside her at the same time. They had become one, *finally*!

"By the Heavens, you're tight!" Aesir growled as he thrust. He kissed her and kissed her while his hard shaft slid in and out of her receiving body.

Mercy Rose felt delicious pleasure as Aesir Blacknight finally made love to her. More importantly, her heart sang because he loved her. Her hands traveled over his firm muscles and then as the pressure built inside her, she pressed his lower back, took him deeper, and suddenly her valley was throbbing and squeezing him where they were joined. Mercy Rose had never felt anything so wonderful as her pleasure climbed, she reached the pinnacle and fell over the edge into bliss.

Aesir Blacknight slowed so that he could feel her reach the heights of her pleasure. He closed his eyes, and the pulsing, throbbing surrounded him. As Mercy Rose caught her breath and squeezed, Aesir gave a knowing, crooked smile. Rising on one arm, he pulled her leg higher over his hip.

"Again!" He commanded, and then he surged hard. Inside his head, the wolf begging for satiation, howled in triumph as Aesir thrust hard again. Mercy Rose gasped in surprise as his hips crashed into hers, then harder still and she completely shattered once more. The first time was wonderful, but the second time her inner walls squeezed harder, pulsing stronger. As she started to cry out, Aesir's mouth came down on hers, and he covered her cries with his kisses. His tongue danced with hers as her inner valley pulsed and held him.

Aesir was almost driven mad with hunger for more of her. He rolled over until she was on top of him and showed her how to ride him. He was between her strong legs and inside her. She rode hard as he caressed her breasts, ran his hands over her sides, and then firmly grasped her hips and thrust up. Mercy Rose moaned as he moved, his thumb finding her most sensitive spot and rubbed. She exploded once again.

Falling forward she slumped onto Aesir's chest and he chuckled deeply as he hugged her tightly and kissed her temple. He could not get enough of her, and his mind whirled over the many ways he wanted to take her, to plunge and thrust until his heart burst but this was the first time for her, and he knew he had to calm the lustful wolf howling loudly inside him. Rolling her onto her back once again, he slowed his thrusts and increased his kisses. She gasped with need and demanded, *"More!"*

Mercy Rose's skin glistened with sweat, and the sweet smell of her passion took Aesir to a level of pleasure where he had never been before. His hips began to move again and then moved faster until he could hold off no longer and he finally released. Pumping his seed into her womb every muscle in his body flexed as he emptied his shaft and filled his heart!

Aesir Blacknight did not want to let go. Even though his body was satisfied his heart was not and he wanted her again and again. As he withdrew from Mercy Rose's body, she winced.

"Now I understand why it is called making love." Mercy Rose sighed and fell to sleep. Aesir hugged her to his chest and let out a long slow breath. His heart slowed and he wallowed momentarily in the peaceful pleasure of being with her, *his Love*. He memorized the rise and fall of her breathing and the silky softness of her white hair, her scent, *their* scent. He slowly closed his eyes and slept.

CHAPTER THIRTEEN

Swan Glory was awake. After what seemed like eons, she was released from the crystal cage Aesir had been forced to put her in. While she understood that it had been necessary to save her life, it had been hard just the same. Time flowed differently while she was in her crystal swan form, and now she felt frozen inside and could not seem to thaw. The Queen of Jior had warmed her with her healing power, and she was free, free of the crystal cage, free of the sickness from the iron, and free to go on with her life, but a part of her still felt caged.

She wanted to shapeshift into her swan form and fly, but she was weak and afraid. The memory of being shot with an iron arrow as a swan and later being turned into a statue was stopping her, but it was hard to resist that part of her nature at the same time. She was very conflicted.

The door to her room was slowly opening, and Captain Joziah entered. He precariously carried a tray with a steaming cup and a bowl of broth. Setting down the tray on the small table next to her bed, he pulled a chair closer and smiled at her while arranging her pillows and blankets, then the dishes and folding a napkin over her lap.

Captain Joziah Caulder was a nice surprise that she found upon waking from being a statue for so long. His gallantry and care for her when she was sick, touched her heart. He had swept her up and carried her to this room when Aesir had been too weak, and he had helped take care of her ever since. Well, he was taking turns with the others in truth but the handsome Captain was frequently nearby or standing guard just outside the room.

As he sat down, Swan Glory noticed he had dimples on his cheeks when he smiled at her. An errant blonde curl fell over his forehead. She motioned for him to move closer and she reached forward and brushed the curl out of his eyes. Her light touch lingered on his temple. Captain Joziah blushed a little and cast his blue-eyed gaze down as if he was not sure what to do. He would rather face a violent battle than embarrass himself in front of a Lady. Swan Glory gave a whispery laugh, and he looked up at her.

"You laugh at me, my Lady?"

"No, brave Captain Joziah, I laugh because you make me happy. You are so gallant, unpretentious, and kind. Completely unafraid of me though you know what I am." Her face fell as she said those last words.

The Captain sat straight in his chair like a good soldier and looked at her lovely smile, her sleek blue-black hair falling over her shoulders, and her long graceful neck. He had little experience with courtly manners or talking to ladies, despite being Captain of the Queen's guard, and despite his popularity with women. Still, flirting with this beautiful creature was beyond his skill.

"You kissed my hand as I slept." She teased.

The Captain turned red again, but before he could affirm or deny his actions, she laughed again and reached out her hand to him.

Captain Joziah reverently took her offered hand and after hesitating for a moment kissed the back of her fingers. His lips lingered there longer than was appropriate and he closed his eyes in bliss before looking up at her. Swan Glory gave him a winning smile, turned her hand, and held his. He placed his other hand over hers and stared at her with obvious infatuation. After a few moments, he remembered himself, cleared his throat nervously, released his hold on her hand, and turned toward the bedside table. He gave the cup of tea to her, and she sipped it gracefully. A small drop of tea hovered on her bottom lip which she licked off with the tip of her pink tongue. Captain Joziah was deeply engrossed in watching her, and his mouth fell open.

Swan Glory drank her tea but had no appetite. No matter how Captain Joziah tried, he could barely get her to eat a single morsel.

"My Lady, you must eat and regain your strength."

"Is that an order Captain?" She smiled weakly.

"If it will get you to eat then, yes, I order it."

"Do you know what I wish?" Swan's eyes were so heavy she could barely keep them open, and she shivered as if she were cold.

Captain Joziah leaned over her, took her teacup away, and pulled the blankets higher over her shoulders while he answered. "Anything you wish, my Lady, I will do."

"I wish you would kiss my lips, not just my hand." Her eyes were closed, and she smiled sleepily.

Captain Joziah was shocked by her wish, but he had said he would make her wish come true. He would like to have leaned over and placed a gentle kiss on her lips, but she had fallen asleep. The Captain refrained from kissing her because that would not be the right thing to do. He wanted to wait until she was fully awake before he allowed himself that pleasure. He finished tucking in blankets around her and sat next to her while she slept.

Later that morning Queen Lily came in, and after giving an account that Lady Swan Glory had woken briefly and had some tea, the Captain left to see to other duties. Prince Vannier came in, and they quietly discussed the best timing to return home. The spring season was fully upon them, and as the weather warmed, the snow would begin to melt. Streams would widen with rushing water, and the land on the way back to Jior become too muddy and treacherous to pass in some areas, as rocks loosened on the towering cliffs. Vannier had some concerns that the way home would become increasingly more dangerous and pushed for leaving as soon as possible, as it was the best course of action.

"My Lady?" The sound of their voices woke Swan Glory, and in her quiet voice she called out to the Queen.

Queen Lily moved over to her bedside. "How are you feeling today Swan Glory?"

"I am better, thanks to you."

"That is wonderful!" The Queen beamed. "I think you need to gain strength, but you should be completely well very soon."

"I've been sick for so long that I don't know how to be well, I think." Swan Glory smiled. "Seven years as a statue is a very long time." Then Swan Glory closed her eyes and fell back to sleep, her energy spent.

"Seven years!" Queen Lily gaped at the sleeping girl wondering what she meant. She looked at Vannier who had heard the girl's proclamation also.

"I think we need to have a frank discussion with Aesir Blacknight," Vannier declared quietly.

An hour later Mercy Rose returned to Swan's room, and Lily and Vannier left to seek out Aesir Blacknight.

They found him in a study filled with books and scrolls. He was so deep in thought that he did not hear them come into the room until Vannier spoke his name. He turned and stood, placed his hand over his heart, and bowed to the Queen.

"My Queen, how is my sister today? I visited her earlier and know she woke briefly but now sleeps. How much longer do you think it will be until she is completely well again?"

"Aesir Blacknight," Angry, Vannier interrupted ignoring his questions, "You have some explaining to do. This time we want *all* of the truth and no more lies!"

"What my over-protective son is trying to say is that Swan Glory mentioned she had been a statue for *seven* years. We would like to know, is this true and how this can be? Because we were under the impression *you* cast the spell turning her into a statue, but for seven years!"

Aesir Blacknight slumped just a little and gestured to a fireplace where a warm fire burned and comfortable chairs were set.

"My Queen, Prince Vannier, please make yourselves comfortable, and I will explain everything." The Queen sat down, but Vannier was too tense and stood by her chair instead. Aesir Blacknight sat in the chair across from her. His eyes pleaded for understanding.

"My sister and I," he started slowly, looking the Queen directly in the eye, "grew up in a small castle on the outskirts of Skoria. As I am sure, you can understand it is dangerous for Swan Glory to be around humans and so we stayed far from the haunts of men. Our parents died when we were young, and we only had servants to take care of us, but they were always a little afraid of Swan Glory and her shapeshifting abilities. Preoccupied with my own *gratification*, I left to pursue my studies as a Blue Sorcerer when I was a young man and didn't see it. I have always had a gift of sorts, manipulating the elements as I have already divulged." He paused momentarily to look meaningfully at Vannier.

"While I was gone, a hunter shot Swan Glory when she was flying in swan form. I was sent for immediately, but by the time I reached her, she was very ill. The hunter's iron arrow had done its worst to her. I should tell you I found that hunter who shot her. I killed him. Then I bound Imda, a Ny-

Komnir to watch the castle so that I could hunt for a cure and until Swan could fly again." A burning look of rage hardened Aesir Blacknight's features, but he went on. "I struggled with my limited knowledge of healing to try and cure her. I have no power over iron; it is the one element I cannot bend to my will. Fever took Swan Glory and her blood was poisoned; she grew worse and worse, so close to death." Aesir Blacknight stopped to collect himself again before continuing. "I spent most of a year trying to help her. In the end, all I could do was watch her become more frail, poisoned by the iron. It looked hopeless. Because of my love for my twin and our bond, the thought of losing her was completely unbearable. I brought her here hoping the cold would help the fever, hoping the power I could take from the dormant volcano would somehow help heal her, but it was never enough. So, I did the only thing I could think of; I turned her into a statue to stop the progression of the fever and poison, and gain time to find a cure! I had servants here in the beginning, but they eventually left us and spread the tale of a swan made of diamonds. The outlaws we ran into a few days ago, have been searching for my castle to steal her in her crystal form. I raged for days and covered the entire mountain range in hoarfrost, ice, and heavy snow so that she would be safe from men. With Imda to watch over her, I left to search for a way to bring her back to me."

He gestured at his study filled with scrolls and books. "I searched through these books and scrolls and many other places for seven years to find a cure to make her well again, but I could find nothing. I was devastated. Then, I heard of a Ny-Failen Queen in Jior who had healing powers and could work miracles. I thought it was a fictional account of King Forlorn Icefall and how he had rescued you from a Black Sorcerer's tower and I had heard about the Great Jiorian War. In my desperation, I hoped your goodness and compassion would extend to helping us, and here we are. After seven long years of seeking a cure for my sister, you have come and saved us both. She is still not completely healed. The last barrier to a full recovery is that she *must* change into her swan form, it is imperative!"

Aesir Blacknight fell silent as Queen Lily and Vannier tried to understand everything he was telling them. The fear and desperation in Aesir's voice touched their hearts, and Lily was glad that Swan Glory and Aesir Blacknight's ordeal was over.

"Aesir Blacknight," the Queen began, "Why didn't you share this information with us from the beginning? I am happy with the outcome, but it might have helped, had we known all."

"I felt your distrust of me in Jior and had to ready myself for another disappointment. As I told you before, I would have said or done anything or let you believe anything to get you here to help Swan Glory. I thought if you saw us, you would instantly think us Ny-Komnir and you wouldn't help. When Mercy Rose used her power to read me in Jior, I thought she would divulge everything and imagine my surprise when she did not."

"Speaking of Mercy Rose," Vannier cut in controlling his frustration. "What of her? Obviously, you two have formed an attachment. When I confronted you a few days ago, you did not profess love for her, in fact, you left me believing otherwise. Though Mercy Rose has not come right out and said that she loves you, I fear she does, and I fear you will break her heart. I am charged by her father with protecting her."

Aesir Blacknight rose to his feet, delaying his answer. The fire in the fireplace flamed blue, and Aesir narrowed his eyes at Vannier. "What would you have me do? I am partly Ny-Komnir and she Ny-Failen! You confront me at the precipice of my sister's fate and ask me to explain my feelings for one so far out of my reach! Have I not suffered and bent my knee enough to the Ny-Failen?" He knew he should not have made love to her the night before, but it had been impossible to resist. Now, he had no idea what to do.

"Peace!" Queen Lily rose to her feet between the two and stood between their glares. "Be at peace Aesir Blacknight and let me tell you *my* story. Sit down! *Both* of you!" Aesir Blacknight and Vannier finally sat down.

"Am I to understand that you feared prejudice from the Ny-Failen of Jior?" The Queen asked as she also sat back down.

Aesir Blacknight would not look at her only stared angrily into the flickering blue flames of his fire.

"My greatest love, my husband Lorn is part Ny-Komnir, from his father's side."

Aesir's eyes flew to the Queen's face in astonishment. Vannier sat rigid in his chair. He was unreadable with this announcement, but he had clearly known.

"Aesir Blacknight, Ny-Komnir *are* Ny-Failen who have descended away from the Creator. They left of their own accord and evolved into a species apart from Ny-Failen turning their backs completely on the Creator. Yes, most became evil and fell beyond redemption but at the beginning of time, Ny-Failen and Ny-Komnir were one and the same. The difference Mercy Rose sensed and the difference I felt when I healed you from your arrow wound, and your sister from her sickness, derives a little from that evolution. It is a bit more complicated than that true, but it is also by degrees of *choice and distance* that your ancestors willingly descended from the Creator. It is embracing evil that makes them the creatures they are. That is not to say that you are of their kind because you are their descendant. It is a matter of your choice. When I withdrew your energy to help me heal

Swan Glory, I felt as if I went back in time taking energy from my husband when I gave birth to Vannier." She leaned forward and placed her hand over Aesir's. "All of this is to say, do not be so quick to find prejudice where none exists. We are different in Jior."

"What of Mercy Rose?" Aesir Blacknight asked, the suspicion in his voice palpable.

"She is a grown woman. She can make her own choices. Despite your parentage, if she loves you and you love her, we would welcome you with open arms." The Queen sat back again and looked expectantly at him.

"My Mother was Ny-Komnir! Now you know, would you still welcome me? If I were to marry Mercy Rose and keep her from Jior, from her father and mother, from her family?" He looked pointedly at Vannier and spat, "From her *obligations in Jior*, what then? Would you still welcome me? You know after everything that has happened to Swan Glory, I cannot allow her around humans or ever leave her again. We will have to live here in exile, hiding from the covetous eyes of men so that she will be safe and never suffer iron and the arrow again."

"Do you love Mercy Rose?" Everyone was surprised when Vannier pointedly asked the question.

Aesir Blacknight took a long moment to glare at Vannier and his question, but he turned his eyes to Queen Lily and softened his gaze before he spoke. His anguish rippled across his face and his distress could be heard in his words.

"My Queen, Mercy Rose is like a rare flower blooming in the purest snow. She is delicacy and grace and possesses compassion to rival your own. She is fiercely loyal to her family, her Ny-Failen morals, and ideals. She has helped me through the last part of this journey more than I can describe. To simply say I love her is not enough. Don't you see? I am torn in two. I cannot leave Swan Glory, and I cannot take her to Jior and risk her life further which means, I cannot have Mercy Rose because I will not exile her from the family that she loves so dearly for my own selfish needs and this simple emotion called *love*."

"Did you not tell me love *is risk?*" Mercy Rose's voice called out from the doorway. Everyone turned and looked at her, wondering how long she had been standing there and how much she had heard? As she walked toward them, she continued, her voice indignant and her eyes blazing signifying she had heard everything.

"You said love is risking everything mind, body, heart, and soul. Yet you claim love is simple? Love does not sound simple to me, and you make decisions for me before even asking what I want, what I can or cannot do? Or what Swan Glory wants, and can or cannot do? You have decided to keep her from the company of others under the guise of protecting her, but really you are sentencing her, and yourself, to lives of complete loneliness! You claim it is out of love, but it is really out of fear! And in doing so, you not only deny yourself love but deny Swan Glory the chance to find love! And you deny *me*, my love."

Walking forward, Mercy Rose stopped in front of them all, but it was Aesir Blacknight she was staring at as if only the two of them were in the room. Queen Lily and Vannier looked stunned at Mercy Rose's outburst, and the look on their faces revealed shock that Mercy Rose and Aesir Blacknight had had a deep discussion about love.

"My Lady," Aesir Blacknight stood and took her hand. He stared into her eyes and implored her with his gaze to trust him. "Mercy Rose, I understand what you are saying, and yes, I have made hard choices for Swan Glory, but I have done what is best to protect us both. Now, I implore you to trust me for a little while longer. Will you trust me until my sister is on her feet again and can shift into her swan form? Will you do that?"

Vannier shifted uncomfortably in his chair. "Aesir Blacknight you should know if Mother remains away from Jior for too long, Father will come searching for her, and he will bring the entire Jiorian army. He was against her coming in the first place. He will also bring Jagged Edge, Mercy Rose's father."

Aesir Blacknight's brow drew furrowed with either anger or worry, it was hard to tell which and he looked out of ice-blue eyes that glinted with a feverish desire. A note of desperation entered his voice as he pleaded with the Queen.

"My Queen, when do you think my sister will be well enough to shift into her swan form? So much is dependent upon that one last triumph over this sickness. Then we will all be free to make our own decisions." Aesir Blacknight turned and looked directly at Mercy Rose when he spoke those last words.

"She has just awoken for the first time today and looks much better." Mercy Rose answered before her grandmother could, "Perhaps a day or two more?" Turning toward Lily she implored with her eyes.

"Yes, I believe that should be enough time." Lily rose to her feet and eyed Mercy Rose carefully before she went on, expressing a note of sadness, "Swan Glory is on the mend, but even if she cannot change into swan form in two days, we must be going."

"She is asking for you." Mercy Rose turned back to Aesir Blacknight who suddenly looked much relieved, excused himself with a bow, and raced out the door leaving Mercy Rose behind.

#

Swan Glory was much improved by late afternoon. Aesir Blacknight, with a firm command, released Captain Joziah to his other duties. Captain Joziah placed his hand over his heart and bowed to Swan Glory, holding her gaze with his dark blue eyes for a moment, before leaving the room to return to his duties. Queen Lily arrived, spent some time with her patient, and was greatly pleased with her improvement. Everyone visited Swan Glory, and there was great joy in the castle that she appeared so much better. It looked like the possibility that she could shift into her swan form would soon be a definite reality. An air of anticipation was in the air and Queen Lily and Vannier were anxious to bring this trip to a conclusion.

Aesir Blacknight spent the entire evening with Swan Glory encouraging her to eat. Mercy Rose felt as if she were an intruder, so she took herself back to her room and spent the evening deciding on what she should do. Aesir Blacknight had not asked her to say at Hoarfrost Castle with him, though he had vehemently professed his love for her. She had heard him say he could not keep her with him because taking her away from her family would prove too hurtful to her. That took the choice from Mercy Rose's hands. Now, as she thought the matter through, she wondered; what grown woman did not leave her mother and family when marrying a man dictated it? It was another right of passage as a woman she should experience. Eventually, she would have to take that important step in every girl's life. Where was her heart in all this and just what was she capable of?

Reliving the previous night with Aesir Blacknight and remembering the perfection of his male body, Mercy Rose suddenly realized that though Swan Glory had his attention during the day, he would always return to *her* at night. It was a different kind of love between them. Was that enough? She had to admit to herself that she felt a little left out. Aesir Blacknight and Swan Glory had a closeness that he and

Mercy Rose had yet to achieve. She had to decide if she was willing to be an outsider? Possibly, for the rest of her life.

The hour grew late, and Mercy Rose had fallen asleep with her worries. It was hard to decipher her feelings and if she fell asleep waiting for Aesir or if she went to sleep and not bothering to wait for him.

The tension in Aesir's body was almost to the point of being painful, and his biggest desire was to relieve his pain within Mercy Rose's embrace. Somehow, she always took away the agony that he had lived with for the past seven years. Here, on the brink of completely being rid of that pain, Aesir realized that he was losing his ability to endure. He sought out Mercy Rose more and more.

Reaching out with one finger he lightly brushed a lock of hair away from her face. Mercy Rose was a beautiful white flower buried in the cobalt sheets and furs of her bed. Aesir shuddered with desire for her, and the wolf inside began to growl with growing hunger, but he tamped down on his lust and got lost in watching her sleep. He had been thinking about how life would be without her, and he thought about how life would be with her if they were to marry. During his conversation with the Queen and Prince Vannier earlier that day, he had not divulged his desire to make this beautiful creature his wife, but he realized, perhaps too late, it was one of the desires he must bury for now, perhaps forever. The other, the demon of jealousy, roared inside him and screamed for complete possession of her, or she would surely belong to Trail Blazer. There was a war waging inside him between the wolf, the demon and the man that he was, and the man he wanted to be. Then there was that secret part of him, that hidden *other* that had lain dormant for seven long years and now strained to be free. Everything depended upon Swan Glory.

Aesir Blacknight realized he would get no answers to any of his dilemmas until his secret self was freed. He could, however, love Mercy Rose while she was here and part of his life now before she found out the truth about him and left him. He decided he loved her too much to use her for his physical gratification and stood to go.

Turning away, Aesir was suddenly brought to a halt as he heard her whisper his name. Turning back, he looked into the glittering amethyst eyes of Mercy Rose, who held her hand out and beckoned to him. He went.

CHAPTER FOURTEEN

It was to be their last day at Hoarfrost Castle as the plan was to leave the next morning. Prince Vannier was anxious to head for home. He did not like being away from his family, and he wanted to know what happened at the Eastern Barracks. Queen Lily had spoken with Aesir Blacknight and his sister Swan Glory and determined she was fully healed but still had to regain much of her strength. Today was the day Swan Glory would try and shift into her swan form and complete the final stage of her recovery.

Aesir Blacknight had asked them all to wait in the large dome room. Queen Lily, Mercy Rose, and an impatient Vannier waited. Captain Joziah had also joined them and his usually calm demeanor bordered on the edge of nervousness. He was pacing but suddenly stopped and stood straighter while looking toward the far doorway.

Finally, the twins appeared. Aesir Blacknight entered with Swan Glory leaning on his arm. Dressed in a flowing white gown, she looked bright next to her twin brother dressed in a loose shirt of dark cobalt. The noonday sun had passed by outside and cast dancing prisms of color through the diamond and sapphire dome above them.

As they approached, Aesir Blacknight addressed them in his strong voice.

"My Queen, Prince Vannier, and my Lady, Mercy Rose," he began formally as he approached. "Today is the day my sister and I have waited for seven long years to arrive. At long last, the wound is healed and the sickness has been vanquished!" Aesir's handsome face was glowing with hopeful anticipation, and Swan Glory smiled shyly beside him. He turned to her, "This is the last test Sister, you must shift into your swan form. *Free us!*"

Vannier looked at his mother with sudden trepidation and saw her brow furrowed too. What was the meaning behind Aesir Blacknight's words? Mercy Rose was completely unreadable as her expressionless face was turned toward Aesir Blacknight and Swan Glory, watching and waiting. Captain Joziah stepped further into the room and stood close behind the Queen as if he were guarding her.

Swan Glory released her brother's arm and stepped forward tentatively. Her bare feet stepped silently on the cold floor. She seemed nervous about shifting in front of so many people and looked back at her brother for assurance. Though they were twins, Aesir Blacknight was a head taller than his sister, and he almost looked menacing looming dark and intense behind her. His eyes held a feverish gleam, and he clenched his fists in anticipation.

Swan Glory continued to hesitate. Her long hair was unbound and flowed long behind her. Her arms were hugging her chest as if she were cold. She looked past the Queen at Captain Joziah and then looked away and continued to hesitate.

"Swan?" Aesir's voice cracked with strain, "Why do you not shift? This is part of your nature, who you are! I can wait no longer!"

Swan Glory was staring again at Captain Joziah who frowned serious and disturbed. Aesir Blacknight stepped nearer, and his eyes followed where she was looking. "Is it him?" Aesir raised his voice in a snarl and pointed toward the doorway, "Captain Joziah you must leave, *now!*"

To the rest of the people in the room, it looked as if Swan Glory was afraid and did not want to shift for some reason. The Queen took a step toward her as if she was going to intervene, but then Swan Glory spoke out, "No Aesir! I, I will do it."

Taking a deep breath, she readied herself. Raising her face to look at the dome above them, she gracefully reached up with her arms. Closing her eyes, she swayed a little, and her form began to change. Before the eyes of everyone watching, the beautiful maiden shimmered and wavered. Her arms grew feathers and turned into wings, then the rest of her body shortened and shapeshifted into a large beautiful white swan. She let out a trumpeting cry that sounded vaguely human, flapped her huge white wings, and leaped into the air flying up to the high ceiling and circling above them. All eyes were facing upwards watching the white swan finally fly. All except for Mercy Rose who had never stopped watching Aesir Blacknight. Suddenly, she cried out as Aesir clenched his teeth, bent over, and began to tremble violently.

"Aesir!" She shouted and started to move toward him.

Aesir Blacknight was not watching his sister fly either. His face had transformed into a mask of pain and his face tilted downward as he clenched his teeth and fisted his hands on a cry of pain. Then he gave a mighty shrug, his shirt tore away and two massive, feathered wings spread out behind him as he shapeshifted. His cry of pain turned into a shout of joy, relief, and triumph!

Aesir Blacknight was winged! Black feathered wings glistened in the bright light of the room. His arms and wings spread out to their full span and gave a mighty flap. Finally, he was free! When the rapture of freedom finally passed, Aesir Blacknight looked at Mercy Rose and then briefly at the Queen and Vannier. Wordlessly, he leaped into the air and flew up to the huge dome, and circled with the white swan.

The white swan and black-winged Aesir Blacknight circled the huge dome together. Swan gave a trumpet of joy and Aesir had the look of pure ecstasy as they flew in unison, wings flapping together in rhythm. Their feathers reflected the blue and crystal light from the dome. To those watching below, it was a rare thing of beauty to see the two flying together and was not a sight any of them would soon forget.

After what seemed like only a few minutes of flight, Aesir Blacknight and Swan Glory landed. Swan shimmered and wavered, elongating into her human form again, but Aesir Blacknight arched back and stretched his arms and wings wide and rejoiced in the freedom he now had. He gave a mighty flap of his beautiful black wings. The spell was *finally*, completely, vanquished and the rapturous look on Aesir's face spoke of his relief from being wingless for so long.

Vannier stepped forward eyeing Aesir Blacknight's *black* wings.

"You said you were wingless!" Vannier practically snarled.

"I was!" Aesir spat angrily. "For seven long years, I have been denied! I told you my sister and I had a special bond, and now you know the full of it. When I cast the spell turning her into a statue, it was to save my twin from dying, but it had a side effect on me. She could not fly but neither could I. My wings were gone, imprisoned as she was and now you know why I was so anxious to get her well and to shape-change. I thought once I broke the enchantment on her I would get my wings back, but it did not happen. That is when I realized the spell had not been completely vanquished. Now, we are *both* completely free."

"But the ne'amh chomhara! *Heaven's Mark*! It is not there!" Mercy Rose exclaimed loudly. Everyone turned to look at her, and her grandmother gave her a look that questioned how Mercy Rose knew that.

Not waiting for Aesir Blacknight's answer, Vannier approached his mother. "Come Mother, let us prepare to leave at first light. We are finished here." He took her arm, and they turned away. After a long searching look at Swan Glory, Captain Joziah also turned away and followed the Queen out of the room, as was his duty.

CHAPTER FIFTEEN

Swan Glory was exhausted and returned to her room alone. Aesir Blacknight disappeared after his great revelation in the dome room. That evening Vannier did not leave his mother's side, and Captain Joziah returned to his men. There were many preparations to make, and the soldiers had to be ready to leave at first light the next morning.

Mercy Rose returned to her room. She did not know why but she felt like crying. A great sadness had overtaken her when she saw Aesir Blacknight had black wings and he looked more like a Ny-Komnir, more like demon-kind than anyone she had ever seen before. More importantly, he was even more of a mystery, more distant from her, now more than ever. The thought that she had given her body and her heart to him and yet she still knew so little about him, terrified her in a way that she could not explain. After everything they shared, he had not told her this greatest secret. There was a great deal of unbiased acceptance that her family would have to offer Aesir Blacknight for him to be fully part of their family. Not asking her to be his wife, suddenly made sense, but would he ever? The answers were not simple, and now, not exactly a mystery, as to why he was not asking her to stay with him.

Taking a deep breath, she analyzed her feelings. When she read him in the Great Hall back in Jior that fateful day, she had not seen this. She realized now she had seen the wounded Swan Glory and her healing was Aesir's future, she had assumed. With her power, she had seen their direct Ny-Komnir bloodlines from their mother, and now she realized she had ignored that because she was so fascinated by him and, yes, in love with him.

How did she feel now? What difference did it make that his wings were black and that he was the son of a Ny-Komnir? That he was a Blue Sorcerer with unimaginable power? Would he choose to follow the Creator? Would he choose to be Ny-Failen? Or descend? He lied to her or withheld the truth at the very least, but still, he could love. He loved Swan Glory, and he claimed to love Mercy Rose but was it enough? Where would their love take them? Aesir Blacknight could not leave Hoarfrost Castle but could she stay?

That was one question she had not dared to even think of asking because she was afraid of the answer. Yet the answer to that last question would determine her future. Realizing, somehow, she had let herself become the kind of woman she never wanted to be. Saying the words in her mind, they echoed, "unmarried, not even bonded" and "no longer a virgin" "unwanted." She remembered her mother's advice that she should wait until she was married and give herself to her future husband. Though she truly did not feel ruined, she wanted Aesir Blacknight more, and she was different now because of it.

The wind howled outside, and a late spring snowstorm was showering large white flakes of snow and ice over the mountains. It was very dark outside having no moon to light the jagged peaks that loomed around them out in the black night.

Mercy Rose stood by her fire and contemplated her future at Hoarfrost Castle or her future in Jior alone. She did not so much as hear his presence as much as she smelled him. That crisp, cold winter scent that always followed Aesir Blacknight invaded her thoughts. He came up behind her and reaching around offered her a single sapphire rose on an emerald-leaved stem. The rose glittered in the firelight, and Mercy Rose smiled slightly as she took it.

Aesir's hands slid around her waist, and he pulled her against him.

"Forgive me," Aesir Blacknight whispered. He placed his cool cheek next to hers and hugged her close.

Mercy Rose took a deep breath and relaxed into his embrace. As it always did when he was around, her pulse leaped, and butterflies fluttered in her stomach.

"What is there to forgive?" She asked absently thinking how complicated a creature he was. Wolf-born and the swan's wing, sorcerer and black-winged, Ny-Failen or Ny-Komnir?

"Indeed." He spoke softly as he held her. Mercy Rose wondered briefly if he was still winged or if he had shapeshifted and hidden his black wings away. She did not want to turn and find out. Right at this minute, she was frozen in his arms battling the love and desire she felt for him in her heart. If she turned, they would have to discuss the future, and she was still so unsure about her desires and needs and completely unsure about what he wanted.

Aesir Blacknight turned her in his arms and answered one of her questions. Though he was standing shirtless before her, his wings were gone, and his eyes searched her face. They finally faced each other, and it was as if they suddenly had to confront the decisions of the future, together. He glanced at her bags by the door.

"You are leaving." He pronounced with slightly angry finality.

"Grandmother and Uncle Vannier are anxious to return to Jior, to home." She could not meet his eye.

"And you are anxious to return home to Jior and to your Trail Blazer?" The jealous demon inside Aesir snarled with fury, but he remained calm on the outside.

Mercy Rose's chin tilted upwards indignant, and she drew herself up proudly to her full height. Though she only came up to his shoulder, she put every ounce of dignity into her demeanor so that she could say what needed to be said but she remained silent.

Aesir stepped closer, so close that her breasts pressed against his bare chest. She breathed in and closed her eyes memorizing the clean, fresh, winter scent of him, like snow coming on the wind. His arm went around her, and he held her close.

"You hold me too tightly, Sir." Whispering the same sentiment, she made the first time they danced together. Her voice quivered as a single tear slid down her cheek.

Aesir lowered his head and kissed her. He kissed her slowly, gently and his arms held her against him. Then they were standing next to her bed, though Mercy Rose did not recall moving over to it. The candle by the bedside painted her in its golden glow. Aesir's eyes were burning with desire as he looked at her. Then he was pulling her robe open and looking his fill. As if he had every right to, he reached forward and pushed the gown off of her shoulders. It slid to the floor as he caressed her bare breasts. She opened her mouth to protest, she really was going to, but his touch silenced her. Standing naked before him, he lowered his head again and kissed her deeply. His hands caressed her and then he was lifting and placing her on the bed. Before he joined her, he undressed and then lowered his body on top of hers in a smooth sensual slide.

Mercy Rose was going to stop this, she had meant to but he was reverently kissing her breasts, and his hand was smoothing down her hip. Her aroused body did the talking as she slowly opened her legs to receive him. Aesir guided his warm, silken shaft into her, and Mercy Rose arched, closed her eyes, and gasped with pleasure as he thrust and spoke.

"I said you would be *mine!*"

Aesir Blacknight was angry with Mercy Rose. At the same time, his heart was aching because he realized when he saw she was leaving him that he was not sure how he could let her go. Even now as his body moved in rhythm with hers, and her soft gasps took him to escalating heights of pleasure, he did not know how he could be without *her*, but how could he ask her to stay? In his heart, part of him wanted her to stay of her own volition. It would be like choosing him. It was partially his pride that would not ask her to stay, partially because he could not take her from her life in Jior.

He did not want his lovemaking to be angry because this could be the last time, if she truly wanted to leave him. At this moment, he did not want to stop and analyze his feelings or think about what he wanted; he just wanted to join with her, to touch her and possess her. The look on Mercy Rose's face was elation and sadness at the same time. She clung to him, and as she reached the heights of her pleasure, Aesir memorized the feeling of her body clenching around him, holding him tightly. Then he rolled over pulling her on top of him as he had the first night. This time though, Mercy Rose did not ride him, she disengaged from him and made him turn over.

Left unsatisfied, Aesir endured her examination of his ne'amh chomhara. Now that the magic spell encompassing both Aesir Blacknight and Swan Glory was broken, his ne'amh chomhara was visible again. As if someone had freshly drawn wings on his white skin with dark silver ink, the beautiful picture was the undeniable indication that Aesir Blacknight was a winged Ny-Failen. Aesir felt her feather-light touch tracing the raised lines of wings on his back. When she finished, he rolled over, and he took this opportunity to turn her onto her stomach. Lifting her hips to his, he thrust his hardness back into her sheath, and she moaned with newly found pleasure.

Aesir caressed her back and thrust hard into her wet sheath. Part of the demon in him slipped out, and he thrust harder as if he were punishing her for leaving him. Mercy Rose was gasping with each stroke, and he leaned forward embracing her from behind. His hand brought her to pleasure, and then his body finished. Resting his forehead on her shoulder, he clung to her as his seed pumped inside her. Holding her tightly, he shuddered as her inner valley squeezed him in return. It was his turn to moan with pleasure as he realized no other woman would ever satisfy him. This time when he disengaged from her and held her in his arms she cried and clung to him. There was no falling into a peaceful sleep. She was choosing to leave him for reasons of her own. He waited until his body recovered and then he made love to her again and later again as if each time was the last until it was almost morning.

CHAPTER SIXTEEN

Swan Glory sat in a chair by the fireplace in her room and forced herself to finish her dinner though she had no real appetite. She wanted to regain her strength. It was heavy on her heart that tomorrow, the Queen of Jior, Prince Vannier, and Mercy Rose would return to Jior. Along with them would go the handsome Captain Joziah Caulder. She wanted to weep. She had only known him for a short time but had quickly come to care deeply for him. It seemed like interminable hours had passed since she transformed and he left the dome room with the Queen, as was his duty. Now, as the night grew older, he had not come to see her as she had hoped and her heart was deeply saddened because of that. Fearing that seeing her in swan form was too much for a human male, she sighed resigned to the facts of her existence.

There were many things that she did not fully understand. If Aesir loved Mercy Rose, why was he letting her go? Swan Glory knew he deeply loved her because, as his twin, she knew his heart. She also knew his stubborn pride. Why, if Mercy Rose loved Aesir, was she leaving him? She had thought Captain Joziah was forming an affection for her, but he had not called on her even to say goodbye. His leaving on the morrow, would not allow any feelings they shared to grow. The later the night progressed, the more heart-sore she grew, hurt by his absence. Sitting back in her chair, she tried to see into her sad and lonely future.

An idea had begun to form in her head. The only alternative was to run away. If she was gone, then Aesir could go to Jior and be with Mercy Rose. Swan Glory could find a clear mountain lake and live out her life as a swan gliding across the cool water. As a swan, her heart could not break over inconsistent Captains who did not even care enough to say goodbye. How to hide from Aesir would be a problem. The bond they shared would not allow her to escape his notice for long and he would eventually find her.

It was very late when a soft knock on her door roused Swan Glory from her troubling thoughts. Walking to the door, she opened it expecting to find Mercy Rose or Queen Lily but outside her door stood Captain Joziah Caulder. Swan Glory was a little flustered and did not know what to do. She opened the door wider, smiled at him, and invited him in.

Captain Joziah had cleaned up, and his golden hair was damp from washing. His black and silver Jiorian uniform had been brushed clean, and he was newly shaven. Swan Glory smiled at him self-consciously and smoothed her hair back, realizing it hung unbraided and unruly down her back, and swept the back of her legs.

"Have you come to say goodbye, Captain Joziah?" Swan Glory asked as she closed the door. As he walked further into her room, she admired him from behind, his broad shoulders in his black and silver Jiorian uniform, and the way his golden hair curled just long enough to touch his collar. His long silver sword and ornate sheath had been shined to a polish and Swan Glory was saddened that he seemed completely prepared to leave. He turned toward her with a serious look on his face.

"My Lady, I have come," Captain Joziah stammered a little and swallowed. "I have come to speak to you."

"Captain, won't you please sit down?" Swan Glory motioned to the chairs by the fireplace, and he did as she suggested, though he seemed stiff, nervous, and uncomfortable. She sat down in front of him, folded her hands in her lap, and began before he had the chance to.

"Before you say anything Captain Joziah, I want to thank you for helping take care of me throughout my recovery. You know I understand most humans are taken aback when they see me transform into a swan and it is-it is-off putting. So, you…you don't need to apologize for being uncomfortable around me now. I understand completely and I do appreciate, *so much*, that you have come to say goodbye. I will always remember and deeply value our short friendship."

The Captain gaped at her for a few moments while she spoke to him and then he pulled his chair a little closer.

"My Lady, I have come…" He cleared his throat nervously then, his eyes alight with a revelation, and he seemed to change what he was going to say. "May I tell you a story?" A new thought occurred to him and he gave her a winning smile showing off his dimples. She nodded her head encouraging him and smiled back, just glad to have the time with him.

"In Jior, before your brother addressed the King and Queen about healing your sickness, there was a young girl. Her father, an angry old brute, was petitioning the King to *force* his daughter to marry a man the father had chosen for her. The man he chose was old and very wealthy, but the young girl did not want to marry him. Before the King could rule, a young soldier stepped forward confessed his undying love for the girl and said she had promised to marry him. So, before the King was the problem of who the girl should rightfully marry? The father thought he was doing what was best for his daughter, and his own pockets I might add, but the young soldier was *her* choice. They were desperately in love and she already promised to marry him. So, you see the dilemma before the King. Do you know what he decided?"

Swan Glory was engrossed in the story and also in the Captain's smooth masculine voice. She shook her head.

"He found for *love*. The very wise King of Jior pronounced that the girl should be able to marry the soldier as she promised. When the father heard the King's ruling, he was enraged and claimed the girl was dead to him and would have no dowry from him. The King had compassion for the young couple and offered to pay *double* the dowry for the girl. They went off together, married, and lived happily ever after."

"That is a lovely story Captain Joziah." Swan Glory sighed.

"My Lady," Captain Joziah reached forward and took Swan's hand in his, "I know we've only known each other a very short time but well, I've come to ask if you will return to Jior with *me*. If your brother does not consent, I suspect if I petition the King for your hand in marriage, he will find for love again and permit us to wed. I make a good wage as Captain of the Queen's guard and can support you. If you will have me?"

"Captain Joziah, that is a sweet story with a lovely ending, but our story is different." Her sweet voice was sad. "I am not of humankind, and I cannot give up that *other* part of myself. I cannot ask you to be married to a woman part of the time and a swan the other part. What if you grow to despise me for what I am? What would our children be?"

"I could never despise you. I will love you all the days of our lives, and when you are in swan form, I will protect you with my very life, and our children will be loved and wanted." He went down on one knee in front of her and kissed the back of her hand and said passionately. "Marry me Swan Glory! Be my wife!"

Swan Glory took a long moment to consider. She was swept away by the Captain's offer and by the Captain himself. His large blue eyes implored her, and she smiled shyly at him.

"Before I give you my answer Captain Joziah, there is a wish of mine you have yet to fulfill." The Captain's eyes sparkled, he rose, took her in his arms, and kissed her on the lips.

CHAPTER SEVENTEEN

Aesir Blacknight walked alone through the long, empty hall of his castle. His boot steps echoed against the walls, and his wings rustled behind him, the black feathers glistened with iridescent colors. Outside the doors, the Queen, Prince Vannier, and the Jiorian soldiers were preparing to leave. The courtyard bustled with activity, men talking, horses snorting and stamping, the company reading to leave. He approached and bowed with his hand over his heart.

"My Queen, I will never be able to thank you enough for all you have done for Swan Glory and myself." His black wings twitched a little behind him. "I hope you will accept this small token of my deepest and most sincere appreciation." He handed her a large parcel and the Queen removed the blue cloth wrapping to reveal a large book. The cover and spine were encrusted with emeralds set within scrolling golden lines and when she opened it, she saw many beautiful drawings of leaves and various plants.

"It is lovely Aesir Blacknight. I thank you."

"I know you don't need it, but it is a book detailing various healing plants and their uses. I *obtained* it from a Green Sorcerer during my search for a cure for Swan Glory. It has information that might be of use to you or one of your descendants someday. It is in no way enough to express my thanks, but I hope you will accept it as a small token of my deepest gratitude anyway."

"Thank you Aesir Blacknight; it is a beautiful and precious gift. I am immensely glad that everything turned out well for you and your sister. I wish you both the best."

Prince Vannier stepped forward and was about to take his leave of Aesir Blacknight when Captain Joziah Caulder with his sister approached. Swan Glory was covered head to toe in a soft gray cloak, her lovely face was outlined by the dark grey fur bordering the hood. Her gloved hand rested lightly on Captain Joziah's arm. Aesir Blacknight frowned at the Captain but then spoke to them all.

"Ah, my sister has come to offer her thanks and farewell."

"I *have* come to say goodbye but to *you* Brother. Captain Joziah Caulder has asked me to marry him with the King's permission," she nodded to the Queen, "and I have accepted him. I am going to Jior to live out my life as his wife."

Aesir Blacknight's beautiful black wings jerked in agitation, and he gave her a shocked, crushed look. "Swan! You can't be serious. You hardly know him! Besides, there are hunters in Jior! People who *eat roast swan!* You will be in danger every day of your life! I cannot allow it!"

"Aesir, I love you, but for seven long years, my life has been dark, empty, and cold. I appreciate everything you have done for me, more than I can say. I know there are risks and I am willing to take them so that I may live a real life. I love Joziah, and he loves me and will protect me. I am going to Jior with or without you, but my hope is *with* you."

Aesir Blacknight shook with rage, and his wings twitched with agitation as if they wanted to take flight. He was at a loss, he had only just regained his sister, and now she was leaving him. He stilled as Mercy Rose approached from out of the castle. All eyes turned in her direction. It seemed as if she had made her choice.

The Queen walked toward Mercy Rose, took her aside, and spoke to her before she joined the group.

"Mercy Rose," the Queen spoke softly to her granddaughter who could not meet her eyes. Mercy Rose started to speak but before she did her grandmother went on.

"Captain Joziah has asked Swan Glory to be his wife, and she has accepted him. She is coming to Jior with us."

Vannier watched as his mother took Mercy Rose aside and was speaking to her. Captain Joziah and Swan Glory moved toward the horses, and she mounted the horse of the soldier who was killed by the outlaws. Tears of sadness flowed down her cheeks, but she smiled at Captain Joziah through them. He looked back at her with eyes full of worship.

Vannier was moved to pity, and he approached Aesir Blacknight. He spoke calmly and with great compassion.

"Aesir Blacknight, before I married my wife Summer Rain, there was a man who tried to take her from me. I would have killed him before I allowed that. Summer Rain is my one true love and that is hard to find in this world. Once a man does find a woman with whom he connects, heart and soul, life becomes desolate without her. It seems to me that the only man standing in the way of your being with Mercy Rose is *yourself.* Your sister has found love and hope for her future. Tell me. What *now* is holding you back from going to Jior and marrying Mercy Rose?"

Aesir Blacknight turned his eyes away from Mercy Rose and looked directly at Vannier. He slowly spread his black wings behind him as if they were enough to answer Vannier's question. He shuddered as if with rage and his ice-blue eyes sparked with anger.

"I have Ny-Komnir blood!" His voice was an angry growl and his hands fisted in front of him. "I am not worthy of her. Will her father or your father, *the King,* consent to her marrying one of my kind?"

Vannier looked at him with eyes full of compassion and understanding before answering him.

"The difference between Ny-Failen and Ny-Komnir is only a matter of choice for the Creator or not. I have come to know you Aesir Blacknight, and I confess, despite your questionable methods, I believe you to be an honorable man in your heart. You have a choice to make and I will speak to my father and Jagged Edge, on your behalf." Vannier waited while Aesir Blacknight lowered his wings and stood watching Mercy Rose speaking to the Queen then he looked over at Swan Glory who sat on a horse waiting to leave him. She implored him with tear-filled eyes.

"What would bring you peace Aesir Blacknight?" Vannier asked finally.

#

Mercy Rose rushed from her bedchamber down the long hall and quickly descended the stairs. She dressed carefully in a pale blue gown with lavender and violet roses embroidered down the front of the bodice, long flowing pleats, and violet ribbons down the front. Her hair was meticulously styled in braids and curls and held in place with sapphire and amethyst pins.

Since returning to Jior, she had thus far been able to avoid Trail Blazer. He always seemed to be lurking somewhere, trying to get her attention or corner her alone. Directly upon her return from Hoarfrost Range, he had stalked her relentlessly but today would be the final confrontation or revelation.

The Great Hall was filled with people, and Mercy Rose picked her way through them so that she could take her place toward the front. Her cheeks were flushed with excitement and her heart raced. Today was the day she had waited for an entire fortnight to come. The hall quieted as the King of Jior, with the Queen on his arm, entered the hall. Taking her place beside her mother Princess Lyra Song, who also stood by the Queen's throne; Mercy Rose smoothed her skirts nervously and looked around. Her usual calm composure was hard to find this morning. As the Queen seated herself, Mercy Rose gave her a worried smile. Queen Lily reassured her with a confident nod.

Across the room, Captain Joziah Caulder stood at attention and managed to look handsome, nervous, determined, and fierce all at the same time. Next to him stood Jagged Edge who had his arms crossed over his chest and stood staring moodily at the floor. When the Great Hall doors opened, all heads turned to look and everyone hushed.

Aesir Blacknight and his twin sister Swan Glory entered. Swan Glory was radiant in a cobalt blue and dark violet dress. Her long black hair spilled down her back and swayed across the backs of her knees. A collar of priceless cobalt sapphires graced her long white neck. Her cheeks flushed and she hesitated slightly when she saw how many people were crowding the great hall. Aesir Blacknight discreetly patted her hand holding tightly to his arm and led her boldly forward. The twins came to a stop in front of the King and Queen. Aesir Blacknight bowed with his hand over his heart, and Swan Glory made a deep, graceful curtsey.

King Forlorn Icefall looked the twins over with a wrinkled brow and stroked his short white beard thoughtfully. He had heard about what happened at Hoarfrost Castle, but this was the first opportunity he had to meet Swan Glory in person. She was glorious, though she looked as if she would like to take flight and leave the assessing eyes of everyone in the hall.

"So, you've come." the King grumbled at Aesir Blacknight. Smoothing his stern look, he turned his violet gaze. "Lady Swan Glory, finally we meet. I am pleased that you are well after your long ordeal and I am glad my wife arrived in time to heal you."

"Thank you, my King. I am very grateful for all that Queen Lililaira Gem has done for us."

Swan Glory blushed a little and curtsied again to the Queen, bowing her head reverently. King Forlorn Icefall was the largest man she had ever seen, and she was overwhelmed by him. He had not shifted and did not display his great white wings, and for that she was grateful. Swan's eyes looked toward the Queen of Jior who gave her a reassuring smile, making her feel less conspicuous and anxious.

Swan Glory had never been around so many Ny-Failen or humans for that matter and her eyes quickly searched the room for Captain Joziah Caulder. He stood on the Queen's side with another man Swan Glory had earlier learned was Jagged Edge, Mercy Rose's father. Captain Joziah gave her an intense unreadable look and then her attention was caught by the King who was speaking again.

"My wife and my granddaughter have come home safe from their journey to Hoarfrost Range. What more do you come here to ask of me?" The King addressed Aesir Blacknight.

That was Captain Joziah's signal, and he strode forward, bowed to the King and Queen then turned toward Swan Glory, offering her his arm, she walked to his side, and they both turned toward the royal couple.

"My King, my Queen," Captain Joziah began confidently. "I have come forward to seek your permission to *marry* Lady Swan Glory. I would also ask to keep my position as Captain of the Queen's guard, but if I cannot marry Lady Swan Glory and keep my post, then I ask to be released from service."

King Lorn frowned at Captain Joziah and Swan Glory. He took his time before answering but finally spoke.

"You are human and she is Ny-Failen. In Everclearing it is forbidden for the two to mate. What is my Queen's counsel in this matter?" He turned toward Lily, and she seemed to consider it.

"Captain Joziah, this is not Everclearing. This is Jior. In this special situation, I would grant it because I believe love is more important than the law in this matter. You will promise to love and honor our Swan Glory? Be faithful to her forsaking all others for all of your days?"

"I will, my Queen." Captain Joziah looked very serious.

"I would like it if you would remain Captain of my guard. If it is your desire to stay on then it will be so."

"It is, my Queen. I would prefer to keep my post as your most loyal and faithful Captain."

"Because of your exemplary service to us and because my Queen wills it, it shall be so." King Forlorn Icefall grumbled, but truly he was not as stubborn as he tried to appear. He would grant any wish of his wife's desire. "I will deal with Lost Morning when the time comes."

"One last thing, my King," Captain Joziah hesitated before being dismissed. "I would ask; I know it sounds a strange request, but I would petition you to outlaw the hunting of swans in Jior. Make them protected by the King of Jior-for-reasons of which I will not divulge at this time, but I believe your Majesty is already aware of."

The hall was silent, and most of the Ny-Failen in the room understood the reason behind Captain Joziah's request. Beside him both Aesir Blacknight and his sister held their breath for it would be the only way Swan Glory could safely remain among humans.

"I understand your request Captain Joziah." The King began, "and the reasoning behind it. I will grant it. Let all swans be protected from being hunted from this day forward.

My proclamation shall go out." His voice echoed and fell like a huge gavel.

For the first-time Captain Joziah let out a relieved breath he had been holding, and smiling, turned toward Swan Glory. He lifted her hand and kissed it as they turned to move aside together. Both of them were ecstatically happy.

King Forlorn Icefall turned the full force of his commanding violet stare on Aesir Blacknight. Silence filled the hall. Standing alone, Aesir Blacknight drew himself up tall and stared back almost insolently. Mercy Rose stood by her mother and held her breath.

"Aesir Blacknight!" The King said with some ire. "You come too frequently to my hall!"

"Aye, King Forlorn Icefall, I've come once again to beg your indulgence." Aesir Blacknight stood straight and tall, looking the King right in the eye. The tone of voice he spoke in though, indicated he was not about to beg.

"I have had a disturbing report about you from a most reliable source." The King turned his gaze toward Jagged Edge who stared moodily at Aesir Blacknight.

"My wife also gave me surprising news. None of what I have heard about you makes me eager to grant *any* request of yours. Since the day you barged into Mercy Rose's birth celebration, I've regretted letting you live. Now I regret it even more after having heard of all the half-truths you've told. I warn you to tell the truth to me now. It is only at the request of my family; I will let you plead your case."

Aesir Blacknight stood still for a moment, and an insolent smirk crossed his face, but then he looked toward Mercy Rose and saw her pale at his hesitation. He wanted to tell her again, as he had told her many times since they left Hoarfrost Castle, that there was nothing that could keep him from taking her as his wife, not even the impressive King

Forlorn Icefall. Jagged Edge scowled at Aesir Blacknight as if to say, '*show some respect boy!*'

"My King, my Queen," he bowed reverently toward Lily. "I've come before you today, to ask for your permission to marry your granddaughter, Lady Mercy Rose."

The people in the room stirred and began to speak in hushed voices. Trail Blazer's mouth fell open in shocked denial, and he drew breath to protest, but then Prince Vannier was suddenly standing next to him and giving him a look that said he had better hold his tongue.

King Forlorn Icefall looked none-too-pleased and sat back in his chair though he knew the request had been coming. After a long perusal of Aesir Blacknight, he looked at Jagged Edge.

"Jagged Edge, do you agree to this union?" The King asked, and Jagged Edge stepped forward.

"I have given my permission, but only under the condition that you consent and that it is what Mercy Rose truly desires."

"Before I answer Aesir Blacknight," the King continued, "I once told you I needed to know who and what I am dealing with for the sake of my family. I understand you have told me a few *lies* in that respect."

The King frowned displeased, but then he waved at Aesir Blacknight indicating he should hurry up and answer.

"Before, when I came to plead with Queen Lililaira Gem to heal my sister, yes! I did lie."

Cries of shock and disbelief rang out from the crowd, and Trail Blazer smirked. Jagged Edge looked thunderous, but he already knew the boy's secrets.

"Previously, I stated that I had not completed my education as a sorcerer, but I actually have. I am a fully educated and very skilled Blue Sorcerer." Aesir Blacknight announced with some pride, "*AND*," his voice rang out over the astonished comments of the people in the room. He turned his head and stared directly at Trail Blazer and sneered.

"*I am winged!*" Aesir Blacknight shrugged and shapeshifted in front of everyone's eyes. His wings slowly unfurled and stretched out. His beautiful black feathers glistened with blue-black iridescence, and he gave a brazen snap of his wings while the room broke into an uproar. Then he folded his wings on his back and waited for the tumult to die down.

Trail Blazer pushed his way forward, and his voice gained everyone's attention as he strode toward the center of the room. "I protest! King Forlorn Icefall you cannot allow Lady Mercy Rose to marry this Ny-Komnir!" He shrugged his shoulders, and his beautiful white wings shifted from his back and he repeated the same insolent snap. He stood opposite Aesir Blacknight, the black-winged and the white-winged confronting each other.

King Lorn just glared at them both. Of course, he knew about Aesir Blacknight because Lily had divulged everything that happened on her journey to Hoarfrost Castle from beginning to end. This confrontation in front of everyone was, in the King's mind, a test of Aesir Blacknight's resolve, his courage, and a test of his love for Mercy Rose.

"Trail Blazer, what claim do you have on Mercy Rose?" the King glared at him realizing he would have to consider his claim.

"King Forlorn Icefall, it is *my* wish to marry Lady Mercy Rose. I have been courting her for months now and I insist you consider my claim, as I am more worthy of your granddaughter than this *Ny-Komnir!*"

"I will kill you if you stand in my way!" Aesir Blacknight snarled and took a fighting stance toward Trail Blazer who glared back at him ready to attack.

The King glared at the two of them menacingly and shouted. "I'll be the one killing if you two don't stand down!"

Then he turned his glare back on Aesir Blacknight.

"I have not seen a black-winged Ny-Komnir in many, many years," King Lorn grinned maniacally. "The last time, I ripped his black wings off and tossed his broken body to the ground from the highest clouds. Tell me why I should not do the same to you?"

"Because, my King," Aesir Blacknight spoke loud glaring at Trail Blazer before he turned and looked at the King, "I am as much Ny-Failen as I am Ny-Komnir. Your father was a wingless Ny-Komnir but none of that matters, what matters is the reason I have come before you. I love Lady Mercy Rose and she loves me," he said this last to Trail Blazer directly. "Jagged Edge has given us his permission to marry with the stipulation that you also approve, only because you are the King and her grandfather. Out of my deep respect for the Queen and my Lady Mercy Rose, I humble myself before you and the Court and ask your permission to wed your granddaughter."

"How far have you *descended?*" King Lorn leaned forward resting his elbow on his knee narrowing his eyes at Aesir Blacknight as he rumbled this last question.

Aesir Blacknight turned red in the face. With arms raised and fists clenched his wings spread wide as he arched back and angrily dared to yell at the King.

"I HAVE NOT DESCENDED! I AM NY-FAILEN!" His shout echoed as he declared for the Creator.

The people in the Great Hall fell silent, and all that could be heard was the heavy, furious panting of Aesir Blacknight.

A slow tear fell from Swan Glory's eye as she watched her brother and felt his pain and humiliation-his fear.

"Mercy Rose!" It was the King's turn to bellow now, breaking the silence. She left her mother's side and walked toward the center of the room to stand between Aesir Blacknight and Trail Blazer. "Granddaughter, two men make a claim for you. Which is your choice?"

Mercy Rose was stunningly beautiful in front of the entire court as she walked forward and faced her grandfather and grandmother. Trail Blazer took a step toward her as if by his looming presence he could force her hand somehow. Aesir Blacknight stood back, watching her as the green demon of jealousy roared within at this, the final test. She would have to declare for him in front of everyone and finally put to rest the question in his mind regarding her feelings for Trail Blazer. Even after everything they had been through and had done, he still held one small kernel of doubt.

"Grandfather," smiling, she began, "I chose Aesir Blacknight."

The entire room erupted in exclamations of joy and some of dismay. The Queen beamed happily at her, and Jagged Edge who was not surprised at Mercy Roses' choice just nodded his head as if reaffirming his consent too.

When the noise died down enough, the King took a deep breath and made his proclamation.

"Aesir Blacknight you have my reluctant permission to marry my granddaughter Mercy Rose." The King of Jior announced and then he stood, descended the dais, and walked toward Aesir Blacknight. Trail Blazer glared at them both and sneered with disgust at Aesir Blacknight then turned and stalked angrily from the room. While the rest of the crowd cheered the King's proclamation, King Lorn stopped very close to Aesir Blacknight.

Though he was smiling, he warned in a low voice so that only Aesir Blacknight could hear, "Hurt her just once, and I'll kill you."

"You'll have to get in line because Jagged Edge has already threatened me as has every other male in your family." Aesir Blacknight growled back in reply, holding his ground, face-to-face against the King.

King Lorn grinned wider bearing his white teeth at Aesir Blacknight before he turned toward his granddaughter, softened his features, embraced her, and kissed her cheek.

After embracing her grandfather, Mercy Rose turned toward Aesir Blacknight and smiled so brightly he had to go to her and take her in his arms. Her arms slid around his waist. Resting his forehead against hers, he closed his eyes. The room erupted into happy exclamations and applause as people cheered the happy couple.

"Thank the Creator!" Aesir Blacknight gave a relieved exhale.

CHAPTER EIGHTEEN

The heavily beaded gown slowly slid off Mercy Rose's shoulders as the lacing down her back loosened. One by one the ribbons pulled out of their eyelets and flowed free. She stepped out of the gown, removed her stockings, and slid under the sheets of her bed. She laid back and stretched her slim, beautiful body luxuriously amongst the pillows and soft blankets.

With reverence, Aesir Blacknight gently laid the bridal gown across the back of a divan, and then he too undressed. Mercy Rose watched him, the way his body moved as he removed his dark blue coat. How his shoulders flexed, and his torso lengthened as he drew the deep blue shirt over his head. The ripple of his stomach muscles accompanied his movements. Smoothing his hands over his head, he reached the black tie that bound his long black hair. He pulled it out and let the length hang free well past his shoulders to his waist. Bending, he pulled his boots off and his trousers until he stood completely naked in front of Mercy Rose.

Though this was not the first time she had seen his naked body, she was once again spellbound by his masculine beauty. He was decidedly, deliciously *male* and every ripple of muscle under his smooth white skin and lean torso, made the wonder of him more and more desirable to her. He was giving her that crooked smile, and she finally remembered to breathe. Sliding under the sheets next to her, Aesir leaned on his elbow and ran his fingers down the side of her breast. Mercy Rose's pulse leaped with his caresses as she watched his every move.

She had a flash of memory back to the first time they had ever danced and realized that even then, the fluid, masculine movement of his body had fascinated her, as it did now. His arm went around her slim waist as he swept her into the starting position.

Today was their wedding day. Swan Glory and Captain Joziah Caulder, Aesir Blacknight, and Lady Mercy Rose had been married in a dual ceremony. Jagged Edge had walked Mercy Rose down the aisle, and Vannier had gladly offered to accompany Swan Glory. King Forlorn Icefall had presided, and it was a jubilant affair.

Now Aesir was her husband, and he was kissing her, caressing her and she reciprocated. He whispered words of love and adoration, and her body responded to him with fire and passion. Aesir's lean body moved over her, and he kissed her breasts. Her blood rushed through her veins, and her heart beat fiercely. She was almost panting with need and raised her hips to him. He teased her and held back from entering her. His ice-blue eyes sparkled at her as he tugged gently on her bottom lip with his mouth.

Aesir knew just where to touch Mercy Rose and just how to bring her to completion. He had left the lamps burning so that he could watch her, see her desire rising and the pleasure overtaking her face as he made love to her. It increased his pleasure to watch her and, the reality of them together, took him to heights of passion beyond where his imagination could fly. Now he was done teasing.

Mercy Rose watched as he gently pulled her leg higher over his hip and then he was reaching down between them. The muscles in his arm rippled as he grabbed his hard length and guided himself into her waiting body.

It was, she decided at that very moment, the most erotic part of lovemaking, that moment signaling their ultimate joining. Something about his deliberate movements; taking hold of himself, finding her, and slowly sliding together, making them one. This act was so masculine, so intimate, and *perfect*.

He was watching her face as he filled her. Licking her bottom lip in anticipation, head thrown back, her nipples hard and her face flushed red. Sheathed fully inside her, she bit down on that full lip and closed her eyes in ecstasy, arching a little more, taking him deeper. Joined with her completely now, Aesir Blacknight made love to his wife.

#

Early the next morning, Mercy Rose stirred as Aesir's movements woke her. He had risen from their bed and was quickly dressing. Outside a far distant rooster crowed welcoming the coming morning. Her brow furrowed as she watched him, wondering. He quickly pulled on his trousers and boots but left the shirt and coat. Purposefully, walking away from her, his broad shoulders shrugged as he shifted and his large black wings snapped open. Without sparing her a glance, he walked toward the huge windowed doors on the balcony and threw them open. Stepping forward, bending his knees slightly, all in one smooth movement, he leaped into the sky.

Mercy Rose, covered only in her long white tresses, raced to the balcony to watch him go. He was already gaining altitude as he was suddenly joined by something large and white in the sky. He whirled through the air in a graceful flip around the huge swan, and they flew up together into the morning light, leaving Mercy Rose behind.

The End

The Gray King

CHAPTER ONE

When the Gray King entered the court of King Forlorn Icefall of Jior no one knew what to expect. When he requested a future marriage contract between his son and one of the Ny-Failen of Jior, it was met with less than cheerful acceptance.

The Gray King came from a faraway place called Sorn that existed on the furthest northeastern coastline of Vedt. People in remote northwestern Jior barely knew it existed as people from Sorn never ventured that far north. The Gray King entered the Great Hall of Castle Jior with an appalling air of arrogance. The man himself was bent, wizened, and sickly, an unimpressive figure. The Gray King had not so much as requested an audience with the King of Jior, as much as he *demanded* it. As everyone knew, King Forlorn Icefall was not one to give in to anyone's demands but had no other reason to deny the King of Sorn. Also, the Gray King had a large number of soldiers camped outside the walls of Jior and he refused to leave Jior until he was granted an audience. He was making everyone within the city very nervous and the complaints were getting annoying. King Lorn was not intimidated by the small show of force but reluctantly gave in allowing the Gray King into the Great Hall of Castle Jior. At the time, he had no viable reason to deny the request for an audience.

Multi-colored glass panes allowed bars of light to paint the Great Hall in a myriad of jewel-toned hues. It was the late morning sun shining through those windows when the Gray King and a dozen of his soldiers entered the hall. They appeared non-threatening giving the impression of putting on their best show of grandeur for the Jiorian court. Though their presence seemed to suck the color out of the bright sunlit day.

Accompanying them, was a boy. Dressed all in gray ill-fitting clothes, the boy was a dull gray smudge among the soldiers in glimmering silver armor. Thin, with dark circles under his large eyes, the boy had a long awkward nose that seemed too big for his face, and a head full of silvery-gray hair that hung lank and dirty over his features. He was, by Ny-Failen standards, an ugly little boy who occasionally wiped his nose on his sleeve and stared down at his overly large feet. The boy darted a look at King Lorn and revealed a large purple bruise on his right cheek. He was so pathetic that he drew pity from everyone in the room who laid eyes upon him.

Many Ny-Failen of Jior gathered to watch and listen as the king and his soldiers from the land of Sorn entered the Great Hall. Among the Ny-Failen were King Forlorn Icefall's two sons, Vannier and Dark Star, also Jagged Edge, Princess Lyra Song, and several other Ny-Failen women, including Queen Lililaira Gem, who was always by her husband's side. Almost unnoticed, darting in and out amongst the crowd, were three rambunctious little girls. One of which, was the youngest daughter of Princess Lyra Song and Jagged Edge. The two younger girls with her were Dark Star's little girls. Several of Jior's humankind soldiers stood on guard along the outer walls of the hall. In addition, nobles, retainers, and other members of the court were in attendance that day and so the hall was full of curious on-lookers.

The Gray King was of humankind. His tall, lanky form was hunched as he leaned heavily on a long ash wood staff. The staff was ornately decorated with fine plates of engraved silver and had a large white crystal sphere surrounded by raven feathers at the top. It was the only item of the Gray King's raiment that could remotely designate the man as a king. However, when the Gray King let down the hood of his gray cloak, a tarnished silver crown was revealed atop thinning gray hair. His face was lined with age and looked as if it were chiseled out of stone. His pallor was gray, his cunning eyes gray, his lips grayish, dry, and cracking. When the Gray King spoke, it sounded as if he were greatly winded and he wheezed as he breathed, stopping frequently to catch his breath and cough.

"King Forlorn Icefall of Jior." The Gray King addressed Jior's King in a weak voice and stopped to catch his breath. "I am, well, my subjects call me the Gray King. To my *face* they call me the Gray King, behind my *back*, I have no doubt that they call me an assortment of foul names." He stopped, gave a rueful grimace, and took a few deep breaths which seemed necessary for him to have the air to speak again.

"I have come from Sorn. I am sure you have heard of my little kingdom residing on the northeastern coast of Vedt. It is a rocky barren place. We live off of the sea, but our wealth comes from large silver deposits found throughout the land of Sorn. You might say even our blood runs silver." The Gray King gave a short bark that would have sounded like a laugh had he the breath. He gave another little cackle but had to stop to draw air into his weak lungs again.

"Welcome, King of Sorn." King Forlorn Icefall, informally known as King Lorn, sounded wary. His eyes scanned the delegation with the Gray King. He counted twelve soldiers covered head to toe in silver helmets and silver armor with silver swords at their sides. They stood solid and unmoving in tight, disciplined formation behind their king. King Lorn's gaze finally rested on the boy who stood in his drab gray, dirty clothing with his head bowed, eyes lowered and his hands slack at his sides. Occasionally, the boy shuffled on his feet or it would have been hard to tell whether the boy lived and breathed.

"I have heard of the Kingdom of Sorn and am aware that high-quality silver comes from those far northeastern reaches of Vedt. We have had long-standing trade agreements with Krickgold and thus our silver comes from their mines. Regardless, tell me what brings you so far north to Jior?"

The Gray King looked around almost as if he had forgotten his purpose there and then his gray eyes alighted on the boy. As he looked at the boy his eyes almost burned under bushy white eyebrows that drew together and dropped into a furrow. The corners of his mouth fell into a scowl. His long-fingered hand rose and he crooked a long finger, pointing at the boy.

"This is my son, Ashen. His mother called him Ashen Arrow. Such nonsense does not seem fitting, but that is the name *she* gave him and I didn't really care. Regardless, my son is one of *you*, a Ny-Failen as was his mother whose only purpose in life, was to provide me with an heir. Ashen, the produce of my loins, is a pathetic little creature and is not all I had hoped for but he is all I have got and someday will inherit my kingdom and rule when I die. Only because he shares my blood and is the very *last* of the line of Sorn, will this be so."

The crowd stirred with the Gray King's revelations and many murmured amongst themselves.

"Who was his mother?" King Lorn, a little astounded, leaned forward and regarded the boy with renewed interest and a spark of sympathy in his eye. As always Ny-Failen children captured a special place in the King's heart.

"Oh, I don't know." The Gray King snapped angrily and breathed heavily. He waved an age-spotted hand and barked. "*Bright*-something-or-other, I don't remember her name.

She is gone now and I don't like speaking of her. She is immaterial to my visit to Jior anyway. I only mention it because I know of the Ny-Failen's aversion to mating with humans and it seems a sound principle."

"It is true that the Ny-Failen no longer mate with humankind which is why your son is such an anomaly. That a Ny-Failen woman would *willingly agree* to bear you an heir is a hard notion to grasp." King Lorn sounded his hidden accusation with a heavy look of doubt.

"Yet, she did agree as here he stands! I said it is not something I care to discuss because it is not relevant." The Gray King interrupted. "He is my heir, of *my* bloodline which is of ancient royalty, venerable, and pure. He is the *last* of the Sorn bloodline and, as my heir, he will someday need a wife to carry on the lineage and so I have come to arrange a marriage for him."

Now King Lorn stared in disbelief. A gathering storm of anger began to cloud his violet eyes and he leaned forward giving the Gray King the full weight of his displeasure in his glare.

"In *my* Kingdom of Jior, arranged marriages are never a consideration. *If,* as you say he is truly Ny-Failen-which I doubt-I would not force any Ny-Failen woman into a marriage they did not choose."

"Oh, I don't want just *any* Ny-Failen," the Gray King snarled back. A cruel, calculating smile overtook his thin lips. "I want one of *your* blood-line." Stabbing his long finger toward the king he spoke loud and clear. "Only the royal offspring directly sprung from the King of Jior, Forlorn Icefall himself will do for *my* son!"

King Lorn was filled with building fury. He was almost speechless as he stared at the Gray King but managed a low angry growl.

"I said no!"

"King Forlorn Icefall, I am prepared to bargain for a girl of your royal lineage. Not one of those *winged* ones though. I can't have her flying away anytime she chooses. In exchange, I will give you enough pure silver to pave the streets of Jior or fill your coffers to the rafters. Much better quality than that tin from Krickgold. Anything you desire I am prepared to make a trade. You get an alliance with the Kingdom of Sorn, as much silver as you want, and in return, a female of your bloodline will be the queen of one of the oldest, most revered, and wealthiest countries on the entire continent of Vedt."

"I have given you my answer. I will *not* bargain away any one of my family to someone who comes to my hall and claims to be a king from a country I've barely even heard of."

"Are you saying *my* son is not *worthy* of the great King Forlorn Icefall's consideration?" The Gray King narrowed his eyes in warning.

"I am saying that I do not consent to an arranged marriage at all, under *any* terms. Besides, my daughter is already married."

"Do you take me for a fool? I know Princess Lyra Song is married. As is her eldest daughter, but you have others to choose from, other granddaughters close to my son's age that will suit. He is ten years old and will be of marriageable age in ten more years. You will have plenty of time to prepare a girl of your bloodline to breed. Choose one of them, any will do, and we can draw up the marriage contract and form a profitable alliance." After his tirade, the Gray King's chest was heaving, almost gasping for enough air just to converse. King Lorn wondered if the old man would live to see the next ten years.

A murderous glower marred King Lorn's handsome countenance and he leaned forward on his throne, tightening his fists, and spoke through clenched teeth.

"My answer remains, no! I have nothing against the boy, but my grandchildren are not for sale, barter, or alliance, now or ever! You will not have any Jiorian Ny-Failen to marry if I have a say about it."

The boy, who stood motionless throughout the entire conversation, finally looked up at King Lorn. He stared out through the long strands of his unkempt gray hair, with large silver-gray eyes. His face held a look of wonder that someone would refuse his father the Gray King. Then he looked around at these people who were so defiant. In the crowd, he spied three little girls who had come forward to stare at him. Dressed in fine lace and satin of lavender, pale green, and blue, he stared at them with wide eyes. The tallest girl, wearing the pale green dress, looked to be closer to his age and was staring back at him with curious, intent, scrutiny. Taking one step forward, she stood in a ray of colored sunshine that streaked through the multi-colored glass window above and painted her with its light. She gave him a shy, hesitant smile. The boy quickly looked away but covertly kept looking back at her through the hair falling over his eyes. The little girl in pale green continued to stare at him, gracing him with her sweet smile.

"I am not a patient man, but I can be reasonable." The Gray King went on. "I see how my offer comes as strange, or even archaic, and perhaps as somewhat of a surprise to you. When a king of my caliber offers an alliance, it is not a decision to be hastily made. I had hoped that the promise of silver would attract you and make you more amenable to the offer. I would have thought that someone of Kullorn's bloodline would not balk at such an arrangement, the offer of silver and a beneficial alliance." The Gray King stopped to catch his breath. "I have traveled a great distance to procure this marriage arrangement and to guarantee my royal bloodline will continue. If you would like some time to think this over more carefully, I will consent to wait until tomorrow for your decision on which of your granddaughters you have chosen."

"You can wait until the Hells freeze over! Do not waste your time because my answer will be the same. Now, leave Jior and do not bother to return." King Lorn was on his feet now and the sound of his voice was terrifying as it boomed throughout the Great Hall. The boy flinched and watched the massive King of Jior. A hush fell over all of the people watching and all eyes turned toward the Gray King expecting him to comply.

Prince Vannier and Prince Dark Star stepped forward, hands on sword hilts, and stood ready to come to the protection of the king. Jagged Edge took a step forward to stand in front of the little girl in the pale green dress as someone pulled the other two little girls out of sight.

"I will not be dismissed so easily King of Jior. You have one chance to change your mind. The youngest, wingless of your granddaughters will suffice for my son. She can even be ugly for all I care, but he is Ny-Failen and *my* heir deserves an equal to mate with and carry on the royal Sorn bloodline."

"My guards will see you *out!*" King Lorn spoke with venomous finality.

The royal Jiorian guard advanced and surrounded the Gray King's delegation. With swords drawn, they stood ready to defend the King and Jior.

The Gray King stood for a moment. His bent body shuddered with indignation as he gasped for air, furious at being thwarted. Both hands clutched his staff as he leaned heavily upon it. The boy had not moved until now he took a step away. He looked up at his father then hunched fearfully as if expecting a blow.

"I am sorry that it has come to this King Forlorn Icefall. I am sure you will come to see it my way in a very short time." The Gray King suddenly coughed and hacked, a wet, gurgling sound of sickness emanated from his chest. He pursed his lips and spat violently on the floor of the Great Hall. A wet black spot landed before the throne and splattered outward.

Everyone took a step back, repulsed by the disgusting act.

As if, now that he had gotten that out, the Gray King seemed to breathe a little more easily, he began a soft mumbling. He waved his ash wood staff in a small circle over the spittle, quickly building his incantation. As he mumbled his spell the black spot began to spread and grow slowly. Tendrils of black evil expanded outward like spilled ink and crawled sluggishly across the white marble floor. The people in the hall gasped and quickly moved back further as the spot slowly grew as if it were a living thing.

The boy began sniffling silently and quickly wiped away tears with his dirty sleeve.

King Lorn roared with indignation and called his guards to advance. The Gray King quickly finished his spell and raised his staff again. With a word and a gesture, Jior's guards were frozen in their tracks. The black spot of evil continued to slowly crawl outward and soon it was as large as a platter.

"This little blight is a reflection of your ignorance in accepting my magnanimous offer." The Gray King spoke loud and clear now. "Let us just call this *incentive* to bring you around to my way of thinking. I will remain camped outside the gates of Jior until you comply. I'm not asking much from you only one silly little Ny-Failen girl to assure my royal bloodline continues. This blight will spread, thoughtlessly devouring everything in its path, until you find wisdom and agree to a marriage contract with Sorn. See me, King Forlorn Icefall, when you decide to accept my generous offer as *I am sure you will*."

A devious smile spread across the Gray King's cracked lips showing his sharp gray teeth as he turned and stalked out of the hall. His soldiers turned stiffly, followed him out and they left the black blight to spread. The boy cast a last sorrowful look at the King of Jior and followed his father from the hall.

#

For the next several days the black blight grew, spreading sticky, corrosive, and giving off a foul stench. It thickly covered the floor of the Great Hall devouring everything in its path and began to climb up the walls. The only thing it did not corrode was the marble floors and stone walls, but everything else that was not solid stone was eaten up by the black foulness. Soon it began to crawl up and leak under the hall's doors and to eat away at the carved wood until it turned into visceral liquid and dripped, falling in black clumps. Black inky tendrils slowly progressed down the hallway and in all directions. Soon, it would reach the stairs going out of the castle and climb to the upper floors in a matter of days.

Attempts to clean it or dam it up failed. A man stepped one foot in the visceral stuff and was immediately engulfed, sucked down into the blackness, and was gone with a horrified scream.

King Lorn was in a state of fury. He met with Prince Vannier, Prince Dark Star, and Jagged Edge, and they discussed various courses of action. Wishing Sorrell Brand, his oldest friend, and advisor was in Jior and not away in Krickgold, he considered the next course of action. Nothing they tried stopped the evil from spreading into the castle. King Lorn immediately sent for Aesir Blacknight who was a Blue Sorcerer, and when he arrived his magic was powerless to stop the spreading blight. He did succeed for a short time in slowing it down, but the black evil eventually overcame his efforts and continued to grow, stain, and devour.

Almost sentient, the evil began to eat away at the mortar of the floors and a few large stones fell through into the rooms underneath. It left holes in which the blight began to leak through to the lower levels dripping like black, viscous rain. In a matter of days, like the insistent roots of a tree, it grew down slithering onward threatening to consume the entire castle. Eventually, it looked as though its path would take it toward the river that ran under the castle and supplied their clean water. The whole castle would soon be unlivable covered in the black blight. As it was, the horrid smell was almost unbearable and there was no escape except to the furthest reaches and highest towers of the castle.

King Lorn decided to take a more direct approach. Having some experience with evil sorcerers, he realized once the Gray King was dead, the magic he created would cease to exist and so they mounted an attack on the Gray King's camp.

Outside the massive black walls of Jior, the Gray King waited in his gray tent. His troops stood guard and never seemed to move from their posts. They lit no fires for warmth nor did they erect tents for sleep, they only stood still at attention, as if waiting.

King Lorn struck at the Gray King. Jior's soldiers, led by Commander Jagged Edge, charged out of the massive gates. They rode at speed of horse with swords drawn with the intent to kill. The King, Prince Vannier, and Prince Dark Star attacked from the skies wielding long Ny-Failen pikes, swords, and iron arrows. When their combined force quickly reached the camp. Jior's warriors engaged the enemy with brutal ferocity and righteous vengeance. Sorn's soldiers fought with great skill and hardly a single enemy soldier fell or gave way. King Lorn's black demon-forged sword and greater strength finally succeeded in felling one soldier. His mighty sword stroke cut the soldier in half. As it fell, no red blood spilled but liquid silver oozed out from the wounds and quickly healed the fallen soldier, regrowing an arm and a leg, a head, and so on, until each half solidified into a full-sized soldier. Now, there were two. Where one enemy fell it rose again and another rose with it. Soon, Lorn was faced with a force of enemy soldiers that grew the harder they fought.

Shrugging his broad shoulders King Lorn again took to the skies. He flew up and outward toward the huge tent where the Gray King was. He landed next to the tent and charged inside with his black sword ready to strike. The Gray King stood calmly within and as soon as King Lorn entered he pointed his ash wood staff, shouted a command, and froze the mighty King of Jior. His body caught, suspended within the threshold of the tent and he could not move. Trapped like a bird in a net, Lorn struggled with unseen bonds. The more he struggled, the more it constricted until it held him so tightly it became difficult to breathe. Soon Lorn was completely immobilized and he could barely expand his chest to draw in air. His wings were spread behind him, useless. Lorn's face turned red and then his vision began to blur as he was slowly strangled. Outside he could hear the sound of his men battling an enemy that would not die and only grew stronger the harder Jior's soldiers fought. The more of them they wounded or killed the more Sorn's forces grew.

The Gray King approached and knocked Lorn's demon-forged sword from his hand with the end of his staff. He waived at the boy and ordered him to fetch the King of Jior's sword. The boy did as he was told and darted forward to retrieve the black sword. He was barely able to lift it but dragged it back a few steps by grasping the hilt with both hands.

"Ah, I see you have come to negotiate my kind and generous offer." The Gray King said calmly while Lorn struggled to draw breath.

The Gray King finally released Lorn enough so that he could draw in air. Lorn's eyes moved to the boy who watched with a terrified look on his face, as a tear trickled down the gray dirt on his cheek.

"I will foster the boy. Leave him in Jior with the Ny-Failen. That is all I am willing to agree." King Lorn continued to struggle against unseen bonds. All the time he was caught, he realized back at the castle, the evil black blight continued to spread throughout his home threatening everyone he loved, and eventually, his entire kingdom. Outside, Lorn could hear the clash of weapons and the screams of his men as they were wounded or killed in the battle raging behind him. His sons and his men were out there still fighting.

"No, I don't think that is good enough." The Gray King answered in an unsatisfied, clipped tone. "Besides, *I* must raise my son to be a strong ruler of Sorn not some milk-sop of a Ny-Failen."

"But yet you claim a Ny-Failen female is good enough to continue your bloodline!" Lorn scowled and continued to strain at his unseen bonds.

"Yes, yes, there is great *power* in Ny-Failen blood. I will concede that it is my true desire to have that power." Done talking, the Gray King whirled and walked toward a table where a parchment lay unfurled. "This is the marriage contract. It is completely unbreakable. You will give your oath, sign and seal it in your king's blood. Before ten years' time, when my son turns one and twenty, we will return to collect his bride. The wedding can be done swiftly and without fanfare or expense, then we will go back to Sorn to begin breeding the next in succession."

The Gray King waived his staff and as if gathering in a net, King Lorn was dragged slowly forward toward the table. He turned the parchment and grabbed Lorn's right hand yanking it toward him. Pulling the short silver dagger from Lorn's belt he made a long, deep slice across Lorn's palm and pressed his bleeding hand to the parchment. Then the Gray King gestured sharply to the boy.

The boy came slowly forward still awkwardly clutching the huge black, demon sword in his arms. The Gray King snatched one of the boy's hands and he almost dropped the sword but clutched it to his chest with his other arm. His other hand was caught in the Gray King's boney claw, and holding it out, he cut deeply across the boy's palm. The boy bit his lip and fought not to cry out, tears of pain rolled down his cheeks as his father pressed his bleeding hand to the parchment. A small red smear was placed next to the larger one. Then the Gray King pressed the two bleeding palms together. His eyes rolled back in his head showing only grayish-white orbs as he mumbled an unintelligible spell. Binding the boy and the King, the deal was sealed in blood and pain.

"Vow it!" The Gray King ordered, his fetid breath blew in King Lorn's face, and his clawed hands squeezed the two bleeding hands together tightly. The boy winced in pain and bit his lip so that he did not cry out.

King Lorn's fury was overflowing, but his body was still frozen as he snarled. "This contract is forced under extreme duress it is not valid. *I do not consent!*"

"The marriage contract is valid. I have your blood and the boy's blood. That binds you both until the wedding is completed and the marriage consummated. If you want your castle freed from the black blight of your refusal to bargain with me then you must vow. Give your oath to uphold the marriage contract and I will release you and your castle. You will have ten long years to prepare one of your granddaughters for her happy nuptials."

Lorn struggled and strained more violently against the force that was holding him captive. He was starting to apprehend that he had no choice at the moment, but also realized he had ten years to find a way to thwart the Gray King's plan.

"Vow it! Or the black blight envelops your entire kingdom and all its people!"

"I vow it!" King Lorn finally snarled through gritted teeth, giving in only because the boy was clearly in pain as the Gray King crushed their bloodied hands together with inhuman strength and because his kingdom was at stake. Inwardly, he made another vow never to give in to this enforced agreement begotten by such evil methods.

"Now you Ashen! Vow it!"

"I vow it!" The boy quickly gasped through his pain. Silent tears streamed down his face.

"Excellent!" Grinning triumphantly, the Gray King released their hands, rolled the marriage contract up, and slipped it into a rune-carved silver scroll case. He tucked it into his robe with a very satisfied gleam in his gray eyes.

"You may go now King Forlorn Icefall. Your castle is freed from your blight of ignorance. Ashen! Return the King's sword to him!"

Ashen slowly walked forward cradling his injured hand and dragging the sword forward. He gave the King of Jior his sword with a sorrow-filled, silver-eyed look. King Lorn momentarily looked at the boy with pity. With his bloodied hand, he grasped his sword by the hilt but before he could turn and raise it to strike, the Gray King plucked the air in front of Lorn with two fingers and pulled back like drawing an arrow in a bowstring. He released. King Lorn violently flew backward out of the tent and was sent careening into the ranks of the fighting men. Leaping to his feet, he was in time to watch as the Gray King, his soldiers, and the encampment, shimmered, faded, and vanished as if they had never been.

CHAPTER TWO

{Ten Years Later}

King Lorn spent ten years searching for a way to protect his granddaughters and his kingdom from the Gray King and his ill-gotten marriage contract. Refusing Lily's offer of healing, Lorn let the cut the Gray King had made, heal naturally. A long, thin, white scar on the palm of his hand became a constant reminder that his blood and his oath, extracted under extreme coercion, had sealed the fate of one of his beloved granddaughters.

There were three granddaughters of King Lorn's who would be old enough to wed the Heir of Sorn when the time came. Princess Lyra Song and Jagged Edge had a young daughter, named Rain Song. She would be nineteen years of age when the contract came to maturation. Prince Dark Star and Lady Dawn Rusher had two daughters, Aerial Dawn and Autumn Day. They were eighteen and sixteen years of age respectively. At only sixteen, Autumn Day was immediately ruled out as too young to wed and so the choice fell between Rain Song and Aerial Dawn.

Beautiful and vivacious, Aerial Dawn was a winged Ny-Failen. Since the Gray King had expressly commanded no winged Ny-Failen for his son, she was ruled out. That left only one choice, Rain Song.

Lyra Song's youngest daughter Rain Song was an ethereal beauty like her mother. Born quite a few years after her sister, Mercy Rose, she was quiet and mature beyond her age. With soft delicate features, almond-shaped green eyes, and the same long, silvery-white hair and pearly-hued skin characteristic of most all Ny-Failen women. The girl had an enchanting voice when she sang and was known for her compassion, intelligence, and sweet, generous spirit. She could not read minds like her father Jagged Edge, but she seemed to have an uncanny intuition about people and events. She was also wingless and of an age to marry.

With parental horror, Jagged Edge raved that he would not relinquish his daughter to the forced marriage with the Heir of Sorn. Lyra Song turned her sad pleading eyes to her father and begged him to find another way. King Lorn feared the black magic of the Gray King and consulted Lost Morning, the leader of all Ny-Failen, about how to avoid going through with the illegal marriage contract. They worked with sorcerers and wise men of humankind to counteract any magic the Gray King might bring. The human sorcerers turned out to be mostly charlatans and frauds and were deemed useless. In the end, they could only wait with their strategies and defenses in place and hope that they would be able to prevail against the Gray King and his son.

Frequently, King Lorn relived the moment when he had been forced to give his word. *"I vow it!"* His voice intoned the angry litany in his memories and nightmares.

The black blight that the Gray King had used as one of his tools to force the King of Jior's hand, had indeed vanished that day ten years past, leaving a dark stain on the white stones in the Great Hall that could not be cleaned or chiseled away. Many of the blackened stones remained in the walls, almost decoratively, like an image of a climbing tree trunk with expanding branches. It spread up and over the massive high walls like an artist had painted a gigantic black oak and King Lorn left it, looking at it every day as another reminder of what was to come.

Before the dreaded date when they predicted the Gray King would appear at the gates of Jior expecting a wedding; King Lorn had intended to gather his Ny-Failen family to Jior for a deadly confrontation.

As she grew, Rain Song for her part in the anticipated tragedy, was brave and subdued on the subject. In the years before the Gray King was expected, she told her mother, father, and her grandfather that for fear of the Gray King's evil magic, and to spare bloodshed over the marriage contract, she would agree to go through with it, for the sake of her family and Jior's people. Everyone hoped that it would never come to that.

#

One month before the Gray King and his son were expected to return to Jior, a small contingency of men was spotted making its way through the northeastern passes of the Violent Mountains. Scouts rode toward Jior at breakneck speed to report thirteen armored and heavily armed men had been sighted coming north. They described in detail the flag they flew; a black raven on a field of gray. King Lorn speculated that perhaps this small contingency was the advance guard coming early in preparation for the main party. Regardless, they assuredly were from Sorn and it was feared that it was truly the Gray King approaching.

King Lorn and his sons, Vannier and Dark Star, took to the skies and flew toward the approaching men and saw that indeed it truly appeared to be the Gray King, come at last. Though it was a smaller party than they expected, and only made up of soldiers on horseback and a few pack horses. They thought about confronting them on the road but were wary of taking on the Gray King's magic outside of Jior's walls without their preparations in place. They decided that solidarity of the Ny-Failen was needed and flew back to the castle to wait for the men from Sorn to come to them.

It was late afternoon when the Gray King and his men were reluctantly allowed entrance into the City of Jior. They rode through the streets under the eye of the people who knew the evil intent of their visit. Most of the humankind did not revile or deter them but watched with detached indifference because Ny-Failen doings were hardly their concern.

Part of King Lorn's plan was to appear as if the Ny-Failen of Jior were resigned and accepting the marriage contract. He was going to spring a trap for the Gray King and his son who had finally reached marriageable age. First, Lyra Song was going to try and compel him to annul the contract with her Ny-Failen power, but they needed to get the Gray King alone. So, they were patiently awaiting the opportunity. Afterward, they would deal with his heir more expediently. In addition, Aesir Blacknight had been sent for immediately and he was called to battle the Gray King's sorcery. Having studied the magic the Gray King used ten years previous, Aesir Blacknight felt ready. A white arrow was also launched to bring Lord Lost Morning, Leader of the Ny-Failen of Everclearing.

#

The large gate in the walls surrounding Castle Jior opened and the Gray King rode forward on a spirited gray and white-spotted stallion who tossed his black mane and flicked his black tail with agitation. Down the cobbled walk to the massive stairway that fronted castle Jior, they came. Within the castle courtyard, the King dismounted along with twelve soldiers from Sorn and they strode across the vast courtyard in military precision, their silver armor glimmered dully in the fading afternoon light. The sound of their heavy boots beat in rhythm as they advanced. The door to the castle slowly opened and the shadowed doorway beckoned.

The Gray King was encased, head-to-toe, in fine silver armor heavily decorated with runes, symbols, and a raven engraving spread-winged across his chest. His face was hidden under an ornate, crowned helmet that was the only indication that he was the king. He had a long, charcoal-colored cloak that hung behind him like broken wings. He strode in with arrogant determination and did not falter or even stop to let his eyes adjust from the bright light of the sunny day to the dark, uninviting corridors of Castle Jior. A chatelain bowed and led him into the castle without greeting or instruction. The massive doors to the Great Hall opened slowly and the Gray King entered followed by his twelve men. Armored and helmeted like their king, the soldiers flanked him in phalanx formation like the deadly tip of a sharp arrow.

King Lorn was seated on his massive throne, a look of pure smoldering fury on his face. His twisted silver crown adorned his white head and beside him sat the beautiful Queen Lililaira Gem. To either side of the throne stood Prince Vannier, Prince Dark Star, their wives, sons, and daughters. All were surrounded by every Ny-Failen of Jior except for Aesir Blacknight and Mercy Rose who were at Hoarfrost castle. Jior's soldiers of humankind lined the walls, armed and ready if a fight should ensue.

Apart and to the forefront, stood Princess Lyra Song, and next to her was her daughter. Her husband Jagged Edge, was on their other side with his hand gripping his sword hilt tightly. Lyra Song placed an arm protectively across her daughter's shoulders. She was ready to call on her compelling power in a show of motherly protection.

The Gray King approached. His shielded face turned from side-to-side observing everyone present. Bending his head, he removed his crowned helmet. Holding the helmet out to the side expectantly, one of his soldiers stepped forward and took it from him. Following his lead, all of Sorn's soldiers bent their heads and removed their helmets in perfect unison, revealing their human faces. Every movement was done with practiced unity, revealing one impressive, highly-trained military force.

Many of the Ny-Failen of Jior restrained their looks of shock when they saw the young man who stood before them. It had to be the same little boy who had come to the court ten years previous, except now he was grown and, obviously, a strikingly handsome, Ny-Failen male. The Gray King's son was very tall and blessed with regal features. His hair was shaved down to the white skin on the sides of his head and the glimmering dark silver length fell straight past his shoulders to his middle back. Eyes of similar silvery-gray swept them all with veiled curiosity, and strong confidence. As a Ny-Failen, he had the same pale white skin as most of them, a long straight nose, high cheekbones and gently pointing ears. His slightly slanting silver-gray eyes were intelligent, confident, and pensive. The bow shape of his mouth was tense and unsmiling. He held his head high and proud with a taint of arrogance. The only indication of possible nervousness he revealed, was a slight hesitation before stepping forward to the middle of the floor in the Great Hall, to confront the King and Queen of Jior. They were not going to make it any easier on the Gray King's son and offered no greeting.

The hall was silent as the sun shone through the multi-colored glass windows and dust motes danced weightlessly in the air. Despite the cheerful beams of light, the atmosphere was expectant and tense with recollections of the last time the boy visited.

Before the Gray King's son addressed them, his gaze again traveled over all of those gathered before him. His hard, gray stare momentarily found those of the girl in white and held. A flicker of surprise, recognition, and longing flickered in his eyes but vanished as quickly as it appeared, replaced with a look of confirmed, and predicted expectation.

The girl in white lifted her chin slightly and stood bravely under his assessing gaze though a deep pink blush colored her cheeks. Dressed all in white with iridescent jewels gracing her hair and dress, she sparkled like a diamond. Beside her, Jagged Edge looked as if he would like to spring forward at any minute with a burst of violence.

Tipping his head slightly to the King and Queen of Jior, the tall impressive, Gray King's son, surveyed the King of Jior as if committing his royal features to memory, then he nodded once in acknowledgment.

"King Forlorn Icefall and Queen Lililaira Gem of Jior. I am the King of Sorn and I have come about the marriage contract you made with my father known as the Gray King." His voice was deep and strong. He spoke direct and confidently as if used to addressing royalty.

King Forlorn Icefall gritted his teeth and in an insulting tone spat, "Where is the *old man* who came ten years hence?"

"The Gray King is *dead.*" The announcement rippled through the room with gasps of surprise and more than a few expressions of relief. "My name, you probably won't recall, is Ashen Arrow of Sorn. King Forlorn Icefall, I beg your indulgence while I relate my story and the reason I have come. As I said, my father the Gray King, died these four years past. Since then, *I* have been crowned King of Sorn and have made it my duty to be a fair and wise king where he was *not*. As a result, I have rescinded every law, discharged every debt, and recalled every edict the Gray King ever made during his rule. Anything the Gray King would have done; I do the opposite. Now, his oppression and abuse of the silver miners, fishermen, and the citizens of Sorn has ended. Every slave and prisoner the Gray King held; I have granted them all freedom. Where once was strife, there is now peace. The Kingdom of Sorn is finally free of the Gray King's evil. Now we recover from hundreds of years of tyranny brought by his bloodline." King Ashen Arrow swallowed nervously and cast a quick sorrowful glance at Rain Song before he continued.

"My last act as King of Sorn is the *dissolution* of the marriage contract the Gray King forced upon Jior through his magic and evil coercion ten years ago."

Princess Lyra Song almost swooned. Her hand flew to her mouth to hide the cry of relief she gave upon hearing this announcement. King Forlorn Icefall sat up straight trying to hide his shock and the hope that suddenly bloomed in his heart. Many let go exhalations of held breaths and expressions of joy reverberated throughout the room as people reacted to the news.

King Lorn raised a hand for silence as he was not finished with the boy. Leaning forward on his throne he glared with suspicion. It all seemed too easily done to his mind.

"It all seems too easily done to me. Undoing the Gray King's evil magic cannot come without a cost." King Forlorn Icefall who had been looking forward to a fight, scowled at him.

"What are you not telling me?"

The young King of Sorn looked a little defiant as if he had nothing more to reveal, but King Lorn glared at him. *"What are you not telling me?"* He repeated forcefully.

"Nothing at all." The King of Sorn dismissed him. "Do not concern yourself. Only take the relief I offer your family."

"Tell all!" King Lorn demanded again. Knowing for certain there was more to learn. He cast a quizzical look at Jagged Edge to see if he read the boy's mind, but he only looked frustrated.

Ashen Arrow scowled as if he did not want to divulge anything further, while King Lorn waited glaring at him with violet, burning eyes that would not be denied. He leaned forward suspiciously. A strong agitation began to grow within Lorn's mind and he could feel, like a prick of a dagger at the back of his neck that something was wrong with this entire situation. It niggled at him and he was determined to get all the information possible.

"I know there is more to this dissolution than you are letting on. For the safety of my kingdom and my granddaughter, I demand to know. You are withholding information, a reason, a consequence?"

The young King of Sorn flushed with anger in return and narrowed his eyes at King Lorn in further defiance. He raised his chin, still stubborn in the face of the King of Jior. He reached out his hand to the soldier who held his crowned helmet as if preparing to leave.

"Boy," the King's voice rose menacingly, a last warning rumbling up from deep inside his chest. Every nerve in his body tingled. His skin began to itch and his heart thundered strangely. Some instinct whispered to him that there was more to learn. He was determined not to let the matter alone or let the boy go. "We have ways of getting the truth from you and I am not averse to using them. Do not make me command it again. Tell all!"

Ashen Arrow knew he was temporarily defeated but it mattered not one bit. He shrugged one shoulder impertinently and scowled back. Confronted, he let out a frustrated breath but continued to remain stubborn. King Lorn slowly stood quivering with agitation knowing to his bones something was not right with this whole situation. His large white wings unfurled slowly and stretched out behind him. He loomed over the boy with a menacing narrow-eyed look that said he would brook no further insolence.

Descending one of the steps from the platform where his throne was, he continued to intimidate the King of Sorn with his show of strength and power.

The King of Sorn closed his eyes and huffed with impatient frustration at the King of Jior's obvious coercion tactic and then stared fearlessly at King Lorn. Again, he shrugged with one impertinent shoulder as if none of it made any difference.

"Before the Gray King took to his deathbed, he revealed to me one caveat to the contract you and I were forced to consent to with our blood and oaths. *I must* marry a Ny-Failen of Jior and complete the marriage contract, as I vowed before I turn one and twenty or…" He hesitated to continue.

"Or?" King Lorn prompted impatiently. A slow trickle of sweat traveled down his spine.

"*My life* will be forfeit. In one month's time, *I* am cursed to die if I do not fulfill and *consummate* the marriage as per the agreement with Jior. I believe this final magic the Gray King wrought was his greatest evil. By king's blood pact agreed upon by you and I, who still live, it is unbreakable except by the death of one of us because the Gray King would force his way even in the end. I am…" he faltered a little, his eyes darting once again to the girl in white, but he went on bravely. "I am releasing Jior and your granddaughter, of the contract to marry me consigning myself to death so that *she* will not suffer such an ill fate as the Gray King had intended to force upon her."

"Why are you here then? Why come all this way just to cancel the marriage contract, if you are so intent upon dying, why not just die in Sorn?" Jagged Edge interrupted suspiciously.

Ashen Arrow blanched a little paler, visibly affected by the unexpected inquisition. He looked almost vulnerable at that moment before he looked Jagged Edge straight in the eye. Holding his hand out as if pleading for *understanding*, and in a soft sorrowful voice explained.

"Because," he hesitated as his entire demeanor changed, softened. His silver gaze shifted to the beautiful girl in white, as if he knew it was she who would have been his betrothed. He spoke directly to her. "Because *if* she waited…*if* she dreaded every day for the past ten long years, the horrible prospect of a marriage forced upon her…if she feared what might happen if she didn't go through with it…I could not bear it. I *had* to come and release her fear and trepidation of the Gray King's wrath. If she was kept prisoner by the machinations of that evil, deranged, cruel king…I could not go to my grave without first freeing *her*, my Lady…well the one who *was* to be mine."

The hall was completely silent and still. Not a breath stirred the air after this declaration. Tears streamed down the faces of some of the ladies as their hearts broke for the beautiful young king standing in front of them who was sentenced to die. Some of the men's faces held looks of relief and some of triumph. No one spoke for a long time. Queen Lililaira Gem was visibly shaken and held back tears of compassion.

Finally, the silence in the hall held so long that Ashen Arrow of Sorn stirred. Out of his cloak, he pulled a long, thin silver scroll case and held it out to King Lorn who recognized it at once.

"King Forlorn Icefall, I return to you the blood that was forcibly taken and with this final act, I release your oath and your granddaughter from this awful fate worse than death."

"Wait!" King Lorn demanded and seemed to have to force the words out. "When a sorcerer dies, his magic dies with him. How do we know you will die if you do not fulfill the contract? How do we know the old man did not lie to you on his deathbed to force you, with fear of death, to go through with it?"

"Take a good look at the case King of Jior. Recall that inner-sight I know all Ny-Failen have and look, and you will see this last curse remains. I feel it. It is bound to me like the Gray King's fist clenching about my heart. Then you will know that his wishes will be fulfilled or I die."

King Lorn stilled as he had done many times in the past and he looked with that inner sight all Ny-Failen have and he *saw*. Every Ny-Failen within the hall trained their vision and saw. Wrapping around the silver cylinder and flowing outwards, the black tendrils of evil that had blighted Jior ten years earlier, seethed around the case and bled out, snaking its invisible tendrils out to coil around the body of Ashen Arrow and enveloped his heart with black, visceral, deadly magic. Every Ny-Failen with sight could see that the boy was somehow bound by that curse that lived beyond the Gray King's death and sealed his son's fate.

Then every Ny-Failen's gaze flew to the girl in white and peered at her. Many sighs of relief were released as they realized she was at least free of the Gray King's magic. Princess Lyra Song hugged her daughter with joy that she was truly free.

"The Gray King feared I would not go through with the marriage contract after he died. He thought I was weak and worthless, and knew from the beginning I would work to free Jior from his evil. In the end, he tried to guarantee that, in this, his will would be done and the bloodline of Sorn continued."

He went on in a strong determined voice, "But I will sacrifice myself for a love that I will never know, so that *she* may be free." He said these last words to the girl in white who stood with tears brimming in her eyes, watching the beautiful King of Sorn sacrifice himself for her who should have been his bride, his wife, his love.

Ashen Arrow of Sorn took two steps forward and gently placed the silver scroll case on the marble steps before the king and queen. Then he turned slightly, placed his hand over his heart, and bowed low to the girl in white who stood frozen, trembling in shock and sorrow. When he straightened, he gazed at her for a full minute as if committing her face to memory and then he turned and strode from the hall.

The Ny-Failen of Jior let him go.

CHAPTER THREE

Out of the towering black gates of the city of Jior, swiftly rode the young King of Sorn and his men, to begin the long journey back the way they had come. Darkness had caught them and rather than travel the Violent Mountain roads during the night, they made camp a little over a mile from the huge black walls surrounding Jior. The men were tired and the horses needed rest before returning to Sorn. Despondent, they sat silently around their campfires and rested for the night.

As if even the beauty of a full complete orb was denied him, the moon shone above just shy of full. It hung, shining straight above Jior in the clear night sky and cast the forest in a white glow almost as bright as daylight. The towering, black-barked trees in the forest of the surrounding Violent Mountains, stood like silent sentinels watching through the peaceful night. There was no peace for King Ashen Arrow of Sorn though.

On the road to Jior, Ashen Arrow had been plagued by terrifying dreams of the Gray King. In those dreams, his father ranted at him in joyful glee that the marriage contract would soon come to fruition. He urged his son on. It was as if Ashen Arrow had somehow brought his father's ghost with him. The Gray King visited him night after night instructing him on getting the marriage quickly done and over with, and consummated as soon as possible. His face appeared large in Ashen's mind and his voice repeated the frantic, insane mantra over and over until Ashen thought he would go mad from hearing it.

In those dreams, Ashen defied his father and shouted at him that he was going to end the marriage contract and would not marry the girl in Jior. As if still alive and before him in the flesh, the Gray King flew into a rage unlike Ashen had ever seen when he was alive. Lashing out, he called him a coward and a failure. His mouth frothed with gray saliva as he raged and continued to spew foul names at Ashen. His insistence that the marriage go through or Ashen would die a long, painful death with torment that would last beyond the grave, drove him even more relentlessly to dissolve the marriage contract and thwart his father's evil. The litany continued each time Ashen tried to sleep, to the point that he no longer could sleep through the night. The only time he had any relief from the Gray King's rantings was when he was awake. Determined to thwart his father's plans, Ashen took heart knowing that he was doing the right thing, and ignored the fact that he had one short month left to live.

Forefront in his mind, something nagged at him. The question as to why the Gray King wanted this marriage so badly that he would curse his only son to such depths and for all of eternity. Ashen could marry anyone and father children to carry on the Sorn bloodline. Why must it be a Ny-Failen and why one of Forlorn Icefall's lineage? Though it was true most all of the Ny-Failen were found in Jior and Everclearing was out of reach. Jior was a solitary choice with little alternative.

It was not a simple evil manipulation cast from beyond the grave that had driven the Gray King. Even taking into consideration his father's considerable conceit and the possibility that Sorn's ancient ancestry was untarnished royalty; Ashen could not put a name to this, his father's madness. All Ashen's speculations were fruitless and the reality struck him that he never had, in all his life, understood his father's evil machinations. Lastly, Ashen feared that somehow his subconscious was so riddled with guilt and the need for affectionate companionship that the dreams and abuse of his mind, were of his own making.

#

Ashen Arrow of Sorn leaned his tall frame against a thick tree and stared up at the almost full moon. The only sound he heard was the crackling flames of his small fire and the gentle breeze swaying the trees around him. This night he had chosen to take his bedroll apart from his men and he stood alone with his thoughts and contemplated the long road home and his inevitable death. His hatred for the Gray King had strengthened his courage, but his resolve to free the girl he was betrothed to, wavered as he remembered the girl in white, whom he had seen in Jior.

She was unlike anything he had ever laid eyes on before and she was certainly the most beautiful girl of his acquaintance. The moon's bright white glow above reminded him of her luminous pearl-white skin and long, white hair. He had not gotten close enough to see her eyes and imagined what color they would be. Ashen intuitively knew it was the girl dressed in white that was to have been his future wife, not only by the reactions of the two people by her side but also by a strong feeling he had when he looked at her. It was like *recognition*. When Ashen had announced she was free of the contract, the two Ny-Failen beside her reacted with obvious joy and unconcealed relief. That hurt Ashen deeply, but he would not admit that to anyone nor explore that hurt further. No part of his mind or heart could allow thoughts that they might still go through with the contract or that she might, against all the odds, *want* the marriage. It could not be tolerated to allow any hope that there was a way to avoid his death or her terrible fate.

Since the day the Gray King died, Ashen had spent years searching for a way to undo the evil curse that gripped him. Under his father's tutelage, he had learned black sorcery with the single goal of undoing it all when the Gray King died. Even now he could feel the tendrils of his father's curse constricting his heart. Eventually, Ashen had to admit defeat in his efforts and he simply ran out of time. This curse was the only lesson the Gray King had neglected to teach him. Defiant to the end, Ashen had been determined to return to Jior, undo his father's evil, and release the girl who would have been his. In the recesses of his heart, he secretly yearned to glimpse her fair face one last time.

It was the Gray King's evil face that continued to haunt his dreams during the journey to Jior, berating him as a coward, a weakling, and a traitor to his own blood that also drove Ashen Arrow. So great was Ashen's hatred for his father that he rejoiced in the satisfaction it gave him to thwart the old man's plans to his dying breath.

As he continued to gaze up at the bright moon, Ashen heard the sound of wings beating the air and suddenly the moon darkened behind the huge shadow of something flying overhead. The King of Jior circled once above then swooped down. His huge white wings beat the air and he landed a few feet from Ashen's fire.

A surprised Ashen Arrow straightened as King Forlorn Icefall approached. Outlined by the silvery moonshine from behind and bathed in the golden glow of the fire in front, the impressive King of Jior stood for a moment before he finally took a deep breath and spoke in a tone that commanded attention.

"It is a brave thing you do, giving your life for someone you have never met." King Lorn spoke calmly but his wings pulsed in agitation.

"It is not bravery it is defiance and revenge. With my last breath, I will spit upon the Gray King's grave, upon his plans and every hope he had that his bloodline would continue." Ashen Arrow spoke with unveiled venom. "The day you and

I were forced by blood to sign that terrible contract, I vowed I would do everything in my power to thwart my *father*. And so, I have."

"You are so unlike the Gray King." King Lorn's voice took on a speculative tone. "I only met him briefly, but without a doubt, his evil was unbound. You are different. Perhaps it is because of your mother's blood?"

"My purpose in life has always been to be completely the opposite of the Gray King. And yes, it has been my hope that I resemble the mother I never knew instead of the father I have only known." His voice sounded sad.

"Alright, but you did not try and convince us that you are not evil and go through with the marriage? There is much for you to gain by forcing us to keep our side of the bargain."

Ashen hesitated for a long minute and dropped his gaze from Lorn's.

"Was that her? In the hall? The girl in the white dress. Was *she* to be the one I would have wed?"

"Yes, she was the only one that would qualify. One of my other granddaughters is winged and the Gray King expressly said no winged one, the other is too young to marry. I did consider some form of trickery but it shames me to say I was leery of the Gray King's magic. Though we were prepared to fight it with everything we have."

"I almost failed when I saw her, I knew it must be her, the girl in white." Ashen's voice went soft and he stared into the flames of the fire, lost in his memories. "She was so beautiful! I almost forgot my purpose and my hatred, but I could not hurt one so lovely, so delicate and graceful. I could not sentence her to an unwanted marriage, to what the Gray King had forced upon her, and take her so far away from her family and everything she loves. I could not do it just to save my own skin."

King Lorn watched the young King of Sorn and his heart felt heavy. He contemplated the situation for many long moments. He had not shifted and still stood winged beside the fire, a large and imposing presence. Eventually, compassion, pity, forgiveness, and a strong prompting in the back of his mind, took hold of his anger and doused it like water on a flame.

"Ashen Arrow, the Ny-Failen of Jior have not been idle. We have worked diligently for the last ten years to combat the evil magic of the Gray King. We were not unprepared to meet him in battle this time. I confess you took us all by surprise when you announced you would rather die than hold us to the marriage contract. You seem to be an honorable young man and I have come to a decision. I am asking you to return to the castle in the morning. Stay in Jior for a while and let us see if we cannot undo the magic spell that would seal your death. Let us work together to truly thwart the Gray King's last work of evil."

Ashen Arrow looked somber as if he did not want to give himself room to hope. He shook his head.

"I have tried for the last four years. Nothing I have done has succeeded. It is one short month until my birthday and, on that day, I will die, sentenced to the Underworld for eternity. I can feel it taking hold. I am in his evil death grip and I am out of time. It is too late. I must return to Sorn, to name my successor and put my final affairs in order."

"Give me a fortnight. Come back to Jior and work with us to undo this evil. If we fail and you still wish it, you will have time to return to Sorn, to die in your home." King Lorn's soft entreaty reached out to Ashen.

Dared he hope? A beautiful, ethereal face flashed out of Ashen's memory and he remembered the girl in white. He closed his eyes and tried to banish the memory but the sight of her was emblazoned on his mind.

"Thank you for your generous offer King Forlorn Icefall. I will contemplate it and you will have my answer in the morning."

King Lorn nodded once, "A fortnight, give me that much." Then he spread his wings and leaped into the night sky.

#

A short time after King Forlorn Icefall flew back to Jior, Ashen Arrow of Sorn felt the delicate prickle of a new presence and he was visited again. A small figure stepped out of the darkness and approached his fire. Cloaked in black, the figure stood silent for a few moments and then reached up with gloved hands and lowered the dark, concealing hood.

Standing in front of Ashen Arrow was the beautiful girl he had seen in Jior's Great Hall. Ashen startled, a little shocked, and looked around as if searching for a place to run to. He stared into the darkness behind the girl and did not see anyone else.

Stepping into the light of the fire the girl worked at the fingers of her gloves and pulled one by one, removing them while she spoke.

"Do not be alarmed, I am alone." Her voice was sweet and musical, gentle and assuring.

"How did you find me?" Ashen Arrow asked in a very un-king-like tone of voice.

"Well," she looked a little embarrassed, "one can see very far from the tall towers of Castle Jior if one but looks."

"How did you get here? This is a long way from the castle."

The girl shrugged and did not answer right away, but moved closer to the fire. The night was fair, but there was a cool breeze blowing and the warmth of the flames was inviting.

"As children my brother, sisters, cousins, and I used to play in the catacombs beneath the castle. It is easy for children who can see in the dark. We discovered many tunnels, most of which were caved in or blocked. Over the years we secretly worked to open a few of them to see where they led and, well, the way out of the castle was clear and I had to come."

"Why?" Ashen Arrow choked, his voice caught and he cleared his voice, fighting to sound normal. "Why have you come?"

"I, I wanted to speak to you." Bravely, she held his gaze and it took a moment before he could respond. He examined her beautiful features, high cheekbones, delicate swooping eyebrows over almond-shaped eyes, and her soft red lips against pearl-white skin.

He straightened as if suddenly remembering himself, remembering that he was a doomed King. Stooping to throw another stick on the fire he took a moment to collect himself, strengthen his resolve and stand tall. The look on his face was almost angry.

"You should not have come. You should be at home, safe in your bed."

"Never-the-less, I have come because I wanted to speak to you and ask, why you wish so badly to die?"

Taken aback, Ashen Arrow stared at her before he could finally answer.

"My Lady, forgive me, I have very little experience speaking to young girls. Most of the females at Castle Sorn are older, mostly servants and I have very little to do with them. The Gray King was the kind of man females ran from and so ran from me as well. After the Gray King died, I tried to change all that and some did come back around a little, but still very few remain. My point is, I have no social graces or fine words with which to converse with someone like you."

"I understand what you are saying but there is no need for formality around me. I am-*was*-the girl you were supposed to marry. Now, it seems you would rather die than be wed to me!"

Ashen Arrow looked horror-stricken and took a step forward shaking his head.

"No! No, My Lady, you misunderstand. It is not that I don't want to marry you! I just thought…the marriage contract was coerced, forced upon your grandfather and myself. I could not make you suffer for what evil the Gray King intended despite the fact he is now dead. That is all. I…you have no idea what he had planned!" Ashen stopped speaking and closed his eyes, he took a deep, frustrated breath before he could continue. "It has nothing to do with you, but it has everything to do with you. You deserve better than an evil king's son!"

The girl took a few steps toward Ashen Arrow and he took a few steps back. A hurt look crossed her face and she stopped. Ashen looked at her bathed in moonlight with her white hair spread across her shoulders and the brave look she painted on her face.

"It is a noble thing you do, dying for the sake of someone you have never met before. It is a great sacrifice." She repeated the same thoughts her grandfather had spoken an hour earlier, but softly, sounding frustrated as she went on. "Maybe if we had more time to get to know each other or court each other or something besides just meet and wed or meet and *die*. I've been given no choices, nor have I been asked my preference in this entire situation."

"I assumed, as did your grandfather I think, that you dreaded this union. Your father, the tall man with the red hair I believe, looked as if he would like to kill me right then and there rather than relinquish his daughter to Ashen Arrow of Sorn." Ashen hesitated and then went on. "It is for the best. Someday you will meet a good man, I have no doubt, and you will fall in love and get married, have many children, and the happy future you deserve. *I* have nothing to offer you, only a lifetime in a forced marriage and sorrow."

She did not speak only stood looking at him for so long that Ashen grew uncomfortable and finally filled the long silence with a false royal attitude.

"My Lady, your grandfather was just here not an hour past. He entreated me to return to Jior in the morning and work with the Ny-Failen to try and break the curse of the marriage contract. I beseech you, go back to the castle before you are missed and if I make the decision to stay, I am sure you will hear of it and then…"

Ashen could not go on because he could not contemplate what might happen if he decided to stay and break the curse. The beautiful girl in front of him looked at him with large, liquid eyes of pure emerald green. Her nearness caused his breathing to catch and his blood to surge. The soft flowery scent of her blew to him on the gentle night breeze and he had to stop himself from stepping forward to capture more of it. He suddenly itched to take her into his arms.

"I don't even know your name?" Ashen Arrow asked.

"I am Rain Song. Named after my mother Lyra Song, and because it was gently raining when I was born. It is my Ny-Failen name." Her voice was like music on a gentle breeze and Ashen watched enraptured as her small hand reached up to pull away a white strand of her long hair that had blown across her cheek.

"Rain Song," he breathed just barely making a sound. *"Beautiful!"* He closed his eyes as if he were in pain. Then he seemed to come awake, straightened, and looked away.

"Lady Rain Song, you must return to Castle Jior at once. I will, of course, escort you and see you safely back but you must go. If you will but show me the way you've come. It grows late and…you should go."

"King Ashen Arrow," she spoke forcefully and stepped forward to lay a delicate hand on his arm. "Please, come to the castle tomorrow as Grandfather asked, as soon as is possible. Let us help you end this curse your father put upon you and let us-*let us*-you and I, start anew. Please, will you do that, for me?"

The sound of his name on her lips was like music in his silent heart. He wished so much that he could take her in his arms and kiss her, tell her that everything would be alright, but he had only just met her and it would not be true. He held no hope that there was a chance to break the curse his father put on him and so he committed the sound of his name on her lips to his memory and moved past her to get his horse.

"I will get my horse and take you back to the castle."

Rain Song turned and watched Ashen Arrow stride past her. She surveyed his long, dark silver hair gleaming in the moonlight, his straight back and broad shoulders moving away in the night. He no longer wore the silver armor that he had worn into the Great Hall that day but wore a simple dove-gray shirt and coat. It did nothing to hide his soldier's physique. Her breath caught and her heart beat frantically watching him go. He was very attractive and noble and brave. She sighed; a delicate sound drowned by the breeze.

Ashen Arrow returned shortly leading a large gray and white spotted stallion with a long flowing black mane and tail. While Ashen had been saddling his horse, he made a very rash and self-indulgent decision. Rather than lead the horse and walk while Rain Song rode, as he should do, he was determined to sit on the horse behind her and hold her in his arms. He told himself he would allow this one indiscretion, this one lingering touch of her, this one closeness so that in his remaining days, he would have this memory to keep.

As if he were greeting Rain Song, the horse nodded its head when they reached the fire. The sound of his silver bridle tinkled with the movement. She smiled and walked toward the horse and patted his long black mane.

"My Lady, this is my horse, Tarnish." He rubbed the horse's nose affectionately, "He is a temperamental beast and will suffer no other rider, but myself. I will put you up and ride behind so that he does not throw you off. Unless you refuse such familiarity in which case, I will do my best to gentle him while you ride."

The thought instantly entered Rain Song's mind that Ashen Arrow could have temporarily borrowed one of the other soldier's horses for her, but she did not suggest it.

"Ah, no, that will do." Rain Song spoke without further hesitation. She was an accomplished horsewoman and knew that no horse would throw her, but she was curious about riding in front of Ashen Arrow. His arms would be around her and his large body pressing very close. She walked forward and reached up to the saddle, she was going to place her foot in the stirrup and swing up, but Ashen Arrow was instantly behind her, his hands were around her slim waist and he was easily lifting her into the saddle. She was wearing a pair of dark-colored trousers and so straddled the tall horse easily. He placed her in front and then he mounted behind her as promised.

The horse sidestepped, easily adjusting to the weight of two riders, and moved sedately on when prompted. Ashen Arrow snaked his arms around Rain Song and took the reins in hand. He waited while she adjusted to his nearness and then he realized what a mistake he had made. The beautiful girl in the saddle in front of him was so tantalizing he almost leaped off because the temptation to crush her in his arms was so great. She was sweet-smelling and when he had put his hands around her small waist and lifted her, his fingers almost went all the way around her slim torso. She was feather-light and felt so enticing now that he was close to her. Ashen had to steel himself against the temptation to lean forward, rest his cheek against her hair and pull her even nearer. This was going to be harder than he thought but would be worth every minute she was this much in his arms. He would remember this night for the rest of his short life.

Rain Song was overwhelmed by the feel of Ashen Arrow's undeniably attractive presence and warmth surrounding her. She was astonished at the ease with which he lifted her into the saddle. When he mounted and his strong arms encompassed her, his legs clamped snuggly behind hers, her pulse raced and she wanted to lean back into his embrace and feel every breath he took. Instead, she held herself rigid reminding herself that he was a stranger. Adjusting in the saddle a little, Ashen Arrow guided the great gray stallion through the woods and onto the road leading back to Jior.

Ashen had never been this close to such a beautiful and delicate lady. It was not lost on him that she was his kind, Ny-Failen and she was so tempting. The feel of her almost touching him was astonishing and when she brushed against his chest with the movement of the horse, he had a hard time controlling himself. His body was flaming with desire. He tried to concentrate on directing Tarnish and not on the feel of her in his arms.

They were silent on the way to Jior except for Rain Song giving an occasional direction. The night was fair and the moon lit their way. Ashen had never enjoyed riding his horse as much before and wished the night would never end. Rain Song smelled so good. Covertly, he breathed in deeply of her scent and committed every detail of her to his memory. Her long silvery-white hair and slim perfect body tempted him beyond reason. His arms were around her grasping the reins, holding her in place. It was almost sensual. Ashen kept Tarnish at a walk the mile back to Jior's walls to draw out the ride as long as possible. Rain Song finally eased back and leaned against his chest. Ashen was so thrilled by this small intimacy that he dared to rest his cheek against her head for just a brief moment before he remembered who she was and who he was and that she was *not* for him.

Gesturing to the deeper shadows on the trail before they met the glittering black walls surrounding the city, Rain Song directed Ashen Arrow toward Jior. It was a long, moonlit ride up a steep trail to the city of Jior and it curved back into the mountainside. Along the tall black walls and behind the thick bushes that proliferated there, she explained a secret entrance could be found.

Ashen finally led Tarnish to a halt and reluctantly swung down when they arrived at their destination. He stretched his hands up to Rain Song. She reached toward him, and he lifted her down. Tarnish was a very tall horse and as she slid from the saddle, she put her hands on Ashen's shoulders and once she reached the ground, she looked up into his silver eyes. They stood thus, her arms slid down his chest and his hands on her tiny waist for a long moment. Ashen desperately wanted to pull her close, lean down and taste her lips.

Rain Song badly wanted Ashen Arrow to lean down and kiss her, but the moment passed, and nervously, he stepped away.

"My Lady, lead on and I will make sure you are returned safely to the castle before I leave you."

Rain Song nodded, and turned to go, but then stopped. She reached for his hand and held it, skin to skin, and made him look at her.

"You will come tomorrow, and try and break the curse, as Grandfather asked? You will! Promise me? *Please!*"

Ashen looked at her for a long time before he drew himself up tall and looked down his long straight nose at her. Trying to harden his heart against her entreaty, her beautiful eyes pleaded with him, and her luscious mouth quivered with emotion. Ashen bowed and raised her hand to his lips in what he hoped was a gallant courtly gesture, then he kissed the back of her hand.

"If my Lady wishes it, I will come." Ashen's deep voice held regret and resignation.

"Promise?" She asked more strongly as she held his hand in a long lingering touch.

"I promise." And so Ashen Arrow of Sorn, felt as if he had just sealed, not only his fate but hers as well.

CHAPTER FOUR

Ashen Arrow had intended to answer the King of Jior by riding back to Sorn early the next morning. Rain Song's visit changed everything. She had extracted his promise with eyes of emerald green and he would not break that promise. The fleeting moments riding with her before him on his horse, his arms around her, and her soft touch when she held his hand, made it impossible to deny her.

After explaining the King of Jior's request to his men, all his soldiers gladly acquiesced. They were in no hurry to return to Sorn so quickly and the lure of hot cooked meals and cold ale for the next fortnight enticed them even further. They were all packed and mounted in no time and were glad there was a possibility something could be done for their young King.

When they returned to the castle the next morning, the King of Jior himself was standing at the top of the stairs at the black castle's entrance as if he expected them. The day was fair and blue skies spread above them. Ashen could almost feel the faintest bit of hope dangerously taking hold of his heart.

"King Ashen Arrow, your men can stay in the soldier's barracks and I have a room in the guest tower for you. We can start immediately trying to break this curse and keep at it until you are free. I have a feeling we will all be free in a way, once that contract is irreversibly broken bringing harm to no one."

"Thank you, King Forlorn Icefall. Your offer was a surprise and you have my deepest thanks. My men and I appreciate your hospitality. They could use some rest and some decent food." Ashen Arrow almost smiled.

Just then the tall man with long hair the color of dark red blood came out of the castle. Ashen Arrow knew this was Rain Song's father who had stood at her side the day before in the Great Hall. He unconsciously stood a little straighter.

"Commander Jagged Edge, as you are aware, this is the King of Sorn, Ashen Arrow. I have told you of my offer to help rid him of the Gray King's curse." King Lorn introduced them formally.

Jagged Edge stood cloaked in smoldering disapproval and only acknowledged Ashen Arrow with a brisk nod of his head. He stood for a moment longer with a frown on his face that only deepened after a few moments. Finally, he stopped trying to read the young King's mind and greeted him.

"King Ashen Arrow. My wife and I are deeply grateful that you have released our daughter from that cursed marriage contract."

Ashen Arrow raised his chin and gave Jagged Edge a look that said *'I just bet you are!'* but instead of answering, he gave him a regal tilt of his head and a single nod.

They went into the castle and King Lorn led Jagged Edge and Ashen Arrow to a great library filled with books and scrolls. A heavy desk, small tables, and a few large stuffed chairs were placed in front of a large, unlit fireplace. They spent the afternoon discussing the efforts Ashen Arrow had employed to break the Gray King's spell. Neither King Lorn nor Jagged Edge was a sorcerer and they knew nothing of magic. They had immediately sent for Aesir Blacknight, who was a Blue Sorcerer, in hopes that he could help. They also sent for Lost Morning who had greater wisdom, the Creator's patronage, and more power than all of them put together.

King Lorn was frustrated because he usually employed the might of his mind, the skill of his sword, and the strength of his muscle to defeat difficult problems. This, however, was a matter of sorcery and he was powerless against that. After a few hours consulting a few of the many books and scrolls they had collected over the past ten years, they discussed different courses of action. Ashen Arrow admitted he had years of tutelage under his father the Gray King, but that all of his lessons were in black sorcery and intended for evil. Though this was an evil curse, none of those lessons revealed a way to break it.

They brought out the silver case that Ashen Arrow had presented to King Lorn the day before. It was the scroll case that held the marriage contract. After discussing it for much of the afternoon, they finally admitted defeat for the day and decided to wait for Lost Morning and Aesir Blacknight to arrive, as their initial efforts proved useless. Ashen Arrow was escorted to a huge chamber in the tall guest tower, where he was intended to stay. He was invited to the Great Hall for dinner with the family later that evening. A bath with steaming water was waiting for him.

After Ashen Arrow left, King Lorn looked expectantly at Jagged Edge, "Well?"

Because of their long-standing relationship as king and commander, father-in-law and son-in-law, Jagged Edge knew exactly what Lorn was asking and he shook with frustration. "He is well shielded like Aesir Blacknight is. He has learned to block his mind and I cannot read him. However, I do sense that the boy has allowed himself to hope and it seeps through his defenses."

King Lorn leaned against the large desk in the room and crossed his arms over his massive chest.

"Jagged Edge, I want you to consider something." King Lorn began, "I had to relinquish my daughter to you, against my better judgment at the time because you were Lyra Song's choice. A few years ago, you had to relinquish Mercy Rose to Aesir Blacknight because he was her choice. Many a father has had to give up his daughter to a man for husband inevitably, as you know. There is one obvious choice in this matter and I ask you if this curse cannot be broken in any other way, would you consent to the marriage if Rain Song chose it? I know Sorn is a long way from Jior, but I have a sense about this and he seems an honorable and intelligent young man, nothing like his father."

Jagged Edge stared at King Lorn in growing outrage. After a few moments, he closed his eyes and breathed deeply calming himself. Looking back upon his history with Lyra Song and how badly he behaved when she was a captive of Lord Borosilis of Ondrea, Jagged Edge felt a twinge of guilt. Ashen Arrow did appear more honorable compared to how Jagged Edge had been in the beginning. His love for his daughter quickly wiped that guilt away and he just brooded silently before King Lorn. His green eyes sparked with frustration and, yes, he had to admit, a severe desire to deny the whole situation and hold his youngest daughter close.

All the Ny-Failen of Jior had felt as if they had little choice before Ashen Arrow came and released Rain Song from the marriage contract, and they were going to fight it with everything at their disposal. Jagged Edge had even contemplated sticking his dagger in Ashen Arrow's heart if it came to being forced into going through with the marriage. Ashen Arrow had removed his helmet just the day before and stood before them all, noble, kind, compassionate, a true Ny-Failen King. Jagged Edge felt Rain Song's hopes flare with something akin to joy and immediate attraction. She felt relief and a small bit of anxious anticipation that the handsome, young King before them all was to be her husband. When Ashen Arrow announced his intentions to release her, Rain Song felt slightly affronted and had a moment of disappointment. When her mother, Lyra Song, had hugged her with tears of joy, Rain Song felt a small bit of numb relief to be released from her obligation to marry a stranger, an evil King's son, and facing the inevitability of leaving Jior.

Jagged Edge came back from his ruminations and snapped at the King of Jior.

"I understand what you are saying, but that doesn't mean I have to like it!"

"You know the easiest way to end this curse, they could marry. Fulfilling the contract would save the young King of Sorn and possibly Rain Song would gain a good man for a husband. She is of age to marry and don't you think she should be given a choice in the matter?"

"NO!" Jagged Edge stormed around the room and yelled. "I don't understand you! For ten years we have searched for a way to prevail against the Gray King's black magic and get out of this marriage contract and now, all of a sudden, you are for it?"

King Lorn endured Jagged Edge's outburst, then he growled menacingly under his breath, "How did you treat my daughter when you first met? It is very different when the boot is on the other foot! Do not accuse me of taking the side of the Gray King, I am simply exploring all the options and trying to save a good man."

"I will not let my daughter make a bad choice based upon pity. Furthermore, I intend that Rain Song shall never meet him. While he is here, I will keep her far away from the Gray King's son!"

"Rain Song has a right to make her own choice, make her own decisions if it affects her future!"

"It is *my* daughter's life at stake, not yours. I cannot read him or hear his thoughts! I cannot tell if he is truly as noble as he appears or if a snake lies under a hidden façade. You would have me risk giving Rain Song to a boy you have only known for a few hours? You know what his father was like!

I fought with you in that battle ten years ago. I do not forget the Gray King's evil magic and this is *his* flesh and blood you want me to give my daughter to? I'd rather let the boy die!"

King Lorn strode toward Jagged Edge and stood looking down at him with smoldering anger. The two were rarely at odds but this intense moment was fraught with dangerous potential.

"Do not think for one moment, I would risk Rain Song or any female in my family if I were not completely assured of her safety and happiness. I only ask that you consider it. Ashen Arrow is Ny-Failen and I sense that he is a good man, but I would never allow my granddaughter or her mother, *my daughter*, to be hurt. I would protect them to my dying breath, but I will have your full cooperation in trying to break this curse Jagged Edge and then we shall see what transpires."

Jagged Edge stood defiantly in the face of King Lorn's demands for a few moments. Then he nodded his head once, barely assenting, turned, and strode from the room. His anger poured off of him in hot waves.

CHAPTER FIVE

Later that evening, the family gathered for dinner in the Great Hall. Long tables had been arranged and were heavily laden with rich foods and many delicacies. Heavy silver chalices were filled to the brim from pitchers of cold ale, spiced cider, or wine.

Rain Song attended dinner as usual, in direct defiance of her father's wishes. She dressed with special care this evening when she heard King Ashen Arrow of Sorn was going to be dining with the family. Her curled, upswept hair was topped with a skullcap decorated with small emeralds. The long flowing dress of lavender silk she wore was embroidered with tiny violet flowers and laced with pale green ribbons that enhanced the color of her emerald eyes. At age nineteen many of the women in her family had been courting or were betrothed. For the last ten years, Rain Song had considered herself betrothed. Though marring what should be a happy status, was the fear of the Gray King and the assumption that his son would be just as cruel, devious, and evil. Now that she had seen and met Ashen Arrow, and he revealed himself as something completely opposite, Rain Song was finding herself in a more encouraging mind. Notwithstanding how strikingly attractive he was, he was gallant, considerate, kind, gentle, and brave.

As with any visiting dignitary, King Ashen Arrow of Sorn was seated at the head table to King Lorn's right and Queen Lily was next to her husband on the left. Though he was dressed informally in a dark gray soldier's uniform, he looked every inch a king. The Sornian king's guard who had accompanied him to Jior were all seated at other tables across the room from the family and dined with some of

Jior's other soldiers as guests of the King of Jior. The Princes of Jior, Vannier, and Dark Star were interspersed throughout the other tables with their wives and children. Prince Vannier's identical twin sons arrived late as usual and quickly seated themselves in their accustomed places. The King of Jior stood and addressed the entire company welcoming everyone and introducing the King of Sorn. Then he bowed his head, and they all said a prayer of thanks to the Creator, and the meal began in earnest.

Ashen Arrow had never seen such grandeur, never witnessed such happiness and people at their ease. Soft music played in the background and there were more beautiful women dressed in colorful finery and bedecked with costly jewels than he ever believed he would see in one place. No one was sick and no one groveled, and the servants seemed happy to bring the excellent meal.

Conversation between King Lorn and King Ashen Arrow was strained at first, but then the topic turned to Sorn and the silver mines there. Ashen explained the changes he had enacted since his father's death four years earlier. He briefly mentioned his uncanny ability to sense the deep veins of silver proliferate throughout his realm. Iron ore was also plentiful there, but Ashen admitted he kept far from those mines without exactly saying why. The Ny-Failen understood such an aversion and no one questioned him.

For the entire dinner, Ashen was painfully aware of Lady Rain Song at another table across from him. He found himself unable to eat much and he drank the excellent ale sparingly. Rain Song's beauty sang out to him from across the space separating them and he could not keep from staring at her. The vivid memory of her riding upon his horse, held tightly in his arms, made his heart race and his body tighten with longing. Ashen had to constantly remind himself that she was not for him and he finally dropped his gaze to his plate and forced himself to eat.

With smoldering irritation, Jagged Edge watched the young King of Sorn, who frequently stared at Rain Song. Though he could read most people's minds, out of respect for their privacy, he shielded his abilities and avoided reading his wife and his children's minds and those of humankind as well. There were a few Ny-Failen he simply could not read as with King Lorn, Jagged Edge's son Storm Rider and Lost Morning the leader of the Ny-Failen. His son-in-law, Aesir Blacknight, blocked him with blue sorcery and now this young man's mind was heavily barred with solid walls like cold steel. Whether intentional or not it made Jagged Edge suspicious and very bad-tempered. He disagreed with King Lorn's insistence that they try and work to remove the curse from Ashen Arrow and he seethed all through dinner. Needless to say, Jagged Edge did not eat but drank heavily.

Rain Song tried not to let show her obvious fascination with King Ashen Arrow. Covertly she watched him, taking in every aspect of his mannerisms and appearance. He had bathed and the sides of his head were freshly shaven bare to just behind his ears. His crest of long hair was clean and shone like tarnished silver. The gray jacket he wore had ravens and strange symbols embroidered onto the collar and down the front, in black, white, and silver thread. As foreign and unfamiliar as he looked and dressed, Ashen Arrow radiated a kind of male allure that drew Rain Song's eye and her imagination. No man had ever made her heart skip a beat until him and when he looked at her with his silvery-gray eyes she became flustered and warm. The curve of his bow-shaped mouth shot an arrow of longing straight into her heart. She was also aware that he stared back at her most of the evening too. His eyes were dark and brooding, unreadable and fiery. He never smiled.

Rain Song had to tamp down on a flare of irritation when her cousin Autumn Day, who was sitting beside her, leaned in to whisper, *'Isn't the King of Sorn handsome?'* and proceeded to list all the attractive qualities that Rain Song had just been observing, echoing her own thoughts. Autumn Day went on questioning everything about Ashen Arrow, *'Why do you think he and his men shave the sides of their heads? What do you think the runes on his coat mean? Is he a Black Sorcerer like his father?'*

After the evening meal Rain Song usually sang, but her mother had asked her not to this evening. Lyra Song told her that to do so might bring her to the unwanted attention of the King of Sorn and they did not wish to give him the wrong impression. Jagged Edge had expressly stated his desire that Rain Song not go within eyesight of Ashen Arrow at all, but she had blatantly disobeyed.

This was the first time King Ashen Arrow had been this close to other Ny-Failen and he was surprised as he began to feel slightly at ease with the company as if he belonged. Still, the overly formal evening seemed to last forever and finally, Ashen Arrow slipped from the Great Hall. During dinner King Lorn had spoken briefly of the many high towers of Castle Jior and, ever since Rain Song had mentioned seeing his camp from there, he was curious to go up and see the view for himself.

Seeking solitude, Ashen Arrow climbed the long flight of stairs toward the top of the high tower. The scuff of his boots on the stone echoed flatly off the curving walls. He emerged out into the night and was amazed at what he saw. The full moon was a bright white orb overhead and the cool mountain breeze caressed his face. High upon the tall tower, the moonlight made the black crystal walls of Jior sparkle and glitter with iridescent colors and Ashen rested his hands upon the smooth, cool stone. Behind the castle, to the west, a massive, towering waterfall plunged down the mountainside and the distant roar of the water echoed for miles. The view of the city below was spectacular with warm golden lights twinkling throughout the valley. Large iron stands held huge fires lighting the cool evening and he could see row upon row of trees in a courtyard far below. The faint scent of burning pine spiraled upward through the air. Ashen had to admit that the Kingdom of Jior was a very beautiful and peaceful place.

He stood there for a long time watching the moon in the arms of wispy clouds waltzing their way across the sky until they posed almost directly over the waterfall. The bright rays cast by the moon made the water look like falling liquid silver. A soft scent of spring flowers wafting up from a massive garden far below, mixed with the crisp scent of water as if it had just rained. Inhaling deeply, he relaxed just slightly and tried to forget his cares.

Behind him, the slow opening and closing of the tower door distracted Ashen and he turned as the sound of soft footfalls came close to where he was standing. He straightened, his senses tingling and then flaring with heat, as he saw who was coming toward him. Lady Rain Song stepped out of the shadows and into the moon's bright glow. She was luminous and delicate. The ribbons down the front of her dress swayed with the gentle evening breeze.

If anything, under the moonlight, Ashen thought her even more beautiful than she was at dinner in the warm lamplight. His heart ached and his body tightened, his arms flexed with a desire to hold her. Fisting his hands at his sides he frowned because her mere presence was torture to him, a reminder of what he could not have.

"My Lady," Ashen Arrow bowed deeply. When he straightened his eyes met hers.

"King Ashen Arrow." She made a delicate curtsey, dipped her head gracefully, and gave him a tentative smile. She tried to sound as if she were surprised to see him.

"What are you doing here?" He had to force the words out and truly he realized he was not sure what to say to her. He tried not to sound rude or affronted but he was irritated because she was a temptation beyond what he could endure.

"I often come here at night, especially when the moon is full. It is a beautiful place to sit and think."

Somehow Ashen had sensed that. If he were completely honest with himself, he had hoped that she would come up to the tower tonight. Now that she was here, he regretted her presence because he had an overwhelming yearning to touch her. Trying to turn his heart to stone and stop his desires from running rapid, he moved away and turned his back to her. Placing his hands atop the cold stone rampart, he closed his eyes and took a deep breath calming his racing heart.

She moved up beside him and placed her hand on the low wall next to his and they shared the view in silence for a while.

Pointing, she turned and revealed, "Just there is where I saw your campfires last night. It is how I knew where to find you."

Ashen did not speak but his mind flashed back to riding Tarnish with her in the saddle before him and the feel of her in his arms.

Rain Song turned her head and looked at him for a long moment when he did not answer her admission. He was so blatantly masculine. Everything about him shouted male, strong, protective, attractive, seductive, and so appealingly forbidden, it took her breath away.

"My Lord, did you make any progress today? With Grandfather and breaking the curse?" Rain Song asked, absorbing his hard profile in the moonlight and committing it to memory.

"No, my Lady, not that I expected to." Ashen's voice was stern and impatient. "Please, will you…please just call me Ashen."

"Alright, *Ashen*. And you must call me Rain Song." He could hear the smile in her voice. She was pleased that he had invited her to such informality. She touched his arm and he turned toward her. He was a full head and shoulders taller than her and she looked up into his beautiful silver-gray eyes.

Ashen's arm warmed where Rain Song placed her hand and he forgot himself for a moment and laid his hand over hers. In silence, they stood that way for a few minutes until Ashen realized he had stepped closer to her and was staring down at her lips, her beautiful face turned up toward him. He quickly broke the contact and stepped back. Searching for something to say, he went on.

"Our efforts were useless and so we decided to wait for some Ny-Failen named Aesir Blacknight and Lost Morning. King Lorn feels that one of them may be able to break the curse. I do not hold on to any hope. I have tried for four years. I read every magic scroll the Gray King had and searched through all his writings. Nothing I tried seemed to make any difference and I know his magic like the back of my hand. Each day I feel his evil curse getting tighter and tighter around me. When I turn one and twenty, my heart will be crushed and I will die."

Ashen had been walking away from Rain Song and she followed listening to his deep voice and watching the play of the moonlight on his hair. They reached a stone bench that faced the waterfall and Ashen gestured for her to sit. Rain

Song sat down on one end so that he could sit on the other and so they stayed side-by-side for a few minutes silently watching the moon above, moving in to kiss the waterfall.

Filling the silence between them Rain Song asked, "Why do you and your men shave the sides of your heads? I've never seen anything like it."

Ashen gave her a quick look then began speaking reverently.

"I watched your grandfather fight the Gray King's men when we were here ten years ago." As if he did not want to remind her of that hated day, he hesitated before haltingly continuing his story. "He was the most outstanding warrior I had ever seen and I instantly wanted to be like him. When we returned to Sorn, I sought out our best warrior and asked him to train me. He agreed and became my Mentor much against my father's wishes and I became unbeatable as a warrior thanks to him. He was a good man but had been badly scarred by a fire in his youth and the side of his head and face had been burned. The hair would not grow back there. My father liked to ridicule his ugliness and so, to displease my father and emulate my Mentor, I began to shave my head, but on both sides so that, whenever the Gray King looked at me, he would see my Mentor's influence and my desire to emulate King Lorn. Then I ordered all the soldiers to shave their heads for the same reason. It became a tradition that stuck and now all of Sorn's warriors shave the sides of their heads. It shows unity and rebellion against everything my father stood for."

"Oh, that is very admirable of you. It shows you are a great leader and I do like it!"

Ashen did not say anything but a slight smile fleetingly passed over his lips. After another long pause between them, Rain Song asked him the real question she wanted the answer to.

"Ashen, why did you not consider marrying me to break the spell? Surely all the good that you have done in Sorn means that it is no longer the dreaded place it once was when your father lived and the danger has passed with his death."

Ashen hesitated for another long moment choosing his words carefully. "My Lady, as I told your grandfather, I could not hold you to a lifetime in an unwanted marriage. Our oaths were forced upon your grandfather and I, through blood and pain. It can only be broken through blood and pain. The contract is explicit on how it is to be done. I cannot just marry you one minute and annul the marriage the next to free you. I cannot marry one of the humankind. I cannot marry just any Ny-Failen, it must be one of King Forlorn Icefall's blood. I must wed and *consummate* the marriage." He stopped and said more quietly, "The magic will know, through blood and pain, the contract must be fulfilled. If it was my father's wish, nothing good can come from it."

Rain Song was glad for the darkness because she was blushing deeply over the connotations of what he was saying. It had to be her Ny-Failen blood and her pain that sealed the deal and fulfilled the agreement and the spirit of the contract.

"My Lady, I am a realistic man. I do not give in to fanciful hopes or self-pity. I willingly give my life to free you so that you may have a happy future. Though I will admit after meeting you it is more difficult to go to my death knowing what I could have had, but it makes no difference. Every plan of the Gray King's will be thwarted and you will be free."

"Ashen, what if, what if I do not *wish* to be free?" Rain Song took his large hand in her small one and turned toward him on the bench. She continued to hold his hand until he turned to look at her.

Ashen was staring at the moon that had reached the sky above the waterfall and looked as if it sat directly on the pouring waters. The night was so bright and the stars were all around them. She was holding his hand and willing him to look at her. When she asked that last question, he could not help but frown. He looked down at her hand, delicate, soft, and warm, clasped inside his large one, hard, rough, and cold. Her gaze was entreating.

"My Lady," he started slowly, his gaze traveling up to look into her green eyes. "I do not speculate upon what might or might not be. I deal with simple facts and then I move on. You cannot want to marry me and I have chosen my path already. I am only here now for purely selfish reasons and because you made me promise to come back to Jior and give your grandfather a chance to break the curse. If that is possible and the magic is undone, I will leave for Sorn alone, and you will go on with your life and marry someone more deserving of you, someone, who can make you happy. There is nothing else to be done."

Rain Song reached up to cup his cheek with her other small hand. He closed his eyes and lifted his hand to hold hers there. She moved her other hand and it drifted to his shoulder. Moving closer she pulled him down to her and he leaned forward. Their lips met soft and tentative. Behind them, the moon smiled upon their first kiss.

As if a floodgate had been released, Ashen pulled her to him. Rain Song had kissed him and he was flying. His blood rushed in his veins and he wanted more and more of her. One of her hands slid around his neck and the other sifted through his hair as she fit perfectly in his arms. His warm lips were on hers and he tilted his head and kissed her deeper. He tentatively tasted her and she him, and then suddenly, their tongues were dancing in a feverish rush as if they could not get enough of each other.

Ashen's chest felt as if it would explode with joy and the desire that rose inside him was almost unbearable. His arms were around Rain Song's slim body, and he held her close, everything else be damned! After a few moments, his body was crying out for more of her and he had to stop. He drew away quickly and gently set her away from him. His hands were still clutching Rain Song's arms and it took all his strength to release her.

He stood suddenly and turned. Walking away from Rain Song he raked his hands through his hair and tried to calm his throbbing heart. Once he was composed, he turned to look and see if he had frightened her.

Rain Song was overwhelmed by the passion that flared between them. The taste of him was on her lips and she burned inside for more of him. Her breathing was fast and her breasts were tight within her bodice. Flashes like lightning shot through her body and downward to land in a place she had never paid much attention to but was screaming for release now.

"Lady Rain Song," Ashen Arrow stepped back toward her. He took a deep breath and pulled himself up as straight as he could. "Forgive me, I lost myself for a moment. I am deeply sorry. I did not mean to frighten you. I never meant…"

Rain Song surged to her feet and strode angrily toward him. "Stop it! Just stop! You did nothing! Drop this cold noble detachment you hide in and allow yourself to *feel*. I kissed you and you kissed me back. It is what I wanted. *I want you* Ashen Arrow to kiss me *again!*"

Ashen hesitated only for a moment. He was not strong enough to deny her. He leaned down. Reaching forward he held her face in his hands then pulled her to him and kissed her, long and slow. His hunger for her was building at an alarming rate, his arms went around her tiny body and he delved deeply into her sweet taste. He kissed her long and hard then, pouring all his desire and passion into that one kiss as if it were the only one, they would ever share.

Rain Song was overwhelmed. Ashen Arrow was kissing her with the desperation of a man who was soon to die. His arms went around her and she was amazed at the feel of him pressing against her, warm and strong. He took a step backward and sat on the low wall behind him and pulled her even closer. He was sitting down at her height now and she was standing between his legs her arms around his neck. She could feel his desire pressing hard against her belly and she was being swept away by their shared passion. Pressing forward she clutched his shoulders and became lost in the feel of his hands on her back and sliding along her curves; lost, they gave into a shared craving for closeness, for touch, for warmth and affection.

Suddenly, the kiss slowed and Ashen gently pulled his lips away from hers. Rain Song opened her eyes and studied him. His eyes were closed and he was breathing hard trying to compose himself. Slowly, his arms loosened as he leaned forward, he rested his face against the hollow of her neck and just held her. Her arms were around his shoulders and together their breathing slowed, calmed. His breath caressed her and he moved his face to lay directly on her soft skin as he allowed her to comfort him. Breathing deeply he inhaled her scent and shuddered as if he were holding back his hunger with all his strength.

She kissed him gently along his shaven temple and stroked his hair. She held him until he was ready to let go. His warm breath blew across her skin and she closed her eyes, a wave of euphoria overtaking her.

Finally, he stirred and raised his head. He lightly kissed her once more then rose to his feet. He towered over her a moment before offering her his arm.

"My Lady, come, it is late. I will escort you to your chamber." As if he could not get enough, he raised her hand to his lips and kissed it in a final parting. Rain Song was overwhelmed by him, by his maleness, and by his extreme control. She was glad of it because she realized while he was kissing her, that she could have given herself to him right then and there if he asked it. This gentle giant from Sorn was stealing her heart.

Ashen Arrow stiffly escorted Rain Song to her chamber door and then, very formally, he bowed and left her without a word. It took every ounce of control he possessed not to follow her in and lay her beneath him. He was tense and hard and aching to hold her and to be held by her, but his heart knew what his body did not, she was not for him. He tried to tell himself what happened at the top of the tower, with only the moon to witness, could not happen again, or his resolve to leave her here in Jior would completely crumble and she would be lost.

CHAPTER SIX

Entering the large guest chamber he had been given earlier, Ashen Arrow looked around. It was a huge, richly decorated suite on the second floor of the guest tower. Picking up his saddlebags, he left and ascended the stairs until he reached the very top of the tower. This chamber was much smaller, circular, warm, and inviting. The smooth, dark wood paneling gave the room a comfortable peaceful atmosphere and Ashen felt much more at ease here. With a word, he used his sorcerous power to start the fire in the fireplace and it burned white and hot very quickly. Lighting a few of the lamps the same way, he dropped into a comfortable stuffed chair in front of the fireplace. It was not his intention to sleep, but his eyes grew heavy as he stared at the flames and relived Rain Song's sweet kisses. Soon he was asleep and then his father was there.

The specter of the Gray King stood before him, bent and wizened just as Ashen had last seen him. Disheveled in dark gray robes, he was scowling at Ashen with a look he was well familiar with. He began degrading him immediately throwing curses and accusations, mocking him. Ashen thrashed in the chair as vile words rolled off of his father's gray tongue like fist blows. Coward, betrayer, weakling, and fool, the names Ashen was so familiar with stung him in the dream.

"You must marry the Ny-Failen girl! You weak, pitiful, failure of a man. Marry her! Whisk her away and stick your cock in her immediately. You know you want to. *She* wants you to! Prove yourself a man! Marry and bed the whore! Do not fail me boy or I will haunt you until your dying day and even beyond the grave!" The Gray King was frothing at the mouth and spittle was flying with his words and dropping like acid.

Ashen mumbled in his sleep "No! I will not do it!"

"You will do it or I will bring vicious retribution upon you! Worse than you ever dreamed. There will be a reckoning for your disobedience and you will die long and slow in horrendous pain! For an eternity, you will burn within the pits of the Hells beside *me*. I will hound you until the end of time's existence! Do it! Marry the girl! Bed her! Consummate the marriage immediately! Do as I command!" The refrain continued until Ashen remembered he was dreaming and woke up wishing he would have dreamt of Rain Song, with all his heart.

Wiping the sweat from his face Ashen rose and left the hot room and returned to the tower where he had shared sweet kisses with the lovely Rain Song. He relived the memory of her. His body remembered her tiny form pressing against his and he wanted to howl and curse. Denying his heart's desire was going to be the hardest thing he had ever done but it did have to be done. Cursing his promise to return to Jior, Ashen faced the dire realization, he needed to stay far away from Lady Rain Song.

#

Aesir Blacknight arrived the following morning from Hoarfrost Castle. He came flying in, his black wings gleaming with dew in the growing morning light. Landing upon the topmost high tower of Jior he found that he was not alone. A tall, young man with silvery-gray hair and intense gray eyes, stood leaning against the wall watching the sunrise over the mist-covered Violent Mountains. Aesir Blacknight approached the man who straightened at the sound of Aesir's arrival and turned toward him. A slight look of surprise colored his handsome face as he scanned Aesir's black wings. Aesir Blacknight spread his wings dramatically, showing them off then shrugged his shoulders, shapeshifted and the wings were gone.

"You must be the Gray King's son." Aesir Blacknight spoke first. His tone of voice was a little bit sarcastic and his crooked smile did not reach his ice-blue eyes.

"The Gray King is dead. I am Ashen Arrow, King of Sorn. You must either be Lost Morning or Aesir Blacknight."

"I am Aesir Blacknight." He tipped his head slightly with his hand over his heart in the traditional Ny-Failen welcome. "Greeting the sunrise?"

"I do not sleep much and the view is peaceful. I have watched the moon set and now the sunrise." Ashen Arrow answered without pretense.

Aesir Blacknight cocked an eyebrow. "I see. Perhaps it is the anticipation of your wedding night that keeps you awake or maybe it is your conscience that keeps you sleepless? Forcing an innocent girl into an unwanted marriage is not a very honorable thing to do."

A look of fury suddenly marred Ashen Arrow's face and he wanted to grab this man by the throat and shake him. They were almost of equal height but Ashen was a few inches taller and he knew he could easily pommel this Aesir Blacknight. His fists clenched at his sides and he had to remind himself that his man was there to help him. He stepped closer just to intimidate this cocky newcomer and he spoke low and menacingly.

"It was your King who summoned you here, not me. Perhaps before you talk of things which you do not know, you should speak to him." Ashen Arrow turned and stalked away.

Aesir Blacknight smiled a wicked smile, satisfied that he had almost provoked the King of Sorn to violence. With a low chuckle, he followed the angry young man down the stairs to the Great Hall.

They found King Forlorn Icefall and Jagged Edge at a table breaking their fast. Ashen Arrow nodded once to them and went to sit alone at an empty table. Aesir Blacknight joined King Lorn and Jagged Edge and they solemnly acknowledged his presence and thanked him for coming. As they ate their morning meal King Lorn informed Aesir Blacknight of the reason they called him to Jior. Aesir Blacknight listened with surprised interest and cast curious looks across the room at Ashen Arrow.

During the course of their conversation, Rain Song too had entered the Great Hall and went directly to sit next to Ashen Arrow at the same table. He was turned toward her and was giving her a very intense look. His brow was furrowed as if he were in pain and Rain Song was speaking softly to him. King Lorn, Jagged Edge, and Aesir Blacknight watched the young couple together. A servant approached them with a tray of food for the two to break their fast. Rain Song was pushing the tray toward Ashen Arrow and was entreating him to eat. She poured him a cup of cider with her own hands and placed it before him. Ashen looked sullen and resolute and Rain Song looked strong and determined. She smiled frequently.

"Doesn't look to me like the wedding is off." Aesir Blacknight observed leaning toward Jagged Edge. "King Ashen Arrow looks at Rain Song as if he were a hungry wolf and she the prey."

"Do not provoke me Aesir Blacknight or you will regret it and I will thank you not to speak of my daughter as if she were an animal to be hunted." Jagged Edge warned.

Aesir Blacknight smirked at Jagged Edge. "I've been threatened twice already this morning and I have only just arrived. It has been a productive day already!" He gave a short laugh, drank his ale, and ate heartily.

Later, they took the silver scroll case to an upper chamber they called the war room. There was a long table in the center of the room that had maps spread out over it. Shields of all colors and insignia decorated one wall and weapons of every kind were on the opposite wall. There were numerous swords, axes, maces, spears, and long white wooden pikes with sharp silver blades. At the end of the war room, were tall thick glass windows that let in the sunlight. They removed all the maps and placed the silver scroll case alone in the middle of the table.

The thing seemed to give off a feeling of evil and made everyone uncomfortable. They all gathered and even though Lost Morning had yet to arrive, they discussed everything they tried so far to break the curse.

Aesir Blacknight approached the table with a scowl on his face and spent many silent minutes examining the case with his Ny-Failen sight. He could see the black tendrils of evil seething around it and snaking off to invisibly wrap its malevolence around King Ashen Arrow. As Aesir Blacknight tried his blue sorcerous power on the scroll case, it began to shake and rattled violently on the table. He intensified his efforts and it began to spin, creating a silver blur, until it looked as if it would shoot off the table and injure someone. When he stopped it stilled and Aesir Blacknight shook his head in frustration. Then he tried his Ny-Failen power over metal. He experimentally tried melting it, changing the silver metal to gold or sapphire, and nothing he did held.

"The thing is cursed well. It surely resists my magic and my Ny-Failen powers. I cannot change its nature or destroy it and thus release the curse. So, it appears it is not tied to Sorn's silver."

"I have spent hours holding spells on it and had similar results. Once it spun off my table and struck me unconscious for half a day." Ashen Arrow volunteered this knowledge and bade them, "watch." Ashen picked up the scroll case and concentrated. His silver-gray eyes turned brilliant blue and the scroll case began to glow. The runes and markings engraved on it glowed as if a fire were lit inside it and they began to shift and rearrange. It glowed red hot in Ashen's hand and he endured the burning pain for as long as he could then dropped it. His hand was not burned, but his brow ran with droplets of sweat as he stopped his magic. The runes and engravings returned to their original script.

"It seems to hold particular malice toward you, King Ashen Arrow. I was struggling to keep it on the table. You almost seemed to rewrite the runes before it burned you." Aesir Blacknight picked up the scroll case and continued. "Yet it can be picked up and held by anyone. I can open it and even remove the marriage contract within. It seems fairly harmless, but for Ny-Failen we can see what evil it holds and I sense that it still has secrets to unlock."

His eyes scanned the document within, he read toward the bottom and then spoke aloud.

"This marriage contract, sealed by blood and by oath, between King Forlorn Icefall of Jior, the Gray King of Sorn, and Prince Ashen Arrow of Sorn, cannot be broken, annulled, or void under any circumstance. All parties agree that on or before the day of Ashen Arrow of Sorn's one and twentieth birthday, this contract shall conclude in the marriage and immediate consummation between Ashen Arrow of Sorn and a female from the line of King Forlorn Icefall's royal Ny-Failen bloodline. By blood and by pain it shall be fulfilled and the Gray King shall rise again."

"What is this rubbish?" Jagged Edge shouted impatiently. "What does that mean 'by blood and by pain?'" His face was red with frustration.

"I would like to know what 'the Gray King shall rise again' means." King Lorn spoke, a similar look taking over his face. "I was not allowed to read the contract before I was forced to sign with my blood and declare my oath."

All eyes turned to stare at Ashen Arrow.

"Nor I, if you recall. I was only a boy ten years of age. It was forced upon me as well." He held up his right hand and showed them a thin white scar across his palm. The same scar the King of Jior had on his hand.

"I assume it refers to the Gray King's bloodline continuing, at least that was the main purpose of this whole arranged marriage. He somehow sired a Ny-Failen child and coerced a Ny-Failen of Jior to assure his bloodline would continue with a Ny-Failen father and mother." Aesir Blacknight volunteered then speculated. "This cannot be valid if neither of you willingly entered into it." He scoffed and threw the parchment back onto the table. Of its own accord, the parchment rolled up again and slid back into the silver case, like a live thing.

"Yet it seems we are to be held to it even though the Gray King is dead. For some reason, it remains in effect. If we can't find a way to break this dark magic, Ashen Arrow of Sorn will die." King Lorn reminded them all ominously.

"Then let him die!" Jagged Edge shouted at King Lorn as if Ashen Arrow was not standing at the other end of the table. "He has declared that he is willing, rather than force Rain Song into an evil, unwanted marriage. Let us give up this useless effort and be done with it. My daughter shall not marry the Gray King's son!"

"There has to be another way! I am not yet willing to admit defeat!" King Lorn argued back at Jagged Edge's rage.

"We could marry and I could save him." A sweet gentle voice spoke from out of the shadows in the back of the room. No one had seen her slip in, but now the men turned to see Rain Song step forward. Ashen Arrow had known she was there but had not said anything nor had he looked at her. He just drew a kind of strength from her presence. At the import of her words, Ashen turned pale, closed his eyes, and pursed his lips as if he were in pain.

"No! I will not allow it!" Jagged Edge roared. "You should not be here Rain Song! Go and seek your mother. I will decide what is best for you."

"Father, no one has asked my preference in this situation. I will not see a good man die because you and he, and everyone else decided what is best for me. I can make my own decision in this."

"No!"

This time it was Ashen Arrow that spoke with barely controlled ferocity. "Lady Rain Song, I will not marry you and sentence you to a miserable fate. This is pointless. King Lorn, I told you the magic cannot be broken except by my death. I appreciate your efforts but I have accepted my fate. There is no reason to continue to feed this false hope." Ashen Arrow turned and walked toward the door. He paused, his hand on the door latch, and he turned his head to look at Rain Song who stood staring after him with a look of shock and hurt on her lovely face.

"Boy!" King Lorn intoned in his loud demanding voice that no one ignored, stopping Ashen Arrow from leaving. "You *will* give me the fortnight I asked for to work this problem. Lost Morning will be here tomorrow and *you will wait*. I command it. If he fails and you are so determined to die then you may go and do so."

Ashen Arrow left the room without another word.

CHAPTER SEVEN

Tarnish's hooves beat the earth as if he were punishing it. Out into the forests surrounding Castle Jior, Ashen drove his gray stallion giving him his head and letting him fly over the ground. Fury clouded Ashen's mind and he was determined to outrun his problems if only for a little while. King Lorn's final words echoed in his mind, but it was Rain Song's words that echoed in his heart. *'We could marry and I could save him.'*

For one fleeting moment, Ashen had allowed himself to think that they might carry out the marriage contract and truly save him, in more ways than one. He squashed the hope because in the back of his mind was a secret he carried like a noose around his neck. He knew marrying Rain Song and consummating the marriage was not the end of the Gray King's evil, somehow it was only the beginning. Though, in what form, he was not entirely sure. He only knew he was two more days closer to his birthday, closer to his death.

Tarnish had been running on a wide trail but slowed of his own accord as it narrowed and became steeper heading up a mountainside. As the horse calmed and Ashen's mind became a little clearer of his anger, he heard the sound of hooves coming up behind him. Someone on horseback was following him. Ashen's senses flared and he knew with painful yearning who it was.

Lady Rain Song rode up to him. Her hair had come loose and swirled around her shoulders like windswept silver. Her horse was winded. She had ridden hard to catch up to Ashen and had not even stopped to grab a cloak. The skirts of her forest green dress blew back over the horse's haunches and she was breathing hard. Her face was flushed, her eyes glittering and she looked magnificent.

Ashen leaped from Tarnish's back and stormed toward Rain Song. He grabbed her horse's bridle before it even came to a full stop and he let his fury have its head.

"Woman! Are you determined to torture me?" His voice was harsh. "Don't you realize you put yourself in danger every time you are alone with me! Go back to your home and leave me be!"

"I will not!" She swung her leg over the saddle and slid to the ground. "I will not be ordered around like a child. You, Father, Grandfather, you all have decided what is best for my future and none of you take into consideration what I want!"

"Trust them. There are things you do not know or understand."

"Then tell me!" She pleaded exasperated. "Explain these things I do not know so that I *can* understand. Do you think you are the only one hurting here?"

"I am for certain the only one dying." Ashen gave her a cynical grin.

Then he turned and walked away not seeing the look of shock and fear that she gave him. She shouted at his retreating back. "I was there you know! That day the Gray King brought you to Jior as a little boy to demand the marriage contract. My cousins and I were standing in the crowd and I saw you. I was only a little girl, but even then, I felt a connection with you. I have waited ten years for you to come for me. Yes, I was terrified of the Gray King, but part of me knew in my heart that *you* were not evil like him. I *knew* you were different from your father."

"I am no different, his putrid blood flows in my veins. He taught me his dark magic over the years and I curse the day I was born and the day he made that marriage contract."

Ashen stormed away from her going further up the trail. Rain Song followed.

"You *are* different, I know it!" She stopped in her tracks and gasped with a sudden realization. "Is it me? You don't want *me*? Do you think you could not love me?" Rain Song's voice caught a little and her hand flew to her throat in a shocked gesture as if she just realized he was trying to tell her something.

"Is there someone else? You love another?" Rain Song's eyes were wide, staring at him.

Ashen whirled around and looked at her, his face was a mask of torment. His long strides took him back to her side and he grabbed her. He crushed her in his embrace, lifted her, and kissed her passionately. One of his hands was in her hair and he tilted her head so that he could delve deeper, taste her, plunder and feel her lips on his, her body pressed tightly against his.

Their lips and tongues fought almost violently, then they danced, and then they waltzed. He kissed her until they were both breathless. The kiss came to a slow halt as the music of desire hummed in their veins. Plucking her bottom lip one last time and kissing her gently, he set her down and took a step back from her.

Ashen had intended to scare her, chase her away by giving her a small demonstration of what he is capable of but it just seemed to strengthen her resolve. Though he also wanted to show her the passion he felt for her and expressed it in that kiss, and she felt it. Stepping toward him, her eyes entreated him to trust the feelings that he saw within their emerald depths. He could see she was trembling and had felt her shiver when she was in his arms.

Ashen nodded his head thinking he succeeded in scaring her. "You see what I am capable of? I could tear your clothes from your body, take your innocence and leave you broken.

I cannot be trusted around you. I can barely contain myself. My hands itch to touch you and I long to feel your naked skin against mine! What is worse, I want to steal you home, take you with me and make you my own, but I cannot sentence you to that fate. It is what the Gray King badly wants for some reason I have not figured out yet and I cannot give in to him! *I will not do it!*"

Rain Song nodded her head as if she understood. Embarrassed for some reason, she bit her lip and looked at him uncertainly and wounded. He closed his eyes and took a deep breath then told her what she wanted to hear.

"There is no other." He slowly confessed as if he had not wanted to admit it and give her any false hope. "Only you, my Lady."

She smiled slowly and looked relieved. Then she grew thoughtful for a few minutes and looked around a little. Something sparked in her eyes.

"Come with me!" She took his hand and led him up the narrowing trail. One hand held her skirts up so she could lead the way and the other held tightly to his hand.

They climbed up and up until eventually, the steep mountain began to level out. After walking along a trail, they came out of the forest into a clearing. A small, crystal blue lake stretched out before them. It was an immensely beautiful and peaceful place. The sun shone warm overhead out of the blue sky and reflected on the still water. Birds sang in the trees and a gentle breeze caressed their faces. She led him along the lake edge until they came to a grassy area that bordered a small sandbar. In the distance, they could hear the delicate trickle of a creek that emptied somewhere into the lake.

At a small grassy area, Rain Song pulled Ashen's hand and commanded he sit down. She sat as well and then began to remove her shoes and stockings. Pointing at his boots she ordered him to do the same. He arched a brow at her that said he thought her slightly insane and she looked back at him and repeated her command. Shaking his head in bewilderment, he did as he was told.

Taking his hand again, she tried to pull him to his feet and he rose. Lifting her skirts in one hand he watched as she walked away and stepped carefully out into the cool water. She led him out onto a submerged sandbar and pulled him along with her. He retained her hand and steadied her so that she would not fall as they wadded further out. Her skirts were draped over one arm and her ankles and legs were visible under the crystal-clear water.

"As little girls, we would run from our nurses and come up here. We rode our ponies without saddles, stripped to our bare skin, dove in, and swam the summer afternoons away." She laughed and he frowned. "I remembered this place when we were down below and I hoped you would like it here and find peace. Have you ever done anything similar, where you are from?"

"I ran away once. The Gray King caught me and beat me bloody. I never did it again."

"Oh Ashen, I am sorry!" Stricken, she looked at him with such compassion he had to look away. Still holding her hand, he let his gaze travel across the mountain lake, and then he seemed to remember something.

"When I came to Jior ten years ago, your grandfather offered to foster me. I instantly knew the Gray King would not allow it, but as a boy, I used to pretend that King Forlorn Icefall of Jior, truly wanted me. It was the nicest thing anyone ever offered to do for me and I have greatly admired the King of Jior ever since. I deeply regretted that I could not stay. I think I would have liked growing up with you and your cousins."

Happily, Rain Song smiled up at him. All afternoon she continued to laugh and entertain him with tales. She pointed out the small fish in the lake water beneath their feet. She told him stories of how her father rescued her mother Lyra Song from an unjust death at an evil Lord's hand and how her grandfather rescued her grandmother from a Black Sorcerer's tower and killed a black-winged Ny-Komnir. She kept watching the sun and looking around as if waiting for something. He finally asked her.

"Are you looking for something?"

"Yes, it is almost time. I hope they still come here." She pulled him back to the shore and then turned back to the lake and watched. Suddenly, she whispered excitedly and pointed, "There!"

Ashen watched as a flock of brilliant red cardinals flew over the lake. They circled and then settled in the trees across from them. Some of the birds landed by the lake edge and flicked droplets over their bright red wings bathing in the clear water. Ashen and Rain Song watched spellbound by the beautiful birds until they all flew away. Rain Song sighed and went to sit in the grass and let her feet dry. Her slim, delicate feet and white ankles poked out from her skirts and Ashen tried not to stare at them. He was sitting very close to her and he was sorely tempted to kiss her senseless, but he refrained and tried to find joy in the sunny afternoon with her.

He wanted to hear her laugh again and so he gathered a few pale green leaves, spread them over her skirts, and placed one in each open palm of her hands. His eyes glowed brilliant blue and he whispered a brief spell. The leaves began to move on their own and morphed into brilliant green butterflies that flitted around her and beat their iridescent wings in her hands.

Rain Song gasped in surprise and wonder. She laughed as the butterflies settled and then flew off. After a few moments, they turned back into green leaves again and drifted to the grassy ground. "That was lovely! Thank you Ashen." She gazed at him with sweet fascination.

As the afternoon shadows lengthened, they sat in companionable silence watching the breeze on the lake and an occasional animal coming to drink.

Later, Rain Song turned to look at him and smiled sweetly then she grabbed her stockings and began to put them on. Pulling her skirts up almost as high as her thighs, one at a time she gently pulled each stocking up her slim, pearl-hued legs. Ashen's mouth went dry as he watched. He stared at her perfectly smooth skin and marveled at how lovely she was. His heart raced and he wondered if she were purposely teasing him? Her every move was seductive, though the look on her face spoke of inner purity. He pulled his boots on as well and rose to give her a hand up. Pulling her to her feet she leaned against him. He was too tall for her to kiss him so all she could do was stare at his lips. She bit her lower lip enticingly and he could not hold back. Leaning down and lowering his head, he kissed her gently, then took that lower lip between his teeth and pulled. His tongue met hers and he kissed her more deeply, more gently than before, then pulled away. He looked down her pearl white neck and stared for a moment at the low neckline of her dress where her breasts heaved like two pillows of pearly softness barely hidden under the deep green material delicately bordered with ivory lace.

"We had better go back." Ashen's voice sounded deep, sensual, and regretful. Rain Song nodded and smiled. Ashen watched her and realized just what an innocent she really was.

They walked hand in hand down the trail and retrieved the horses who had been calmly eating the grasses where they left them. Ashen put his hands around Rain Song's waist and lifted her into her saddle. She swung her leg over and settled her skirts and put her feet in the stirrups. Before he could walk away, she bent and kissed him, one last time.

She put her hand against his cheek and smiled as she said, "You see, you spent the entire afternoon with me and you did not hurt me or take my innocence even when I shamelessly showed you my legs. I trust you Ashen even if you do not trust yourself."

Ashen took her hand from his face and placed a kiss on her palm and one on the pulse in her wrist before handing her the horse's reins. Before he let go, he squeezed it gently and said, "It doesn't mean that I didn't want to or that I didn't think about it. You are playing with fire, my Lady, be careful you do not get burned."

Ashen had a stern look on his face when he turned his back to her and Rain Song shivered at the coldness in his voice. Watching his long lithe body as he mounted his horse, stubborn confidence rose within her. She was determined to make him see the goodness she saw in him.

CHAPTER EIGHT

Rain Song did not see Ashen Arrow at dinner in the Great Hall nor did she find him atop the tower later. She spent the evening feeling thoroughly thwarted. Realizing she had less than a fortnight to…what? She stopped her thoughts, unsure. Had she truly decided she wanted to marry him? Did she think she loved him or was she just attracted to his handsome face and overwhelming masculinity? Marrying him meant she had to leave her home for a place she knew nothing about with a man she barely knew. She would have to leave her mother and father, her grandfather and grandmother. Her sister Mercy Rose was going to give birth to her third child and Storm Rider had two young sons that Rain Song adored. Jior was filled with Ny-Failen and she truly felt as if leaving would cause her more sorrow than she could bear.

As she went up the stairs toward her bedchamber she looked around and realized her feet had somehow taken her up the wrong staircase to the guest tower. Suddenly, she found herself at the very top at Ashen's door. Rain Song looked around guiltily not quite realizing how she had made this mistake but before she could analyze her actions or turn to go, the door opened.

Ashen stood framed by the golden glow of the lamps inside his room. He was shirtless with a white cloth thrown over one shoulder, holding a sharp, short dagger. It appeared to Rain Song that she had interrupted his washing but was unsure what the dagger was for. He just stared at her for a moment then stood back and beckoned with a tip of his head for her to enter. She went in.

Ashen quietly closed the door behind Rain Song. He walked to the washstand where he had been shaving the sides of his head, neck, and face. While she watched, he waved his hand across the stone wall and it shimmered and became a fine silver, reflecting mirror. He finished his last bit of shaving, wiped water and soap from his skin in smooth movements lifting his chin until he was clean and dry. All the while he watched her, watch him, through the reflecting glass holding her eyes with an intent stare.

Rain Song stared at Ashen's broad shoulders and muscular back in awed fascination. He was lean and beautiful with the body of a warrior. The muscles in his shoulders and arms rippled with the slightest movements and he was a perfect specimen of raw male power. Her heart skipped a beat as he turned toward her. He placed the cloth down and let her look at him. Though she was used to the pale white skin of the Ny-Failen, she had never seen a *man* this undressed. Ashen was perfect, smooth-skinned, and almost hairless. The muscles in his chest twitched and his flat stomach was lean and segmented, hard and narrowed down enticingly. She could see the striations in the muscles of his shoulders and arms, and her eyes followed the ridges of his ribs down to his sloping hips. A few laces of his trousers were loosened and open. Rain Song had to stop her eyes from wandering down any further. Blushing she looked away.

The tower room was round though not very large with a high peaked ceiling and walls completely paneled with dark polished wood. The lamplight made the room glow golden while a window let in a pool of white moonlight and revealed the stars in the night sky. The room was comfortable and inviting. A large, dark wood, four-post bed stood against one wall hung with dark wine-colored drapes. A small table held Ashen's untouched dinner and a pitcher of ale. The fire kept the room comfortable and two chairs sat companionably in front. It just now began to seem very close and overly warm to Rain Song.

Ashen went to her, circled her like a predator would its prey, and stood behind her for a moment. The many things he wanted to say to her flew through his mind. His eyes went to the large bed in the room and then his mind went to the many things he wanted to do to the woman who had come to his bedchamber in the middle of the night. For her own good, he decided he needed to teach her a stronger lesson before she tempted him any further. She just had to realize how dangerous he was and how teasing him by being around him was tempting the evil in him to do no good. Reaching out he pulled her close. He rested his cheek against her head and kissed her soft, sweet-smelling hair. His hands moved down her shoulders and he caressed down to her wrists, then up again until he boldly cupped both of her breasts. He kneaded her through the silken material of her dress as he kissed her cheek and neck while she gasped with shock and mounting pleasure.

Rain Song closed her eyes and leaned back into Ashen allowing his caresses and his kisses. Her skin was flushed and she was breathing hard. Feelings like she never had before began to churn inside her body as Ashen kissed and touched and heated her. She felt slightly light-headed as he slowly loosened the lacing at the front of her dress and slid his large hand down inside and took hold of her bare, warm breast. He continued to touch her. His kisses grew heated, his breathing heavy, and his hands grew bolder.

Then he stopped and scooped her up into his arms. He strode over to the bed while kissing her passionately, not giving her a moment to catch her breath. In seconds, she was beside him on the bed. His hand was pulling up the material of her dress and reaching under and smoothing slowly up her leg. His touch traveled over her knee and to the top of her stocking and up. Rain Song pushed away from his kisses gasping. She was overwhelmed by Ashen and the things he was doing to her and making her feel. As his large hand reached her bare hip, he stopped kissing her and stared into her eyes. His silver gaze was burning bright with desire for her and he was barely in control.

An angry, cruel look took over his features as he whispered to her, "Are you ready to be burned?"

Rain Song's breath caught. She remembered the warning he gave her earlier that day and was shocked by his words and by his actions. Ashen's hand branded her hip under her skirts but had moved no further and he had not looked down at her bare breasts revealed to him. His breathing was heavy and the desire in his eyes was ignited from smoldering to a flickering flame. She did not understand his anger. Worse, she did not understand her own actions or why she went to him. All she knew was that she had to see him but this was not what she wanted, not like this, with him angry and she so unsure of herself. She tried to stop trembling.

"Ashen," she whispered, calling him back to himself. Looking into his eyes. Sensing his anger and self-loathing, she whispered calmly, "Ashen, not like this-*please*."

A pained resolved look crossed his face and Ashen let her up. He moved away and sat on the edge of the bed, turning his back to her while she rose and righted her clothing. She tied the last lace and smoothed her hair back. There was a vigorous chorus of questions echoing in her head. Her heart was thundering between her breasts and her body was screaming with denial. Ashen had not looked at her or spoken and Rain Song was not sure what to say to him. The only sound in the room was his heavy breathing and the crackle of the fire.

Rain Song was Jagged Edge's daughter and she had uncanny intuition. She suddenly realized what Ashen was doing and knew he meant to scare her yet again. She also knew that if she went through with what he had started on the bed, he would hate himself afterward and so she had stopped him. It was a battle of wills they were locked in now while he tried to push her away as she tried to pull him nearer. More than ever she was determined to save him from himself. She knew that because of their actions tonight he would be gone by morning. He was even now scalding himself in self-loathing for intentionally scaring her with his actions and was planning to leave.

"Ashen, I came to remind you of your promise to me." Her voice was strong and fearless. "You promised me you would try to break this curse. Lost Morning will be here tomorrow. If you leave before the fortnight you agreed to, I *will* have Grandfather follow and bring you back."

Ashen kept his back to her and continued to stare at the fire as if he would like to throw himself in. She approached him and bent to whisper in his ear. Her soft lips almost grazing him she spoke gently. "I have come to love you and I will *not* let you go."

He heard the door close gently as she left him.

#

That night, as he drifted off to sleep in the chair in front of the fire, the Gray King took a different approach in Ashen's dreams. An empty mug of ale slipped from his fingers and fell to the rug on the floor. Ashen's father sat in the chair opposite him still a ghostly specter, but for once he was calm. If it were not for the flashes of emotion rippling over the Gray King's face, Ashen would have thought he was almost docile. He leaned forward, hands resting on the arms of the chair.

"Ashen, she wants you." He spoke calmly. "What is stopping you now? Marry the girl. Take her to your bed. It is what you want as well."

Looking up, Ashen narrowed his eyes. He could endure his father's curses and yelling because that was what he was used to, but this calm conversational tone was almost unnerving.

"She said she wanted to marry you. She is willing! There is no need for further delay, no reason for hesitation. Marry the girl."

"No!" Ashen growled and sarcasm stung his words. "I'll not give in to your schemes and plans. Something is not as it seems in all of this, *Father*. What is it that you truly want?"

The Gray King sat back in his chair and gripped the arms tightly as if he were barely holding on to control. Surging to his feet he calmly walked over to the chair where Ashen slept and circled behind him. Whispering, tempting, and cajoling in a seductive voice.

"You have everything my boy. My kingdom is yours. My wealth is yours. Now take your Ny-Failen bride. You felt her soft curves, saw her round, luscious breasts, and heard her passionate sighs. She wants you, wants your body between those lovely white thighs. I'm long past dead and not caring for such things, but you have your whole life to live. The love and affection you've always craved will be yours. Why embrace death when you can embrace that lovely girl. She said she loves you! *She loves you!* It is as good as done. She is yours! Marry her Ashen! Do it, boy!"

As if weaving a spell in the dream the Gray King circled Ashen whispering on, tempting him. Visions of lying in a dark empty iron cell, gasping for air, flitted through Ashen's mind. Pain tore through him like burning acid and his flesh smoldered with eternal fire. His bones felt broken and his eyes were blinded by raging waves of pain that smote him like the angry lashes of a whip. The heavy sense of time, long agonizing days, years, and centuries hit him and he realized the tortuous future that awaited him in death.

Ashen bolted awake in his chair and looked around. The whispering ghost of his father was gone. His hand shook as he ran his hands through his hair and down his face as if he could wipe away the memory of this most terrible dream. The next thought that came to his mind was of Rain Song. She was so lovely, so sweet and innocent and she had said that she loved him. He wanted her like he never wanted anything before in his life, but something still plagued the back of his mind. The words of the marriage contract, his father's constant insistence over the years, the haunting dreams and the threat of the curse, a long painful death.

Ashen's eyes slowly opened, centered on the empty chair across from his and for a long time, he sat thinking. Then he rose, dressed, and sought the heights of the tall tower where he and Rain Song had shared their first kiss. During the rest of the night, while he waited for the sun to rise, he remembered every kiss and touch, and her words repeated in his mind like a promise.

"I have come to love you and I will not let you go."

CHAPTER NINE

A bolt of white light hit the landing tower of Castle Jior. Lord Lost Morning suddenly arrived. King Forlorn Icefall was standing on the tower already, looking downward. He greeted the leader of the Ny-Failen and they gave each other a brotherly embrace. Before leaving the high tower, Lost Morning joined him at the parapet and also looked down at what earlier had King Lorn's attention. The sound of ringing metal upon metal echoed faintly up to them.

"Who is that warrior in silver armor being attacked by five men?" Lost Morning inquired.

"He is the reason I have asked you to come." King Lorn answered frowning down at the warrior battering away at five men at once. "That is Ashen Arrow of Sorn."

"So, the Gray King has finally returned with his son to force the marriage contract." Lost Morning sounded anything but pleased.

"The Gray King is dead and Ashen Arrow, his son, has released us from the marriage contract. There is a problem with that plan though and that is why I have called you here. Let us go and rescue those five men and I will explain everything once the young King of Sorn has a cooler head."

King Lorn and Lost Morning spread their wings and swooped down to land at the edge of the practice field.

#

Ashen Arrow was furious over what he had done to Rain Song. His dreams had been particularly harrowing that night as the Gray King's attack was cunning and sinister. Now, he was taking his fury and frustration out on the practice field. He trained hard with his own men not knowing how the soldiers of Jior would take to his unbridled ferocity. His men were used to it and gave no quarter. Ashen asked for none. They attacked him from all sides. Ashen whirled and blocked with inhuman speed as his shield and sword battered back his five opponents. If the soldier fell or was beaten out of the circle drawn in the dirt around them, it was considered a killing blow and was scored in Ashen's favor. The fallen soldier would rise from the ground and back out of the circle. The first beaten soldier ripped his helmet off and wiped the sweat from his brow as he stood and cheered on his comrades. Ashen now faced four attackers. One by one they fell to his might, skill, and rage. Ashen remained undefeated. The last soldier only yielded once his arm was broken and Ashen stood in the middle of the practice field looking for any more attackers.

His chest heaved like a raging bull as he gulped in air from his exertions. He turned and saw King Lorn and another winged man watching him from the edge of the practice field. He drove his sword hard into its sheath and ripped off his helmet, flinging back his dripping wet hair. He had a small cut on his cheek and his blood mixed with his sweat as it ran down his face. One of his soldiers ran up and took his helmet and shield. Ashen's rage was barely quenched after his rounds with the sword and he almost invited King Lorn to spar with him but judging by the look on the King's face he wisely decided against it.

Ashen removed his gauntlets as he approached and stood in front of the two, winged Ny-Failen. One hand moved to grip the handle of his sheathed sword, so tightly his knuckles turned white. The other hand slapped his gauntlets on his thigh in an impatient manner.

"Ashen Arrow, King of Sorn, this is Lord Lost Morning the Leader of the Ny-Failen." King Lorn introduced them.

Ashen Arrow was in no mood for bowing and scraping and making polite niceties so he said nothing, just stood glaring at them. A fit of insolence was swiftly adding to his mood. Lost Morning placed his hand over his heart and, tilting his head, greeted the King of Sorn.

"So, you've come to rid me of my curse?" Ashen Arrow could not mask the sarcasm he felt.

"King Ashen Arrow, I have yet not been fully informed of the reason I have been called here. King Forlorn Icefall does not often summon me, but when he does, I know it is for good reason."

"This is the reason!" Ashen wiped the blood from the side of his face and held his hand out to Lost Morning. He spoke with all the anger and frustration burning in his head. "My blood! That is what it has always been about. Though the Gray King is dead he still dictates from the grave and would have his way. He would force me to marry a Ny-Failen of Forlorn Icefall's bloodline to carry on his royal lineage or *I* shall die. That is his final decree and my curse. Despite my efforts to release Forlorn Icefall's granddaughter from the marriage contract, he insists I stay in Jior and try to release the curse so that I may go on with the life that has been so good and fulfilling to me. That is why he has asked you here. It is a fool's errand, I fear."

King Lorn was not going to suffer Ashen's bad temper and he walked up and stopped, nose to nose with him. Not many men were as tall as King Forlorn Icefall, but Ashen stood just shy of his height. Now, he held his ground while King Lorn growled down at him.

"This is Lord Lost Morning from the Creator's city of Everclearing. He is the leader of all Ny-Failen which includes you. You will address him with respect and reverence or I will turn you over my knee and swat you like the little boy you behave like."

Ashen Arrow remained stubborn and the two faced off, neither planning to back down. It wasn't until Lost Morning spoke to defuse the situation that Ashen finally yielded.

"King Ashen Arrow, perhaps we should speak later when you have had a chance to cool down from your sword practice. That man has a broken arm and it should be seen to. I look forward to speaking with you later." Then he spread his wings and leaped into the air and flew back to the castle.

"What is this truly about Ashen Arrow?" King Lorn demanded.

Something flickered in Ashen's eyes and King Lorn caught a fleeting look of regret and sorrow before it was quickly replaced by flaring rage again. He looked away and refused to answer. King Lorn knew the boy was too stubborn to talk and so he turned to one of his men who was standing by. He pointed.

"See to it that man is taken to the Queen so she may heal his arm. You," he spat pointing a finger into Ashen's chest, "Clean up and meet us in the war room and bring a better attitude with you." Then he bent at the knees and shot into the air.

Ashen Arrow smirked rebelliously into the gust of wind created by King Lorn's wings as he took flight. Removing his armor, he went to the river to cool his rage. Alone at the water's edge, he stripped off his boots and clothes until he was completely naked. He dove into the river and the cool water shocked his heated body as it swallowed him whole and the bite of the cold took his breath away. He swam underwater until he surfaced gasping and, with long smooth strokes swam further out into the wide slow-moving river. He trod water in the deep middle and looked into the distance where the massive waterfall fed the river with a torrential downfall. He was miles away from the waterfall and here the river coursed slower as it widened. Ashen could see the distant mist caused by the force of the waterfall striking the rocks directly below it and could hear the rushing waves tumbling and echoing out over the canyon with a roar. The majesty of the white cascade called to Ashen, humbling him as it reminded him that he was no more than a tiny fish in the huge vastness that was the River Jior and the wide world beyond. Awed by the beauty of nature he swam up the river toward the waterfall fighting the water as it gained speed coming toward him until he could fight no further. Then he finally gave up the fight turned onto his back and let it float him back the way he had come until he struck out, swimming back toward the shore. Laying in the grasses at the river's edge, he closed his eyes and let his temper cool and his head clear.

The King of Sorn lay, alone under the clear blue skies and realized what was happening to him. The Gray King's ghost was slowly driving him mad with his haunting, curses, foul language, and threats. In turn, Ashen was behaving badly toward people who were only trying to help him. It was not just how he had treated Rain Song that bothered him, but he had been insolent to King Lorn. Embarrassed to have behaved so badly toward someone he revered so much, Ashen felt ashamed. How his father would smile with malicious glee if he knew what chaos he was causing inside his son's heart and mind. He thought again about the night before with the lovely Rain Song and even the icy cold water of the river could not cool his scorching desire for her.

Their relationship had not been slow in developing. It did not meander from simple attraction to teasing affection, slowly evolving into a lukewarm love. It had been more like an immediate spark upon first sight and then flared into a blaze fueled by a passionate, enduring love. Ashen realized he did love Rain Song to the point of desperation and pain.

Last, he stopped to think about what his father would do, were he in Ashen's position. The Gray King would not have hesitated to immediately take Rain Song as his wife days ago. His father certainly would not have loved her or anyone, he would have used her for his purposes. Ashen rose and grabbed his clothing and boots, dressing quickly. His life's goal had always been to do the *opposite* of what his father would have done and now that Ashen's head was clear, he knew what he had to do or, more accurately, what he could *not* do; marry Lady Rain Song. He must thwart his father no matter what, even if it cost him his heart and soul in addition to his life.

CHAPTER TEN

King Ashen Arrow strode into the same war room where they had met the day before with Aesir Blacknight. He was the last to enter and the others stood waiting, quietly talking among themselves. His eyes and senses did a quick sweep of the room looking for Rain Song and he was relieved she was not there. After what he had done to her the night before, he was in no hurry to see her and was sure she was in no hurry to see him. His blood still burned through his veins with hungry desire and his hand remembered the touch of her soft breasts. Even the ice-cold water of the river did not douse the fire that burned inside him for her. It intensified every day he was in Jior, as did his anger and frustration over the whole situation and what he could never have. The lack of sleep, his father's haunting, and impatience to be back on the road to Sorn, were driving Ashen slowly to an exhausted state of madness. Time burned and his birthday was swiftly approaching. That coupled with the craving for Rain Song's body was making Ashen more and more frustrated each day and he was having a hard time controlling his rage. Before he had started this farce of trying to release the curse, he had only his life and his soul to lose. Now, during his last days on the earth, he lost his heart too.

Lord Lost Morning appeared to be different from the Ny-Failen of Jior. Dressed in a long white and silver coat and a light breastplate of iridescent silver scales, he glowed with an inner light that made Ashen want to squint when he looked at him. As tall as King Forlorn Icefall, Lost Morning was something from the Heavens and Ashen momentarily regretted being so rude at their first meeting, but he was not about to apologize.

"King Ashen Arrow, Forlorn Icefall has informed me of the details of the marriage contract and the curse you are under. He seems to think that our combined efforts can somehow break this curse and that you may return to your home free of it. I confess I believe your actions have been noble and wise beyond your years. Your concern for the people of Sorn and for Lady Rain Song is honorable. I am willing to offer my help if you will accept it."

Ashen Arrow fisted his hands at his sides and realized he had to go along with this charade because these men would not let him leave Jior without continuing to try.

"I appreciate your help, Lord Lost Morning. I am willing to do anything to save Lady Rain Song, even unto death." Ashen could not think of anything more to say but could not resist looking over and smirking at Jagged Edge who was practically gnashing his teeth with the usual anger and frustration he exhibited around Ashen Arrow.

Aesir Blacknight took up the conversation from there and related all the spells and magic he had tried to end the curse. He and Ashen both demonstrated the spells they tried and the effects they had on the silver scroll case. It spun wildly as it had before and when it came to rest, it opened and the parchment peaked out. Aesir Blacknight removed the marriage contract and handed it to Lost Morning who read silently.

A small frown slowly crossed Lost Morning's brow as he silently read and when he looked up, he stared directly at Ashen Arrow as if he had suddenly figured something out. Before he revealed anything, he turned to King Lorn.

"Forlorn Icefall, please tell me again how this contract came about? How you could have come to make a blood oath for such an agreement?"

King Lorn described the Gray King and his visit to Jior that fateful day. He told of the evil blight that grew and grew until it threatened to poison the water that supplied the castle and how it devoured everything in its path. He told about the fierce battle they fought and the Gray King's silver soldiers who multiplied as they were cut down. Described how the Gray King had frozen him with magic, cut his hand, and forced his blood oath. King Lorn's voice softened as he told about the scared little boy who was also forcibly cut and his hand crushed into a painful clasp, sealing the deal. As he related the tale, he held Ashen Arrow's gaze and tried to impart the truth that none of this was Ashen's fault.

"So, you see Lost Morning, the boy and I were equally coerced into the marriage contract. Now Ashen Arrow has brought us news that the Gray King died four years ago and he is trying to make everything right. Somehow, he is still bound by the curse. If he does not marry a Ny-Failen of my bloodline by his next birthday, keeping the terms of the contract, Ashen Arrow will die. I simply will not allow the Gray King to win." King Lorn finished his story.

Lost Morning re-read the parchment and then set it down. Turning to Ashen Arrow, he held out his hand.

"I wonder if you will allow me Ashen Arrow, I have certain powers that can reveal much that remains unseen. It doesn't hurt and is only done with a simple touch."

Ashen Arrow looked doubtful about submitting but he was fearless and wordlessly held his hand out to Lost Morning. Lost Morning approached him and clasped his hand. His eyes began to change from deep violet to brilliant blue and flared. A bolt of energy flowed through Ashen Arrow and he began to sweat a little but stubbornly held on while Lost Morning delved into his mind, his blood, and his soul. Suddenly, the silver case on the table began to rattle violently. A horrible wailing noise issued from the end of the case as it began to spin even more violently than before.

Ashen quickly let go of Lost Morning and as soon as he did, the case stilled. Lost Morning held a contemplative gaze on Ashen for a long time before he stepped back and returned to his place by the table.

"Ashen Arrow, tell us how your father died, *exactly*." Lost Morning stood looking not at Ashen, but at the scroll case.

None of the men in the room had ever seen Ashen Arrow smile before but now he did and it was not a nice smile. He leaned both hands on the tabletop and began his story.

"When I turned sixteen years of age, the Gray King felt I needed a little *tutelage* in the art of laying with a woman. He claimed it was a right of passage to becoming a man and would be preparation for my wedding night and he sent a woman to my bedchamber. She was an experienced older woman of about five and twenty, and my father adamantly claimed she was beyond childbearing age. It was only to be once but she secretly returned to my bed several times after that first night. It seemed I was a quick learner and very adept at what she was teaching me. When the Gray King found out she was with child, he had her *killed* in front of my eyes. He said he would not suffer a bastard." Anger smoldered in Ashen's eyes and they grew dark and menacing as he looked back into his past.

"The Gray King was very old and you will recall his health was failing. After he killed the woman, he told me that, once my future wife had a child, a similar fate awaited her as *we* only needed a son. That night as he lay weak in his bed, I went into his chamber, stuck my dagger into his chest, and ripped his heart out *as he did mine!*" As if to emphasize his point, he pulled out a long dagger hidden in his boot and tossed it onto the table. The blade was dark red with dried blood.

Silence filled the room as Ashen's tale unfolded and all eyes stared at the dagger laying on the table.

"I hid the blood and wound with my sorcery to make it look as if he died in his sleep of his sickness. As heir, the nobles and counselors of Sorn crowned me King. At the time, I thought, as you did King Lorn, that the Gray King's sorcery would die with him. I quickly learned I was wrong."

Then his voice broke the silence that fell over the group and pleaded quietly.

"Please, I beg of you," he spoke directly to Jagged Edge. "Do not reveal any of this to Lady Rain Song. I could not bear it if she knew."

Not a man in the room blamed Ashen Arrow for his actions. Many of them nodded their approval. Jagged Edge looked at Ashen Arrow with a small measure of begrudging respect. King Lorn unexpectantly placed a hand on Ashen's shoulder and nodded once as if to convey his sympathy and understanding. He turned to Lost Morning.

"Lost Morning, what have you learned." King Lorn asked.

"Forlorn Icefall, I see within our young King of Sorn a very haunted and troubled soul. He is indeed under a terrible death curse that would doom him unto eternity, but I also can see that deeply hidden, *you* are indeed under a similar curse."

King Lorn looked a little startled at Lost Morning's words but waited until he was done explaining. "It is buried within the curse and is hard to see but its evil flows from the scroll case to Ashen Arrow and faintly encircles you also. I do not think its intent is to kill you Forlorn Icefall, it is only meant to force you to keep the contract and assure the marriage is fulfilled. When Ashen Arrow's father pushed him too far and forced him to kill him, it released his greatest magic and the worse part of the curse."

Lost Morning unrolled the parchment and read. "It is here in these words, *'By blood and by pain it shall be fulfilled and the Gray King shall rise again.'* My fear is that because of your blood oath, Forlorn Icefall, you will eventually force the marriage rather than let Ashen Arrow die. Ashen Arrow will marry Rain Song and upon the consummation of the marriage, the Gray King's *soul* will be released and he will possess Ashen Arrow and rise again in *his* body. Ashen Arrow's soul is meant to replace the Gray King in the Hells. I believe the Gray King knew he was going to die before the ten years passed and would not be here to force the marriage. So, he pushed Ashen Arrow to kill him and hid his soul in the scroll case, and assured it would be brought to Jior. Either way, Ashen Arrow is meant to die, the Gray King will have a new body and a young Ny-Failen wife then she too would die as he revealed, once she bears him a son."

"Are you saying this is my fault? That killing him was part of his plan?" Ashen Arrow was outraged, but there was no real force to his words as he realized he had known or at least suspected this treachery all along. This possibility had plagued his subconscious since his father's death and was the true reason he was so adamant about releasing Rain Song.

"Yes, I am saying that it may have been his plan all along. Your father was human, elderly, very ill, and dying anyway. He pushed you past any man's breaking point until you were driven to kill him. Think back Ashen Arrow, before he died, he must have cast the spell. Because he was murdered, now his soul resides within this curse. If you marry Rain Song you release the Gray King's soul and he will possess *you*, his own flesh and blood, and live again. Either way, everything that Ashen Arrow is, will be gone and the Gray King will rise again inhabiting your young immortal Ny-Failen body, replacing your soul. Ashen

Arrow, you were always meant to die and Forlorn Icefall was always meant to see that it happens."

"Then we have no choice," Ashen spoke into the silence that now hung heavy in the room. "I truly must not marry Lady Rain Song and I must die so that the Gray King's plan may not succeed. She will be safe."

No one spoke to contradict him and so Ashen Arrow, King of Sorn, straightened to his full height, gave them all his most noble, humble bow, and left the war room.

CHAPTER ELEVEN

Ashen Arrow packed his few things and planned to leave at first light. He had wasted enough time and the number of days until his birthday was swiftly dwindling. He was out of time. Having had no restful sleep since coming to Jior and, when he did sleep, his father haunted his dreams and left him little rested. Now, he no longer tried. The lack of sleep and the revelations about the scroll case, along with the sexual tension Rain Song created in him, made Ashen very irritated. He barely held onto his sanity. When he was packed and ready to go, he went to the wall and conjured a reflecting mirror, poured some cool water into the basin, pulled out his dagger, and began to shave the sides of his head. The carefully studied action of shaving his temples required all of his attention and calmed him, forcing him to concentrate on one thing only. The new day's growth had to be maintained or the hair would grow back. The soft scraping noise and the sound of his breathing relaxed him.

Aside from emulating his long-gone mentor, Ashen did not stop to think deeply about why he daily practiced this ritual, but he did it through habit and to concentrate on something other than his problems.

A firm knock sounded on his door and Ashen cursed under his breath. Changing his grip on his dagger to an underhanded attack position, he went to the door and yanked it open. Unlike his visitor from the previous night, he had not sensed anyone's presence. King Forlorn Icefall did not wait to be invited in, he just walked into the room. He looked down at Ashen's packed saddlebags and nodded his head as if he understood. They stood in silence for a moment before the King of Jior began to speak.

"Ashen Arrow, there was a time in my life when I too was ruled by a father who was evil incarnate. I never stopped to question the things he did nor did I try to deter him. Quite the opposite, I helped him for many years. It wasn't until he was killed in battle and I later met my wife, Lily, that I began to see that there are many trails a man crosses in his life but it is the one he chooses to walk down that is the most important. Despite how it seems in hard times, you *always* have a choice. I have learned you can always gain forgiveness and be redeemed."

Ashen did not answer King Lorn immediately, only stood contemplating his words and his presence there.

"The Gray King held King Kullorn in high esteem and I believe he wanted the evil and viciousness Kullorn was known for, to be part of the next generation of Sorn through an alliance with a female of your line. That is one reason he was so adamant that your family join with Sorn."

Lorn nodded slowly. "Your father's arrogance about his royal blood and his desire to unite with mine is not surprising. I had begun to suspect as much after meeting the man. Only one evil despot would care about mixing bloodlines with another evil despot."

Ashen reflected on everything Lorn was trying to tell him and he nodded reluctantly.

"I never thanked you," Ashen answered him calmly, changing the subject, "for offering to foster me ten years ago, even if it was under duress. I would have killed to stay here in Jior and I thank you now for making the offer even though I knew the Gray King would not allow it. He wanted to mold me into something evil like himself. Imagine my lack of surprise when I learned he just wanted to possess my body so that *he* could live again. Though it was part of his plan, I am not sorry I killed him."

"Lost Morning said Ny-Failen blood is more potent and imperative to creating this type of magic. That is why he insisted on Ny-Failen blood. In fact, now I recall, the Gray King even admitted it to me the day we were forced to sign the contract." King Lorn stared sympathetically at Ashen, "Ashen, I am not saying you did wrong killing your father. It certainly gave you another choice. It allowed you to become the man, the *King*, that you are. That is my point." The King of Jior walked over to the fireplace and leaned against the mantle and a full minute passed before he turned and continued. "Ashen, if you were my son, I would not stop fighting to free you of this curse until the very last minute. I would not admit defeat. By leaving tomorrow and consigning yourself to death, you are giving up. If I had my way you would stay here and give Lost Morning a chance to work his magic. He is from the Heavens and has power from the Creator that you and I cannot even begin to understand. I ask you to give him a chance, even up until the last hour, *keep trying*."

"King Lorn, is this you talking or the curse? Lord Lost Morning said we were both bound by it and that you would try and force the marriage."

"The curse does not change the man I am. I am convinced I would keep fighting this regardless."

"Then, I appreciate what you are saying, however, there are *other factors* that make my staying here longer more difficult and I fear, for the safety of others, I should leave."

King Lorn crossed his arms over his massive chest and gave him a narrow-eyed look that Ashen could not define.

"Let me ask you something Ashen Arrow." King Lorn's tone grew menacing. "Do you think I am the kind of king that isn't aware of *'other factors?'* Or the kind of grandfather that would let his granddaughter prowl around in the dark, running after a strange man alone? Or do you think that I do not know what goes on in my kingdom enough to know what happens between two young people on top of a tower or at a secluded mountain lake? Jagged Edge may be able to read minds, but I know what my family is up to in *my kingdom*."

Ashen shrugged non-apologetically.

"So, you know Lady Rain Song and I have been spending time together. It means nothing. She has romantic ideas about trying to save me but I know a lost cause when I am faced with one. It is true, Lady Rain Song is my biggest regret in all of this, but I will take memories of our stolen moments together, beyond my grave."

"Do you love her?" the King calmed and asked quietly.

Ashen avoided the question he did not know how to or even want to answer. He stalked over to the washstand where he carefully placed his dagger down and leaned against the stand as if he needed the support. He could not turn to face King Lorn and to speak words of love would weaken his resolve.

"Has she told you that she loves you?" The King asked.

Ashen ignited and he whirled on King Lorn shouting, "What I feel or what she feels is irrelevant! I can say that I want to make her my Queen and spend the rest of my life making her smile but what good does it do?" He waved his arms, "What good does any of this do? I am a dead man! I will not marry her and leave her the wife of an evil despot who has possessed the man she *thinks* she loves. I may love her with all my heart and soul, but I *must* leave her for her safety and happiness, as I have said a thousand times. As her King and her grandfather, you must let me go!"

King Lorn bristled, and then it was his turn to shout. "I would throw you in my dungeon and keep you for as long as it takes, but Rain Song has asked that I implore you to stay willingly. One more chance, that is all I ask. It is all *she* asks.

Give Lost Morning one more chance to break this curse and then we will both let you go."

Ashen Arrow slumped, his back against the wall, and ran his fingers through his long hair. After a long silence, he spoke sadly. "If *she* asks it…" He did not finish his thought and could not meet King Lorn's eyes.

As if he had gotten the assurance he was waiting for, King Lorn strode toward the door. Before he went, he stopped and patted Ashen on the shoulder, and said quietly, "Get some sleep Son," and he left.

Ashen slowly slid to the floor and sat against the wall, his head in his hands, as if he had not the strength to rise.

A small, soft hand smoothed his long hair back from his weary face and Ashen looked up into the large green eyes of Rain Song. She was kneeling beside him and looking at him with all the love in her heart. Leaning forward she kissed him on the cheek and then took his hand pulling him. He rose to his full height and towered over her. Leading Ashen, she walked over to the bed and gently pushed him down. Ashen laid down and she slid next to him fully clothed. She cradled his head on her breast and he fell asleep in her arms.

CHAPTER TWELVE

The clouds ruled the skies the next morning and rain threatened to fall. King Lorn and the others gathered together for the morning meal and to discuss a new plan of attack against Ashen's curse. When he entered the Great Hall with Rain Song on his arm, no one said a word. The Ny-Failen of Jior had a new sort of respect for Ashen Arrow and all that he had done for a girl he never intended to know. Now, with the end coming so close, they did not begrudge him his time with Rain Song. Though King Lorn had not divulged what he knew of their secret meetings together, he did command a certain leniency for the couple. Watching them now, he hoped that his trust was not misplaced.

Ashen guided Rain Song to sit first at a long bench across the Great Hall where the morning meal had been served. She lowered herself down gracefully, never taking her eyes from Ashen Arrow. He sat next to her with only an intimate distance between them. As the day before, she served Ashen Arrow and appeared to be prompting him to eat something. Ashen Arrow did as she bid and only had eyes for Rain Song, not noticing anyone else in the room who may be watching.

Jagged Edge was watching from his usual place at the head table and King Lorn could swear that he heard him grinding his teeth in frustration. He stared at his daughter and Ashen Arrow with his typical simmering intensity. The conversation continued around him. Lost Morning expressed his confidence that he could end the curse that very day.

"I will break the curse this morning. I believe that it is a possession spell instead of a death curse, but the two are intricately bound together. In the end, no evil can withstand the power of the Creator."

Across the room, Ashen Arrow had risen to his feet. Bowing low, he lifted Rain Song's hand and placed a lingering kiss on the back of it while they stared into each other's eyes like long-lost lovers.

"Don't bother Lord Lost Morning because I'm just going to kill him." Jagged Edge had been watching the hand-kissing and began to rise to his feet.

King Lorn placed a heavy hand on his shoulder and commanded, "Sit down Jagged Edge and cool your temper."

Ashen Arrow approached the table and went directly to King Lorn. There was an unmistakable look of respect and gratitude on Ashen's face when he looked at Lorn. He inclined his head to the King as his morning greeting, with a secret understanding relayed in his glance. Turning to Lost Morning, he greeted him with unveiled respect.

"Lord Lost Morning, Aesir Blacknight, and Commander Jagged Edge," Ashen greeted them one by one with unaccustomed patient formality. "I am eager to start when you are ready. First, I must inform my men that we will be leaving this afternoon, as soon as is possible. I need to get back to Sorn so that I may name my successor. There is not much time until my next birth date and I have a long way to go." He did not need to voice his confidence that their efforts would prove futile once again.

They all rose to their feet and King Lorn frowned at Ashen Arrow but he did not see, he had turned to cast a last longing look at Rain Song. No one spoke as Ashen Arrow left the hall, and they all retreated to the war room to prepare.

When Ashen met them a short time later, he was greeted by five, winged men. Lost Morning of course, always remained winged. Also standing winged were King Lorn and Aesir Blacknight who was the only black-winged Ny-Failen. Surprisingly, Vannier and Dark Star who were also winged were in the room. They all stood arrayed around the table with wings spread and somber looks on their faces. Jagged Edge had not yet joined them. Ashen stood at one end of the table and they all waited for his arrival. The dagger with the Gray King's blood on it and the silver scroll case and parchment lay in the middle of the table next to a small brazier as implements prepared for battle and ready to be engaged.

Outside the wind began to increase and raindrops splattered heavily on the windows in the war room. The sky crackled with a bolt of lightning and thunder rolled overhead. They waited for Jagged Edge to come.

Ashen Arrow suddenly straightened and looked behind him as Jagged Edge entered with Rain Song on his arm. Ashen was about to protest, but Lost Morning spoke first.

"Ashen Arrow, the powers of the Creator do not function like men's sorcery does. We do not need familiars, potions, spells, vessels, or any such instrumentation to call upon the Creator for the power to dispel evil. However, I believe that rather than free the Gray King's soul into the world, we should briefly contain it and then send it permanently to the Hells where it belongs. Aesir Blacknight agrees with me and his blue sorcery will capture the Gray King's soul into the parchment where the terms of the marriage contract are written in his magic and sealed with your blood and Forlorn Icefall's blood. Once bound, Forlorn Icefall will burn it ending the Gray King and releasing you both, once and for all."

Ashen was a little angry that Rain Song was there and in danger. "What is to stop the Gray King's soul from entering me or anyone of us for that matter when it is loose? And what part do I play in this?"

"You must light the brazier with your dark magic to bring the Gray King then remain still and let us extract the possession curse from you. Aesir Blacknight assures me what remains of the magic will be drawn into the parchment and burned as well then you will be free. All Ny-Failen from Jior have the protection of the Creator and so we do not fear the Gray King's soul overtaking any one of us. It is only you, we have to be concerned with."

"Why is she here?" Ashen pointed at Rain Song without looking at her. "Lady Rain Song could be in danger. We do not know what could happen." He turned and appealed directly to Jagged Edge. "For her protection, she should leave."

"I am staying Ashen." Rain Song answered him and gave her father a look that said even he could not budge her. Her back was straight, shoulders squared, and her face held a courageous, stubborn look.

Ashen shook his head, resolved to what he considered was madness. "At least stay back from the table as far away from danger as you can."

Lost Morning began as soon as Rain Song stepped back far enough from the table. Jagged Edge stood in front of her with arms folded, as a protective presence, looking as thunderous as the storm raging outside.

Ashen Arrow was infuriated at not being obeyed and violently tossed a ball of white fire into the brazier igniting it with a flaring burst. The flames died down slightly and remained contained.

Wings spread and hands held outward, palms up, to receive the Creator's blessing, Lost Morning bowed his head, closed his eyes, and began to pray.

"Almighty Creator," Lost Morning began, then he looked up toward the heavens, eyes glowing blue and his face illuminated in a rapturous glow of worship. As if standing in the bright light of the sun, he shone. He switched to speaking in the Ny-Failen language to call on the Creator. Ashen could not understand it, never having heard it before, but King Lorn and the others seemed to understand. At some pauses in Lost Mornings praying they answered him back in the same language.

As soon as the prayer began, the silver scroll case began to vibrate. Outside the Storm's thunder boomed and shook the windows at the other end of the room. Aesir Blacknight began chanting only softer with a low voice as an undertone to the prayers. His blue sorcery flickered forward and turned the fire in the brazier and the few lamps in the room to burning blue flames. The entire room was cast in a sapphire glow. Ashen just watched only slightly impressed because he had never seen blue sorcery which affected the elements. Aesir's Ny-Failen power over metals began to work and the scroll case began to glow as if it were stoked in a forge.

The longer Lost Morning's prayer continued the more the scroll case shook and then it was violently spinning and clattering on the table. Ashen began to feel hot and sweat broke out on his forehead. He felt as if he were burning in a forge as well. Suddenly, he was yanked forward by an unseen force. With both hands, he braced himself from pitching headfirst onto the long table and into the brazier. He fought to stand against the power that was pulling him. He had to resist raising his hands to his chest where the strong force of the curse clutched at his heart refusing to let go.

The room was whirling as if the outside storm's wind was blowing inside the room. The shields on the walls rattled violently and a few crashed to the floor. Maps and papers blew everywhere. Ashen thought he heard Rain Song speaking over and over to him, "Hold on Ashen! I love you. Hold on. I love you! Hold on!" Then her sweet voice was drowned out by a low keening. It came from the scroll case as if it had a human voice. Around them, the five Ny-Failen spread their wings side by side as if creating a shelter of calm within the storm.

Ashen suddenly felt as if he was being pulled in two. He gritted his teeth and fought the pulling and tearing that the curse had wrapped around him and through him. He planted his feet wide, braced his arms against the table, and struggled until the force of Lost Morning's prayer was too much and the evil blight finally released him. Like a line snapping, it let go and Ashen went flying back. He was lifted off of his feet and slammed hard into the door. He looked as if he were pinned against it by an unseen force, but it was also him trying to stay upright on his feet. He gasped with astonishment and relief at the feeling of *freedom!* The darkness, anger, and evil that had clutched his heart for many long years were gone!

Lost Morning kept up his prayer, a calm, confident presence in the storm. The wind tore through the room and the keening became a wailing howl and then morphed into an enraged ranting scream. The Gray King's voice cried out in fury at being torn from its temporary shell. As they fought the magic holding his soul in the scroll case, they could see the ghostly form of the Gray King rise from its hiding place. The Gray King turned and looked at Ashen, pointed a finger, and shrieked, *"YOU worthless failure!"*

Aesir Blacknight swiftly lunged into action and grabbed the parchment. It seemed to act like a sponge as Aesir held it up chanting his blue sorcery even stronger. With Aesir's final command, *"Beyaka vila minum!"* The Gray King's apparition whirled, writhed, and fought gnashing his teeth and wailing. *"NNNNOOOOOOO!"*

Lost Morning's prayer was ringing out louder now. A blinding white light lit the room and the sun burst through the windows from behind him. His large white wings fanned out and shone in the golden light and Lost Morning was illuminated in bright gold as his prayer intensified. All the winged Ny-Failen in the room spread their wings further encompassing the group and continued praying.

Ashen started to slide to the floor a swath of blood from the back of his head smearing down in a streak as he fell. He was clutching his head fighting anew with the unseen force that was threatening to tear him apart. Rain Song, upon seeing the blood, screamed his name, slipped around Jagged Edge, and ran toward him. She grabbed his arm and helped him as he struggled to stand. A look of terror was on her face when she saw how pale Ashen was and how badly he was shaking. Taking huge gulps of air, he struggled. The muscles in his chest bulged and the veins in his neck stood out in stark swollen ropes. Ashen's entire body clenched as he fought against the Gray King's magic while trying to push Rain Song back out of the way of danger. Jagged Edge was beside her trying to pull her away but she was fighting to stay at Ashen's side.

Aesir Blacknight succeeded in trapping the Gray King in the parchment and Lorn picked it up and threw it onto the blue flames of the brazier. Then Aesir Blacknight began to use his Ny-Failen power and the silver scroll case started to melt into a molten pile of blackening silver.

The Gray King's death-eaten apparition writhed and let out another horrified scream, each more terrible than the last. Again, and again, they echoed as Lost Morning's prayers beseeched the Creator. Blue sorcery burned him with sapphire flames, engulfing the Gray King as he fought. Suddenly, as if sensing part of himself remained in the world, he looked around frantically and his burning hand reached out and grabbed the dagger with his blood on it. In a last act of defiance, the Gray King drew back and threw the dagger at Ashen, but it was Rain Song's back that was in the path of the deadly, flying dagger.

Through pain-filled eyes, Ashen looked up in time to see the Gray King's ghost grab the dagger and as it flew toward Rain Song he lunged, wrapped his arms around her, and whirled around. He sheltered Rain Song in his protective embrace when the dagger found its mark. Ashen grunted a little and slowly released Rain Song. He slid to his knees and then fell forward, the dagger deeply embedded in his back. The last thing he heard was Rain Song shouting his name as the wind tore through the room and the rain sang its song.

CHAPTER THIRTEEN

Queen Lililaira Gem was immediately sent for and she bathed Ashen Arrow in golden healing light until his wounds were healed. He was going to be fine after his harrowing ordeal, he just needed rest, she prescribed.

Ashen slept for three days. The lack of peaceful sleep for the past many weeks and the impact from the curse tossing him around like burned ashes from a fire left him completely spent. The removal of the curse, striking the door so hard and hitting his head, and the dagger stabbing him, used up his reserves of energy and so he lay pale and weak. He looked as if he had been tortured nearly to death, torn apart and remade into something new.

Rain Song stayed by his side in case he woke or his condition worsened the slightest bit. Lyra Song entreated her to leave him in the care of her grandmother, but Rain Song would not consider leaving. She stayed by his side night and day.

On the third day, he finally woke and looked around a chamber he did not recognize. Rain Song was standing at the window looking out into a bright sunlit day. He lay there watching her for a long time and memorized her bathed in golden sunlight and the way her hair fell to her waist in soft white gleaming waves against her slight beautiful form. Looking down at himself he found that he had no wounds and realized he did not even have so much as a headache. He was not wearing much either so when he sat up from the bed and swung his legs over the side, he held the sheet over him.

Sensing his movements Rain Song looked over and found him trying to stand. She ran to him and pushed him back down.

"Ashen! Please stay in bed. You are very weak!" Rain Song admonished him.

"I…" his voice came out in a dry rasp. "Lady Rain Song, you are safe? Is the curse truly broken? The Gray King is finally gone?"

"Yes, thank the Creator! Ashen! You are free!" Rain Song smiled radiantly at him. "Grandmother said the dagger did not hit anything vital, but that you needed rest as you lost a lot of blood and were exhausted. You should get back in bed and let me bring you something to drink and eat. It will help you regain your strength." She was pushing him back, covering him up, and arranging the pillows for him.

"Lady Rain Song, I am well. I do not have to lay abed like an invalid." Though his back was sore where the dagger had stabbed him, he realized he felt quite well. Smoothing his hand over the sides of his head he felt the many day's growth there and understood how long he had been down.

"No doubt you feel well enough to get up but will rest until I get you something to eat. Stay in bed!" She ordered firmly.

Ashen gave her a crooked half-smile and then leaned back resting against the pillows. He allowed her to fuss over him until she was satisfied that he was settled comfortably back in the bed. As soon as she was gone to fetch food, Ashen flung the blankets off and left the bed, striding over to where his clothes lay. They had been washed, his shirt stitched where the dagger had cut it and his boots had been shined. He was looking around for his dagger intending to shave the sides of his head and face, but he could not find it. Stopping a moment, he tried to assess how he felt. His heart was light and the anger and frustration were gone from his mind. Probing deeper within he realized the heavy feeling of doom had been lifted from his entire being and he realized his father was truly vanquished. The Gray King had left him completely and Ashen was *free*! He closed his eyes and breathed a huge sigh of relief.

When Rain Song returned carrying a tray, she found Ashen out of bed, standing half-dressed and a little wobbly on his feet. Her brow furrowed in irritation; Rain Song watched him standing there staring at her. The smooth muscles of his bare chest flowed with his movements. Her breath caught. Ashen was so beautiful and male she thought she might swoon. Even after watching him for days in a sickbed, she marveled at how magnificent, masculine and so very enticing he was to look at.

Ashen went to her and relieved her of the tray and set it on the nearby table. She pushed him down into a chair and told him to "eat!" Ashen reached for the cup of cold ale that she brought and downed it in a few gulps. He was very thirsty, ravenously hungry, and ate silently while watching her pour him more ale. After a good portion of the food was gone, he finally sat back and contemplated what he wanted to say to her.

"My Lady Rain Song, I…" he hesitated and was unsure how he was going to say everything that was in his heart. "I need my dagger so I can shave." He realized he was having a hard time figuring out what should be said to her. Before, when he was a prisoner of the curse, he had nothing to gain or lose and so conversation had been perfunctory. The few times he had been alone with her were like stolen moments in time when he had let his guard down and had nothing more to lose. Now that he was completely free of his curse and the Gray King, he had little idea how to go forward. He had a lot of thinking to do.

Rain Song nodded and silently slipped from the room again and he was able to form a coherent thought. She returned a short time later with a bowl of steaming water, a bar of soap, and a sharp dagger. He tried to rise from the table, but she pushed him down and moved behind him. Placing a long cloth over his shoulders, she lathered up a brush with the soap and water and spread it over the right side of his head. The soap gave off a crisp pine scent and was appealing and relaxing at the same time. He leaned his head to the side as she pulled the long length of the rest of his hair back exposing one side of his head where the fuzzy gray growth was filling in. She followed the path of shorter hair and began, with slow sure strokes to shave his head in the fashion he normally wore it. Moving behind his gently pointing ear, he tipped his head forward and she shaved down the back slope of his head the way she had watched him do a few nights back.

Ashen closed his eyes and relaxed into the feel of Rain Song's hands against his skin. He was acutely aware of her body and movements behind him. When she was finished shaving the hair down to the skin on one side, she moved to the next. He never would have thought that such a simple task as shaving the sides of his head could be so sensual. With Rain Song's delicate hands on his skin and her smooth deliberate movements, her presence so close to him; he was beginning to think he might not be able to handle her nearness. He wondered why she was so quiet as she said not a word while she worked, only diligently focused on her task. When she finished shaving the sides of his head, she shaved his chin and neck.

If Ashen thought her shaving him was seductive and soothing at the same time, when she brushed his long hair and braided it tightly down the crest of his head, he thought maybe he had died and gone to the Heaven's. She tied off the length with a thin leather strip and removed the cloth from around his shoulders. Wiping off the excess soap and water she stood in front of him at the table. Replacing the instruments on the tray she busied herself cleaning up. She did not seem to be able to meet his gaze and Ashen grew concerned at the solemn look on her face.

Gently, Ashen took her small hand and pulled her between his legs, and circled her small waist with his large hands. Her eyes were downcast and she almost looked as if she were about to cry.

"How is it that you know how to shave a man?" Ashen teased just a little, trying to catch her eye.

"I watched you the other night." Her voice shook just a little and she continued to look down.

He smoothed a hand across the side of his head, "You did a fine job. Thank you, my Lady."

Rain Song only nodded. Ashen put one finger under her chin and made her look at him. They stared into each other's eyes for a long moment.

"My Lady, what distresses you? I would like to see you smile."

She took a few moments to answer him and then she looked into his eyes. "Now that you are well, you will be leaving, returning to your kingdom. You told me before, you would return to your home, alone."

"Aye, I will." He said gently. "I have responsibilities there. A kingdom to rule."

"I understand. You are a King and have responsibilities. I know you never intended..."

Ashen had enough of talking and he pulled her closer into the circle of his arms. His hands were in her silken hair and he was overwhelming her with a passionate kiss. He tried to be gentle but she tasted so sweet and he was desperate for her. He drank her kisses, tangled his tongue with hers and slipped his hands along her curves, felt her warmth and tenderness.

As with every other time, Rain Song was again swept away by Ashen's kisses. He held nothing back but showed her with his kiss, his very deep desire for her. When he slowed and placed softer kisses on her cheeks working his way to her neck, she leaned back just a little to give him more of her to kiss. She could hear his rapid breathing and feel the tension in his muscles as his arms struggled not to hold her too tightly or take their mutual hunger too far. She knew he was holding back.

In truth, Ashen wanted to lift her onto his lap and get her as close as he could. He was wishing that she did not have such a large *damned* amount of material to her dress because he could not get close enough to feel her body or touch her bare skin. As soon as his lips found the swell of her breasts, she gasped and trembled. Smoothing her hands over his bare shoulders and down his arms, she clung and arched into him. Ashen had to drag himself up from the depths of desire he was falling into and find the strength to stop. He swept a few more kisses up her neck and then placed one last gentle kiss on her lips.

They stopped. Each breathing hard. His forehead resting against hers, eyes closed, he fought to gain control. Rain Song's intuition told her that they had crossed some kind of barrier in their relationship, but she did not dare let her assumptions match her heart's wishes.

Ashen finally made her look at him again. "Rain Song, did you think I did not want to take you with me? I know what I said before, but now you are out of danger and I am truly free. I want to make you my wife and my Queen, but I know how hard it will be for you to leave your family and Jior, and live in Sorn." His last words flowed freely, words he never expected to utter, "Will you? Be my wife?"

"Ashen," she whispered in that breathless longing way she had of saying his name. "I have known since the day I saw you ten long years ago that we were meant to be and I have known that it could happen. But you are a King and now you are free of your father and his curse. When you first came to Jior you had no intention of leaving with a Ny-Failen bride from Jior. Are you sure this is what you want? Now, you are free you could have any woman."

"There is no other I will accept. I want *you* Rain Song to be my wife and if you are willing, I will speak to your father today. I may be King of Sorn, but I am also a Black Sorcerer. Your family may have rid me of the curse, but I doubt they did it so that I would marry you after everything we have been through and for me to take you away from them. Still, I will ask your father for your hand if it is what you want as well."

"There is nothing dark in you Ashen or I could not love you as I do. I want nothing more than to be your wife." She smiled shyly at him and then he hugged her close. He held her tightly in his arms, his elation flowing through him and warming her. He was smiling as he whispered in her ear, "You *will* be my wife if I have to throw you onto my horse and take you away in the dead of night!"

Chapter Fourteen

Jagged Edge was in the practice arena. He was sparring with one of his men and instructing him on the finer points of swordplay when Ashen Arrow came striding down the path from the castle. Looking up, he was only slightly surprised to see the young King of Sorn out of his sickbed and coming purposefully toward him. Jagged Edge made him wait while he finished his lesson. Once he was done and the young soldier left, he begrudgingly turned toward Ashen Arrow and acknowledged him with a glare of angry green eyes. Eyes so much like Rain Song's.

"Commander Jagged Edge, I would speak with you." Ashen Arrow was not the slightest bit as intimidated as Jagged Edge would have wished.

"We are in the practice field, pick up a sword." Jagged Edge gestured toward the row of practice swords. "Shall we spar?"

Ashen Arrow gave Jagged Edge a grin that indicated he would like to do so very enthusiastically. He took his coat off and choosing a weapon, stepped onto the practice field. As soon as he was close enough Jagged Edge made a vicious swipe toward his head. Ashen Arrow smiled and easily dodged the swing, countering with a backhanded blow. Jagged Edge caught his sword and danced out of the way. Circling, he returned Ashen's blow with three more in fast succession, and Ashen was forced back a step. Thus went the next quarter of an hour of intense sparring and it seemed as if the two were evenly matched.

"I want your permission to marry Lady Rain Song." To distract Jagged Edge, Ashen Arrow suddenly interjected his appeal between hammering blows, and it worked. Jagged

Edge momentarily straightened from his fighting stance and had to leap out of the way of Ashen's next sword stroke toward his middle.

"No!" Jagged Edge countered and doubled his blows, forward slash, backslash, forward thrust, each one getting harder and more vicious.

"Why do you deny me?" Ashen Arrow was countering the blows as fast as he could and barely missed stopping one. He ended up with a slight cut to his arm. Jagged Edge smiled with wicked satisfaction that he had drawn first blood as a red stain spread across the arm of Ashen's dove gray shirt.

"Despite the fact that the curse has been removed and Lost Morning assures me there is no longer any danger from the Gray King, I will not relinquish my daughter to a Black Sorcerer."

"There is no more darkness in me. I learned the black arts only so that I could defeat the Gray King. I think you know that!" He parried a vicious thrust and countered.

Jagged Edge began circling and made a swipe at Ashen's head who just barely ducked in time to avoid being decapitated.

"I love her." Ashen stopped and took two steps back giving ground. "I will make her my wife and the Queen of Sorn."

Ashen Arrow had been ill for three days and was recovering from more than just a head wound and a stab in the back. He quickly began to tire. Jagged Edge renewed his onslaught and Ashen Arrow went completely on the defensive. Concentrating on deflecting each of Jagged Edge's blows, Ashen decided it would be better to let his future father-in-law win the match.

"You are not good enough for Rain Song and she does not know what is best for her. I do! You will not marry my daughter!" The last sentiment was hammered down on Ashen's sword, a blow emphasizing each word.

Ashen deflected the last strike dropped the point of his sword to his side and stepped back yielding to Jagged Edge. When he was sure Jagged Edge was no longer swinging his sword, he tossed his sword to the ground at Jagged Edge's feet and went down on one knee.

"Then take my head Jagged Edge because I cannot live without her." He bowed his dark silver head to Jagged Edge in invitation.

Jagged Edge's anger cooled instantly when he saw the King of Sorn on his knee in front of him, yielding, willing to die for his youngest daughter. His ire deflated completely. Running his free hand through his long dark red hair Jagged Edge cursed and then just stared at Ashen Arrow bowing before him. After a few tense moments, he sheathed his sword.

"Very well. If Rain Song wants the marriage, I will consent but if you hurt her, I *will* take your head." Jagged Edge offered Ashen Arrow his hand and helped him rise to his feet.

"Commander Jagged Edge, I would rather die than hurt Lady Rain Song. You can rest assured I will take good care of her and I hope you visit Sorn often so that you can see what a wonderful wife, Queen, and mother she will be."

"Be assured, I will be checking on you." He growled and bent down to pick up Ashen's sword. "Come, before I go break the news to my wife…I need a drink!"

#

King Lorn and Lost Morning stood upon a high tower watching Jagged Edge slash and stab at Ashen Arrow. They placed a small wager on who would prevail and made comments about this or that maneuver.

When Ashen Arrow stepped back, dropped to his knee, and bowed his head to Jagged Edge, King Lorn commented, "Oh, that was well played. I guess I owe you ten pieces of silver Lost Morning, looks like we will be having a wedding after all."

"Forlorn Icefall, have you not yet learned? Love always wins in the end."

#

A week later, King Ashen Arrow of Sorn and Lady Rain Song, daughter of Princess Lyra Song, and Commander Jagged Edge, Granddaughter of King Forlorn Icefall of Jior, were wed. Lost Morning officiated in a ceremony held during the late morning hours of a beautiful summer day. Rain Song was swathed in shimmering layers of gossamer silver silk. Her radiant smile was infectious. Tiny diamonds shimmered in a veil that floated on her curls and hung from her braids like rain from a silver-lined cloud. King Ashen Arrow received his bride with a victorious smile and an appreciative glimmer in his eye. After Lost Morning pronounced them husband and wife, he said a long prayer to the Creator and gave thanks for the victory over evil. He blessed the marriage and bade Ashen Arrow kiss his new wife. Kiss her he did, quite thoroughly. In front of the entire gathering, Ashen Arrow took her into his arms, gallantly swooped her into a dip, and devoured her lips in a long, sensual kiss. Rain Song's arms gracefully slid around his neck embracing him lovingly.

Blooms of deep blue and pale pink and long strands of emerald green ivy filled the great hall where the wedding feast was held after the ceremony. Their fragrance filled the air along with the rich scent of bees' wax candles. Tables brimmed with roasted meats and expertly cooked vegetables that sent enticing aromas through the air. Bread and pastries filled with jams and fresh berries, puddings, and honeyed fruits made a colorful display. As they ate, they celebrated the happy couple and an end to ten years of fear. No one had ever seen Ashen Arrow or Rain Song so happy and comfortable with each other. Lyra Song expressed her joy to Queen Lily, her mother, that her daughter seemed so happy and at ease with her new husband. Jagged Edge was sullen and moody. He still glared at Ashen Arrow as if he would like to stick a dagger in his chest.

As the wedding celebration went on, King Lorn decided to have a talk with Jagged Edge. He approached with a consolatory pitcher of ale in his hand and refilled Jagged Edge's chalice.

"Jagged Edge, it is a swift flight for me to go to Sorn. I will check on Rain Song frequently if it will ease your mind."

"It is hard to think of my youngest daughter as a woman and a wife, let alone the Queen of a far-off country." Jagged Edge grumbled into his ale.

"Did I ever tell you years ago, I was going to hunt you down in Celtica for breaking Lyra Song's heart? I had very satisfactory visions of taking your head from your shoulders for everything that happened to her." King Lorn gave him a wicked grin. "When you left her with a broken heart, I was going to kill you *slowly and painfully*."

"What stopped you?" Jagged Edge did not look surprised.

"Lily. She convinced me that Lyra Song loved you and that no matter what retribution I took I could not change that. It is the same with Rain Song. Though I admit, I was not happy at the beginning with the match. I believe all things worked out in the end and I feel that Ashen Arrow is a good man, will be a great king and an even better husband."

"I will consider your *wise* counsel Forlorn Icefall." Jagged Edge, not placated in the least, raised his cup he saluted Lorn and they drank. "And, thank you for *not* taking my head off."

The wedding celebration continued long into the evening hours and Ashen grew more impatient for the wedding night. He watched his new wife with growing intensity and finally when his patience ran out, he whispered in her ear that they should retire for the night. She gave him a terrified look but wiped it away as quickly as she could. He lifted her hand to his lips and kissed her wrist trying hard to calm the hungry anticipation throbbing through his entire body. She left to go prepare and Ashen waited impatiently for enough time to elapse until he could go to her. Finally, when he could wait no longer, he left to seek his bride.

Ashen found Rain Song in the chamber that had been prepared for them. Flowers decorated the room and their sweet floral scent filled the air. A huge four-post bed intricately carved with scrollwork and twisting vines was the central focus of the room. Rain Song was waiting for him, but she had not taken her wedding dress off and prepared for bed. Instead, she paced the room like a nervous colt. She was wringing her hands and was clearly upset.

Ashen, who had little experience with women and none with young virgins, realized he was going to have to proceed very slowly. He took off his sword belt, then his coat, and removed his new dagger from his boot, then the boots went off and everything else until he stood in nothing but his trousers and shirt. Moving toward her, he untucked the dove gray shirt, while he watched Rain Song watch him. Her eyes were huge and slightly frightened. She trembled, reminding him of a deer's alert terror right when it senses a hunter; head raised, muscles bunching before it took flight. A delicious sense of challenge rose in Ashen's breast and he stalked toward her. She flinched as if she truly wanted to run.

"You're trembling. Why?" Ashen reached out and patiently ran his hands over her arms trying to calm her.

"I, I," Rain Song swallowed and blushed a little. "I have never…"

"I know, my Love." Patiently, Ashen leaned down and kissed her forehead. "I will try and reign in my passion for you so that it will be...did your mother give you any instruction?"

"Yes," she whispered. "And two of my aunts did as well." She smiled.

"We have kissed and I have…well, before, that one night when you came to my room and I tried to scare you off, you did not seem the least afraid of me then. Why are you now?"

"I don't know! I am sorry! I did not think I *would* be so frightened."

"You are frightened of me?"

"I am frightened of how much I want you, of how much I love you. I know we have kissed and embraced a little before, but I am frightened of displeasing you and not being *enough* for you Ashen."

Ashen laughed just a little and shook his head. He swept her up and pulled her close then took her over to the bed. Setting her back on her feet, he sat down on the edge and turned her so that she could look him straight in the eyes. Slowly he tugged, loosening the lacing down the front of her wedding dress. His delectable bow-shaped mouth curved in a patient smile. He was careful not to move too quickly and he began to speak to her in a soft tone trying to soothe her fears.

"My Lady Rain Song, you are wrong to fear that you would displease me. You more than please me already. I have burned for you more days than I care to count. We will go slow. Now kiss me and stop worrying." He smiled at her and Rain Song stared at how beautiful he was. She traced the curving slope of his lips with her fingertips as she cupped his face with her small hand. She bent forward.

Tilting her head, she lightly kissed and smoothed her lips across his. Ashen kept unlacing her dress and when her tongue met his, he slid his hands inside and smoothed them over her breasts. As he teased her nipples over the material of her underdress, Rain Song caught her breath on a gasp. Gently, she bit his bottom lip and sucked it. Ashen groaned and raising a hand to the back of her head pulled her in for a deeper taste.

They had shared kisses before and Ashen hands had ventured to a couple of the wonderful places they wanted to go, but this was different. Gone were the barriers to their happiness and the dark veil of fear was lifted. Now the light of their love shone through. This was right in every sense of the word. She was his wife now and he did not need to stop or hold back his hunger for her. He felt her hands move to his sides and she was pulling his shirt up to his shoulders and he had to stop kissing her so that she could remove it from him completely and let it drop to the floor.

Gazing down she stared at his broad chest and boldly put her hands on him, warming his skin where her touch explored. Ashen pushed her dress off of her shoulders and it floated to the floor with a slight rustling and lay in a gossamer heap of silver. He ran his hands over her quivering curves looking at her pearly-white skin and, slowly shaking his head, spoke with astonished wonder.

"I have never seen anything as beautiful as you Rain Song." Ashen was amazed, "And *you* are *my wife*. Please do not be afraid of me. I will be as gentle as I can. I promise."

"I won't be afraid Ashen. I trust you." She smiled tentatively at him and tugged the last bit of silken material from her body, letting it slide to the floor. Standing completely naked in front of him Ashen's mouth fell open in awe. Her breasts were larger than he had first thought and now it was he who was nervous because she was so small and delicate. Her pearl-hued skin glowed with warmth and she was stunningly beautiful.

Ashen lifted her, stood, and turned toward the bed that had been turned down for them. He laid her on the cool sheets, divested himself of his trousers, and then slid down beside her. His desire for her was hard, satiny smooth, and almost hot, waiting impatiently for the act to begin. Smoothing his hand down over her hip he gentled her, he warmed her body with his hands and dipped his head to kiss down her neck and her breasts. His kisses followed down to her soft, flat stomach. Ever since the first time he lifted her onto his horse, he had a fascination with her tiny waist and he kissed each rib and traveled across her belly and kissed down her hips. The scent of her heat and desire rose to entice him lower, but Ashen contained himself and kissed no further than the gentle slope of her hips. His hand, however, delved between her lovely thighs to caress her where she most wanted and needed, to prepare the way.

Rain Song pressed back, her heart pounding in her chest. Every nerve tingled delightfully with Ashen's nearness and when he touched her, she cried out, "Ashen!"

The sound of his name on her pleasure-filled gasp drove Ashen mad with desire and he moved between her legs. Settling, he pulled one of her legs over his hip and teased her entrance with his hardness and gentle pushes into her warmth. His lips descended to her breasts and she arched against him almost frenzied for more of him. Kissing her passionately, Ashen eased home and with one careful thrust, finally, completely, made her his.

Rain Song's entrance was slick with her desire for Ashen and when he slid inside her, she gasped with a shock of pain, but his gentleness and slow caresses enticed her to relax and so she accepted his intrusion. The wonder began. As if he was not sure how much time to give her to adjust to him, Ashen waited, breathing hard, shuddering with the effort it took not to move. When Rain Song moved experimentally against him, he eased carefully out and then back in, showing her the way. It was a natural, fluid movement and was pure in its simplicity. His gentle undulating hardness inside of her warm softness was the most wonderful thing either of them had ever experienced.

Rising on his arms he looked down at their joined bodies and watched his hips withdraw and enter again. Slender pearl-white legs clasped him and her hips met his thrusts, causing him to groan with satisfaction. When he lay completely atop her and her arms were around him caressing his back and pulling him in deeper, Ashen's heart flamed with satisfied yearning and utter fulfillment. She was loving him and the affection and acceptance he always longed for were *finally his.* In a life that had been so filled with darkness and cold, she gave him the light and warmth he needed most.

As their lovemaking reached its peak Ashen's thrusts became harder and more urgent, his kisses more ardent. Rain Song clung to him and as she reached the summit her body had been climbing toward, she cried out in fulfilled joy.

When Ashen felt Rain Song reach her completion he gave a final few thrusts and burst. Throbbing and emptying into her body's safe haven, Ashen sank into Rain Song's total embrace and whispered to her of his unending desires and all the love in his heart.

Finally, the marriage between Jior and Sorn was consummated in love, passion, and peace.

CHAPTER FIFTEEN

Ashen Arrow was insatiable when it came to making love to Rain Song and they spent the days after their wedding sneaking away for passionate encounters. Rain Song for her part, could not get enough of Ashen's attention and affection. They explored the different ways to make love and in their secret moments, he spoke of his hopes for their future. Ashen's other saving grace was that his dreams were finally peaceful and completely devoid of his father's specter. It confirmed to him that the Gray King was truly, finally gone. Instead, his dreams were filled with hope for the future. Without his father's ghost constantly railing at him over his failures and telling him what to do, he became calmer and more confident in his decisions and his actions. He spent a lot of time with King Lorn in deep conversations discussing ruling a kingdom. Ashen learned from him whom he had always revered and admired since that fateful day King Lorn had defied the Gray King.

Rain Song and Ashen returned to the mountain lake, undressed completely, and swam in the cool waters under the hot summer sky. He made love to Rain Song in the water, and on a blanket under the sun, she climbed atop and made love to him. Ashen folded his hands under his head and smiled up at his beautiful wife riding him like a stallion. Their joy in each other was complete, but the day quickly came when they needed to say goodbye to Jior and Rain Song's family.

Ashen was torn. The duty he owed to his people made him anxious to get back to Sorn. Dark, evil, black magic, and years of hardship and cruelty had marred the place with terrifying memories and dread. There was much work to be done to repair centuries of damage. Though it had been an evil and desolate place while he was growing up, he had made many changes since the Gray King's death. It remained sad, dark, and certainly no place for a gentle lady. Ashen had no idea what was needed to make Castle Sorn a home, but he hoped that Rain Song would bring new brightness to its dark halls and wipe away its tragic history. Another part of him did not want to leave Jior and take Rain Song away from her family, though she valiantly attacked preparations for leaving her mother and father, and everything she knew and loved, to go with him.

Rain Song's intuition became stronger as the days went by and she knew as she made her preparations what to take. She felt that she should take this or that mirror, these pillows and that these colors would do well in Castle Sorn. Large brightly colored hangings and rugs, as well as small pieces of furniture, glass vases, and luxurious curtains, were stowed carefully away at Rain Song's direction and Ashen let her do anything she wished. Out of Jior's wealth, they took what her instincts told her to take, but she could not pack the love of her family.

On the day of Ashen's twenty-first birthday they had a grand celebration and Ashen never knew such love, happiness, and acceptance. The next day, they were set to leave Jior as the sun rose over the Violent Mountains in a thousand hues of pink, gold, and orange. White clouds covered the sky in shapes like dragon scales and wispy feathers. Despite the beauty of the morning, the mood was somber as the Ny-Failen of Jior gathered to say goodbye to Lady Rain Song and the King of Sorn.

Four wagons filled with presents, supplies, and Rain Song's belongings had been packed. One of the wagons held the deconstructed four-post bed Ashen and Rain Song had occupied since their wedding night. Ashen had mentioned to

King Lorn that there were no furnishings at Castle Sorn fit for the delicate Lady Rain Song. The King consulted with the Queen who already had matters in hand having worked with Rain Song to see to it the newlyweds had enough furnishings from Jior to make a fresh new start. Vannier sent a white wood bow and white arrows with Rain Song and entreated her to summon him if ever she needed anything. Dark Star sent dozens of young trees and seedlings with them to begin a garden in Sorn. He promised to visit in the very near future and use his power to make them flourish. Once food, ale, cider, water, and every necessity they could fit in the train of wagons was ready, there was not much else left to do but to head out of the gates of Jior and ride toward the Kingdom of Sorn.

A company of ten Jiorian soldiers, hand-picked by Jagged Edge, were sent along with the soldiers from Sorn and they would travel along with them for safety. There were numerous servants from Jior going along to assist and offer every help and comfort they could for Lady Rain Song's sake.

Finally, the time came for Rain Song to say goodbye to her family. Tears of leave-taking pooled in her green eyes as she hugged her grandfather and grandmother for what felt like the last time. She smiled as she said tearful goodbyes to her aunts and uncles, cousins, and friends. When it was time to say her farewell to her mother, she clung to her and cried while they spoke in quiet tones. Lyra Song assured her that they would come to visit Sorn in little over one month's time which eased the pain of Rain Song's departure.

Last, Rain Song turned to Jagged Edge. His face had been caught in a frown since the wedding and it deepened as he watched the preparations. He calculated everything his daughter would need for her long journey from a military standpoint, but when the moment came to look upon her face for the last time, he hesitated. He wanted to hold her close and not let go. After a tearful embrace, Jagged Edge held her at arm's length and looked at his youngest daughter. All the words he wanted to say were sticking in his throat. Ashen was standing by her side as they said their final goodbye to each other.

"Rain Song, I will miss your smiling face and your beautiful singing. I wish you the greatest happiness in your new life. Your mother and I will leave Jior to visit you in one month. If your husband is not giving you the best of care that you deserve, I will kill him and bring you back home." He was giving Ashen Arrow a malevolent grin and Rain Song laughed at him, but Jagged Edge was serious. Ashen Arrow nodded his head in acknowledgment of the threat.

Then it was Ashen's turn to say goodbye to Jagged Edge. They clasped hands with strong crushing grips, each trying to make the other flinch. Jagged Edge tried once more to break through the walls of Ashen's thoughts, to no avail. Ashen Arrow gave him a wicked smile as if he knew. He surprised Jagged Edge by pulling him into an embrace and whispered into his ear, "I will protect her with my life."

When they parted Jagged Edge responded in a quiet voice so that only Ashen Arrow could hear, "Good because that is what it will cost you if you don't."

Then they were off. Rain Song mounted a dappled white and gray mare with a long rippling white mane and tail and rode beside Ashen on Tarnish. Hiding his face, the King put his silver crowned helmet on and led the entire procession out of Jior heading for the Kingdom of Sorn.

CHAPTER SIXTEEN

It was early fall when the leaves were just beginning to change colors from rich greens to brilliant reds and golds. Travel to Sorn would take at least seven long days. Word spread ahead of them that the King of Sorn and his Ny-Failen bride from Jior were passing through Vedt on their way to the coastal land of Sorn. Outriders rode ahead to scout the way and for the most part, they traveled unmolested. Ashen Arrow took them along the border between Skoria and Skogur because it was the swiftest route. The weather was fair and they traveled swiftly.

Taking his bride to Sorn was the final battle Ashen had to fight. He knew what awaited them there and his dread was a powerful presence in his mind. After the beauty and vivaciousness of Castle Jior, he did not know how she would react to seeing his desolate castle. Her disappointment was something he could not abide. It was the ghosts of the past that gave him the most trepidation but he reminded himself that his father was dead and his evil spirit truly vanquished.

After three days of travel outside of the Violent Mountains, they were abruptly challenged by soldiers from Skogur. Two of them sat on horse in the middle of the road. The party halted in a small gully that was strategically placed in the perfect spot for an ambush. Ashen Arrow raised a hand to stop his caravan and gave Rain Song a sideways glance that she could not read. It disturbed her nonetheless. There were only two confronting their number of twenty-three warriors from Jior and Sorn combined. Five soldiers from Sorn rode forward and spread out in a perfect line in front of the rest of the caravan. Jior's soldiers split into two groups of five and rode along to the side, effectively boxing in Rain

Song and the wagons. Ashen Arrow put his crowned helmet on and alone rode Tarnish forward, very casually.

The two soldiers made no move closer but waited quietly as Ashen Arrow approached. Neither one of them looked surprised when they all heard a great rumbling. Suddenly, coming from the end of the gully and riding very fast toward them, came at least twenty more of Skogur's soldiers. Dust rose from their horse's hooves and the ground trembled as they neared the spot where King Ashen Arrow waited. Foot soldiers joined the others and the ranks stretched back revealing at least fifty more. With a great deal of stamping and show of force, Skogur's cavalry in front spread out, blocking the road with a long line of heavily armed, mounted soldiers. While foot soldiers waited in ranks behind.

One of the first of the two Skogur soldiers gave Ashen Arrow a yellow-toothed grin that said he spotted easy pickings.

"You must be the young King of Sorn we heard about?" The soldier spoke to Ashen Arrow while he surveyed the company from Jior. His eyes came to rest on Lady Rain Song and he shifted restlessly in his saddle.

"I am. What of it?" Ashen asked mildly. His deep voice carried strongly to everyone in the gully, though he was not shouting.

"You're trespassing on Skogur lands." Some of Skogur's soldiers laughed at this remark and the one who had designated himself as spokesman, shook his head with mock sadness.

"I'm afraid it is going to cost you a heavy toll to travel through Skogur. I'd say what's in those wagons might ought to just about cover it."

King Ashen Arrow calmly removed his helmet and his long silver-gray hair gleamed in the sunlight. "The price you are asking is high and one I'm not willing to pay. Besides, you and I both know that this is a free road on the border between Skoria and Skogur. You've no right to tax me anything."

The Skogur soldier did not answer right away, but again looked around Ashen Arrow directly at Lady Rain Song, his stare traveled around to the soldiers with the company, assessing their soldiers.

Rain Song for her part was distressed at a large number of men blocking the road in front of them. She was not sure how Ashen would take to being held up like this and being so greatly outnumbered. Her intuition told her that this confrontation was not going to end well.

"Willing or not, we'll be taking your weapons, any coin you got, and those wagons." The second soldier cut in sneering. "Or you'll just have to go back to the Jiorian hole in the ground you crawled out of."

"What my brother is trying to say is that there is no way you'll be going through Skogur lands unless you pay us the toll." The second soldier added helpfully.

Tarnish shifted nervously underneath Ashen Arrow but he remained silent. The sound of singing metal rang out as Jior's soldiers, surrounding Lady Rain Song, drew their swords and watched, ready for a confrontation.

"Tell you what I am willing to do. You Skogur scum shove off and I'll let you all live." There was an amused sound to Ashen's voice as he made his threat and the smile he gave them was frightening.

The Skogur soldiers all laughed. "You're greatly outnumbered! So, I suggest you hand over the wagons and pay the toll."

He sneered at the Jiorians. Jior and Skogur had always been at war and though the last few years had been quiet, there was still a shallowly buried animosity between them.

The Jiorians were not surprised at the scorn from the Skogur soldier. The second soldier made the next demand.

"And because we have a problem with the company you keep, we'll also take your fine horses but you can walk away with your lives. Unless you'd rather fight then we'll take those too!" He shouted louder, "we like spilling Jiorian blood!"

"After you're all dead we'll take everything anyway and I will personally take that *woman* and make her my whore for the night." The first soldier grinned lasciviously and licked his lips

Ashen's voice grew deep with fury. "That woman is my wife and the Queen of Sorn! You're not worthy to lick the bottom of her boots. And because of your insult to her, *all* of you shall die." Ashen Arrow wheeled Tarnish around and returned to join the line of Sorian soldiers.

"Protect the Queen!" His deep voice shouted out and then he put his helmet back on his head and readied to lead the fight as he rode back to his soldier's he shouted louder. "Kill them all!"

While Ashen was speaking to the soldiers, Rain Song remained quiet on her gray spotted mare, watching and listening. Around her, Jior's soldiers tensely waited to see what would happen. It was clear that a battle was inevitable. When Ashen commanded his men to kill all the Skogur soldiers, she went cold at the malevolent sound of his voice.

As Skogur's soldiers advanced toward them, Ashen reached into one of his saddlebags and withdrew a black bag. Untying it he reached in and pulled out what looked like a handful of silver chess pieces. In an underhanded toss, he threw the pieces. They glittered faintly, tumbling in the air with the sunlight glinting off of them, before landing in the dirt in front of him. As he tossed them, he shouted *"Saigh-hure pawns!"*

As the pieces hit the ground the silver pawns began to shimmer and quickly grew until there were five large silver soldiers, larger than most of the humankind, standing on guard in front of their group.

Rain Song gasped with horrified recognition. These were the same silver soldiers that had accompanied the Gray King ten years earlier into the Great Hall of Jior. She had seen them with her own eyes when she was a little girl the first time she ever laid eyes on Ashen Arrow. Rain Song had also heard about the battle outside of Jior's walls and understood that these warriors could not be killed, but would simply multiply as they were cut down.

One of the older Jiorian soldiers next to her must have recognized them as well because he mumbled under his breath. "At least now we're not outnumbered."

It remained that they were a company of about twenty-three live soldiers with about four wagon drivers and four servants in their group. They all prepared to battle.

King Ashen Arrow had drawn his sword and he and his men charged with a loud battle cry. The silver pawn soldiers engaged the enemy with deadly precision. They came together with a thunderous clash of sword and horse, silver and flesh. Ashen Arrow was magnificent in his light silver armor that shone in the autumn sunlight. His long sword flashed as the two forces collided and the fight began.

Rain Song's horse reared, frightened by the commotion, and she fought to keep her seat. As the battle raged, Rain Song stared watching Ashen, and said a quick prayer to the Creator for his safety. Jior's soldiers were stationed around and behind her. The people in the wagons drew whatever weapon they had at hand. The horses pulling the wagons stamped and some reared with fear. Some of Skogur's soldiers tried to ride around the soldiers from Sorn and attacked the Jiorians with the fervor of long-held hatred for each other. Jior's soldiers were highly skilled and fought with deadly accuracy.

The silver pawns Ashen Arrow created began to multiply as they were cut down in battle. They fought with stiff precision and easily held off the men attacking on foot. Ashen's sword rang as he struck at his attackers on horseback. His men fought with graceful brutality and skill that rivaled the Jiorian soldiers. The scream of injured men and frightened horses echoed through the gully with the clash of steel hitting steel. It was not the Jiorians nor Sorn's men though, who screamed.

Rain Song finally got her mount under control. With the massive number of Skogur men coming against them she feared they would all be overwhelmed and killed. She whirled her horse around intent on finding the wagon with her bow and the white arrows Vannier had given her. Although she had faith in Ashen's abilities, there were too many soldiers from Skogur coming at them. She decided they needed the help of the winged Ny-Failen. The bow and arrows were stored two wagons back and she kicked her horse forward to reach them and also to get out of the way of the fighting soldiers crowding her.

The Jiorian soldier beside her went down as the two Skogur soldiers, who had been leading the others, battered their way past him. Their eyes gleamed with triumph as they kicked their horses pursuing her. Right before Rain Song reached the first wagon, she felt two strong arms grab her and pull her from her horse. She screamed and kicked, fighting the hold the soldier had on her. Wheeling their horses around, he and the other soldier rode back the way they had come toward the press of Skogur's soldiers fighting, taking the new Queen of Sorn with them.

Ashen Arrow heard Rain Song scream and he looked over in time to see her being carried away. He roared in fury and took off after them. Rain Song continued to thrash and fight her capturer then she remembered the dagger in her belt, grabbing it, she stabbed downward at the soldier's arm. Biting his flesh, the dagger sliced causing him to drop Rain Song and she hit the ground hard. The wind was knocked from her and her ankle twisted, but she could not spare the time to catch her breath or assess any other damage. She leaped up and with a limping run headed toward Ashen. She heard the sound of pounding feet as the second soldier, seeing she was free, leaped from his horse and ran after her. Because of her hurt ankle, he was much faster, he quickly caught up to her. Grabbing her from behind he held her tightly against his chest while holding his knife against her throat.

Ashen Arrow was more than fifty paces away when he shouted and gained the attention of the man holding onto Rain Song, threatening her with his knife.

"Ashen!" Rain Song screamed reaching toward him. She had dropped her knife in the fall from the horse and could not defend herself.

As if the soldiers on both sides of the battle, knew the danger the Queen of Sorn was in, they seemed to stop and watch what might unfold.

Ashen yelled at the top of his lungs, "Let her go!"

The soldier tightened his grip and grinned at Ashen as if he felt he had the upper hand. Ashen was not to be denied his wife. Though he was standing fifty paces from the man, he reached his hand up and caught the air as if it was solid and he gripped it with clawed fingers. The man holding Rain Song was laughing but then his laugh cut off as if he was being choked by an unseen force. He began to gasp for air. Everyone saw the moment when Ashen's hand clenched the air closed and he pulled viciously back mimicking ripping the man's neck out.

Rain Song felt the soldier's hold on her loosen and she pulled away turning to look just enough to see the soldier's face turning blue. Then, as Ashen pulled his clawing hand away quickly, an invisible force ripped the man's throat out. Blood splattered Rain Song's face and chest as the man let go and he fell, face forward, dead.

Ashen's black sorcery had ripped the man's throat out from twenty feet away. Blood splattered and, free now, Rain Song whirled and ran into the safety of her husband's arms.

#

During the battle with Skogur's soldiers, was the first time Rain Song had ever seen her husband use black sorcery and it frightened her a little. She realized he had been given no choice by the men from Skogur when they announced their plans to loot the peaceful caravan on the way to Sorn. The battle had raged on and though the Sorians were outnumbered, the attackers from Skogur were frightened by Ashen Arrow the Black Sorcerer, and by the silver pawns that exacted a heavy toll. They soon fled as they realized what they were up against and that their superior numbers could not win the fight.

Ashen, though pleased that he and his men prevailed, was furious over what happened to Rain Song. She was splattered in blood from the man who grabbed her and he had killed. Once they took to the road again, they only traveled a short distance until Ashen found a river where water could be fetched and she could wash the blood off of her. The young King of Sorn's anger was inconsolable and he posted the silver pawns on guard around their hastily erected camp. The people from Jior traveling along with them, looked at Ashen Arrow with new respect tainted with fear.

Pails of river water were heated and, inside the king's tent, Rain Song was undressed by one of the female servants they brought with them. She fought to take her mind from reliving the battle and what Ashen had done to the soldier who grabbed her. Never in her life had she been in such danger.

The black sorcery he had been forced to use, unnerved her as she had never seen anything like it before. Though she had known he was raised by the Gray King to use dark magic, actually seeing it used was another matter. Her mind was a whirlwind of fear, rationalizations, and denial. Recalling that she had never seen a battle much-less been in one, the shock of the death being wrought around her caused her to grow cold and numb.

Before Rain Song's bath had even begun, Ashen ducked into the tent and with a sharp nod at the servant girl, bade her leave. Rain Song looked up at him and it was as if she were seeing him for the first time. He was blood-spattered as well. The raven emblazoned on his silver chest plate was dripping red with the swiftly drying blood of their enemies. Towering over Rain Song as if he were an angry giant Ashen stood and stared at her for a moment before looking away. Removing his weapons, he stripped off his light armor and undercoat and tossed the bloody things aside. His boots were still on and his britches, when he turned to his silent wife.

Rain Song for her part was speechless, examining new feelings toward her husband. He had been frightening in his black sorcerer guise but underneath all the magic, the silver armor, blood, and dirt he was still the beautiful, gentle Ny-Failen she fell in love with and married. As he turned toward her, stripped bare to the waist with the blood of his enemies mixing with his sweat, Rain Song had a sudden recollection. It was that moment Ashen raised a hand to halt the caravan when they were first confronted by the men from Skogur. He had given Rain Song a sideways glance, a look she could not read, and had never seen on his face before. It was a look, she realized now, that said, *'Be forewarned! I will do what needs to be done to protect you!'* She now knew he had intended to use black sorcery all along. It was his command to *'kill them all'* that turned her blood cold as the words rang in her memory. She also realized she knew very little about Ashen Arrow of Sorn the Sorcerer.

Her silence and the wide-eyed unsettled look Rain Song gave Ashen, struck him to his core and made him want to howl with sorrowful anger. It made him want to drop to his knees and beg her forgiveness. It made him want to crush her in his arms and tell her he was still the same man she married. Could she not understand that he had been given no choice? Closing his eyes, Ashen took a deep breath and walked over to a stack of clean linens brought for Rain Song's bath. Grabbing one, he went to her and undressed her. Without a word, he lifted her to her feet and then lowered her into the warm bathwater. Rain Song settled back into the bath as Ashen knelt behind her and began to wash the blood from her fair skin. Silently he smoothed the wet cloth over her shoulders, her neck, and face. She settled low into the water and he rinsed her hair until she was clean. Pulling her to her feet, the water ran down her breasts, torso, and legs and Ashen wrapped her in dry linen. As if she were a child, he carried her to their bed where he finished drying her, put her in a soft linen nightdress, and eased her down to the bed. Buried in the thick luscious furs he left her.

Ashen called for the guards and had them take away the bath. Then he left the tent without his shirt, without his sword, without even a word or a backward glance. Rain Song sat up frozen by the strangeness of what had just happened. During the bath she tried to think of something to say to her husband, to thank him for saving her, for his attention and kind consideration, but no words would come. Now, she was not sure how to go forward or what would happen next between her and the Black Sorcerer with who she would spend the rest of her life.

The river was ice cold and Ashen dove in to cool his feverish mind as he had in the river back in Jior. He was anxious to get back to Rain Song, to explain his actions during the attack, but he really could not even explain it to himself. Part of him felt as if no explanation was needed. All he knew was, at that moment when the enemy soldier grabbed his wife, his black sorcery had come unbidden and unleashed. He killed the soldier without much thought only desperate alarm for his wife's safety. So many things could have gone wrong and she could have been killed, leaving Ashen bereft for the rest of his days. Ashen knew that such a loss would cast him into a deep dark place that he would never arise from. His wrath would have no bounds should he lose his precious wife, Rain Song. That fact scared him the most because he knew what he was capable of and was not surprised as he realized the depths of his love for Rain Song. His thoughts went to her reaction, the look of horror on her face when he killed the soldier who dared to lay his hands on her and threaten her with a blade at her throat. Ashen knew at that moment he revealed the darkness within and that was a part his wife would have to settle with because he had no way of stopping it.

Ashen stopped swimming and looked up at the darkening skies above him. The setting sun outlined the mountains towering around him with a faint golden glow. Not a cloud in the sky obscured the stars shining overhead and the deep black of night was rushing toward him.

#

The fire inside the tent, cast a warm red and gold light so Rain Song saw clearly when Ashen returned. His hair was wet as he had just bathed. Silently, he looked at her with his silver-gray eyes. She looked back at him with her eyes like two glittering emeralds. Her soft pearl-white skin was stark against the dark furs of his bed. Turning his back to her, he cast his boots off and his britches until he was naked. Ignoring the dinner of cheese, cold meat, apples, and bread that had been left for him, he slipped under the furs next to his wife. Propping his head up under his folded arms, he closed his eyes to go to sleep as if it had been an ordinary day on the road to Sorn.

Rain Song was only still for a moment then decided she had enough of the silence between them. At the end of everything that had happened that day, Rain Song knew Ashen was not cruel or bloodthirsty. She had a suspicion that Ashen knew she had been afraid of the black sorcerer in him and she did not care. Her love for him outweighed her fear of him and she would face it with her power, the power of her heart.

Rising she moved over and straddled him lifting her nightdress off and tossing it aside. His eyes flew open and his silver eyes flared with hunger, need, and desire.

"Ashen!" She whispered as she leaned over, *"My perfect Love."* Sliding her breasts over his chest, Ashen jerked and his body responded to her instantly.

Those were the words he needed to hear, that she still loved him despite what he was. She lifted her hips and slid his hardness into her body and held him. Her green eyes flashed with rapture as she began to slowly rock her hips. She made love to him deliciously, torturously, deliberately, slow. Her mouth sought his and he hungrily devoured her offered kisses. His hands smoothed over her hips and he thrust up hard inside her causing Rain Song to gasp and take his next breath as her own.

She whispered his name again, "Ashen!" Every caress and movement of their bodies, loving as one, brought them closer. Every cry of his name on her lips told him of forgiveness and acceptance.

"Wife!" Ashen growled almost in warning, and in a passionate, clench he flipped her onto her back and drove himself deeply into the haven of her body. Kissing her hard and long he surged again and again.

Rain Song cried out in her climax and Ashen thrust on, desperate to show his love for her, to share his body, close the distance between them. Branding her with his kisses, he claimed her with the primal hunger that always overtook him when she was in his arms. Her legs clasped around him in the way he longed to be held. As one they moved and relished each other, dispelling the anxious silence between them and holding back the darkness.

When the crisp cool of morning dawned the next day, they headed back onto the road to Sorn. The remaining days of travel were without hindrance or trouble. During the nights when they stopped to rest the men and horses, Ashen made love to Rain Song with insatiable fervor. Rain Song soaked up his attention and was surprised at how gentle and loving he could be and other times so passionate and overwhelming. At times though, as with the Skogur soldiers, he was quick to use the sorcery he had learned since he was a young boy, though he was never harmful or deadly unless provoked to be. He was never cruel. Rain Song accepted that part of Ashen that was the Black Sorcerer, but knew in her heart, he was a good man and she endeavored to show him just how worthy he was of the happiness that had been denied him his entire life.

CHAPTER SEVENTEEN

The forests of Skoria were different than the black forests in the Violent Mountains of Jior. White-spotted Aspens with green and gold leaves thickly dotted the land which consisted of gently rolling hills more than true mountains. There were birch trees and ash trees, late autumn wildflowers growing from rich black soil, and abundant wildlife. They passed unchallenged through the outskirts of Skoria in just two days and swiftly reached Sorn's borders.

The last night of their travels Ashen informed Rain Song that before the evening of the next day, they would see the spires of Castle Sorn. He was moody and almost brooding as he reluctantly spoke of his home. His trepidation overtaking her there increased as he thought about the state of his castle. He knew he would have to purge the halls and rooms of the evil sorcery that was his father's legacy. A legacy he had shown he inherited in more than just land. Though he had sent riders ahead to send the news to his people that the King was returning with his bride, he worried about how Rain Song would react to the gray, dismal Sorn tainted by so much evil.

In their tent, Ashen finished washing the day's travel dirt off and sat shirtless while Rain Song shaved the sides of his head as had become her habit. He remembered the first time she shaved him and he pulled her between his legs as he had that day. Setting the shaving implements aside he gave her a wicked grin and unlaced his trousers slowly, while she watched him free himself. Then he raised her skirts, grabbed her by the bottom, and lifted her onto his lap. Once she was close enough, he guided his hard shaft into her waiting warmth and he made love to her seated. He did not kiss her just watched her face as he filled her. Her eyes grew dark emerald with desire. She rocked against him as he thrust into her, and arched back as her climax took her. Once Ashen had achieved her satisfaction he stood and still connected to her, carried her to their sleeping furs. He laid her down, unlaced her bodice, and feasted on her breasts while bucking hard into her warm sheath.

A hungry fever overtook Ashen and he withdrew from her and rolled her over. Stripping her dress off in one smooth movement he reverently ran his hands over her back and hips. Kneeling behind her he pulled her hips back to his engorged shaft and returned to her. Ashen bucked again hard and Rain Song cried out achieving her climax once again. She gripped the furs and pressed back against him clutching him with her inner muscles and then Ashen came hard inside her. He threw his head back and thrust until he was empty and exhausted. Folding down behind her, he lay with her tightly held against his body. Rain Song pressed her bottom back into him keeping them linked and he began kissing her neck and shoulder while he reached forward and caressed her most sensitive place. Still sheathed inside her, he stroked her to completion once again. He found himself hardening and began to move, his thrusts becoming harder and more desperate. He loved her again until, body entwined with Ashen's, Rain Song fell exhausted into a peaceful sleep.

This loving had been a claiming, a demonstration by Ashen of his power, his lust, and his unending need for her. With his body and each hard thrust, each touch, he let her know…no, he demanded she acknowledge by her submission that this was Ashen Arrow of Sorn, her husband and he would have his way and she would know she was his!

#

The morning dawned gray and cloudy and Ashen was in a dark mood. Despite making desperate love to Rain Song that morning before rising, he could not shake his trepidation. One more day of travel and she would see her new home. He knew what awaited her there and he was not looking forward to it. He did not want to think about what she knew he was capable of with his dark magic. After their camp was quickly packed and they broke their fast, Ashen followed to help her mount and wanted to tell her of his fears. Instead, he remained silent not wanting to reveal his greatest shame just yet. The thought of the bright, delicate Rain Song living in the dank, gray halls of his castle, made Ashen furiously apprehensive as they headed eastward toward Sorn. That place held no good memories only loneliness, remembrances of past degradation, evil, and dark, black, soul-crushing *fear*.

They left the tree line on the border of Skoria and Sorn and the landscape changed drastically. Traveling through the low brush that gave way to tall grasses and then fields of stone, hills with giant rock formations jutted up and green grasses fought to take hold in the rocky earth. Short bushes and clumps of gnarled trees could be seen disappearing into the distance. They moved along an unmaintained road that did not look well-traveled. Sorn's soldiers also became grim as the greenery became sparser. Ashen became even more sullen and unhappy. Any hint of a smile faded and his face became more intense as the vegetation turned gray and dying, and gave way completely to rocky ground. As if in response to their passage into Sorn, the skies darkened with gray clouds over the distant low hills that rose on the horizon. Ashen pointed out a few dark caves where silver mines snaked back under the mountainsides and deep into the earth. Rain Song learned something else new about her husband. Ashen had an uncanny ability to find veins of silver. All he had to do was walk over the earth and he could feel where it lay hidden deep down. After his father died, he diligently found new mines and the wealth of Sorn tripled.

They eventually passed a large river that wound slowly away into the distance. Once they went through hills and some small valleys, they began to smell a salty tang in the air. Rain Song became excited about her first look at the ocean and could hear waves crashing on the beaches the closer they rode. Her heightened intuitiveness warned her of the reason for Ashen's brooding and she guarded her reactions so that she displayed no sense of fear or trepidation at the sight of his lands.

Suddenly, they passed out of the low valley they had been traversing and came to the rocky shoreline. The ocean beyond heaved steel-colored water in giant waves that crashed against humongous boulders scattered down the beach. Overhead gulls screamed at them from clouds heavy with rain. Rain Song expressed her joy at her first sight of the ocean and spoke of how breathtakingly beautiful it was. She truly, instantly, loved it. The rest of the day they stayed on the beach road that slowly climbed upward toward high uneven cliffs. The wagons had a little trouble on the rocky pathways and that slowed their progress especially as the way became steeper.

Ashen fell completely silent and Rain Song spoke about immediately planting the trees from Jior and asked if Castle Sorn had a garden. Ashen's short "no" led her into a one-way conversation about planting one with the seedlings sent by her Uncle Dark Star and then onto questions about the castle itself. She spoke with a suggestive teasing tone in her voice about sleeping in a real bed after so many days of travel and he did not even glance at her. No matter what she tried, she could not draw him out of his dark mood and into conversing with her. She asked about the people of Sorn and that cheered him slightly and he finally did respond to a few of her questions. The castle, he told her, was populated by a few people, mostly soldiers, but he hoped that upon learning there was to be a new Queen of Sorn who brought the goodness of Jior, people would come back.

They came to a rock arch of dark gray stone cut by the wind and waves. The ocean surf violently crashed on the beach in the distance. Passing through the arch they came out on the other side, looked up, and saw castle Sorn high on a cliff in the distance. Ashen looked grim as he covertly watched Rain Song take her first look at his domain. It was a great stronghold with tall spires surrounded by thick walls and battlements. Black twisted trees dotted the landscape and it looked as though not a green thing was to be found. Ravens sat in the barren trees and along the high walls of the castle. Rain Song now understood why Sorn's insignia was a raven. There were hundreds of the black birds everywhere. They perched silently as if they were vultures waiting for something to die so that they could swoop down and feast.

As they approached the castle, Rain Song could see that a few of the tall, towering spires of the castle were crumbling and one had the side caved in. The road they traveled on ascended toward the castle gate which was closed with huge iron bars. Rain Song took in the massive gray stone structure that was to be her new home, the place where they would raise their children. As they approached the iron gates Rain Song looked a little alarmed as she realized her mother would have problems passing through the massive iron bars. Lyra Song could not tolerate iron and so Rain Song frowned and made a mental note to speak to Ashen about it. Ashen noted the brief look of apprehension on Rain Song's face and his grimness settled deeper in his gut.

They passed quickly through the gates and Ashen led them at a gallop toward the main keep. Tarnish's hooves rang hollow on broken paving stones as he left Rain Song behind. The smell of rich dark soil and the salty tang of the ocean permeated the air. Not a green growing thing could be spotted on the road to the main castle. A few women in poor clothing stopped their chores to watch the King return as the long train of wagons passed by. Two dozen workers gathered in the courtyard to greet their party.

Upon reaching the main keep, ranks of Sorn's soldiers stood at attention in orderly rows. Each one had the sides of his head shaved just like Ashen's and their armor was polished and shining. They were a disciplined unit forming a show of strength and solidarity for Sorn's defense.

Rain Song slowed her horse to a walk where Ashen had galloped in and now contemplated her new home. It was a sad place, devoid of life and stained by its past, but she resolved to change all of that and to make Sorn a new, cheerful place entirely. When she reached the massive front doors of Castle Sorn, Ashen helped her dismount. He removed his crowned helmet and led her up five stairs where he stopped her and took her hand in his. Silently, he stared into her beloved beautiful face and the desire to be a better man rose within him stronger than ever before. For her sake, he would build his Kingdom of Sorn into a bright and shining place where the Gray King was a thing of the past and Ashen Arrow's hope for the future stared up at him with sparkling green eyes filled with love.

"My Lady, my Love, you brighten what is dark inside of me. Sorn is a dismal, dying place. You will be the new star in Sorn's sky and will bring light, life, and goodness to it. It is not a home or a happy place, but I hope that when you are crowned Queen of Sorn, the people will embrace you, and together we can revive this place. I only ask you to be patient and work with me to make Sorn a real home."

"Ashen, my perfect Love, anywhere we are together will be our home. I will do everything in my power to make you happy." She smiled at him and melted his frozen soul. Overhead the gray clouds fractured and, as if the Creator were smiling down, painted them in the warm golden rays of the sun.

Ashen's face changed into a mask of joy and he lifted Rain Song into his arms and swung her around. He kissed her with unbridled passion and the people of Sorn rejoiced.

The End

Epilogue

Storm Rider, Mercy Rose, and Rain Song, children of Commander Jagged Edge and Princess Lyra Song of Jior, were among the first grandchildren of King Forlorn Icefall and Queen Lililaira Gem the Ny-Failen King and Queen of Jior.

Legends, fairy tales, and myths came from their stories as they grew to adulthood and started the next generation of Ny-Failen Jiorians. As children of two Ny-Failen parents, they possessed the beauty and power of creatures blessed by the Heavens.

After returning to Jior and marrying, Storm Rider and Moon Dancer conceived a son. King Forlorn Icefall's first great-grandson came hollering into the word with the well-deserved name of Thunder Bird. As Mercy Rose predicted they were blessed with many more children; two more sons, Storm Bringer and Bristle Frost, and a sweet little girl named Silver Star who had white-gold wings like her mother.

They spent most of their days in Jior but as soon as their sons could fly, they spent many months on Javelin Peak with Helm and Glenna and their children.

Each spring, Moon Dancer and Storm Rider returned to the heart of the Violent Mountains and rode the storms, together.

#

Mercy Rose grew heavy with child during the first year of her marriage to Aesir Blacknight. Late in the night, her labor pains warned her that the birth was forthcoming. Her grandmother was summoned by Aesir Blacknight and she was by Mercy Rose's side as her water broke. Mercy Rose cried out in pain as the first boy was born, still, blue, and ominously quiet. A confident Queen Lily held the small body in her arms and blew her sweet breath into his face while her hands glowed golden, bathing him in warmth and healing. Suddenly, he inhaled a deep breath and his blue skin turned pink and then purest white as his bright eyes burst open. The baby coughed and sucked in the pure mountain air, but he had seen death before his birth was allowed and his ice-blue eyes held a solemn, knowing stare that would mark him his whole life.

As Mercy Rose gave birth to her first son, his name crashed through her skull and later she would fittingly call him Moon Shadow, but her body demanded further attention and she continued to strain and push. Night Wing quickly followed his twin brother and he soon began to wail and wave his tiny fists.

Queen Lily laid each tiny boy in Mercy Rose's arms. The silver lines depicting wings, on each boy's back glistened in the lamplight.

#

As time passed in faraway Sorn, Rain Song took over Ashen Arrow's castle with a feverish desire to create him a happy home. Her Uncle Dark Star visited within the first month of their arrival in Sorn. Very soon the entire land grew lush with green life as he swooped over it, pouring his Ny-Failen power over plants into the gray land. The fallen castle tower was repaired and the garden flourished with the seedlings from Jior. New trees quickly took root and grew strong and tall where Sorn's ravens perched and made their nests.

Green and silver pennants, heralding Sorn's new colors, rippled in the ocean breeze from every spire, rampart, and tower of Castle Sorn. With each change and improvement to Sorn, Ashen Arrow lost a little more and more of his brooding and apprehension over bringing Rain Song to Sorn.

When knowledge of the new Queen spread throughout the kingdom, people began to return to Castle Sorn and the population grew.

One month after Dark Star arrived, Jagged Edge and Princess Lyra Song came to Sorn as promised. Rain Song greeted them with delight and the news that their first grandchild was expected.

Ashen Arrow leaned against the gray stone of a high tower in his castle. He watched as his wife ran out and happily embraced her parents who had just arrived in a flurry of commotion. Horses stamped as soldiers dismounted and numerous wagons flowed through the gates with their arrival. Ashen looked beyond the courtyard below out into the distance and surveyed the new life surrounding him in every direction. Astonishment sparked in his silvery eyes at the green grass, willowy trees, and even flowers that now blossomed everywhere. The gray deadness from the Gray King's rule was now domineered by lush greenery. His once dark, foreboding kingdom now thrived with life and prosperity. Ashen smirked at it all knowing how his father would hate it if he were still alive to witness the changes. A little thrill of accomplishment ran across Ashen's shoulders.

The revelation that his child now grew in his wife's womb gave Ashen pause. As if savoring that sweet and hopeful knowledge it echoed in his heart and he shivered with apprehension and anticipation. He watched Rain Song below him and embraced the lusty hunger that always seemed to streak through his body when he saw her. His body grew hard and his unending hunger for her threatened to overrun his control.

Ashen took a deep breath tamping down hard on his lust. He reminded himself that tonight, his beautiful Rain Song would lay naked beneath him, painted by the golden candlelight, and he would once again be joined with her.

Moving away he raised his hand, he let his black sorcery flow. A white flame swirled from his palm and he twirled it with his long fingers spinning it slowly into a sphere. He poured his black sorcery into the ball until it spun so fast it glowed white-hot. Staring at his in-laws and his wife below, he then turned his back to them, his gaze now rested on the white flames he was creating. Raising his hand, he lifted the flaming ball to his lips and turned toward the vast open ocean that crashed behind him. Breathing in, reaching within his heart and very soul, he pursed his lips and blew out a hot black breath. The white flame transformed, took the shape of a flaming raven, caught and filled with Ashen's released darkness before it took wing and flew away out to sea.

Smiling and shining with a freedom he had never felt before, Ashen Arrow, King of Sorn turned and went to greet his family.

Dear Reader:

Thank you for reading my Kingdom of Jior fantasy series. I sincerely hope you enjoyed reading it as much as I have writing it.

Share your love of reading by leaving a review. Your support through reviewing my books is a great help in getting the word out.

As an independent author, your support and reviews of my books allows me to publish more books and inspires me to keep writing!

Now, read on to book five, the Last Ny-Failen, the final book in the Kingdom of Jior fantasy series.

You can find out more about me and my books at:

https://www.wendylanderson.com
amazon.com/author/wendyanderson

Very Sincerely,

Wendy L. Anderson

Made in the USA
Las Vegas, NV
27 December 2022